Take to the Sky

KAREN E. BLACK

Viceroy Power Press

2017

Take to the Sky

by Karen E. Black

Published 2017 by Viceroy Power Press

Vol 3 in the Devereux Cousins Trilogy

Please feel free to contact: karen.black@sympatico.ca

ISBN-13: 978-1-7751431-0-9

Copyright ©2017 by Karen E. Black

Review Highlights

Drugs, bikers, prison breaks and (and what some people would call incest) provide surprising plot twists in this rough-and-tumble romance...set in the '60s and '70s...Black has a flair for historical novels .and she shows remarkable storytelling depth... **-- Kirkus Reviews**

"...courtroom scenes are so well written, I thought I was reading a John Grisham novel but without half the tediousness of his long drawn out court battles. The sexual scenes are also beautifully done, a real part of the plot, not woven in to titillate the reader." **--Book lover "Elsee" (Malvern, UK)**

"...this is an eloquently crafted tale about love, guilt, and human resilience." **- Ben Avery (Victoria, BC)**

"Both Liza and Dace are haunted by the decisions that they made in their youth- his a charge resulting in a jail term, and hers a relationship with an older man which results in a heart breaking decision." **--Nadia (Toronto, Canada)**

"I fell in love with the character of Dace (during the prison riot). His perseverance and resilience, whether making good or bad decisions, can't be matched." **--Francine1898**

"The author is a woman but she really nailed it in portraying a desperate man, driven both by his violent circumstances and his desperate need for his girl, Liza. But as much as I liked him, it was Liza I really cared about..." **-Goalie (Trenton, ON)**

"...a meditation on obsessive love, free choice and fitful fate. "From the Chrysalis" asks us to consider how much of life is the result of choices we've made, and how much is determined by circumstances beyond our control." **-- Joseph A. (Toronto, Canada)**

Feeling for the Air (The Devereux Cousins Book 2) is a brilliantly written coming of age novel. -- Anne Boling for Readers' Favorite

In memory of B.B. and in honor of the boys of St. John's in Uxbridge, Ontario. May you and your families find peace.

Millions of King butterflies to pass through Toronto and surrounding area in two weeks or so.

The striking orange and black monarch butterflies will mass along the Lake Ontario shoreline, then move toward Point Pelee, Dr. Gene Sheridan, butterfly expert and head of the museum division of zoology and palaeontology, said today.

"There has been a great increase in the number of these 'King Billy' or monarch butterflies due to an unusually warm spring and summer," he stated.

Dr. Sheridan is completing a lengthy study of the migration of the monarchs which summer in Ontario but winter in Florida.

(unidentified Toronto daily, August 18, 1953)

Chapter One

Mariposa and Kathleen Aldous — The San

Just one look at so many monarch butterflies and she was hooked for life.

"I spent two and a half years in the San, not the Ritz," Kathleen always tells her daughter Mariposa. "You don't get a lot of stimulation in a place like that."

The Children's Tuberculosis Sanatorium in Toronto didn't even have television in those days. Not that it mattered. You can't miss what you've never had. There were books in the little school library, but the nurses didn't really like her to read. Too tiring. Kathleen had one job and one job only. Getting better.

The San had one thing going for it: it was on a monarch migratory route. Every September, the sky above was studded with thousands of butterflies fleeing Canada looking for sanctuary.

"Lucky you," Mariposa says, watching a butterfly, a little white one, flitting in the June roses.

"Right, I just got TB. Polio would have been worse."

Until she saw them, young Kathleen never gave monarchs or any kind of butterfly much thought. Like most of the kids in the San, she just wanted to go home. Day after day, she stayed on her back, with her hands folded over her chest. Doing what the good girls did. Healing. Getting lots of rest. Beating her disease.

Willpower went a long way in the San. Willpower and prayer.

You want to get better, don't you? the staff would say if a child's disease wasn't following the course they thought it should.

There were lots of monarchs in the nineteen-fifties, way more than now. The brightly colored orange and black insects showed up in Ontario in May or June, but the first ones didn't last for long.

Monarch enthusiasts — and there were lots of them then — asked themselves questions like these:

Did monarchs live anywhere else except North America?

Where did they fly south in winter — to the same places in the States as the birds?

Were the butterflies who made it down south the same ones that left?

If they weren't, how did the monarchs born down in the States know their way back?

Reports also came in of monarchs out west and in sunny California. But how could that be if they flew back to Ontario from down south every spring?

Working out of the big provincial museum in Toronto, a man called Dr. Gene Sheridan and his colleagues had studied monarch populations for years, but they still weren't sure.

The sanatorium staff was kind, but there wasn't a whole lot in the place to feed a curious young mind. Especially a mind like Kathleen's, trapped in a sick body at the wrong time. No television, no electronic bulletin boards and none of those new computers with the world wide web.

As for Kathleen's heart, it was like most little girls' hearts. It wanted more, it just didn't know what.

Kathleen slept a lot in those days, but she didn't have a lot of dreams. Or role models.

Kathleen is still always going on about role models, about making the best of yourself. About having a grand passion and doing something worthwhile with your life.

"To him whom much is given, much is expected," she always says.

"You mean much is required," sixteen-year-old Mariposa replies.

Except for a pediatrician, every last doctor in the sanatorium had been a man and all the nurses were women. Mlle Beaulieu, the teacher who came from Quebec was an exception. She had a paying job, but she wasn't a nurse. It helped that she had no children, so she was somebody in her own right.

In another time and place, especially if Kathleen had been born a boy, they might have expected her to be a somebody. The way people did with boys. The cute ones anyway. Somehow the San boys got the undivided attention of a visiting official, the choicest cuts of meat, the spot with the best view in the hospital yard and lots of chances to 'help' out with small tasks.

Not that young Kathleen cared. There was a reason she had survived tuberculosis—not just because it was the nineteen-fifties and a medicine called streptomycin was making miracle cures. There had to be a reason.

Strep-to-*mice*-in, such a strange name!

Left alone for long stretches of time in her hospital bed, Kathleen read whatever she could get her hands on. "Bookworm," they called her, the same thing people still call kids like that. She was drawn to books early the way some people are drawn to sport, the arts, religion or the great love of their lives. She was looking for something, she just didn't know what.

Until the day the monarchs came.

Resting on her left side, Kathleen studied the windows down at the end of her ward and daydreamed about levitating over all

11

eight beds. She did this a lot. The floor-to-ceiling windows looked faraway but they weren't.

"It's mine, it's mine," somebody shrieked. On the floor space in-between the middle beds, Kathleen's roommates had been playing jacks since they finished supper, but they kept losing the darn ball.

"Shut up, just shut up," she muttered.

Squinting into the setting sun, she chewed the tip of her baby finger. All her nails were bitten down to the quick. A filthy habit. Nail-biting helped her focus, but it also distracted her from everything wrong with her body.

She had to get out of bed, if it was the last thing she did.

"It's now or never," she whispered. She smoothed out the news article she'd found in the paper: "Millions of King Butterflies to Pass Through Toronto Area."

Gosh, you'll read anything, won't you? Nurse Louise said, when she caught her with the scrap of newsprint just last week, but she'd let Kathleen keep it. Torn from the women's section of a newspaper full of stories about murder and Martians landing, the article must have looked harmless enough.

"You pushed me, I got it this time! It's mine!" A roommate yelled.

What a stupid bunch of show-offs! Kathleen hated them all. She was way better off in the younger girls' ward, but she got moved here back in June.

It was still warm outside. *You are my sunshine,* she hummed softly to herself, cracking her bony little knuckles and unbuckling her cramped toes. *My only sunshine.* The monarchs were on their way. She knew this because the paper said so and she sensed it in her bones. How did butterflies know it was time to fly south? How did birds? How did anyone know what to do? Lots of things didn't make much sense.

Like why she was the one who got so sick when nobody else in her grade two class did.

"Okay, it's your turn, get going!" the shrillest little girl said.

Jerking her legs free, Kathleen tore her bare feet from under her top sheet. Everything slid. She made a grab for the book she was hiding, but she wasn't fast enough. It tumbled to the floor.

Nobody noticed. The boys' and girls' wards from the babies to the big kids were usually quiet by 6:30 p.m. so the TB patients could get a long, healthful rest, but down the hall, Kathleen could hear a bunch of ankle-biters squalling and squawking.

Where's Nurse Louise? She was usually in and out of the ward by now. Kathleen could almost tell time by what the sanatorium staff was doing, she knew their routines so well.

A fresh burst of giggles irritated her. If her roommates were trying to rattle her cage, they were doing a good job. Nurse Louise was right. *That's what happens when you girls start to get better,* she said, *you act like fools.*

Look at them! The bums of their skirts were all dirty. They were going to get in trouble for that. But it was their dirty white socks that would really give them away.

"Get lost!" Kathleen tried shouting, but a croak was all that came out of her mouth.

Really, is that the best you can do, Kathleen? she chided herself, the way the San staff did when she tried to pee into a little bottle. As soon as these girls realized what she was up to, they'd spoil things for sure.

Once in a lakeside park, she saw a flock of geese go after one of their own, an injured female.

It's just nature, darling, her mother had said, but Kathleen couldn't get that picture out of her head. *Usually it's the boy geese — the ganders — that get so nasty,* her mother had added. But why? Why didn't the ganders just leave the girl goose alone? Kathleen almost threw up when she saw the geese, but she kept on looking anyway.

That goose's wing was broken, so it couldn't get away. But Kathleen will.

Keep up the good work and you'll be out of here in no time, the director of the hospital told her every time he saw her.

That new medicine was the ticket though, he said. Especially if Kathleen did what she was told, she'd be back home with her mother in Montreal in no time, free to run through butterfly gardens, to go out trick-or-treating at Hallowe'en or ice skating in the wintertime.

She was just a bit sicker than her roommates, that's all. She had *a ways to go*. Which was probably the real reason the other girls didn't want her around. A sick kid wasn't supposed to be in a "well" ward with kids who were almost out.

Half of the stupid retards here can't even read! Maybe that's what the nurses mean when they say Mademoiselle has her work cut out for her.

Gossip bored Kathleen—the same old sloppy talk every day, what this person ate for dinner and what somebody else did or didn't do—but she was all ears anyway. The hospital administration had advertised far and wide to find Mlle Beaulieu, a young woman fresh out of Normal school.

Teaching's such a good job for a girl, Kathleen overheard more than one nurse say. Not that this girl's going to be here for long. *Now if Administration had hired a man instead of a dolly like her, they might have spared themselves a lot of grief down the road.*

Yes, if Miss or Mademoiselle or whatever-she-calls-herself Beaulieu is as smart as she says, she'll sink her talons into one of the interns by Christmastime and split. Why else would she waste her time in a place full of sick and germy kids? Every girl wants to marry a doctor, they say. *A real girl, anyway.*

Kathleen snuck another look at the jack-playing girls. Just wait— Nurse Louise is really going to flip her lid!

Every night she said the same thing: *You big girls are perfectly capable of getting yourselves into bed.* All she had to do was turn off the light.

Taking a deep breath, Kathleen ground her pointed little heels into the mattress. Nobody was looking at her. Maybe she could get down to the floor and crawl.

Dear God, she prayed briefly.

But God only helped those who help themselves. Her mother said that almost every time she visited. Alone. Except she had that man with her last time, a big one with glasses. *I'm your new dad,* he said, but Kathleen wasn't listening. She was sure her mother had come to take her home, but she hadn't. Not this time.

Turn off the tears, her mother said.

You're scaring your new dad, kiddo, Nurse Louise added.

Kathleen squeezed her eyes closed.

She might as well go now. Nobody was paying any attention to her anyway. *Them and their stupid game!* She held her breath and eased off the side of the bed until she felt the cool floor. The next thing she knew, she was down on her belly. *Hey, that wasn't so bad.* She was just a bit winded.

It was only about ten feet to the windows, but gosh, it was a long crawl. Looking to her left, she could see under all her roommates' beds clear to the opposite wall. There sure were a lot of dust bunnies. Kathleen's nose twitched, but she didn't dare sneeze.

Even if she hadn't read that news story about the monarchs passing through Toronto, she'd know they were coming. Monarchs were creatures of habit. They flew the same migratory route at the same time every year. They always had.

What a pain she had to share them with a bunch of dumb girls. But with all those butterflies in the garden, they'd be impossible to hide. Everybody would want to see them: the hospital's caretakers, the gardener, the nurses, the doctors, the patients with privileges, even some of the kids—the walkers, those bad boys who were always getting into trouble, the ones the staff couldn't keep in bed.

That's what happened last year. First there was this loud whirring noise, then everybody rushed outside to see the most amazing sight: swarms of orange and black butterflies: monarchs, poisonous Milkweed butterflies, wanderers, all streaming out of Canada, all headed south.

Or almost everybody had gone outside to see them. Kathleen couldn't get out of bed.

Well, she'd be the first one to see them this time.

Another name for monarchs was King Billies, but Kathleen still hadn't figured out why. *How strange*, she thought, puzzling over the name. It helped take her mind off her tired arms and legs as she hauled herself along the floor. She tried to keep her mouth closed, but her breath was coming in short gasps. What if somebody heard? What if Nurse Louise came in and she was still on the floor?

Oh, gosh, Nurse was going to be so mad when she got here.

What a bitch, Kathleen thinks now. Life's a whole lot easier near Angangueo, Mexico on the butterfly preserve she set up in 1974 than it was in the San. Away down in Mexico, she calls all the shots. She tells people what to do.

She starts each day on her ranch bright and early and stays up long past midnight, but she also enjoys three-hour siestas with her lovers during the long afternoons.

My, oh, my, that Juan-what's-his-name is so sweet, so sinewy, so flexible, so obliging.

If only she were in Mexico right now, away from all this fuss and bother about the dead and dying. She got enough of that in the San.

On a cool June day in Montreal, her day has started out predictably. First, she had a breakfast meeting at McGill University with some pedantic old academic jerks who've been spouting the same crap for years. The usual yammer about the role of the university in the New Age, but mostly about their tenure, their early retirements and their summer cottages.

From her two-hour breakfast meeting at the U, she went to her mother's nursing home in Westmount, helped the old lady eat her lunch and listened to a litany of complaints. Her mother's short term memory might be completely shot, but she sure hasn't forgotten how to complain. Mum's right though. Those lazy support workers aren't doing much. Now if this was Mexico...

It's late afternoon. Kathleen's out in the backyard garden with her girl at last, away from the damn phone. They're both reclining on webbed aluminum lawn chairs.

Kathleen asks Mariposa about the friends she spends so much time with and who are always trying to take over their house, but the girl isn't talking, or at least she's not talking about herself.

All that Mariposa really likes to talk about is the time Kathleen spent in the San.

So Kathleen obliges her. Anything to keep the kid home.

"The San was a good place, but it got a bit lonely sometimes. Most of the patients were a long way from home. People didn't gad about in those days, the way they do now, so parents didn't visit much. If it hadn't been for the butterflies —"

"Oh, Mummy, didn't you have any friends?"

Friends, is that all this kid wants? She should be studying for her SATs. On a weeknight, anyway. Do they still do SATs here? There was talk about banning standard admission tests, a real nuisance because Mariposa needs the SAT for an American school. She has to go to university in the States.

"Well, no," Kathleen says, leaning over in her chair and flicking away a wasp burrowing in-between her toes, "I never hung out with a gang of kids like you do. Not even in high school. But it didn't matter. Because I had a dream, something more important to do. I had to find out more about the monarchs. That's how I got through —"

She was talking about this to her psychiatrist, Pearl, the other day. How she doesn't really need other women. Or men. Men are good for sex, but a woman can take care of such things herself, though maybe not quite as well.

Kathleen values this independence, one of the perks of spending so much time alone in the San.

Looking back, it's spared her much heartache, the three years she spent in the care of kind and intelligent professionals with the grand passion of curing TB.

That, and the fact that against all odds, she was part of something grand too, something greater and more magnificent than herself.

"As a ten-year-old patient in a tuberculosis sanatorium," Kathleen tells Mariposa, "I never went anyplace. Except to the girls' ward or to the garden. Rain or shine, the staff used to push our beds outside. I was such a good little girl, waiting and watching. Anticipating..."

"I thought you said you weren't allowed in the garden."

What a memory the kid's got! Just like her.

"That's right. You've seen the pictures. Nobody went into that garden, at least not the kids. They used to line our beds up on the lawn."

The staff never let the kids out into the garden. The harm they could have done if they were left on their own—running and trampling spring life back into the earth, yanking up May flowers and trilliums and tulips just for fun.

There was another reason the staff didn't want kids out in the garden, but they never said so. They didn't have to. Kids just *knew*.

A small, cumulus cloud drifts lazily across the sun. Kathleen wraps her arms around her chest, feeling a slight chill. It's not really summer yet, but she's spent the last few weeks in Montreal sorting out her mother and daughter. Kathleen's stepfather died eighteen months ago of congestive heart failure — *drat the man!* — so nobody can.

For all that she was left so much on her own, except at the very end when Mlle Beaulieu came and mentored her, the sanatorium was mostly a good place. Even if she had to have years of therapy before she came to terms with her disease — *why did tuberculosis happen to me?*

Even if she still calls her psych, Pearl, every time she's back here in Montreal.

Yes, she was pretty lucky. She sees that now, especially when she hears what happened to kids in orphanages and training schools all over the world and at the residential schools in Canada and in the States. Lots of bad stuff could have happened to a pretty young girl growing up in an institution, but it never happened to her.

Not for her the "romance of the invalid" in Victorian literature either, which she understands all too well. Every December in the San, they watched Dickens's *Christmas Carol*, but she was no Tiny Tim. She was helpless for such a long time at the San — the victim of some freak, random germ — but people took care of the kids there. They really did. The goal of every person on the medical team was to get the children back on their feet, to make them healthy and thriving, to strengthen them into adults who could contribute to society and who might have children of their own someday.

Some of the tuberculosis patients didn't make it, but nobody talked about them. Bodies were buried quietly and efficiently, in Prospect Cemetery in west end Toronto or in unmarked graves on the sanatorium grounds, she's not really sure.

Three children died one night in November her first year in the San. None of the kids in her ward heard a thing at the time. Maybe it was a fluke, losing so many children in one night, but it happened.

You never talked about stuff like that, though. That or your health. You were as plucky as Little Orphan Annie. Things could always be worse. What if you'd gotten polio? Crying and carrying on just made everybody else feel worse.

A priest, a minister and a rabbi visited the sanatorium at appropriate times. In those days, every last man of God was male. Everybody wanted the TB kids to get better, to go back home. Most people did their jobs, unlike those lazy foreign loafers in her mum's overpriced nursing home. And nobody left helpless patients alone with aberrant men either. Like that gardener. Nobody ever let one of the boys "help" him. The sanatorium staff had more sense than to hand children over to strange men. Imagine that—they protected their charges and still kept their jobs!

What in God's name went on at that nasty school in Maitland? She'd heard about Mount Cashel, but now rumours are flying around about St. Matthew's School. Every time she opens up the paper, there's a fresh horror.

What's next, something about that other school in Maitland where all the real bad boys got sent? Somebody was in charge, some adult. And what about the stupid people who hired a bunch of perverts in the first place? Come on now, lots of people in those awful warehouses for hapless, neglected or orphaned children knew what was going on. Even if they didn't talk a lot in those places, they weren't blind.

"Let's get back to the garden," Kathleen says to her daughter. "I never got inside, but I could see it from the window. The monarchs used to spend a night there on the fir trees on their annual flight down south. To Florida, we thought. Imagine—"

"Yes," Mariposa imitates her mother's serene expression, "let's talk about butterflies."

"An award-winning garden was attached to the Children's Sanatorium, but the gardener was the only person with a key. Don't worry," Kathleen always reassures Mariposa at this point because she wants her to grow up strong and resilient, tougher than any man—kind of like herself in fact, "I wasn't the victim-type. The old bugger never touched me. Besides, he only liked boys. Or so I heard."

Mariposa gets up from her mother's side to look over the neighbour's fence. *Those poor boys.* The stuff that's happened to them! Luckily she doesn't have anything to worry about, not even on her early morning runs. At her mother's insistence, she's taken karate for the past three years. She's almost finished her black belt.

Once Kathleen mentions the pedophilic gardener, the fucked-up priests are next. She's been talking a lot lately about the bad priests in the news. Mariposa has no idea what they have to do with her mother's life. Did her mother know somebody who was raped/raised by priests? Except she's never had a lot of friends, so who could it be?

The neighbour's little terrier sets up a frenzied barking the minute he spots her. The mutt never shuts up. Mariposa's room is in the rear of her grandmother's Victorian house, overlooking the garden. The terrier keeps her awake half the night yapping. That and the cool motorbikes racing up and down the back laneway. Mariposa is tempted to toss some chocolate over the fence, but she's afraid of getting caught. It mightn't even kill the damn dog. Pulling first one leg and then the other up to her rear and stretching for a count of ten, Mariposa makes faces at him until he really goes whacko.

"Stop pestering that dog and sit back down here with me," Kathleen says.

Sure thing, Mum, Mariposa thinks, *as long as you don't tell me another story about child sexual abuse.* Not on this lovely June night, the kind she's been waiting for all year long.

Mariposa knows enough. She's almost seventeen, so she reads the paper. She's always been a newspaper junkie. Maybe she'll go into journalism after she graduates high school if she doesn't end up buried alive on her mother's butterfly sanctuary.

Her mother wants her to go to university though. An American one, in Texas or something, closer to the ranch in Mexico. Two universities in Ontario offer a Journalism degree, Carleton and Western. Carleton's in Ottawa, not that far away. Mariposa would really like to stay closer to her grandmother, even if she doesn't see her much anymore.

She sits down beside her mother again. It's that or get into another argument about going out to see her friends.

"Tell me more about the butterflies. How they captured your imagination when they flew so far. C'mon, Mummy. You were such a wise child, an old woman in a child's body."

"Who told you that?"

"Granny! Remember? She used to say that, well, you know — when she still had all her faculties! Before you were ten years old, you'd read all about monarch butterflies in some scientific journal you found. You know that article by the expert from the University of Toronto — what's his name? How lucky is that — that his article ended up on some dusty shelf in the hospital schoolroom? Maybe some medical student was reading it for fun. And then you saw something about monarch butterflies in a local paper, the *Telegram* or the *Toronto Star*."

"It might have been the *Star*," Kathleen says.

"Or did you find the news article first? Whatever — I bet it was just a bit of filler in the Women's Section. They always stick stuff like that there. Look at that old story I found in the *Globe and Mail* microfilm at the Reference library about monarchs leaving Toronto in 1953! That was just a year or two after you left the San, wasn't it?" Mariposa pauses for breath, but when her mother still doesn't say anything, she sails on.

"You were always reading." Mariposa's always had a tough time sitting still, but she stretches out in her lawn chair again. "The backs of cereal boxes, discarded newspapers, forgotten mail, other people's private business. You had your nose in everything! You're not like me. Or else I'm not like you! Except for reading newspapers, I'd much rather fly a kite, run a marathon or ski at Mont-Tremblant. Yeah, Granny told me you were a real nosey parker, a busybody, the kind of kid who got on other people's nerves. Especially hers! So that time—at the San, I mean—you were in the girls' ward reading and waiting. Locked up for your own good."

"A young girl waiting, anticipating…" Kathleen says a little ruefully to her daughter, this girl who also wants to know everything and acts like she already does.

"You know, your eyes get all misty when you hear *Try a Little Tenderness* and you're always humming it." *I like you better that way*, Mariposa thinks, but she's sure as hell isn't going to say so and bust their mood. She's drawn closer to her mother now that her grandmother's in long-term care and they have the old lady's house all to themselves, but if they get any closer, she might tell her about the pot she smokes almost every day.

Or about that boy at Camp Arrowshot, the one with the dark, soulful eyes? It's like she's always known him. Micah Devereux. And it's got nothing to do with sex! Really.

She should know. She's already had sex with a boy down the street—well, sort of—though it happened way easier than she thought it would. He was only up inside her vagina for half a sec. How did that happen? She was in total shock, it happened so fast. She shrieked so hard that he got the hell out. Where was all the blood? Why didn't she bleed?

Hey, don't do that to a guy, he said.

Don't do that to me! she yelled right back.

Yes, Mariposa doesn't need or want sex with Micah. After what happened with her neighbour, sex is the last thing she wants. Yuck. She wants Micah, just not all of him. *Please, please, please*, let him come back to camp!

Of course her mother wants "mother stuff" for her only daughter. She wants her to get an education, to have a dream. No way she wants her tangled up with needy boys or dark, dangerous, improvident men. Her mother doesn't have to say these things to her. She's her mother and she's raised her without a whole lot of help from a man, so Mariposa just knows.

But Kathleen's still quiet, so Mariposa keeps talking to keep the focus off herself.

"The ward—the large, whitewashed room you slept in had four long windows and eight beds in a row. Shades of *Madeline*, one of the few girly books you ever read, just because it was there. Yeah, yeah, I know—you've never liked poetry or fiction, you like to read about real things. Truth really is better and stranger than fiction! Maybe if there had been more books in the San, but there weren't. Just odds and ends from other peoples' libraries, other people's lives that they left around. You liked the San though. Liked the routine. Loved the safety, maybe. They don't do that anymore, do they? Isolate TB patients in a hospital for years?"

They've talked about this before, but Mariposa likes hearing the same stories over and over. When she was real little, she used to make her grandmother read *Cinderella* all the time. Not just because she loved the story, but because it drove her mother nuts to hear this.

"They don't have to. The drugs are better now," Kathleen says decisively. "Way better. They've practically wiped out tuberculosis in North America, you know. AIDs is the new scourge."

Oh, no you don't. Get her mother talking about the quest to cure AIDs and she'll never shut up. The woman's crazy about progress and cures and scientific discoveries. And that new thing the library's getting, the world wide web.

"You were in the San for two or three years, so it's all you knew. I understand that, I really do," Mariposa says earnestly while she searches the grass at her feet for a four-leaf clover. If she finds just one, maybe Micah will come back to camp. If she finds two, maybe they'll both go to Carleton U.

"When I was small, I wanted the same thing—to stay in the same place. That's why I don't like going to Mexico in the summertime."

And she thinks to herself: *thank God I got that job at Arrowshot! Poor me, I have to spend the whole summer up here!*

"But it wasn't enough for you," Mariposa says. "The ward you slept in smelled of disinfectant and urine from the yucky chamber pots under the beds, no matter how hard the orderlies worked. The nursing station was just down the hall."

Kathleen pulls herself up a little in her lawn chair and smiles. With her fair skin, she's never dared sit in the sun for long. It's so aging, not to mention carcinogenic. But the northern sun is weak at this time of day. Besides, Mariposa is home for once instead of gallivanting all over downtown Montreal with her friends and getting up to God-knows-what.

As if she doesn't know that the kid smokes that damn pot! Kathleen's got to head back down south in a very short time anyway. One thing's certain, those illegal loggers are up to no good. They don't give a shit about the monarchs or their habitat. They never have. And what if Juan-what's-his-name forgets her? Not that a boy like him could or would.

A boy like him—she can almost feel his fingertips on her skin, caressing her neck and then sliding to her waist, positioning her hips...

Ah, but Mariposa's such a stubborn kid. She always has been. She just won't let go. She's still prompting her to recite the same old story she's heard before, the only personal stuff Kathleen ever really shares:

"On this occasion—you've always said it was Thursday, September 3, 1953—the nurses were in their workstation, talking and drinking their evening tea, with their tired, aching feet propped up on wooden chairs. You'd seen them doing that sometimes when the orderlies took your bed outside. There was no TV in the San, but maybe they had a radio turned on real low.

You couldn't quite make out the lyrics, just snatches of Patti Page's silly hit, *How Much is that Doggie in the Window?* You couldn't hear what the nurses were saying either, but their laughter floated down the hall."

Kathleen smiles at her daughter, this lovely extension of herself. The girl is so achingly beautiful, the way she was when she took her first lover at the ripe old age of twenty-one.

Why in God's name did she wait so long? It's hard to remember, but she thinks it was something to do with wanting to preserve her virginity for her one true love—whoever he was supposed to be!—and having more interesting pursuits.

Yes, as much as Mariposa goes out of her way to prove she's not like her mother—c'mon, what teenage girl wants to be like her mum?—they're way more alike than she thinks.

Like most Caucasian females in their mid-teens, Mariposa has obtained her full height and pretty much grown into her strong-featured face. But even if she's inherited her father's dark good looks, she doesn't resemble the man in personality or brains at all.

Why should she? He didn't bring her up!

Kathleen culls her memory and concedes that D'Arcy "Dace" what's-his-name was probably smart enough in his own way. The way con men often are. Not that he had much of a chance considering the kind of place he came from. The poor bastard was probably doomed from the start. But Mariposa isn't, on account of nurture and Kathleen's own strong genes.

Whatever happened to Dace, anyway? Kathleen was with him for such a short time. She doesn't remember much about him. Even his surname is buried layers deep underneath everything else she still hopes to accomplish in her life. She had to take off on him like that. She really did. She had better things to do. And he was on the run from something. Well, so was she, except she was chasing butterflies and pursuing her life's work while he was up to no damn good! True, he was her physical type—tall, dark and handsome, but personality-wise, the guy was a total Jekyll and Hyde.

Mummy, Mariposa used to ask, *who's my daddy?*

Papa was a rolling stone, Kathleen would tease, parroting another old song. Because it sounded better than the truth. That her kid's father was basically a sperm donor, an escaped convict who must have had the kind of childhood that encourages trouble and damages a personality, or he wouldn't have ended up like he did.

But, oh: Dace sure was handsome, way too handsome for his own good! And she needed him to get down into the States. Traipsing back and forth between Canada and Mexico, Kathleen got over her agoraphobia pretty darn fast, but the week she met him, she couldn't drive a mile without hyperventilating and breaking out into a cold sweat. She'd gone less than two hundred miles her first day on the road.

Her agoraphobia was probably the direct result of all the time she spent in the San. Which her psych Pearl also thinks. But when something like that's happening, you don't know what's going on. She'd just wanted to get on with her life, to get out of Montreal, to get down to Mexico so bad.

Wait a minute—wasn't Dace from Maitland? That's right, Dace—Dace Devereux, that was his family name, she remembers it now because she looked him up way back when—he had some other connection to Maitland besides the horrible prison he'd fled. His family had property there. Or so he'd claimed.

Whatever, Dace didn't know she was pregnant and she didn't either, or she would have done something about it. Like gone back to him in her fear and despair if he hadn't jumped back into jail.

Well, never mind. She's made a couple of poor choices in her life, but Mariposa isn't one of them.

Somehow Kathleen did it, did practically everything by herself, carried and gave birth to a baby, got her doctorate. Not many women could have accomplished what she had. Even if she was almost thirty, practically an old maid in 1973. Maybe if she'd realized how parasitic a baby is, how they cannibalize a parent — except of course she did. Parents in the animal kingdom, mothers and sometimes fathers, sacrifice everything for their young.

That's what life's all about, in nature.

She was getting on though. And maybe she identified with all those butterflies she'd studied, just a bit. She needed to have a baby, to have Mariposa. It was time.

Or maybe she was under some subtle pressure from her own mother. Informed people like to think that life's all about choice and free will. But it's not. For most of the world, family — biology — is destiny. She didn't want to think about what a pregnancy would do to her body — not to mention her profession — so she just didn't. Then after ignoring her body for a couple of menstrual cycles, it got too late.

So she had the baby and farmed it out for a while. Left little Mariposa with her own mum to raise. What's wrong with that? Look at the rest of the world. Few people raise a child singlehandedly.

The next time she got pregnant, she made a more rational choice. Mainly because she was in a much better frame of mind, so she was more focused on herself. Once she realized her body had decided to ovulate early and no doubt enticed the condom to break, there was still plenty of time to rectify its mistake. From the Morgentaler abortion clinic in Montreal, she went to the nearest hospital and got her tubes tied.

She had to argue with the damn fool doctor — a man! — but no woman in this day and age should count on a man to protect her. Especially if she can't even count on her own body. The surgery wasn't that bad anyway.

How else was she supposed to pursue her life's work and protect the monarchs?

But how ironic that she — sickly little Kathleen — turned out to be such a hale and fertile woman. Who knew?

Kathleen's eyes flicker to Mariposa's hips. Amazing how they have rounded out in the past few years. Expected, but still amazing, just like those masses of monarchs are every single time she sees them.

Dammit, the kid's probably just as fertile as she was. The faster she gets her on the pill, the better.

The girl is wasting so much time at high school, though. Even with her late birthday, Kathleen had graduated long before she was seventeen. And that was after spending several years in the San! Except for Mlle Beaulieu's efforts, the schooling she got there was totally inferior. She was self-taught for the most part, the way smart people often are.

This generation is just so damn spoiled. Mariposa's private school is so cushy, she's never going to want to leave. *Maybe if I enroll her in another school —*

"Go on," Mariposa prompts her again, like she's a forgetful old lady. Kathleen sits bolt upright and glares at her. Oh, for the good old days when you didn't have to explain everything to your kid and be their friend. The nerve of this kid! Nobody in the nineteen-fifties jumped to the conclusion that their mother was senile just because she didn't go on some talk show and 'fess up everything she knew.

Kathleen's still in her forties. And she looks ten years younger because she's always so careful in the sun. She has to be — first she got tuberculosis and then when she finally got her PhD, she ended up spending ten months down in Angangueo, Mexico every year.

But maybe the girl's worried on account of her grandmother, Kathleen's mother whose memory began to fail before she was even fifty. The woman who got to raise her granddaughter "Mary" Mariposa or "Posie" as she used to call her, because she couldn't raise her daughter Kathleen.

No, Kathleen hasn't forgotten anything. She's nothing like her mother, anyway, an artsy little woman who loved to cook up a storm and serve her husband three-course meals. Kathleen takes after — well, who knows? Her mother never said much about her father, either. She didn't have to in those days.

No, Kathleen didn't get to know her real father or her father's people and it's a little late now. The mind of the only person who could tell her — her mother's — is trapped in a more distant past.

How did that happen? Kathleen's a real scientist, not a social scientist, she knows how important good genes are. She knew this from her youth when her mother still had all her faculties. She shudders, recalling all those theories about nature versus nurture in the seventies. Junk science!

Still, she always meant to look up her father, the man who gave her half her genes. She just never got around to it. Too busy. And when it got right down to it, she didn't give a shit. What kind of moron got her mother knocked up and left her when she was barely seventeen?

But maybe she's getting on a little herself now. Doing stuff old people do — revisiting her past, reflecting on things that happened at the San.

She should go back there someday. See if the sanatorium's still standing or if something else has taken its place. For all she knows, it's a museum now.

Not that it matters. As long as there's milkweed and the sanatorium garden isn't paved over, the monarchs will still stop there when they migrate south in the fall.

Kathleen closes her eyes and it all floods back to her — early fall in Toronto, when the monarchs made their annual pit stop at the San on their incredible flight down south. She was almost ten years old. That's all she's got to remember — that she was nearly ten, the dividing line between childhood and girlhood — and swoosh, she's back in that magical place again.

For that reason alone, she's never indulged in illicit drugs. All she needs is her fine mind. For the most part, she's even avoided prescription drugs. She didn't need them after she got out of the San.

There's not a trace of TB left in her body except for a tiny shadow on her right lung.

Her memories are way better than drugs, anyway.

Mary Kathleen Aldous is such a clever little girl, that's the first thing people used to say about her. No, it was the second thing. The first thing they said about her—especially her mum's neighbours and friends—was, *oh, gosh, the poor kid's got TB...*

Down on the floor, Kathleen propped her heavy head on her elbows while she took a brief rest. Her roommates looked busy with their game but they'd bug her if they noticed her. That's how they got their thrills.

As if she would let them. This was her chance. Lots of people saw the monarchs last year, but she couldn't even get out of bed. She was so mad that she cried until somebody said, *Oh, never mind, dearie, they put on the same show every year.*

She crawled on just a little further, her eyes on the floor, until she butted into a wall.

The windowsill was two feet up from the floor. But what if she was wrong, what if they weren't there? *You can't believe everything you read in the news*, Mlle Beaulieu said.

There was no need to worry, though. The instant she hauled herself up to the windowsill, all she saw was monarchs. Hundreds, thousands of them—for all she knew, there might have been millions. They flew at her face, bits of black and orange, fast and thick. She ducked instinctively, but it was all right.

The monarchs couldn't get in and she couldn't get out.

Where were they all coming from? Where were they going? Wherever it was, she wanted to go.

But right then, she was lucky to be standing on her own two feet. Where she could pretend she was one of them, another super monarch butterfly come down from the sky.

From what she'd read, Kathleen knew that the first monarchs leave Ontario when the farmers bring their crops in, when summer dies into fall, when children go back to school.

Somewhere she'd also found out that monarchs were tropical creatures that spent the summer months in Canada and the winter ones in a much deeper south. When the Canadian temperatures dropped, their bodies told them what to do. Or was it the moon and stars? It sounded like a lot of hocus-pocus, but maybe it wasn't. Monarchs were probably just doing what they had to do. Heading south, but stopping when they must. Their wings weren't built to fly in the cold and dark, so at the first hint of sunset, they found a roosting place like the garden at the San. Give them a good wind and they'd be gone tomorrow.

Kathleen's legs were quivering by now. But she couldn't sit down, not yet.

Somebody else must have noticed the monarchs. A capped, skirted figure came out of the garden with a lit cigarette in one hand, moving pretty darn fast. A nurse who'd been on a break or who was meeting somebody there. The nurse didn't bother closing the garden gate. She didn't use the staff entrance at the side, either. She headed straight for the front doors of the San and rushed inside.

There was a whole lot of shouting and the sound of people running. Both double doors of the hospital flew open and crashed into brick walls. A minute later and the whole sanatorium was outside. Well, the whole sanatorium except for Kathleen and her roommates. Her dummy roomies were still playing jacks.

Kathleen shrank closer to the window. She watched the butterflies for ten minutes before they noticed her.

"Hey, look at her! How'd she get over there by herself?" a roommate shrieked. One girl came over and grabbed hold of Kathleen's arm until she saw all the monarchs.

"Ugh, bugs! They're all over the windows, they're trying to get in! I hate bugs!" the kid cried, hastily letting go of Kathleen and then inching back towards the door.

"I'll get Nurse," another girl volunteered.

Kathleen knew the butterflies wouldn't be there for long, that they'd be gone by first light, so it was a real effort to tear her eyes away from the garden tableau, but she did. Her silly roommates, except for the bold girl who went to fetch help, were squashed into the corner closest to the door, too scared to even look.

There wasn't much time left. Nurse Louise was going to throw a fit when she got here. The monarchs were already in a tizzy. There wasn't enough room for all of them to clump together and hang from the trees. But then they saw Kathleen. They whacked at her window pane with those little black things, their antennae and their needle-like legs.

Let us in, let us in!

"Shush," Kathleen whispered, pursing her lips against the window.

"Oh, yuck, she's kissing them!"

Not that she cares. The monarchs wouldn't be back for another year. With any luck, Kathleen would be long gone.

She took her lips away from the window and tried counting the butterflies instead, but it was impossible. *39, 40, oh, there's another one!* Stupid girls, she hated them, she really did. At least she saw the monarchs before they did. Yes, she saw them first, so they were all hers. *62, 63.* How big was a butterfly colony? How many colonies were there? Somehow or other, she had to find out.

She stopped counting them, though. She had to. It was no use, the way the monarchs had overlapped their wings in the trees. If she hadn't known better, she might have mistaken those clumps of butterflies for bouffant orange blooms. These monarchs were way bigger than the ones she'd seen in the spring. The strong, supple branches of the fir trees were sagging.

When some butterflies lost their perch and dropped to the ground, Kathleen almost cried. It pained her to see even a single one fall down.

It was getting darker and harder to see. But that was okay. Her hearing got better after nightfall. That's when she heard the rustling sound. It was so loud that she could hear it with the window closed. At first she thought the noise was coming from the trees, that a strong wind was blowing through their branches and all the leaves were falling down, but it wasn't that. It was the fluttering of all those monarch wings.

When Nurse Louise finally bustled in, headed straight to the window and grabbed her by the shoulders, Kathleen almost laughed in her face. Louise was tall and thin, a bit of a beanpole. Maybe that's why some monarchs had settled on her cap. But how did they get there—was she out in the garden too?

"You can find your own way back to bed," Nurse said, helping her along with a clip on the ear and a push in the right direction. Fresh adrenalin flooded through Kathleen, enough to convince her that she could walk back to bed on her own.

"You," Nurse continued, herding the remaining girls out of their corner, "you little devils!" She slapped at a few of their scuttling rumps with her right hand and then with her left one. Most of the jacks got swept under the beds with her foot.

Nurse Louise was so funny. Kathleen tried not to laugh, but then some of the other girls got the giggles. Soon they were all laughing. *Look at all those butterflies on Nurse's head!* One by one, the monarchs took off from her cap and headed straight for the ceiling but Nurse still didn't have a clue what was going on.

Nurse really flipped when all the girls started laughing.

"What in God's name are all you girls doing out of bed?" she hollered. "It's almost seven! Get into your nightgowns, this instant! You want to get better, don't you? And school's tomorrow! Mlle Beaulieu will whip you all into shape. She sure will! Don't give me those looks! Not that a bunch of sick girls like you ought to be in school. You're too sick!"

One of the girls couldn't quite stop giggling, but the rest of them did. They pulled their nightgowns out from under their pillows and put them on.

Nurse Louise wasn't finished though.

"I have a good mind to write your parents, your guardians and let them know what's going on," she continued muttering, as she circled the room and snapped a succession of top sheets tighter and tighter on their beds. "And let's see what Head Nurse has to say about this! She won't be pleased, that's for sure. Or Doctor. He'll — well, I don't know what he'll do when he finds out, but you won't like it. Just you wait and see, there won't be any treats at Hallowe'en for the girls in this ward. Or maybe he'll cancel *Christmas Carol* and the party! The very idea — you're here to get better, not to fool around! If you were my girls, except you aren't. I'm just the person who works here, twelve hours straight, day in and day out."

Kathleen was the last girl under her covers. Her legs still felt like noodles, but by holding onto her mattress for dear life, she hauled herself into bed just using her arms. Her neck muscles were practically useless, though. And worse in bed. Try as she might, she kept on missing the pillow with her head.

When Nurse Louise finally spotted the butterflies on the ceiling, she did one good deed before she blew out of their room. She opened a window.

"Shut your eyes and go to sleep," was the last thing she said. But Kathleen was still watching the monarchs in their room. They'd gone for the ceiling when they first arrived, but after Nurse turned off the light, they drifted towards the open window. Kathleen felt like she was flying too. She followed the butterflies back out into the garden. It was easy now that she was one of them. A large female monarch with a black body and orange wings, a butterfly who would catch a warm air current tomorrow and soar way up into the sky. The other girls had fell instantly asleep. Kathleen tried to stay awake, but she couldn't.

Her mother was waiting for her with a shovel. "You're not going any place. You're one sick little girl. If I've told you once, I've told you a thousand times—you're just going to have to stay inside and do what you're told."

Kathleen tried yelling, but her voice was no stronger than before. When she was even smaller and she heard people talk about going "into the San," she thought they were talking about a big, black hole in the ground.

In her dreams, in all her nightmares at the sanatorium, her mother got the San, the Sand, ready for her.

"This is for your own good," she said just before she grabbed her daughter and dropped her into a hole cushioned with the velvety remains of dead butterflies, of all those monarchs Kathleen couldn't save.

Chapter Two
Micah Devereux — Here Be Dragons

Dovercourt Grove Park, Toronto, Monday, June 11, 1990

Micah James Devereux might have been conceived for all the wrong reasons — so his mother Liza could fill up the hole his father's flight ripped in her when she was twenty years old — but it doesn't show. For a long time, until he hits his mid-teens anyway, he's sunny and predictable, the book-loving son of his mother's dreams and the delight of his father.

Except for Sammy and Eden who at first glance look different with their gold spun hair, all the Devereux children share a strong physical resemblance, but Micah's the child everybody hopes for, the kind that makes a parent proud. He does well in school, he gets picked for teams and he's that rarity, a kind-hearted person who can put other people before himself. He's even on the debating team and he can play guitar. When he strums *The Girl from Ipanema* in the schoolyard, all the high school girls swoon.

And he's funny, even if he hasn't been much fun lately. *No fair*, say the brother and sister who are next to him.

But he's so boring! Summer, the elder of Micah's two sisters can usually be counted on to protest. All her short life, she's been jealous of the time Micah takes from their father when he's home.

Whenever the children's father René "Dace" Gagnon comes back from his forays and the weather's favourable, Micah's the one he takes out on the Harley. Not that Dace has much choice—his second son Sammy hates the Harley and anything mechanical and his wife Liza Devereux is super cautious about getting on a bike now. She's busy overseeing her large brood and working at *Dazzle Publications* as an editor.

As for the girls, Summer and Eden, they're still too young. Their mother doesn't want them on any bike, not even their dad's. The less they have to do with bikes and bikers, like—well, never mind that. The twins Cory and Cole have just gotten up and started walking and talking, so who knows what wild, dangerous things they'll do, but the less they have to do with bikers, the better.

Liza scowls her head off if she so much as hears the local motorcycle gang roar up Dufferin Street on its way to Rutherford Road or someplace in Woodbridge where the outlaw biker gangs hang out.

And God help the guy if she spots one of the hairy beasts in the vicinity of Dovercourt Grove Park. Lucky for the Devereuxes, the park's practically right in their front yard. Never mind that Dace keeps his Harley in the garage right behind the house. Liza's dislike of bikers and other layabouts is well-known. Her hardworking neighbours aren't fond of freeloaders either.

The family's Edwardian house sits squarely on Southview Avenue, the southern border of the park, so it's easy to keep an eye on what's going on there. Micah has gone over to the playground by himself ever since he was five or six.

The downside of living near the park is the noise. All sorts of people use the park. Come summertime, the beer-fueled parties go on all night long. Some of the neighbours—the high school kids anyway—are worse than the bikers, but who wants a biker hanging around the park? On the rare occasion, Dace goes over to the park to dispatch the offender or Liza does it herself, but they never call the police. For as long as Micah can remember, his parents have been suspicious of the police or people in uniform, but he doesn't think much about it. Lots of people in his neighbourhood hate cops.

Cops and criminals — two sides of the same coin, he hears over and over.

Micah has always taken his father's frequent absences for granted, but lately he's begun to wonder. Where does the guy really live? In one of his planes? He wasn't even on the voter's list, the last time Micah saw one stapled to a wooden hydro post.

Liza notices everything, which is probably why she's the family's chief organizer. Somebody has to be. She draws the line at keeping track of all their school assignments and teacher's notes sometimes get lost in the laundry or their backpacks, but their library books are never overdue, their activities and medical appointments get marked on a washable calendar on the fridge, all their photos are labeled in numbered albums, the basement freezer's filled with make-ahead meals and she keeps an up-to-date list of emergency numbers by the kitchen phone.

She worries about her kids all the time too, something else Micah takes for granted. She's a mother, isn't she?

"You can go over to our old neighbour, Mrs. Campione — she's just over there on Hallam," she says, "if you ever need help. But it better not be because somebody's acting up around here. The Jaffe nanny would help you too. What a prize that girl is! Nobody wants the police coming around here. There's lots of poor people here and sometimes poor people have things to hide."

"Like what?" Summer asks, nosy as usual. "Bad things?"

"What?" Liza always stalls. Maybe she's just irritated with herself for saying too much, but then she bulldozes ahead and overdoes her explanation again. Why's she always doing that? So she'll know what to leave out?

"No, no, not bad things exactly," she explains, "just things they don't want the police to know, like maybe a relative is an illegal immigrant or something. I don't know! We can't all be lucky enough to have been born in Canada, to have access to a health plan like OHIP, to go to school and to work."

She doesn't have much time for the unemployed men who play cards in Dovercourt Grove Park all the time either, but she leaves them alone.

Micah's always read the news, from the time he was in grade three anyway. The *Toronto Star* is delivered to their front door during the week and the *Globe* comes on the weekend. He reads all the news, good and bad. *So why are we still living in this neighbourhood then?* he wonders especially after nine-year-old Sharin' Morningstar Keenan disappears from a nearby park and eleven-year-old Alison Parrott vanishes when she emerges from the St. George subway station, but he never says anything about moving. His Dovercourt Grove Park place, so close to the subway and downtown Toronto, is the only home he's ever known.

Sometimes people talk about things they shouldn't—stuff that's none of their business—but nobody talks about grown men fooling around with little boys if they can help it. They just don't. For a long time, Micah thinks that bad stuff like that only happens to girls.

There's no place else to go anyway. No way he wants to live out in the burbs in someplace like Scarborough. Just in case, he walks his sisters to school, though Dovercourt Public School is just around the corner, up the block a bit and across Hallam Street. He usually hangs around when they're home from school too, while his mother's stuck in the subway worming its way through downtown Toronto, as she returns from the job that helps pay their bills. Micah has kept this up—walking the girls to school— even after he started Kent Senior Public School and Bloor Collegiate, a few blocks south of their home.

Going by the mail that flutters through the slot in their front door Monday to Friday, they sure do have a lot of bills. Their debt skyrocketed after the family moved into a larger, three-story detached house a few doors around the corner from the little dollhouse Liza rented on Hallam Street while she did her master's at the University of Toronto.

You're so lucky, everybody tells his mother, seeing how helpful he is his kid sisters.

You're so lucky, people also tell his father, seeing how Liza's contrived to keep her looks in spite of having all those kids.

But they think his mother is the luckiest person of all, a Canadian born woman with an education, a big family and a full-time job. How did she get so lucky? It's 1990 now, but the women in the seventies and eighties sure didn't get to have it all. *Nor should they* is what some people still think.

Not that his mother acts that lucky, except about her kids. She works as an editor at *Dazzle*, a job she won when her best friend Val Jaffe moved on to work at the *Toronto Star*. But what she really wanted to do, what she really wanted to be, was an English professor. She even started, but she never finished her PhD. She's always writing though. When Micah and Sammy get dropped off by a neighbour from their late night hockey practices, they see the light on in the porch attached to the master bedroom.

Look at that, the driver will cluck, *Your Ma's still up*. There's a big oak desk in the porch, a swivel rattan chair, a Van Gogh print on one wall and a small pullout couch.

Sammy and the girls were all born in the master bedroom. Yes, his mother has some nice digs on the second floor at the front of the house, including her own bathroom with a decades old deep, claw-footed tub. Micah gets to share a roughed-in shower with his younger brother Sammy on the third floor. When they're older, the twins will end up there, too.

Unless he goes away to university, but he'll probably have to go to the University of Toronto. It's so close that his mother used to walk there with him in a baby carrier while she was doing her master's. It was a long walk, but she did it except when it snowed.

Yep, she's pretty amazing all right. Even if she couldn't quite pull off a PhD with another five kids in tow.

Okay, so Micah's begun to resent his mother just a bit. Sure she started out with little but she has way more than other people's mothers do now. She really does.

Why does she take over everything? he fumes late at night when he can't sleep. His dad Dace sleeps with her on their legless king size mattress when he's home, but he isn't carved into the woodwork of the house like she is, he isn't part of the air Micah's got to breathe. Nor has Dace claimed every last nook and cranny in the house, including all the closets. Liza's forever foraging and rearranging. The woman would move walls if she could, she'd alter the very bones of the house.

She already has! The wall that created a tiny corridor leading to the kitchen is long gone. Micah has a dim memory of Liza getting Dace to smash down the wall, how the plaster dust went everywhere and made them all sneeze. What's with her anyway?

Okay, so Dace has the garage, supposedly a double one, not that you'd know it with all the junk inside. When Micah was little, he used to pretend that his father was just sleeping in the garage. He felt so much better, so much safer when Dace was home. They all did. They all do. Not that there's much room in the garage anymore. Home to generations of raucous raccoons and annual influxes of mice, it's bursting at the seams with a motorbike, bicycles, toboggans and a slew of tools, just like all the other junky garages in their neighbourhood.

Liza has always shared the classics she loves with her firstborn son. He's an insatiable reader. He got that one from her for sure. He was practically raised in the cavernous rooms at Gladstone Public Library. One by one, he went through all the novels in the children's department, starting with the 'A' named authors just like she did. Lucky them, Gladstone is just a few blocks from Southview where they live.

Bookcases also crowd the bedrooms and overflow the narrow hallways of their family home. The books, though mostly poetry and novels, are separated into fiction and nonfiction, with the novels alphabetized by the authors' surnames.

Their house on Southview is nothing like his friends' homes. Most of his friends' houses are crammed with canned tomato sauce and cured meats. There's enough homemade wine in their root cellars for everybody. Even the children in these houses drink a little wine with dinner. In the long narrow backyard gardens that are laid out just like his, somebody—a woman usually—grows grapes for wine and vegetables instead of all those useless flowers, the foxglove, the morning glories and the roses that his mother likes.

Best of all, black dressed ladies preside over the basement kitchens of his friends' houses and they're always making food. It's just what they do. They work, they don't loll around reading books, that's for sure. Most of them don't even watch English TV.

Micah has grown at least a foot in the past two years. He's practically starving all the time.

Maybe you've got a tapeworm in there, his dad sometimes jokes.

On the nights that Liza goes grocery shopping at Knob Hill Farms and stops with Dace to have a couple of beers at a local pub if he's home—c'mon, who else's parents do that?— there's hardly any food left in the house, except for frozen home-cooked meals or Styrofoam trays of poorly labeled meat that he would have to haul out of their freezer to defrost and cook.

I'm tired of cooking, Liza has even started saying, which also rubs Micah the wrong way. Other people's mothers don't talk like that. *Nobody eats half the stuff I cook or sits down at the same time, anyway*, she explains—kind of guiltily, Micah thinks.

At least Summer has figured out how to make Kraft dinner— the "Babysitter's Special" as his father has dubbed Kraft macaroni and cheese—though technically Micah and maybe Sammy in a pinch are the only children in the house old enough to use the stove or maybe the microwave.

Micah doesn't know anything about his father's secret life either — not because he couldn't snoop around the mountains of old *Maitland Spectators* and some of those *Toronto Stars* heaped in the garage and find out, but because he really doesn't want to know.

The way his mother calls his father "Dace" and everybody else calls him "René" — *It's his nickname,* she's explained — is confusing enough.

Let his nosy sisters excavate his parents' mysterious history when they grow up. Yeah, let them do some research, coauthor one of those blab books and go on national TV.

Sure he knows there's something bad way back when by the trouble he sometimes sees in his mother's eyes. But the past is the past. There's nothing he can do about it. And he's going to have enough troubles of his own.

Listen to the way people talk — if you want trouble, you got trouble! Trouble finds you, no matter what talisman you hold close to your heart, no matter what God you pray to, no matter what steps you take. You could hide in a cave on a mountainside and it would still find you for God's sake. It finds some people faster, that's all. Maybe it even gets a bit of help. *Whoa,* you think, *where did that one come from? Am I cursed or what? What the heck did I do wrong in my past life?*

You do your best, you take every precaution, you listen to your elders and you learn from their mistakes, but you're still totally screwed.

Or worse, Micah thinks, his mind flashing to the body of a nine-year-old girl in a rooming house refrigerator. What family — what child brings that on herself? Let's face it, a lot of stuff that happens to people is pure evil or monstrous bad luck.

Yeah, let his sisters write their memoirs, like those losers he sees on late night television, the children of dead celebrities, who are peddling books.

Micah isn't even interested in the past as a predictor of the future. Deposited on a remote island with a trunkful of books, he'd read anything, but he'd go through all the science fiction first. Give him a classic like *Brave New World* or *Dune* or a chance to watch *Star Trek* reruns after school and he's in his element.

He isn't sure why exactly, but he figures that if he imagines the worst, it won't happen. What's the use in bemoaning history, anyway? What's the use in whining about what's already gone and done? The future is what matters. It can still be changed.

In his history class, the leaders who have come and gone all sound so moronic and cruel. Look at Hitler. Where did he spring from? How did such atrocities occur in World War II, anyway? No point in even asking his parents. They were both born after the war, so it's his grandparents who must know, who bear responsibility for what happened in the thirties and forties if anybody does. Everything that's ever happened was done in the name of some religion or to keep women and other people enslaved, if not to exterminate them. Do some men really think that they'll live forever, that there'll be no final reckoning and that if they somehow escape and earn the glory of God or Allah, that their descendants won't have to pay?

Look at what the last generation—and this one really is his parents' fault—has done to the ozone layer and look at what they're doing to the educational system right now. All those cuts! It makes him so goddamn mad.

And more and more crap keeps coming out about the goings-on at the residential and training schools in Canada and abroad. Stuff about Mount Cashel and some other real bad shit over in Ireland and down in the States. What's wrong with people, especially the adults? No wonder so many of his classmates and friends take to drink and drugs. Lucky him, he wasn't made that way. Getting drunk or being drugged doesn't turn him on.

No, he really doesn't want to know what happened to his parents before their babies came along and brought them so much joy, well his mother, anyway. Not that his parents are always joyful. Far from it. He just doesn't want to end up totally miserable, his whole fucking life spent, kind of the way he feels right now.

He knows his parents aren't entirely happy because they aren't shy about arguing, much as they try to do it behind closed doors. From what he's overheard, Dace was conflicted about having so many kids and maybe even about having him, but Liza wasn't. It's not his dad's fault, though. What the heck's a guy supposed to do? Get the big snip? He really can't see his father doing that, not Dace. Not to mention he'd probably have to pay cash to get it done down in the States.

Though he was born in Toronto, Dace doesn't have an Ontario health card, something that even the most recent immigrants can get. A good thing he's so healthy. The one time he got sick and he didn't get better right away, Liza dosed him with some antibiotics she got from a walk-in clinic. After that, she kept some penicillin in her room.

But kids are such a big responsibility and fathers are supposed to be financially responsible for them. Or should be. Mothers are too, but bringing home a paycheck is really the father's job. If Micah got some poor girl knocked up even once, he doesn't know what he'd do, so he would have felt the same way as his dad about having so many kids. And in a perverse kind of way, his father's qualms about siring more brats has always reassured Micah that he's his real son. Why would Dace want another kid when he already had him?

When he's in a good mood and his brothers and his sisters aren't driving him crazy, Micah doesn't even blame his mother. She's obsessed about babies, but she's okay, most of the time.

There are worse kinds of obsessions and passions to have, worse things she could do. She could be a drunk, a drug addict, a smoker, the kind of woman who loves too widely and not just unwisely and then what? What would happen to all her kids?

There's a couple of mothers right in his neighbourhood whose kids aren't doing very well.

Micah was an only child while his mother was finishing her master's at the U of T, an act which earned her a steady job and salary and brought some much needed stability into their lives. She talks about this sometimes, like it's a heroic story from her past. Before that, the family relied on a patchwork of resources — Liza's scholarships and student loans, Dace's sporadic infusions of money into their checking account from his American interests and Grandpa's magnificent gift of the down payment for this house on Southview. But did any of this stop his mother from having more kids? Hell, no.

Lately Micah has also begun to recall his early childhood with just a bit of nostalgia, like the other day when their old Greek guy neighbour got a good look at the twins, shook his head and said Micah used to be the only "king"! Yeah, well, those were the days.

Micah had already celebrated his fifth birthday when his younger brother Sammy wrestled his way into the world, a couple of ounces heavier than the ten pound whopper he'd been, but oh-so-much easier to birth. His mother tells this story all the time. Jeez-Louise, she's always talking about giving birth!

Other women are satisfied with their firstborn and maybe one more. An heir and a spare. Yes, that's what most sane women are doing, just having one or two children, hedging their bets.

When Micah was born at his Grandpa's house in Maitland, Dace was away, but miracle of miracles, Dace — and sometimes Micah too — ended up at the rest of the kids' births. All Micah's siblings, except for the twins, were born upstairs in this very house, on the bed or in the bathtub. Little Eden almost came out on the floor. Liza had reluctantly gone to Women's College Hospital for her last birthing.

The way his mother tells it, she had absolutely no help during the births and she still doesn't. Also, the roof is leaking, the paint in the hallway is peeling, half the laundry has gotten lost again, the dishes are piling up in the sink and there are more dust bunnies under the beds. As far as she's concerned, she's singlehandedly raising her kids.

Okay, so there's some truth in this because even when Dace is home, he lies pretty low. He's their father though. Lots of people's fathers aren't around much unless they're unemployed. Some of his friends' dads weren't even in the delivery room. Seeing his mum give birth when he was a kid didn't scare Micah, but it apparently scares the heck out of a lot of grown men. Is that the kind of man his mother wants? Probably not.

Not that Micah cares to know about his father's absences, either. No, he really doesn't need to know everything, like all the females in his damn house, including the sitter and his grandmother who come and go. There's comfort in denial, in not knowing. Happiness for sure. What if it turns out that his dad gallivants around because he's more interested in men than in women, like Micah's friend's father is? Micah doubts this very much, but you never know.

Or that he's hidden another family somewhere? That's what happened to another friend at Kent Senior Public when he and Micah were in eighth grade and what a fuckup—no what a calamity that was. *Yeah, that's right, listen to your mother and call it a calamity*, Dace always says with a little smirk, *Not a fuckup. You'll stand out better that way.*

What if his dad has Mafia or outlaw biker connections, like some of the other guys in the hood, those biker wannabees say? Jeez, what a pack of storytellers those guys are, the guys he hangs out with in the laneway and sometimes—unbeknownst to his mother—in a Bloor Street pool hall. Some say that Dace even wanted to start his own biking club, but if he did, it was a long time ago.

Whatever, Micah would lose his father, the strongest man in the neighbourhood, the one he always points out and says, *hey, that's my dad!* And the neighbours would lose him. Everybody on the little streets around Dovercourt Grove Park looks to his father—the man they call René Gagnon—to help them out with their cars especially, but sometimes they need repairs to their old brick houses or they're mixed up with some thug. Dace can talk sense to most people, probably because just one look at him and you don't give him any guff.

A good thing that when he's home, René "Dace" Gagnon also fixes his own house and works out at the gym as much as he can—to keep himself in shape, he always says and because he was too wild to stay in school.

"Too wild?" Summer sometimes asks. "What's that mean? Are you guys like hippies or something, you and Mum?"

"Jesus," Dace always reassures her, with a little shudder, "not that. Well, okay, maybe your mother is! Who else delivers at home in this day and age?"

"Delivers? She's not having another baby, is she?" Sammy worries. A frown creases his still rounded face and his hair is all sprouted up in points like Bart Simpson's on that new show. "That old guy next-door is scared we're going to run out of room and that we'll all be hanging like bats from the rafters soon."

On the occasions that Liza works late and Dace is actually home, he hangs out at the YMCA at College and Dovercourt Streets. If the twin-obsessed girl from down the street can come over to babysit, Dace takes his older boys with him, Micah and Sammy. He's such a proud papa then with such a fine pair of sons, even if Micah's gotten a bit lazy lately and just sits there on a gym bench reading while every passing woman drags her fingers through his hair.

Micah still wants to go to the Y though, even if he doesn't work out. The big gym stinks of sweat and testosterone and bleach, but he likes watching his father. The guy's in his element there. He can bench press way better than anybody else, except for maybe the local heavyweight champion who made good when he was a teenager but who couldn't leave his mother and the rest of the west end behind.

As if west end Toronto is such a great place, Micah thinks, trying to dismiss the latest newspaper headline about yet another missing girl as he cracks open the sports section of the *Star* instead.

What do men want with little girls, anyway?

Well, some men, not all of them. For a long time, he doesn't understand and when he finally does, the sight of his own sisters and his knowledge about what a pervert might try to do to them makes him sick, just sick. Just let some perv look at one of his sisters the wrong way and he'll kill the bastard with his bare hands. He goes down to the basement bathroom and barfs, calling upstairs just in case somebody has overheard him, "I'm okay, I'm okay!"

Dace also goes downtown a lot when he's in Toronto, but for this kind of "work" as he calls it, he usually wears a suit.

"Doesn't Daddy look sharp?" Micah's grandmother can always be counted on to say the odd time she sees her son-in-law off.

"No, he looks like a criminal," Micah hears his mother say under her breath once, but only once and probably because she was mad about something else. Why the hell else would she say such a damn stupid thing?

Micah isn't sure, but he thinks his grandmother compliments his father like this to encourage him to have more financial responsibility for his children. He wouldn't put it past her. Grandma's a bit sneaky that way. And from her point of view, it's Dace's fault for impregnating her daughter Liza, again and again.

That boy could have and should have gotten a vasectomy, especially after the twins, Micah has even heard her say. *It's an easy enough operation for a man, just one little snip.* Apparently she knew one man who wouldn't get it done and his wife... well, never mind.

And Dace needs to get a snip for other reasons. Liza's kids all look healthy, but you never know. Sometimes illness — especially mental illness — doesn't show up for years. Or skips a generation! Look at her own twins, also boys.

Twins run in the Magill family, her side, so Micah's got the impression that she doesn't mind taking credit for this.

Liza's brothers, the boys are okay now, no thanks to their father, a man Micah's never actually met and isn't especially keen to after listening to his mother and his grandmother talk about him, but right through their twenties, it was touch and go. Oh, the trouble and grief those kids caused everybody! Micah's grandma especially. She almost lost her mind.

Not that Micah's grandmother actually says such things to Dace or Liza. She tries not to interfere, she really does. Grandma is a far cry from the opinionated old ladies in the neighbourhood who are always telling their families what to do. But when Micah visits her over on Clinton Street which he has been doing a lot lately, if only to escape his hellhole of a house and get some peace and quiet to study for an exam, he hears her on the phone talking to one of her friends, or maybe to a sister-in-law. She talks mostly about her family.

As the oldest daughter in a big family who married a man from an even bigger family, Grandma has way more sisters-in-law than Micah cares to count. She even kept in touch with the ones from her husband's side, long after he left. Grandma's never been a grasping woman, but she was poor when she was raising her own children, so she wants more for her daughter's family. Or maybe she just wants more bragging rights about her wonderful daughter, Micah's not sure.

No, whatever the heck Dace is doing, it's not enough as far as the ladies in his family are concerned, which is why Micah needs to get a university degree like his clever mum. Not that Dace's kids ask him much when he takes off for "work," but they don't ask their mother about her job either.

For the most part, for their younger kids anyway, Dace and Liza are just Dad and Mum.

In addition to spiffing up in a suit for God-knows-what in down-town Toronto, Dace also takes frequent and mysterious flights, mostly from the island airport.

Dace doesn't exactly own it, but he has an interest in a small airport just outside of Toronto. He got a pilot's licence down in Mexico that he's kept up for years. This flying business kind of grabs at Micah, especially since his father never takes him along on that kind of ride. Not that he wants to know the nuts and bolts of planes or the business. He just wants to go someplace. Anyplace will do.

But the moment Dace starts grabbing his hair with both hands and arguing with Liza about family time and saying stuff like, *Well, okay then, you'd better make damn sure the kids don't take after me*, Micah knows he'll wake up the next fine morning and find his father gone. He can pretty much count on this. And, yeah, it's begun to piss him off, even if a man's a man and he's got to work.

Maybe if Dace called or left notes while he's away, it would help, but he never does. Sometimes he's gone for weeks and sometimes it's just a few days. He's gotten better though. Once when Micah was real little, he was away for months.

Liza always seems to fall apart the minute he leaves and leans on Micah and little Summer or she'll take the babies to bed with her, but she usually perks right up. She's got to. It's that or go crazy and smother them all in their beds. To be fair, Micah only hears her say this once, but it's enough. It scares the bejesus out of him! What kind of woman—what kind of mother— says such things? Luckily his grandmother's there for dinner that night. And maybe they're all a bit rattled by what they just heard on the six o'clock CTV news.

"Look, Liza, maybe it's too much for you," his grandma sympathizes with her daughter instead of fussing around about herself, which is also strikes him as a bit unusual, " — the house, the kids and always being on your own! I know what it's like, your father was never around much either and then one day, he just up and left while I was in hospital and already half out of my mind! No wonder I nearly went crazy! The doctor said I was completely run down, what with you and the twins and everything else going on. Look at that poor woman a few subway stops over who just stabbed her husband and one of her little girls to death. What was going through her head? She was hardly more than a girl herself, married to man in his forties. You might be better off without him — "

"What, who, Dace?" Liza spins around from the kitchen sink.

Micah's grandmother hesitates just a little, but then she blurts out, "I sure was! You know your dad! I was upset at first when he took off like that, but maybe he did me a favour. That's what the doctor said. Some of the Devereuxes are a bad lot, that side of the family."

Usually Liza lets her mother just reel out all her old stories about her family and what she was doing back in 1945 or in the Great Depression, but on this occasion, she throws an oatmeal-encrusted pot back into the stainless steel sink and sputters through her clenched teeth,

"I'm okay and Dace is too! My only problem is that I don't have a single kid who's capable of picking up a sock or washing a pot. Why's that? What in God's name am I doing wrong? Go home, Mum. The younger ones are sleeping and Micah can't stay up playing Dungeons and Dragons all night." This, though she called her mother earlier in the day and begged her to come over and keep her company.

Much as she always says she wanted them, her kids seem to grind Liza down to the bone when she spends a lot of time alone with them. Weight just falls away from her when Dace is gone, showing first in her face. She'll call her mother or go round to her best friend's place, Val Jaffe's, just to talk. When the kids were younger, she'd move her mother right in with them for a day or two. She never wanted to be a single parent, Micah still hears her say, even if this begs the obvious question: what in hell possessed her to have so many kids in the first place, especially with Dace? Other women know their limits, or should. One thing's certain—they aren't having kids all over the place.

There's already too many people in the world! It's embarrassing. What was his mother thinking? Except for the midwife, nobody else they know has multiple children, unless they've had more than one husband.

From what Micah's grandmother says, it wasn't always like this, but ever since the seventies, women have to and want to work outside the home and so they should. A girl shouldn't be dependent on a man. That's just asking for trouble, it really is. Men leave—and you know, lots of time it's for a much younger gal—and they never, ever do what they say. The next thing a woman knows, she's sixty-five, she's sick and she's on her own. If she's waiting for the government to look after her, good luck! Grandma couldn't feed a kitten on the pension she gets.

In some ways, his mother is just as bad as his grandmother when it comes to this kind of talk. Micah overhears her spouting anti-man to stuff to her friend Val Jaffe and making other controversial statements, though she never says much about his father Dace.

Nobody really talks about Dace. They just don't.

If only she would talk to me like that, Micah sometimes thinks.

Not that he really wants her to. It's just their women's intimacy he craves, because the more time his mother spends with other people, the less time she has for him. Duh. But Liza needs her friend Val Jaffe and her mother. Anybody can see that! She glows, especially after she talks to Val and she always comes back refreshed.

Lucky, because whatever Liza had taken on, whatever crisis is brewing at work, her babies always have unexplained but dangerously high fevers; strep throat rages through the entire family; Summer is just plain difficult, the kind of kid who gets on your nerves; Eden knocks out one of her precious front teeth and Sammy brings home a D in Science and he's only in grade six for God's sake! All that kid does is doodle, drawing cartoons over and over, though they're kind of witty and cute and Liza plasters them all over the fridge.

Please, she has recently taken to lamenting under her breath, so God knows what else she tells her mother and Val Jaffe, *don't let my babies grow up to be psycho teenagers!* Even worse, nobody knows how to clean up the house except her, the taxes aren't done and a mouse has gotten at the kitchen garbage again and no, mice aren't cute at all, she loathes the repulsive, nasty little things.

Micah never goes through the drawers and cupboards or snoops behind the bookshelves like his sisters do, the older and more daring they grow, but he listens to his parents yakking in the front of their old station wagon at the drive-in movies when they think their kids are all asleep or on one of their long, boring summer car trips. Especially if they're talking about him and they usually are. They really don't talk about much else except the plots of boring novels Liza edits or his grandmother's latest ailment or some kind of shit that happened in the distant past and still haunts them, but he really doesn't want to know about.

On the rare occasion that his parents mention bikers, drugs or prison or Liza says, *Surely to God, your old buddy isn't up to the same old shit!* Micah just stops listening.

He's got to or they'll blow his mind.

Summer's all ears if she's awake, but not him. Maybe that's the real reason he's always been so good in school—he has an amazing ability to shut down all sorts of crap. Take that away from him and he might not be as smart.

Here be dragons, he thinks, the moment his parents plunge willfully, carelessly into their murky past.

Dace and Liza clearly adore all their children and are amused by them, but he's the one they find the most intriguing, the one who bears the burden of their unfinished dreams.

He doesn't know how he knows this, he just does.

But the responsibility he feels for so many younger siblings is getting to be a real hassle. It doesn't take a genius to figure this one out. Lucky for his parents, he's been pleasant and even-tempered this long. They've had a pretty good run.

Maybe they should just get off his back and count their blessings, considering what goes on in other places. A couple of guys got themselves kicked out and slept in their friends' garages for months. Or maybe those guys just took off, whatever. They had to go. His parents—well, mostly his mother—only really started to bug Micah after he hit fourteen or fifteen. Even now, extreme irritation only washes over him in intermittent waves.

It's like a switch gets turned on. It scares the hell out of him. The blood rushes up into his head and he hates everybody and everything. If he could just do something about it! Like break out or smash some holes in all the old plaster walls of their house! Or pop some random fucker in the nose! Get the hell out of here.

At least this isn't America, so there's no guns in the house. His mother even got rid of his father's hunting rifle. Years and years ago. She tells this story over and over, like it makes her some kind of saint, never mind that when she's on her own, she could use a little personal protection.

"Where's my oldest son?" she's also started saying a little mournfully, which bugs him even more. "It's like he's already moved out."

"Or been hijacked by aliens!" Dace quips when he's home, trying to be funny, but only making things worse.

No wonder Micah can't stand the sight of them sometimes. They're sucking the bejesus life out of him! He'd like to tell them except he doesn't have the nerve. He daydreams about it, though.

If I could just go someplace, he thinks and dreams all the spring of 1990, when he's turning seventeen. Way out west to the mountains or down east to the coast. He's had his eye on his father's bike for years. Dace lets him tool around on it in the laneway sometimes and he's finally agreed to help Micah get his licence in June. Micah could have gotten his licence last year, but Liza wouldn't let him.

What a beauty the Harley is! Most of the time, that bike's just wasted in the garage. It's in mint condition and raring to go, a real temptation if Micah had access to the key, licence or not. His father keeps his bike way better than he keeps anything else in their house, though he sure does lots of upkeep when he's home. Not much for his mother to complain about there.

"Maybe I'll borrow Dad's bike and go across Canada," Micah announces half-jokingly to his parents one fine spring evening when Dace is actually home. He's never been anyplace by himself except to camp in Algonquin Park and his grandpa's place near Maitland.

His father must think a solo bike trip across Canada is a fine idea because he nods and looks quite pleased, like his firstborn is a chip off the old block. In hindsight, Micah probably should have asked his dad first and gotten him on his side, but she's there as usual, dammit. His mother hardly ever leaves his father's side when he's home, except to go to work.

"Over my dead body," she immediately says, tossing aside another book she just complained she doesn't have time to read. She adds with what sounds like a sob of a relief, "Besides, you're going back to Camp Arrowshot, right? I worked at a day camp one summer in Maitland, but your dad and I never had this kind of opportunity. You'll love it!"

Yeah, sure, Micah thinks. *I don't think so.* Jesus, he's sick and tired of people telling him what to do. Though a camp counselor's job pays a mere pittance and he probably could have gotten a job in construction through one of the neighbour guys his Dad has helped out over the years, he agreed to be a CIT, a Counselor-in-Training at camp last year. Big mistake! That's him though. He hates making waves. Working as a CIT for a month was pure slavery, so working as a counselor all summer long will probably be ten times worse.

His mother will make him go when he'd be far better off traveling on his own. The stuff he'd learn, the experiences he'd have on the wide open road! Just wait, she won't be able to stop him once he's eighteen. The bike trips his father talked about sound so cool. Or maybe Micah can get his pilot's licence—yeah, sure, as if his mother will go for that! Well, another year or two, he'll make and save a little money and she won't have any say.

He hoped and prayed that the directors at Arrowshot wouldn't offer him a job this year, but of course they did. His offer of employment arrived a few weeks ago, apparently delayed by a missing postal code. His mother practically wept for joy and waxed on about the loons, the wolves, the deer, the clear waterways and the good, clean air. The next thing he knew, he was looking for a new sleeping bag, but his own feelings are still quite mixed.

Oh, joy, he can canoe through vast stretches of forests and lakes, when he'd much rather be biking through mountains, lucky him! He's been a camper at Arrowshot for years, but probably because of his athleticism and his co-operative nature, he's one of the director's first choices. If the damn camp wasn't so isolated, it might be okay, but Little Joe Lake is really in the boonies.

"You're so lucky," his mother says, but he takes no pleasure in his acceptance at all. Success comes so easily to him that he takes it for granted.

Though Liza's still watching him anxiously, Micah doesn't bother answering her. It's no use. The woman always gets what she wants. She always has! She's spoiled rotten. Her and all her damn kids. Just then, he hears some high-pitched shrieks from the basement playroom where the twins are zooming around on their Big Wheels, while the girls try to watch *Little House on the Prairie*. Jesus, there are kids everywhere in this goddamn house!

He kicks a section of his father's discarded newspaper on the floor. He slams his fist into the solid oak frame of the doorway on his way out of the living room too, just to make his point. Knowing them, his parents are trading accusatory looks about what the other one could have and should have done, but he doesn't care.

At least the wildlife's kind of cool in Algonquin Park. Speaking of which, that girl might come back to camp! The one who, well, they really didn't do anything. She was still kind of young last summer or maybe he just doesn't feel that way about her. But man oh man, they sure could talk. They had one of those instant connections, the way you do with a complete stranger in a waiting room, never mind that you'll never see each other again.

She—Mariposa Aldous—was so much like him. She couldn't stand being at home either, though she alternated between two real cool places, Montreal and Mexico. Her mother's some kind of academic just like his mother. The bulging envelopes with the long, wordy letters they got from their mothers and never bothered to answer is what drew them together in the first place.

He isn't sure where else he wants to be or even who else he wants to be with, but he wants to be himself, not the latest plot twist in one of his mother's novels. He doesn't even want to be like his father anymore, a strong man, a— He isn't sure what exactly his father is anyway, cool as he is. Micah just wants to be himself. What's wrong with that? Be true to yourself, everybody says. It's what you're supposed to do.

From the hallway, he races up two long flights of stairs to his room at the top of the house, scaring both their tabby cats on the way. It's his parents who are making him so crazy. Look at all his friends, it's what parents do! They fuck up their own lives, so they can fuck up yours. No wonder the whole world's such a mess!

Kickboxing some dirty laundry out of the way, he crosses his room to the window overlooking the street and the park. There's a bar across the window so a small child can't fall out. Yeah, the bar's still in place and here he is, almost seventeen. Like he could just lower himself out the window and leave anyway! It's a thirty foot drop and he's no Spider-Man. But the rope fire ladder is still there, folded on the floor just below the window. Maybe he can squeeze out...

If only he was stupid and lazy enough to chill out with some beer or smoke some pot. He does sometimes, but he's not really into that kind of crap. He wants to be somebody, to do something else.

Right, so he's a real dork because he wants to do something with his life, he just hasn't figured out what. Was his dad ever like this? He fucking doubts it, the guy's so sure of himself. Micah presses his forehead against the cool window glass and looks down into the street. What a waste, hanging around this joint, going to school and looking out for his kid brothers and sisters all these goddamn years.

Maybe if he gets himself a real girl, instead of the obliging ones he fantasizes about at night. That's part of his problem, that's what he really wants/needs. A girlfriend, a real girlfriend, onc who lives in the same place as him. That's why he never wrote back to the Algonquin Park chick like she asked. And she did ask, so that was kind of cool.

But she lives so far away. They couldn't keep up that kind of camp chatter in letters. What would he have done in the wintertime while she went off to Montreal or God-knows-where? He never used to feel this way — that he needed a girl with him all the time or that he really, really wanted to screw one—but it's gotten lonely in this big house on Southview with so many kids running around and his father and even his mother away so much and all wrapped up in each other when they're home. Where's he in all of this? He feels invisible, like a dream child who only comes alive when his parents talk about him.

Never mind that he's so special to them. He's always known this. "He's the sweetest," his mother always whispers, especially if he's just gotten one of the younger kids out of trouble.

"Because he's the one most like you," his father replies, which sounds like a compliment, but for some reason, it always makes his mother mad.

"No, he's not like me and he's not like you either! I don't want him to be like us."

"Oh, Liza darling, you haven't done so bad! He's really a lot like you," Dace tries pacifying her, a lost cause if there ever was one.

"No, he's not, he's himself. He's going to be happy because he's a natural born optimist and I'm sure not," she argues repeatedly with this man, her man, the one who gives a different name every time they cross the Niagara Falls border to shop in Buffalo or go on a summer driving trip. Micah practically feels like he's an American, they cross the border so much, even if Liza usually ends up driving them back by herself to Toronto and is petrified all the way. "It's in his genes all right, but no way he got that from us."

"Who, then?"

"A throwback. Somebody who didn't grow up like us," Liza mumbles with her arms wrapped around herself or the interloper child in the infant seat between her and Dace. Every time she says this, her eyes fill with tears.

"Oh, c'mon, Liza," his father will say as he reaches over to flick a tear from her cheek and then caresses the back of her neck. "You're an optimist too—a secret optimist. You married me, darling. People around here didn't know us then and our families have their own problems, but we had everything against us. We're even — well, you know. It didn't matter to us, but it matters to some people. Everything's going to be all right." And then she leans into his caress and seems to agree.

They're always like this. His mother argues with his father a lot when he's around, but then she just capitulates and does what he wants. "Capitulates" is a new word for Micah, but it's exactly the right word for what his mother does. She's not as easygoing with her children, but maybe she's just thinking: *That's it, that's enough. If I give in to them all the time, there'll be nothing left of me.*

When he was younger, the dynamics of his parents' relationship and their attraction to one another didn't bother him, but it does now. Why don't they behave like other married people? They're old. Dace is past forty, so the woman he still calls "Little Liza,"' which really creeps out Micah, can't be far behind.

Chapter Three

Dr. M. Kathleen Aldous

Far below her, Dr. M. Kathleen Aldous sees little square patches of green and brown and upon closer inspection, black-speck buildings, ant-like figures and tiny toy cars. Can she really see some people? Like all God's creatures who are sentient, even a scientific mind like hers can stray. Sometimes scientists feel things too keenly. They try to create order out of chaos, to make sense of the incomprehensible, to solve the riddle of the universe. If you really want to find out about something, long-term observation, evaluation and record-keeping are what count. She keeps good lab books down in Angangueo with all her butterflies. Only a damn fool relies on memory or her own eyes.

But wait — what's that? A monarch way up here? It might be; monarchs can fly a mile or so high.

Do they see anything when they take to the sky? The orange and black flash of a companion against an iridescent blue sky or just the earth glowing in the sunlight below?

"Mummy, Mummy," a young voice shrieks so sharply that Kathleen almost hits the cabin roof, "My ears hurt! Make it stop!"

An adult responds in a stream of babble even more irritating, "Danny, Danny, Danny! I'm so tired, I haven't slept in days, the baby was up all night. Oh, please, c'mon, Danny, Mummy can't do anything about it right now"

Reasoning with a tiny tyrant, Kathleen thinks, *who does that?* Flying over the Midwest a week or so after her conversation with Mariposa in the backyard, she curses herself for not taking a later flight like she usually does so she can sleep on the plane. But once she got Mariposa settled in at Camp Arrowshot, Kathleen hopped the first plane out of Montreal. Anything to get away from her own mother.

The woman's driving her nuts. She bitches about everything from the dining hall menu to the way the maid cleans her apartment, and then just for good measure, she repeats everything. For God's sake, the woman's in safe, if lazy, hands in her pricey nursing home. Kathleen's pretty tired herself. It was a five-hour drive just to get Mariposa to Camp Arrowshot and five hours back.

Not that she's got much chance of sleeping, seated with a brat pack. The way it sounds, there's at least three or four kids right behind her and to her left, spread out between their parents in two different rows. The mother's not on her own. Kathleen has flown with Mariposa on plenty of planes by herself, though once the kid was old enough, she paid extra to fly her as an unaccompanied minor.

Why don't people control their children if they can't or won't control their fertility? All it takes is consistency and firmness. If a person can train a dog, they can train a child. It's not that hard.

The kicking's the last straw. Spinning her head around, Kathleen glares between the cracks in the seats at the little devil thrashing around on his mother's lap.

"Stop that right now!" she says so loudly that 'it' promptly bursts into tears. So she's the monster now. Big deal.

"Jeez, he's only two," the child's caretaker, an unattractive young woman with a fringe of pale frizzy hair says. "A kid knows when you don't like him."

So give him a bottle and hold his feet. A dose of Tempra before you got on the plane might have helped too, Kathleen nearly snaps.

But instead of giving the overweight and self-indulgent mother some sound advice she'll just ignore, she turns back around in her seat and seethes some more. Dammit, she's grinding her teeth. At this rate, she'll need dentures before she's fifty.

The kid's still squawking. And upsetting her more than it should. She doesn't have time for this. *Life's full of small irritants,* Pearl, her psychiatrist often says. You just had to roll with the punches and focus if you wanted to get things done.

Take her little monarch sanctuary, the Mariposa Monarca Mission, close to the Sierra Chincua and El Rosario colonies in Michoacán. The monarchs come back to the same colonies every year. They have for millennia. Her sanctuary is just below those mountains, near the town of Angangueo.

Even if she does say so herself, she's accomplished a lot of good in the years since they discovered the monarchs' wintering grounds. The sight of so many monarchs still stirs her to the depths of her soul. Largely due to Kathleen's efforts, the monarch population increased last year. But the long-term benefits are going to be negligible if the Mexican government doesn't get off its fat arse and do something soon.

True, the climate's changing, but the illegal logging of fir trees is the biggest threat to the monarchs right now. *We're just trying to make a living,* the loggers say.

Kathleen's mind races, the same way it always does when she faces the possibility that her monarchs might lose their wintering ground. Maybe those firs look like oversized Christmas trees, but they aren't. They're oyamel trees. The distribution of the oyamel fir forest in Mexico has always been extremely limited. The monarchs favour this high mountain habitat for the same reasons the firs grow so well there — it stays cool and relatively moist even when this region of Mexico gets parched during the dry season. But less and less of the original oyamel forest remains. And once the monarchs' overwintering grounds are gone, they won't be able to come back here anymore. They'll be gone.

Most of the locals don't give a crap. It might not be political to say that, but it's true. They're clones of the young mother in the seat behind her, clueless breeders, born and bred. A romantic might daydream that the uneducated are more spiritual and closer to the land, but in Kathleen's experience, this isn't so. Look at her Mexican neighbours. Except for some nonsense about the returning monarchs being the souls of their ancestors, most of them — the women, anyway — cheerfully produce five or six children apiece while the men rape the land. It makes her furious. Fifteen to twenty years later, the cycle repeats itself and a fresh crop of imbeciles arrives. Okay, so her neighbours haven't had her advantages. If she'd been living in Mexico when she got tuberculosis, she would have died. But what are they thinking? *Oh, God, don't get me started.*

Kathleen looks out her window. If only the plane would lift above the clouds. At least she'd have the illusion of getting someplace. The scenery below is sucking the life from her, but she hates flying with the dinky little airline shade pulled down. The Midwest is so, so, so monotonous! Pity the people who live down there, but maybe they don't know any better either, maybe they've never been anywhere else. She knows a lot of people like that, even in the academic world. Narrow-minded people who hate traveling and have no desire to cross the pond or the equator. They pursue the familiar and the comfortable instead.

Kind of like her girl Mariposa and her Cinderella stories. Trying to create some privacy, Kathleen leans back her head and closes her eyes. She could pull out a book or check out the junk in the duty-free catalogue, but she needs to think. She's looked out for the monarchs for years, but it's not enough. She has to get cracking. Maybe if she organizes more people and lobbies for better controls, they can stop the illegal lumbermen and outside profiteers from going up into the mountains and making a huge pile of sawdust out of the oyamel trees.

Not that she can do anything right now.

"Mummy, Mummy!" the brat behind her shrieks again.

Christ, she needs a drink. *Where the heck is the stewardess?* She sits up straighter, trying not to look frantic. She hasn't seen the attendant for ages, not since she first got on the plane and squeezed by her near the cockpit. *What's she doing – goosing the pilot?*

Well, maybe not because just then somebody fumbles with the speaker and the pilot announces some turbulence up ahead. He's going to try dropping the plane a bit more, so don't be scared, ha-ha.

Great, a comedian! Just what she needs. When the plane drops, several passengers yelp while the child behind her chortles mindlessly in glee, but it doesn't bother her. She's flown a lot in the past fifteen or sixteen years, back and forth between Angangueo, via Mexico City, and Montreal, Canada. Half this turbulence stuff is just to spice things up. Big jets practically fly themselves these days. In the unlikely event that both the pilot and the co-pilot conk out, she could take over the controls. No kidding. No wonder the pilots and the stewardesses get bored on these milk runs and want everybody in their seats, so they could slack off and catch a little shuteye or whatever. She looks out of the window again. Have they moved at all or are they just hanging in the air? Although it's not possible, she thinks she can see whole fields of newly emerging soybean plants and small, yellow tasseled stalks of corn.

Possibly in order to look out the window, the man beside her leans in just a little too close. She's done her best to ignore him ever since he got on. White guys are no longer very appealing. The stench of nicotine wafting from this one isn't helping either.

"Hey, there, my name's Freddie Nolan," he says, "What's yours? Off on a little Mexican adventure? Or are you just getting away from the family and meeting a girlfriend down there for a bit of fun? I'm–"

"At this time of year?" she interrupts. They're just coming into the rainy season in Mexico. Does she look stupid? Maybe he is, the big white dope, but she's not. She's got zero interest in his itinerary. She looks him up and down. He's well-dressed, but that doesn't mean anything. It just increases the odds that he's a drug runner.

"I'm not married either if that's what you're really asking me," she says crisply. "I run a research facility near Angangueo. I've had it for years. It was in the paper a few times last year. You might even recognize my name, I'm Dr. Kathleen Aldous—"

Freddie scratches his head, his eyes lighting up even more. "Well, now, so you're a business woman *and* a doctor. Are you like a PhD or a doctor-doctor, the kind that makes sick people well? Whatever, that's great. I like that. You know, your name kind of rings a bell."

"Well, it should. And I prefer to think of myself as a scientist, not as a 'business woman' or a 'doctor-doctor' by the way. I have a butterfly sanctuary near one of the preserves. To describe it to you in layman's terms, we check and report tags and try to smarten up the locals a bit. Fat chance! I don't know what's the matter with some people. They'll do anything for a bit of greenback. You'd think Mexicans were starving. They're not like us anyway, they're used to not having much."

Freddie looks deep into her eyes like he cares. "What do you think of that Roundup stuff all the farmers are using?" he asks. "That sure as heck must be a threat to all sorts of wildlife." Extending one arm across her body and causing her to foolishly shrink against her seat, he points out of the window. "Look at those fields of corn down there—the Midwest is like a breadbasket for America so if that goes, we're pretty much sunk. It's really quite a dilemma—we need food! But what if this Roundup stuff is genetically modifying the corn and maybe us? Are we all going to turn into little green men or will our children just be born with missing limbs?"

So he's not entirely stupid.

"For sure," she says. "If we don't do something about it."

Farmers have just started using Roundup—where did he pick that up? Oh, well, even if she's mistaking his comment and the spark of lust in his eyes for a modicum of male intelligence, it doesn't matter. She's got nothing better to do. A little warning bell, the voice of her psychiatrist goes off in her head, but she ignores it.

With both hands, she smooths back her blonde hair. The movement brings her small breasts into sharp relief while she reappraises him.

He isn't bad looking. At his age, he must do something to keep himself in such good shape, so they have that in common. He's about forty years old and blue-eyed, with a shock of thick, dark hair sporting a splash of grey at the temples. She likes hair on her men and lots of it. Definitely a Caucasian, but maybe she'll make an exception. White men aren't all buttoned-down and passionless like the professors she'd hooked up with at the U were. And Dace— Dace Devereux certainly wasn't passionless. He was no professor, though, not him.

Now why in hell is she thinking about him again? She hasn't thought about him for years.

Her seating companion's older than the hot-blooded boys she keeps down in Mexico, so he might be smarter than them.

Just how smart is he? *Well, let's see.* "Never mind the genetic modification of mankind's future offspring, Roundup is having immediate consequences," she says. "Did you know it's wiping out all the milkweed and how vital milkweed is to the monarch butterfly population?"

The stewardess chooses that moment to make an appearance, clumsily yanking along a loaded cart of drinks and snacks like it's her first day on the job. The girl smiles at the Freddie Nolan fellow and not at her, so she's that kind of female, a man pleaser, but

Kathleen doesn't mind. Dressed in an airline uniform, the girl has a long way to go to catch up to her.

Freddie orders a scotch, another good sign in a man. Kathleen's stepfather used to drink Glenfiddich. He was okay.

"I'll have a double gin-and-tonic," Kathleen says when the stewardess finally tears her eyes away from Freddie's face to smile coolly at her. "Bombay Sapphire."

When the stewardess moves on, Freddie surprises her by picking up the conversation where they left off. Not many people could do that, especially men, unless they felt somehow slighted and needed to set the record straight. Or they were yakking about their favourite subject in the first place! *Goody, I've got a winner here.*

"Yes, I did hear that someplace about the milkweed, just recently," he says after taking a fortifying gulp of scotch. "That's real interesting, your business, though. You're doing such a great service. Making people more aware about the plight of the monarchs, that's what we've got to do. I'm a travel agent myself so I'm thinking about organizing a couple of trips down to the monarchs' sanctuaries in the late fall. There's two or three of them, aren't there, mostly around the same spot? I'll just be checking out the area this time. I know the roads leading up to the reserves are pretty bad and there's not a lot of hotels in the area. But maybe visitors could take day trips out of Mexico City. Do you think that would work? A lot of people are asking for those kind of eco trips lately — probably because of your efforts," he says, still staring into Kathleen's eyes and boldly brushing her arm with one forefinger. "I'd like to get into my own business. My ex-wife," he adds, laughing comfortably, "well, let's just say she isn't a smart lady go-getter like you and she's costing me a bundle."

An ex-wife, I bet, Kathleen thinks, deliberately ignoring his sexist remark about lady go-getters. Well, at least he hasn't said anything yet about having to pay child support.

Kathleen glances at her seatmate's ring finger but she can't see anything. Ring or not, it doesn't matter. If this guy's unmarried, she'll take up knitting. He's much too good-looking to have made it to his late forties on his own. And personable, the way a good salesperson often is.

"February would be better for those kinds of excursions," she volunteers, "although as a scientist, I have reservations about a bunch of tourists tramping around the monarchs' resting grounds if that's what you're really thinking about doing. You'd have to be so careful, so responsible, but you won't see much in the fall. Monarchs arrive in Mexico in November on the Day of the Dead, but they aren't really active then. They've expended a lot of energy flying thousands of miles and it's cool, so they just sleep."

Freddie smiles at her and smoothed back his own hair, but with just one hand. "Really? I don't know their habits that well," he confesses. "I happened across an old *National Geographic* article about them when I was at the dentist's…"

"The article by Dr. Gene Sheridan?"

"I think so. This was a few years back. But it sounds like seeing them should be on everybody's bucket list. What do you think — are they in any immediate danger of extinction?"

"Well, not quite, but they're getting there. If the Mexicans keep up all this illegal logging, it really doesn't look good. And you know, the other stuff, the illegal drug-trade — and for that I really blame Americans because they're the ones who are actually profiting — it certainly doesn't help."

Kathleen pauses a moment to polish off her weak gin and tonic and wave to the attendant for another one. *Damn the girl, she's so slow!* If Kathleen didn't know better, she'd think she was ignoring her.

"Let me tell you," she begins. *It's fun to have somebody to educate,* she thinks, settling into her role. Anything to relieve the tedium of this damn flight.

Chapter Four
Maitland — Trouble

Another thing — if Micah's parents really are so hot for each other, why don't they ever talk about their wedding or even how they met? Instead of about their kids' births and all kinds of other shit? It's like they're hiding something. Maybe they were married before and they don't want to tell their kids. Not that he gives a fuck, but Summer might. You aren't supposed to keep secrets from your kids. Or maybe his mum, but more likely his dad, has done something bad. Not really bad, just bad in the eyes of the law. Or maybe his parents are *Bonnie and Clyde* bad, but how can that be, unless they're brother and sister or something?

It makes him, no, they make him want to puke. He wondered about his parents when he was younger too, except he didn't have the words for what he was thinking then and he does now. Yeah, now that he has the vocabulary, he can almost put his finger on what's wrong in his house.

His parents are just so different: his father, a cool, mysterious person who draws people to himself in droves and his super well-educated mother, so busy and on top of everything with six kids — six! — and an effing job. It's ridiculous. He thinks again about their in-your-face intimacy and dismisses it. He's got to.

Maybe they're like that because they don't see each other much, but it still makes him want to barf. They're his parents!

Sure, you should marry somebody who shares your interests and values, so you can golf and play cribbage together in your old age or winter down in Florida, if you want your marriage to last. Most marriages don't, that's what the newspapers and all those women's rags say. He doesn't exactly look for things, but he reads everything he finds, even "Can This Marriage be Saved?" in his grandmother's *Ladies' Home Journals*, so that's how he knows.

"But they like the same things," his kid sister has recently observed. "Dad likes boxing and wrestling, but they both like books and families and crime shows and they get all gooey-eyed when they see monarch butterflies—can't you see? Remember last year when Grandma came over here and they took off to Point Pee?"

Much as he hates to admit it, Summer's probably the real reason he's thinking about all this stuff. She's scary, that kid. If she doesn't turn into a private eye when she grows up, she'll be a psych. Micah doesn't like figuring people out, but Summer does.

"Point Pelee!" Micah corrects her. "You weren't missing anything," he reassures her. "There's bugs there, Summer, lots of bugs and you know how scared you are of them." That's another one of his stupid chores: he takes care of all the spiders in the bathroom, the ones that come out of the woodwork every spring.

"Point Pee," Summer repeats, just to annoy him. Nobody's that dumb! "But they went to see the monarchs! They should have taken us!" she says, working herself up a bit more. "And just look at all the flowers and milkweed and stuff in our yard! Where's our vegetable garden, anyway? Mrs. Campione's always asking me. She says it looks like our house is in a ditch and it does! Our place is a mess! And Mum and Dad are always touching each other— yuck, it's so gross! They're so much alike, like twins. Mrs. Campione says so, too!"

"*Mrs. Campione says,*" Micah tries to mimic her little-girl voice, but she ignores him.

"The only thing that's sort of weird is that Mum and Dad don't have the same last name. Some of my friends' mothers have their own names, but the kids have the dad's name and we've got mum's."

"Not always," Micah says. "Sometimes a kid has the mum's name if the parents aren't married."

"What if Mum and Dad aren't married?"

Who cares if they are or not, Micah thinks, but she's got him wondering. Not that he's going to let on to his sister, the little brat. He'll do anything for Summer, but she's such a mouthy kid, the kind who sucks all the air out of the room, day in and day out.

Dace and Liza are their parents, for God's sake! He's one hundred percent sure about this. When pressed by Summer, his parents — well, mostly Liza because Dace is usually nowhere to be found — always tell some cock-and-bull story about how they got married on Centre Island in some kind of hippie ceremony with wildflowers and then biked down to Niagara — on the Harley! — and honeymooned in a seedy motel on the American side of the Falls. Yeah, maybe. Micah can almost see his mother on the back of his father's bike in a long white wedding gown, but no way she wore a traditional dress. It was summertime, Liza's time, of course. June, July, August. The months she liked to have her babies. But something in her story doesn't ring quite true, so either she's lying or else she's holding something back, something big, something he's pretty sure he doesn't want to know.

But once Summer gets hold of something, she never lets go.

"Let me see your pictures," she wheedles. If Micah ever gets a kid like her, he'll strangle it with his bare hands. In addition to a bunch of My Little Ponies, Summer collects pictures of lithesome, dark-haired brides in fussy wedding gowns. The brides look a lot like her and Liza.

"Don't you have any pictures, Mum?" she keeps on asking.

"I'm too busy to look for those old snaps," Liza always says. "Somebody took some Instamatics but they're starting to fade. They'll fade worse if I unpack them. And they make me feel a little sad. When you grow up, you'll see what I mean. Dad and I were so young then."

Right. The woman has dour studio portraits of great-grandparents all over the house, a couple of them in formal wedding attire and even one of a great-great-grandparent, but not one of her and Dace.

Once when Micah came home from school and said he had an assignment to research his family history, she'd looked a little green, though maybe she was just pregnant with Eden. After that incident, she rustled up a little family tree from her mother's side of the family, all about the Magills, who are Anglo-Irish too, except they're even more boring. There's not much variety in his family tree, nothing interesting, nothing like the stories that the kids at school tell. In his form alone, there's a Chinese girl and a Pakistani guy, both of them from ancient cultures. Then there's all those Italians and Eastern Europeans whose families escaped persecution and poverty in the fifties and sixties.

Liza has also mentioned the years she spent with her Magill granny in Dublin when she was in her teens around that time. From the sounds of it, Ireland was the absolute pits in the late sixties. He never asked her about Ireland again. Her adolescence sounded so miserable, that he has no desire to visit his roots. Ever. Anyway, he's just as Canadian as Canadian can be. As for the Devereux side of the family, she always claims they don't know much about them.

"But I'm sure they were just the usual," she says. "Farmers who brought their big families over here during the Irish famine. Devereux sounds French, but it's an old name in County Wexford, Ireland."

And then there's Micah's grandfather, his father's father who lives in a big modern farmhouse east of Toronto with his second wife and a little girl, Micah's half-aunt, Dawn. Hard as this is to swallow, his little Aunt Dawn is actually a bit younger than him.

They were there just last weekend. Micah never thought it would happen, but he's starting to hate that place.

There are even more mysteries in his grandfather's farmhouse, things Micah never paid any attention to before, but he can't help himself now. Except for the papers, every bit of mail is spirited away when his family comes from Toronto to visit and the name on the rural mailbox has been scrubbed off for as long as he can remember. Or maybe his grandfather just gets his mail sent to his closest auto shop, who knows? There's nothing to read in the large comfortable house, except the *Toronto Star* and the *Maitland Spectator* which are always delivered without fail and scoured — for what?

Until a couple of years ago, none of the Devereux kids even had a clue what their grandfather's real name is. They just hadn't given it much thought. Why should they? They were busy checking out the kittens in the barn and exploring the woodlot. Oh, yeah and eating Millie's butter tarts. She's good for those. They've always called Grandpa's wife Millie, but Grandpa is just Grandpa. Millie tried for years to get them to call her Aunt Millie, but it never took. The Devereux kids' real grandmother, Grandpa's first wife May, up and died of cervical cancer a long time ago.

Something no girl need die of in this day and age! Liza always chimes in, with sidelong glances at her own daughters, Summer and Eden.

And Dace always acts so different when he goes back home — like he's half-expecting the cops or Darth Vader, who the hell knows, to materialize or an effing nobody to spring out of Grandpa's sugar bush and machine-gun down his entire family, the baby twins and all. This confuses Micah more. C'mon, now! Who would want to kill them? His family's weird, but they're not

Mafia. And even if they're part Irish, they're nothing like those Black Donnellys from down Lucan-London way.

What gets into his father at Grandpa's place anyway? And his Grandpa too, who old Millie, kind of embarrassingly, practically lauds as a freaking prince among men and calls "Hon" all of the time? At least his mother doesn't do that. In fact, she's not appreciative enough of Dace as far as Micah's concerned. But what the heck is his grandfather's name anyway and why is his mother calling her father-in-law "Uncle Norm"? Micah used to think it was just an affectionate name, kind of like Millie's "Hon," because Liza clearly loves the old man, but it's kind of strange.

Who's he trying to kid — both his father and his grandfather get a bit weird, especially at the farm. Grandpa always tries to act real cool and laidback. For a guy pushing sixty, he's still in great physical shape, but something, maybe an old shared history drives him and his son to drink. Though Dace would win a drinking contest for sure.

Dace acts more like a moody teenager than a grown man when he's back home in Maitland.

And Micah's mother Liza is even worse. Look at what happened at suppertime last weekend!

"Dace," she'll try to interfere, with both her husband and her father-in-law looking kind of tense and like they want to push her away, though neither man would dare. Jeez, even old Millie usually has the good sense to shut up when Dace and his father start up and that's saying something.

But not Liza. "You don't have to go over all those old things," she says. "You were a different person then. So was I."

Most of the time Dace doesn't say anything else, except maybe *That kid's crying again!*

But this time he does and Micah really wishes he hadn't, it makes them all so anxious and sad.

In the midst of all the noise and confusion at the supper table, what Dace says comes right out of the blue: "I've got to try to do something," he announces, the urgency in his voice making Micah's ears perk right up and from the looks that Millie and his Grandpa exchange, they go on high alert too, "It's in the paper again—"

"Not here," Liza says, getting up and motioning him into the adjoining family room.

Dace goes with her, but Micah can still hear most of it, their voices are so loud.

"It's the same old shit. It's happened everywhere. I can't just let—Look at this, a couple of guys have sent me letters care of Dad," he says. "I'm going to get in touch with them, find out if they want to talk to somebody."

"But how?" Liza cries.

"It's because of Newfoundland, because of Mount Cashel. All that shit on TV and in the newspapers. People started putting two and two together and asking if the same things happened here too, if the very same Rollan Brothers were involved—"

"What do you mean?" Liza interrupts him again frantically.

"I've heard from some people—they're pushing for a royal commission to investigate matters here as well."

"Who is?" Liza says more loudly, prompting the quieter twin Cory to put his hands over his ears and Summer and Sammy to stop fighting for once, "And these guys you're getting letters from—how do they even know you're still alive, that you've come back to Ontario?"

"They don't know. Nobody knows anything. They're just hoping, darling, and they know where my old dad lives. They know he's still here. A lot of them came from Maitland themselves."

Grandpa looks at them all sitting there at the dining table, their faces agog. He gets up and goes into the family room.

"Don't upset yourself, Liza," Micah hears him say, because he can't stop Dace now. Nobody can. The guy's an avalanche.

"They're going to need my help to get all those bastards who hurt kids," Dace says.

"Don't," Grandpa says again.

"I've seen stuff, I can testify, try and make sure that nothing like that ever happens again," Dace goes on.

"But why has this all taken so long?" Liza mutters as she comes back into the dining room. She grabs at the dessert plates on the table and starts stacking them.

"Hey, let me do that," Millie says, "that's my good china."

Grandpa comes back into the room too, shaking his head. "Never mind the china. Get the kids out of here, Millie. They can watch TV in our room."

What the heck's in the paper this time, Micah wonders. What's he gone and missed? And what exactly are his father's letters about? Hurt kids? As far as he knows, not a single child has been murdered by a stranger in Ontario this past year. Kids may have been slow tortured and killed by a relative or a babysitter maybe, but not by a stranger. What would an abused or murdered child, or children, have to do with his dad Dace anyway?

Last year several priests who worked at Mount Cashel Orphanage down east were charged with sexual abuse dating back to the seventies, but that place is way out in Newfoundland, another cold and rainy place Micah never wants to go. Mount Cashel's only connection to Ontario is through the Rollan Brothers who ran some training schools here too, or at least that's what the *Globe and Mail's* been saying.

And he doesn't know anybody who's ever been in a training school, that's for sure.

"He's got to let this go," Liza says. Little Eden gets up from her chair and wraps her arms around her mother's legs and tries to comfort her like she usually does.

"Why does he want to do this now?" Liza asks Millie, who's struggling to pull a twin out of his highchair.

"You have to ask him," Millie says.

"But he hates the past and he's always said that nothing happened here—to him anyway! I've begged him to talk to somebody, but he won't. Why in God's name go public now? It's crazy! We've got six kids and four of them are boys. Micah's old enough and Sammy is too, to read the papers, to know… "

As if Sammy would read the papers, Micah thinks, *when he's always got his big nose stuck in some comic book.*

"To know what some sick fucks did," Grandpa mutters under his breath as he bangs his beer bottle down hard enough on the Formica countertop to make Dace come back.

An odd look passes between the two men, like they're both sorry. "She's right, son, you can't do this. The past is the past. Let sleeping dogs lie. That's what your mum and me would have done."

"Right," Dace says sullenly and for the first time Micah can remember, he doesn't like his dad very much, "bring Ma into it."

"C'mon, kids," Millie says, now that she's extracted the second twin from his highchair.

"Micah," Liza says. "You need to go." All the adults turn to look at him, trying to be invisible while he shuffles some cards he's pulled out of his pocket. If only he could be back home playing *Dungeons and Dragons* in his friend Tony's garage instead.

"Mum," Micah says, pushing away his empty dessert plate. "You missed a plate. And it's okay. I'm not a kid anymore. I'm seventeen." *Or almost. And,* he thinks, *it's all your fault anyway. I could have been on a motorcycle and halfway across the country and away from all this shit if you'd just let me go. But you won't, you won't.*

"Dace," Liza says, "Please make him go. He's just a baby."

"For God's sake, Mum!"

"Actually, he's not," Dace says, staring across the table at his oldest son like he's a complete stranger. "Not really—Seventeen—that's just about the same age I was when—"

"He's not seventeen until June twenty first," Liza says irrelevantly.

81

"And Sammy and Summer understand more than you think," Grandpa says. "Look at them," he tugs at Summer's ponytail as she passes him, "they're all ears!"

Summer pulls Eden away from their mother by her hand. Millie and Grandpa aren't far behind with each of them lugging a twin who stare over the adults' shoulders with big smiles on their faces. The twins are always thrilled to be carried anyplace.

"Let's get you kiddies to bed," Millie chatters on, like nothing's happening, like the earth hasn't just moved. "We're eating so late tonight." The kettle is singing on the stove, but she turns the element off just before she leaves the room. God knows she'd never leave the kitchen dirty even if a hurricane was roaring in, but with Eden's help, she's already washed the pots and loaded the dishwasher with their used plates and cutlery.

Micah's legs start working. He gets up from the table. He leaves, but he stops just inside the next room. He doesn't want to hear anymore, but he has to.

"Don't you dare, Dace," Liza is saying more quietly.

Something, maybe an old childish tenderness for her, socks Micah in the gut, but it irritates him. Blood rushes to his face and a loud humming starts in his ears. He misses a few words, but when he clues back in, Liza is still going on and on, the same way she always does.

My God, does she never stop? Why doesn't she just shut up?

"It won't endear you to him and that's not where the real trouble began," she's saying. "You know where it was — yes, you do! Don't turn away from me like this now. You started this, I didn't. It was at that awful school," she adds, "when you were nine or ten years old and you wanted to help your sister Rosie — "

God, his aunt Rosie, so she's mixed up in this too. *Thank God she's not here listening to all this crap.*

Micah hears Dace chugging his beer and then he says, almost too casually, "Ah, but Liza, the man who got killed that time was the same kind of man as the priests at that school and he had what some might say, the same *proclivities* as a lot of them. You know what that means, right? Yes, that man, it turns out that he liked slightly older boys and my friend Rick was about the right age, a skinny sixteen or so... His voice had just changed."

Micah is on the stairs when he hears the patio door from the kitchen open and then slam shut. Dace and Liza have gone out into the backyard. He's glad, real glad to have them out of the house and out of his hair.

Christ, he hates family life.

If he ever has a wife and family of his own, no way it'll be like this.

Chapter Five

Black Flies

Round the corner of the house they come, their bodies casting long shadows in Norm and Millie's big backyard. The yard lights flicker briefly and then go out. But it's no use. Liza can't stay outside. They, well, she anyway, is being eaten alive. The black flies, the scourge of every longed-for Ontario spring, are out in full force again.

Re-entering the house through the side door, they hope to find temporary shelter and privacy in the glassed-in porch off the living room, but no such luck. A half dozen wilier black flies have followed them in. Dace runs his fingers through Liza's long hair and dispatches the tiny blood-filled insects in the palms of his hands. One of the bugs transfers to him, but he squashes it in his ear with his fingertip.

"Ah, c'mon, Liza," he says, "you have to like the little bastards, they're so damn easy to kill."

After a few moments of holding each other, they go back into the main house and upstairs. In just this short time, the whole place has quietened down. Norm and Millie are off in their own wing and everybody else seems to be in their rooms, their doors closed.

Dace and Liza take a quick shower together, something they can't really indulge in at home. Some kid is always pounding on the door. Liza's skin feels a little better, especially after Dace soaps her all over and brushes a facecloth across her nipples and in between her legs.

She slips a little in the soapy shower stall and clutches at him. "Funny, isn't it, that a bunch of blood-sucking insects bother me more than some of the jerks we know."

If Dace realizes she's trying to give him an opening, he doesn't bite. At first, it looks like he might, but he doesn't. He bends down and kisses her instead.

Here we go again, she thinks as she steps out of the shower and grabs the nearest towel. *Give him a bit of privacy and this is what he does. He distracts himself with sex. He's going to try and pretend he hasn't heard me, to forget what he started talking about downstairs in the heart of our family. Where he had absolutely no right to talk about anything serious!*

Dace lights a fire when they finally retire to their room. Nights are cold out here in the countryside, even in late spring. They get into bed from the same sides they always use. Maybe it'll be easier in bed. Sometimes it is.

So she tries again, after they make love, whispering what she has to say. Even if in the flickering light coming from the fireplace, it takes all her strength not to fall asleep in his arms.

"What did you mean — was that bootlegger a pedophile too — the one you and your friend shot — accidentally! — when you were just a kid? Everything wasn't in the papers and I know you still don't like to talk about it, but I really should know — I need to know —"

"Do you?" he says coolly.

"I'm scared to talk about this stuff too, but it's time for me to know. If you're going to testify at this inquiry, if you must — if this horror story, if all this poison, has got to come out. God, who's still alive? Look, you've got new lines in your forehead! Shit, I probably do. Oh, stop that!" she interrupts herself as he blows the bangs from her forehead to check for the supposed lines. "Jesus, we're getting old! I can't go on like this and I can't just go look it up at the library like I did before either," she says, while Dace's arms are still wrapped around her and his mother's old quilt is pulled up to his chest and her chin.

"Liza," he says warningly, suddenly flinging the quilt off her and smacking her rear with his free hand, but at least he doesn't jump up and leave. "Stop it. I don't want to talk about this shit anymore." He's a runner sometimes, like the other men she's known, like her long departed father, she supposes. Not that she's had any experience with other men since Micah was born.

"I have to know now," she repeats, curling into him closer and pressing her face into his chest so he won't have to look into her eyes and he can keep his deadpan expression, the one he cultivates for strangers, "on account of what little was in the paper about the death of that awful man, maybe I'm just imagining the worst. I was only fourteen when I went down to the old Toronto reference library and read all that stuff, so for all I know, maybe what happened with the bootlegger wasn't that bad. You know papers, the way they exaggerate some things and leave other bits out. So they can tell people what they think they want to know. I want to—I need to know what happened at that school!"

"Not that bad? No, things can always be worse," he says, giving a harsh little laugh. "But—I don't know. Wait a minute—is that one of the babies?"

"Nice try," she says. "They'll sleep for a while now. All of them. Even Micah and he's always up," she adds, pulling a face. "You can tell me, it's all right. It's hard with the kids always around. But don't you think it would be better if we talked about all this stuff—just you and me?" Okay, so he doesn't like to talk about his feelings and ditto for the long ago past, but he's still cupping her breast with his hand, so that's a good sign.

Ah, sex. It's still so good, in spite of the risk she took having so many children, no matter how many babies she puts between Dace and herself. If she didn't like sex so much, she wouldn't be able to endure all this uncertainty in their lives, they wouldn't still be together, but she does. Maybe there's something wrong with her, if sex is all it takes.

He's the same way. Even when they're at his father's house, nothing stops him from practically drilling her into the bed, though it probably should. Here in this big dream house on two hundred acres of prime farmland near Maitland, there are even more people around than when they're home in Toronto. This house is more soundproof than theirs though. And Dace always puts one hand over her mouth so nobody else can hear what they're doing anyway.

"C'mon, Dace, please let's try," she says, knowing he won't be able to leave her now.

Yes, if they hadn't made love, he might have grinned a little ruefully and then just gotten up and left the room when she asked about that bootlegger. For some reason, he's always let her find out stuff in newspapers, even if she only gets half the story.

And now he's acting the same way about that priest-run school in Maitland on account of what had happened at Mount Cashel! Except he's not alone in his nightmare anymore. Lots of other children went to that awful school. For all she knows, all across Canada, there are hundreds of more men just like him. Men who figured out when they watched the news about Mount Cashel that there are others like them, others who endured the same things. Maybe the Mount Cashel inquiry is even giving them a measure of comfort, who knows? Full disclosure's good, isn't it?

Then again, maybe it's not. Hearing what happened out at Mount Cashel is probably a lot like ripping a bandage off a wound. You mightn't feel a thing if the wound has completely healed, but if it hasn't, you bleed all over again.

Old shit, Dace might have offered over his shoulder as he headed for his usual walk in the bush, maybe—hell, she doesn't know what he does when he goes outside anymore, only what he does when he's inside her.

Besides, he always comes back to ease the terrible loneliness she sometimes feels, that aching what-the-hell-is-the-point-of-all-of-this feeling. He always has.

Early on, she learned to live in the here and now with him. But she still worries. Dace is her husband, her cousin, her lover, but deep down, she fears something terrible might suck the life from him and force him into places she can't go. An ugly, sneaky cancer or maybe even something worse, like a horrible, disabling accident, the fucking police or one of those other guys who used to bother him.

She likes that Dace is bigger and physically stronger than she is—it's the way she's made—but he can be weaker than her in some ways. Partly out of a desire to protect both of them, he's kept silent about certain things, but it's also made it hard for him to shake off his past.

Her hair's everywhere. She looks a mess, but she doesn't care. Dace has made her feel beautiful and desirable, just like he always does in this wonderful house, where they feel safe and Micah drew his first breath.

Yes, if they hadn't just had sex, with him coming in from behind the way she liked and his hands full of her breasts, she couldn't have rekindled this terrible conversation, but they had. *Oh, Christ, what a wicked person I am, but what choice do I have?*

With his arms still wrapped around her, Dace opens his eyes. *Uh, oh,* she thinks, but then she feels him relax and so does she. She's got him now, she hopes, enjoying the small thrill of power she always feels when they make love and he comes and she hasn't, but she still wants to and she can.

This is all she really wants—that they go on and on this way. Lovers forever. That they stay together, keep their children close and their enemies at bay. Screw "Keep your friends close and your enemies closer." She can't afford to do that. She's a mother, six times over. She doesn't want any bad guys near their kids, not for one single moment and neither does Dace.

Whatever happened to him, Dace loves her and he loves his kids. And that's all that really matters, isn't it?

He puts his hand down between her legs again and almost the minute he touched her, she comes. The moon and the stars stay in the sky and she comes again. Everything's going to be all right. Once she knows everything anyway. Knowledge is power, isn't it? It's the reason she keeps a stack of books by her bed and reads far into the night. It's the reason she knows every nook and cranny in her house. It's why she tries to read her children's minds.

Because the more she knows, the safer she can keep everybody else.

You probably can't know everything about your children, a small voice reminds her, but she ignores it.

And who's keeping you safe, the same voice sometimes asks, but it doesn't matter.

Dace is keeping her safe right now.

"Tell me," she pleads with him again.

He's quiet so long that she thinks he's pretending to fall asleep. As if she'd let him! Maybe if that Royal Commission wasn't happening and reminding people of things they'd rather forget, but what some of the priests had done to the vulnerable children way out in Newfoundland at Mount Cashel is still all over the news.

They've danced around this topic for far too long anyway. Oh, the short-lived peace of denial. What's wrong with them? What have they done? Maybe if somebody had advised her, she could have wrung the truth out of him long before now.

Or if she'd talked to a therapist, but she hasn't. No money, not enough benefits at work and not much confidence in therapists, if the truth be told. That one guy at university in Student Health Services was a real jerk.

But when Dace's arms slacken and let go of her, she's not sure if she wants to know after all.

Be careful what you wish for. How many times has she said that to a child when they wish for the moon and the stars?

"Okay, you wanted it, you got it, but you won't like it," he says, suddenly sounding more like a belligerent, bravado-filled boy than the man she loves. "Why the fuck do you want to know all this old shit anyway?"

"Because it sounds like we might end up having an inquiry here and I'll hear anyway!"

"You don't have to get involved. It's not the first time the school's had an inquiry, you know. Some of the parents and kids from St. Matthew's tried back in the sixties, but it didn't go anywhere. There must have been a report though. I wonder what the hell happened to it, where they buried it."

"But that's when you were there!"

"Probably."

"And you're still hoping for a new inquiry? Sounds like a colossal waste of time. Well, you wouldn't be able to go by yourself. It would be all over the news."

"Not everything. Not if I can help it. I'm going to see about testifying under an alias. It won't be the first time somebody has. "

"Oh, sure and I suppose that you and me and the kids would all end up in a witness protection program! What about my job? What about Micah? We can't just move him hither and thither like you can some little kid. And what about my mum and your dad? They're both in their sixties. If we run off and leave them, we might never see them again. And Val, I'd miss her. She's the only person who really gets me, except for you."

"Liza, Liza, you're really getting carried away! You'll go crazy if you come to the inquiry, imagining the worst — "

"The worst? Well, that's a laugh, considering this situation! I went to the trial after the riot while I was pregnant with Micah, so I can certainly handle something like this now. I don't want to, but I can. I'll tell them something at work, I just don't know what."

"It'll probably be held in Maitland in one of those administrative buildings near the courthouse—"

"Why not in the courthouse?"

"It's an inquiry, not an effing trial! But people still have to testify and from the looks of things, the prosecutors are running into a bit of trouble dredging up witnesses. Most of the school's former residents hightailed it someplace else the minute they were grown, surprise, surprise. Some are dead. Looks like the guys easiest to locate were the ones who landed back in jail and stayed there. But they got TV in jail now and conjugal visits, so people are noticing things and remembering other stuff and if they're anything like me, they're mad as hell and they're not going to take it anymore. Remember Lowery?"

"Rick Lowery? Oh, c'mon, you're not going to see him again, are you? Look at all the trouble he got you into before! Where's he been all this time anyway?"

"In jail, I guess," Dace shrugs. "The lawyers for the priests probably should ask for a change of venue if they want to keep those baby fuckers out of jail too, but maybe they can't. 'The times they are a-changin.' They'll get the buggers this time."

"Don't worry, if the lawyers for the priests don't get the location changed, it's because it's in their own best interests," Liza says. But where and how did Rick Lowery figure in the St. Matthew's School scandal? She forgot that he and Dace knew each other from the time they were boys, not just since they were in prison. "They probably think that witnesses from town—the janitorial staff who worked at the school, let's say—will say anything to protect their own reputation or at least the town's. You know what Maitland's like. Shit, if this inquiry goes ahead, I'll have to take some more vacation time, if she lets me."

"Who, that Irina? Just tell Ms. Commie Red to go stuff her job. You don't need to work. I can get enough money for you and the kids, I told you that before. The twins need you and you can finish your PhD, do whatever you want to do. Write that book of yours!

Yeah, some bad shit's coming down and it's all happening in Maitland again."

"But Dace, you can't — you won't be able to — what if it comes out who you really are?" she asks, even though she knows from the faraway look on his face that she can't shut him up now. Why on earth have they even started this? She must be crazy. She is.

With his arms under his head, Dace stares at the ceiling. A stranger's voice comes out of his mouth. The voice is just breaking, as if it belongs to somebody much younger than himself. "Yeah, that bootlegger Turbot was some kind of pedophile I suppose," he remarks, a bit nonchalantly for her liking. "The memory's always there with me — I can't forget about it — but I don't really think about it all that much. I can't really explain why."

Because you're compartmentalizing, Liza realizes, flinching as she recalls some of the closed rooms in her own life.

"Because I can't keep on going there," Dace says, as if realizing this for the first time. "Or I'd go crazy. Except Turbot's thing was for older teenage boys, I guess. He wasn't the worst kind — his victims were older and he wasn't in a trusted position — not that I'm saying that there are or should be degrees of buggery when it comes to kids, to juveniles. It's all just plain fucking bad."

"Shush," she whispers, pulling at his arm.

But Dace shakes her off, desperate not to taint her with what he's saying, she supposes. "But guess what — Just because I shot the bastard — *accidentally* — doesn't mean I'm not fucking glad he's dead! That's what I should have told the court or at least told the parole board when I was trying to get out. He's coming at Rick or he's coming at me, so I still kill him over and over again in my dreams — with pleasure! Yeah, that's me, a cold-blooded murderer, just like all those lying cocksuckers at the riot trial said when those two little perverts ended up dead. Except when I shot Turbot, I really did it and I'm still maniacally fucking glad that I did. Somebody should have offed the rest of Turbot's bastard league a long time ago. There's no cure for people like that and all the stuff they do, it just goes on and on—"

Ricochets down the generations, Liza thinks.

"Like some of the priests from your school, you mean?" She presses her fingertips to her eyelids to tamp back her tears. Well, at least the clerics didn't have their own children to mess up, they just had somebody else's. But if some priests had done bad things to altar boys and such under their care, what was going to happen to the girls they're bringing into the church now?

At last Dace rolls off his back and looks at her again. "You still read the papers, I know you do," he says. He braces his head on one arm, but his dark eyes look lead dull and he leaves the tears on her cheeks. "Look at you—you're the kind of person who thinks you want to know everything, even if it makes you sick and half-mad with grief." He puts his hand on her forearm then and she buries her face in his shoulder. "But shit happens, darling and sometimes when you know things, it's hard to move on. You get stuck. That's what happened to some of the guys I knew from that school and some of the people I met in jail who came from other places. A lot of guys in jail have something like that in their backgrounds, you know. A perv priest, a "funny" uncle, a sick teacher, maybe the squirrelly neighbour down the street. What really kills me is that some of those bastards' victims go back forty years and they're still in the same jobs, doing the same stuff, hurting kids, even after all those kids, all those people have come forward. Did you hear that the police charged some of those Newfie Brothers with molestation back in the seventies, but the charges didn't stick and that they just got around to taking another look last year? Pretty sick, right?"

"But that's out in Newfoundland, darling!"

"Except some people think that those Brothers in Newfoundland came from the same batch as the ones who were working at St. Matthew's here in Ontario and at the training school in Maitland too, another real fucking happy place."

"But what good does it do to tell everybody now? What are you going to 'out' about that school anyway? It's been closed for years now and nobody will do anything about it," she cries, rolling away from him to the opposite side of the bed, then getting up to head for the window, where a thin sliver of the yellow moon hangs like a scythe in the sky.

Dace sits up in bed and stretches out his arms towards her. He's a patient man now, but she knows he won't be for long. If he has to, he'll get out of bed and yank her back from the windowsill. He's angry enough. He scares her sometimes, the way he's always so mad these days.

"Watch it, Liza! Do you want everybody else in the house to hear you? That's enough of this shit for tonight. You asked me and I told you. But I've got to try, dammit. To do something right, to get something right. You know that. Some of these grownup kids who were fucked over would be happy with even an apology from the church! I wouldn't settle for that, but they might. It was all right for a while — especially after Micah was born and I was on the run and it took everything to keep our little ship afloat — but every time we have another kid, I dream more and more."

"Dream?" she asks, turning away from the moon.

He throws himself backwards down on the bed and pulls on the headboard with both hands.

Please don't break that, she thinks. And don't break yourself remembering. Oh, God, why does everything hurt so much?

"Except they aren't good dreams, darling," Dace says. "And they aren't just about that old creep Turbot. I must be getting old or something. I'm remembering a lot of other stuff, things I'm not even really sure happened, but they must have, because other people say they did. School stuff, shit stuff. The kind of things you heard out of the Mount Cashel inquiry —"

"Oh, Dace," she murmurs weakly, totally at a loss for words.

"Christ, I'd like to see that place, all those places burned to the ground. Sometimes I think total anarchy's the only solution."

Liza comes back over to the bed. She drops to the floor to kneel by his side. "But if you really must testify at an inquiry," she says, letting him take her face into his hands, "Will you have to use your real name?"

"Maybe not, but we'd probably have to waste money on a lawyer to find out. That's what stopped me in the past."

No, she thinks, though she sure doesn't say it. *That's not it. My darling, my life, you're scared too, you're scared all the time just like me. And there's a whole lot of stuff you'd rather not remember.*

The Tuesday after that weekend Dace finally makes some phone calls. He's put off doing this for such a long time, but once he gets going, it's not so bad. The more times he explains himself, the easier it gets.

I'm a St. Matthew's boy, he says. Just let him find one official willing to do something and they're all set. *I should have done this ages ago,* he thinks. *The truth will set you free.*

He's willing to testify if there's another inquiry into St. Matthew's, he says. It doesn't have to be a Royal Commission like the one down there at Mount Cashel, just something so people can confront the past. Not that he himself is a victim or anything, but he was at St. Matthew's, and at the training school too, and some bad shit happened there for sure.

Just to be on the safe side, he calls Rosie to tell her what he's doing, but it's the same old thing. They were never close after he got sent to jail. She was just a kid then and except for their father, she had to find her own way. She sounds exasperated now, the harried working mother of two school-aged children. It's six o'clock so she's just gotten back from their father's shop in Maitland. *Where I'm supposed to be,* Dace thinks. *Sometimes Rosie's more Dad's son than me.*

Ah, Rosie, she's always been like this. Closed. Trying to protect herself, he supposes. She remembers things and then she doesn't. How old was she at St. Matthew's — four?

"I don't want to get involved," she says now. "You know that. And let's suppose something did happen to me at St. Matthew's—you know what all the so-called scientific literature says about adult victims!"

"Look, we've been over and over this," Dace says, looking over his shoulder for Liza. She'll be home from work any moment. "You talked to the same social worker as I did—or she talked to you—and it's all hogwash. No way we'd ever abuse our kids, so no way that anybody can take them away. The correlation between victimization and future abuse isn't definitive, anyway. That's what the latest literature says—"

"Daniel, get out of those cookies or your father will kill you. He's cooking dinner tonight if he ever gets home," Rosie shouts off somewhere, almost taking Dace's ear off.

"Yeah, the correlation between victimization and future abuse is not definitive!" she mimics him, speaking back into the receiver. "Says you! What does that even mean? Or are you just paraphrasing that little dolled-up social worker, what's her name? No way I'm giving her a chance to bend my ear again! Besides, I thought Liza was the one studying for her doctorate, not you—"

"In English lit. She likes books and fairy tales."

"I wonder why," Rosie says drily. "Well, maybe she can still have her fairy-tale life because even if they decide you were the one being abused, they won't be taking away her children on account that nobody knows they're yours!"

"Nobody said I was abused, Rosie."

"Well, that's what everybody's going to say if you get on that stand. Why the hell else would you?"

Chapter Six
Domestic Bliss

Micah can't believe it, or maybe he just doesn't want to believe it, because it's always the same damn thing. His parents are up and at it again. Up in his single bed on the third floor of the house, he burrows under his flabby pillow, but he can still hear them for Christ's sake. What do they think? In the open room adjoining his, a kind of walk-in closet that Liza had a skylight installed in, Sammy is completely out of it. He always is. Even when he's awake, the dorky kid's a bit clueless, pretending he's a cartoon character in one of his comic books or some such shit.

His parents' fight will end like all the others. Pretty soon they'll be doing it.

They're just below him and Sammy, in the porch off the master bedroom. At night, Liza's darkened porch is like a womb—hers, Micah supposes, a bit queasy at just the thought. Yep, his parents think they're pretty private and safe down there. That they can be as creative and emotional as they like. That they're free to play out their stupid soap opera lives.

Liza's study is in the porch. From the sounds of it, she's probably carolling out the front windows right into the street. It's midnight on Wednesday and his mother is sobbing, "It's so lonely here when you're away."

What will the neighbours think? It's mid-June and unseasonably hot back here in Toronto.

They should have just stayed at Grandpa's farm in Maitland, but they came back for the dog days of school. Oh, yeah and Liza's job. Every window on the block is open. If his parents wake up the twins in the room next to theirs, they can look after them. The rest of his siblings are just like Sammy. They can sleep through anything.

Or else they've been putting on a pretty good act for years.

Micah hates it when his mother cries.

"Shut up, shut up," he mutters under his breath.

As if she can hear him. All the drama some women make! Liza is even worse than some of the Italian mamas he knows and boy, those ladies sure can hit the roof. What is she thinking? She still has him. And Dace always comes home.

Just watch, this fight is going to end like all the others, with them in bed together. They'll kiss and make up or do whatever it is that old people do. Then Dace will fall asleep—if he doesn't grab a cab to the airport right away—while Liza pounds away on the keyboard of her automatic typewriter until just before dawn.

It's harder to catch his father's lower-timbered voice, but Micah knows what he always says, "Little darling, you know I'm going to make a lot of money—we need money, right?—and it's just for a couple of weeks."

Yep, it's the same old song-and-dance, the same old shit. Why can't his father see it isn't money that his mother wants? She wants love, she wants security! That's what she's all about. Maybe money's the same thing. What does Micah know? He's never been totally destitute, out on the street, broken and broke. He's never been on the run. Not that his parents have been either, as far as he knows. He knows almost zero about them before they had him. He likes it that way.

"Yeah, sure," his mother says. "I thought we'd have enough money for the mortgage this month if we didn't send Sammy back to camp this year. Arrowshot's such a lovely spot right there in Algonquin Park, but it's mostly for rich kids."

"Well, maybe we're not rich, but we could be if I —"

But Liza doesn't seem to be listening.

"Lots of Americans send their kids," she says. "And lots of out-of-province Canadians. It's the wilderness setting that attracts them, I guess, but Micah's really benefited. He's met people there from all over the place. I wonder if we can still get Sammy and Summer into a cheaper camp, someplace closer to Toronto? Sammy's probably all right hanging out at the Boy's Club and he could spend a week or two with your father. He loves it on the farm. You know how he's your father's favourite. They're always out in the fields or the bush together. It's no wonder — Dawn's such a little madam, just like her mother, the kid hardly leaves the house—"

"Ah, c'mon, Liza! Dad's not like that at all! He never showed favourites with Rosie and me."

"But the property taxes are due and we've got to pay the sitter to look after the twins. They're not infants anymore, but toddler daycare for two children really adds up…"

"Maybe Auntie Maeve can quit her part-time job at the store and we could pay her."

"No, Dace, she can't! My mother can't babysit for us all the time and you know it! She's too old to keep up with two toddlers and Summer and Eden are still pretty young. You're always such a hopeful one. Why don't you ever listen to me? Mum can help out a bit, but I really think she does enough. I'm going to have to stop asking her to stay over when you're away. It's driving her nuts! What with Summer and Sammy fighting all the time and the twins roughhousing… You should see them, they roll around the floor like Cain and Abel, the little—"

"I have!"

"I guess I shouldn't call them that, self-fulfilling prophecies and all, but I'm scared the little devils are going to kill each other! And nobody picks up after themselves! God knows what I'm going to feel like when I'm old like Mum."

"Oh, hell, Sammy doesn't have to go back to camp this year! We didn't do stuff like that when we were young."

"And we turned out okay, right? Yes, right! My point exactly. Sammy and Eden will be okay, but if we don't keep Summer occupied, things could go real, real bad. She's a handful, that girl."

"Look, Liza, not going to camp had nothing to do with a kid turning out bad —"

"It's what camp represents! Sammy doesn't care, but Summer begged to go to 'real' camp this year. She loved that Brownie camp when she went for a few days last year — remember? But there's still the expense of getting Micah back and forth on weekends to Algonquin. Or maybe that's paid for, I don't know. It should be, or the cost of the gas is going to eat up what little money he makes. We sure as heck can't drive him! We only have one car, I'm working and you're never here. I'll look into it," Liza sighs as she points out the obvious, stuff so trivial that it makes Micah wonder if she's worried about something else and this is her way of avoiding what's really on her mind. He's caught himself doing that a couple of times. Shit, something else he's gotten from her!

"He can probably take the camp bus, but he has to work. And Algonquin is perfect, just perfect. I've been so scared for him. He's so moody now, I don't know what to —" Liza yaps on.

And then suddenly she's crying again, but this time it's about him, her oldest son, which is way worse. Micah's stomach plummets. He's never been much of a problem to his parents until now. What a mess! At least his mother isn't like this with outsiders or in front of her children. No, outside their house, she's calm and collected. Usually. You never know with her. But she's always digging up dirt and from the stories she tells, she solves problems at work all the time and just puts up with that bitch, her supervisor or whatever. It's downright scary what family does to people, if it turns them into raving lunatics like her!

Or maybe that's just a woman for you.

Micah's still thinking how much he wants to be with somebody, to have a girl like that Mariposa, but not if it's like this. Messy. Emotional. With all this bawling and caterwauling.

Oh, Christ, "caterwauling," that's one of his mother's favourite words! *Stop all this caterwauling*, she says to Summer and Sammy when they're brawling. Yes, if she's anything like his mother is, a girlfriend could be real trouble.

There's another mutter of conversation from downstairs, stuff that Micah can't quite make out at first. "It's all right, Liza," Dace says in his full of pride voice, no doubt happy to deflect trouble from himself. Micah sure as hell would be. "We don't have to worry about that kid. We've never had any problems with him—"

Not yet, Micah thinks.

"You mean, you never had to worry about him!" his mother says. "I sure did. He was so slow to walk and I was on my own for ages with him and sometimes I think he has way too much responsibility here. And he doesn't love me like he did!"

"Of course he loves you!" Dace answers, sounding so astounded and amused and paternalistic that even Micah feels pissed off on his mother's behalf, "He's a boy, darling, he's just growing up! Micah's not like I was. He's been acting kind of pissed off lately, but he's never been any trouble. He'll be okay."

"Hmm," Liza says, apparently calming down enough to make one of those lightning changes in subject that always catch both Micah and his father completely off-guard, "I heard you on the phone the other day—"

"I told you not to listen," Dace explodes. "I thought you were giving the twins a bath."

"I was, but then Summer came along and started playing with them, so I went out into the hall closet to get another towel and you were shouting your head off. What am I supposed to do? I'm not deaf, you know. So are they going to have an inquiry into St. Matthew's or not?"

"I don't have that much influence but it turns out that I'm not the only guy who watched the news out of Mount Cashel and saw some similarities. A lot of people are kind of worked up about this. So many that we're setting up a hotline. I found one guy in the government who thinks he can help us."

"A hotline or a helpline? Help, that's what the kind of people who call in are going to need. I can't keep track of all this stuff and I want to forget it so much. It's crazy. Is this going to happen this summer? Do you think if I looked up your old lawyer Hubert Gold that he could at least advise you about your role at an inquiry?"

Ah, Micah thinks, *so this is what she's really on about. It's that inquiry thing again.*

"Yeah, if you paid the guy enough! Dad paid Gold a shitload just so I could pay my dues last time. Maybe I'll just stop in Maitland on the way back from Cornwall, little darling. Get my bearings, figure out how to get around there, how to steer clear of trouble and beat a path away from the press."

"Well, that would be something—if you could keep from under the radar this time," Liza says dryly, adding, "Gold's not that bad! You have to pay lawyers something. I still see his name in the *Toronto Star* sometimes. One thing about that guy, he always wins his cases. He got some old pervert off just last week."

"Well, we don't want that."

"But if this inquiry goes ahead, I want Micah gone, gone, gone, out of the picture. I won't let anything happen to that boy!" Liza's voice drops and says, "He's my—" but Micah can't hear the rest of what she says, until her voice goes up again. "But maybe the counselors will be busy sailing and swimming and lighting campfires! And remember the light in those cabins, the first time we took him up there? Even if they get the paper, they wouldn't be able to see well enough to read the news —"

"Yeah, those cabins are pretty dark. The kids might as well be in tents. What the hell have we been paying the big bucks for anyway? The cost of that camp is almost what I make on one of my trips down into the States. But, hey, maybe dark's good. Maybe some girl will come along and they'll hang out in the bushes —"

"Oh, Dace," Liza says, but she doesn't sound that sure.

Micah bashes his forehead soundlessly into his mattress. Here she goes again, getting even more dramatic, asking his father for the impossible, for assurances he can't or he won't give.

"Listen to us— We sound so married, so boring, old!" she cries. "I'm scared! What's happening to us? What have we done?" When in her heart, she ought to be thinking: *Oh, God, what have I done to this man? What's wrong with me, clipping his wings and saddling him with so many children? He could have been somebody, he would have been somebody else if he hadn't met me!*

Or maybe Micah's the one who's being dramatic right now because if his mother ever has such thoughts, she's not saying. And taking some responsibility for overpopulating the world doesn't sound like her at all.

"Micah's a bit too young for a girl, isn't he?" she says instead. "He's just turning seventeen! He's real smart, but I don't think boys mature as fast as girls."

"Remember you, remember me?" his father says and of course he's laughing. Then Liza starts laughing and just like that, everything's all right in their world, at least for now.

"Well, if he gets a girlfriend, I hope he gets a nice one, somebody who doesn't take advantage of him and his sweetness. And you never know, he could be gay," Liza says. "Come to think about it, you're right, we were both involved with somebody by the time we were sixteen and he's older than that."

Which is news to Micah because he's always thought his parents were never with anybody else until they met each other. But Dace was in his twenties, so maybe he did have other girlfriends. The guy's not shy.

"Oh, Christ, that boy isn't gay!" Dace says with a predictability that's funny but only because Micah's pretty sure that he isn't gay. Or else he'd be totally pissed off with them for even bringing the subject up. Why don't they mind their own business, anyway?

"Do you want him to be? Come on over to the gym sometime and watch the women fawning over him, he likes that all right. Being gay won't keep the boy glued to your side, you know."

Jesus, they make him sick—their whole damn conversation and them talking about him like this—but Liza has already won this round. Even though he's usually on his father's side, Micah finds this comforting. Because Dace can't go anywhere, at least not tonight and Micah needs him here, even if it's just to dilute her.

Micah escapes into sleep, but they're in his dreams. Doing what they're always doing, looking for the winning cards in their lives.

Chapter Seven

The Morning After

When Dace gets downstairs that morning, Liza's still in her nightgown, sleepy-eyed and begging to be taken again. Why does she have to look so good? If he stops to make love to her, he'll never get out of here. Not that they could do much with four, no three of their offspring around. At least the twins are still strapped into their highchairs, dumping soggy Cheerios out onto the tiled floor.

For a moment Dace stands there, surveying the whole frigging mess, something else Liza wants him to take more responsibility for. He has his own business to tend to though. He has to—*shit, what's that? What the heck did his toes just touch? Some damp cereal or something the cat did?*

Micah has already left, which is just as well. He's a real Nervous Nellie if there ever is one—cautioning his family and the sitter about this or that—but he was going into school early to get some paper for camp signed.

"Aren't they getting too old for this?" Dace says, just as he steps into another little mess, some dry cereal this time. It scatters under the big pine table for the cats to chase around.

"Daddy, Daddy!" both twins shriek, holding out their fat little arms. He hugs them and inhales their sweet-smelling heads.

"Auntie Helen's coming soon," he promises. The babysitter will get the twins out of their highchairs and sweep the floor. Somehow everything will get done. All the kids except the twins are supposed to make their beds, or at least pull their duvets up, toss dirty clothes into a hamper and wipe their toothpaste out of the main bathroom sink. The calendar on the fridge says it's Sammy's turn to feed the cats, but with that kid, you never know.

Dace doesn't have time for this kind of crap. He never does. Liza's right. He isn't home half the time and when he is, there's a lineup of neighbours at the door asking him about a rattle in their car or a leak in their house. Who do they think he is, Mr. Fix-It? But he helps them out if he can. That's what neighbours do and what if his own family needs help someday? Okay, and it makes him feel important. People take advantage, though. From the sounds of it, the neighbour two doors down is having trouble with that old beater of his. Dace tried to tell him it was a piece of junk when he bought it, but he wouldn't listen.

He turns away from the twins, but his little angel Eden's in the way, trying to brush out her own hair. He takes the brush from her, smoothing her curls into a ponytail and secures it with the pink-covered elastic band she's clutching in one plump fist.

"Daddy," she says, "Are you going away again?" Of all his kids, she seems to miss him the most when he's gone. Instead of answering, he gives her a little squeeze.

So far Sammy and Summer haven't even seemed to notice their dad coming into the kitchen, maybe because they're busy bickering at the breakfast table.

What's with his kids—why can't they just get along? He feels like knocking their heads together. He never fought with his sister Rosie, but then she's six years younger than him.

Proving herself the aggressor as usual, Summer slaps Sammy's toast onto the floor, where it ends up butter side down. Dace figures she's just trying to get attention. He'd like to clip her on the ear, but people frown on corporal punishment these days.

Not that he cares what anybody else thinks, but Sammy has to learn to take care of himself.

And Liza's got to get to work, though judging by her current state of undress, her lack of makeup and her tumbled hair, she won't be going anyplace fast. She confirms this, grumbling to nobody in particular, "I'll have to stay late today or there'll be hell to pay. Not that it will make any difference, she'll still remind me of it down the road!"

Dammit, Liza still looks so good. Well, why not, she's just coming on thirty eight. She thinks she's old, but she's not. How could she be? She's four years younger than him.

Right now, she's scrunched into the corner by the stove, pouring herself a cup of black coffee, cramming a piece of dry toast into her mouth and scribbling something on a list.

"Maybe we should get everybody's hair cut for summer?" he suggests.

"No, no!" both girls automatically shriek, their hands on their heads, but at least Summer stops pestering Sammy.

"Stop teasing them," Liza says.

The older kids are eating whole-wheat toast. They must be running out of yogurt and eggs and cereal. Not that Liza eats much in the morning, but that's what she wants the kids to eat. Dace pauses a moment, trying to remember if she's organizing yet another birthday party—Micah's maybe? She goes crazy doing parties for the kids in the summertime. If she isn't planning a themed party in her spare time, she's baking an elaborate birthday cake and freezing it until the next party. But no, Micah's coming on seventeen. He's all boy, for Christ's sake. He'll want to party with his friends and do all the stuff they aren't supposed to do, like drink and carouse.

Dace recalls his last conversation with Liza about how their eldest kid's reaching an age that was so difficult for him. He doesn't like to talk about it, so he tried not to, but they did, back there at his dad's. About that and a bunch of other things, which might explain why he ended up drinking even more beer at his father's the next day. Liza drove all back to Toronto, sitting on the edge of the driver's seat with both hands gripping the wheel.

Funny how opening one can of worms leads to another, not that Liza gave him much choice. She had to know. The goings-on at Mount Cashel orphanage in Newfoundland were rehashed in the news every slow news day last year. Via his father in Maitland, he's still getting news from all the old friends who were getting freaked out by the Mount Cashel news.

Not everybody reads the newspapers, but if you do, you talk and you tell your friends. You have to. The shit in the news is that creepy, that upsetting, that sick. Yeah, well, who wouldn't feel sick, hearing what had happened down there on the east coast. Mount Cashel, Newfoundland is a long ways away, but it's bound to make people relive similar experiences that they had here.

Sure he remembers some good guys in the place where he and Rosie first got sent, but from the sounds of it, most of the Rollan Brothers were cut from the same cloth.

No, he keeps telling himself, *don't go there.* Micah's almost seventeen, but the boy's nothing like he was. For one thing, the kid isn't fresh out of training school, on account of what happened to that fucking priest when he—well, here he goes again. Never mind. For another—

Forget it, he isn't going to think about the penitentiary, about the Big House either.

People talk about confronting the past, about closure and all that crap, but you can't undo the past, you just can't. And you can't change people's minds. As far as most people are concerned, Dace Devereux, a man who no longer exists except in his father's and in Liza's minds, must have been the ringleader of the riot, the boogeyman director of a real live Canadian horror show.

Liza's freshly brewed coffee smells good, but not as good as her. Even though he just had her last night, she gives him a massive hard-on. She always does. There's nothing wrong with him. There was nothing wrong with them!

There's nothing wrong with any of their kids either! Even though Liza's mother — his dear old auntie Maeve — anticipated a host of physical problems, due to her antiquated beliefs about their relatively weak consanguinity. Why should there be? He and Liza went over and over this. Liza talked to doctors. She's bonkers about babies, but not that bonkers. Most of her is pure reason, she just doesn't have any sense when it comes to him and the kids. They're a picture-perfect family. Well, almost. Nobody's perfect.

That's what he told Summer's teacher when she called them in about the kid's bratty behaviour last month. If only he hadn't been at home and gone to the parent-teacher interview.

He doesn't do much of the school stuff with his kids. It makes him so edgy, the minute he steps inside an institution and sits down on one of those little wooden chairs that they always give to the parents. What the hell's that all about, except to give teachers and the school administrators the upper hand? Christ, he's known prison officials who were more subtle.

Liza had to do her woman stuff and step in and calm things down. Christ, she doesn't have to let people walk all over her!

What do you want us to tell Summer and what can we do to help out at home? Liza asked. As if it's their responsibility! That stupid girl-teacher with her super casual clothes, a shirt riding above her tight midriff, cropped pants and a pair of Doc Martens, is fresh out of teacher's college. What does she know about raising a family? What does she know about Summer, his first little girl? It's the teacher's job to control what happens in her classroom, not in his house. Everything's downright copacetic and hunky-dory with him and Liza and their brood as far as he's concerned. Or so he told that girl.

Liza got a little red during the interview and gave him an earful afterwards, but he wasn't that bad.

In the kitchen now, Liza's hair hangs forward, half covering her face but it doesn't take a genius to figure out the kind of mood she's in. He fantasizes about rustling her back upstairs, holding her hands above her head and talking her into using up one of her precious sick days until he hears a familiar noise at the front door.

The sitter's letting herself in with the key they gave her. He swallows an explosive sigh and grins instead. It's early for a drink, his answer to a lot of problems lately. Well, better booze than the horse that nearly hooked him back in the Joint.

He likes the sitter, Helen. A lot. The woman's so low-keyed. She's Liza's age, maybe a little younger. She had her first kid when she was just fifteen.

Fifteen! Summer and Eden had better not get pregnant so young. Sure Helen has her own problems, a family she sends money to down in Saint Vincent, but she doesn't talk about them much. And she's great with all the kids. Much to Liza's dismay, though she wouldn't want it any other way, both babies adore her.

"Good morning, Helen," he says as she beams back at him, "You got here just in time! What would we do without you?"

Goddammit, this place is such a zoo! Liza's probably used up all her sick days taking the kids to dental checkups and doctor appointments anyway.

For just a moment, Dace turns away from the sitter and wraps his arms around his wife. He buries his face in her hair, heartened that she doesn't pull away.

"Hair a man could get lost in," he whispers, though he knows damn well that a smarter man would be scared to have sex with her. Real scared. The twins are over two, so it's high time for Liza to get pregnant again if she wants another baby, which she does. Of course she does! There are worse things than making babies, but she's crazy that way.

He should get a snip, but he won't. He just can't.

Chapter Eight

Dace

Lately Dace feels like he's on a seesaw with Liza, which isn't as much fun as it seems. Up and down they go. Up's good, but when they come down, sometimes they just fly apart.

At least he doesn't have to catch a plane, so he can leave late. The Harley will get him to the Akwesasne reservation in less than five hours, whatever time he leaves. As long as he doesn't get held up at the border for again.

From the back door of his house, he looks up at a clear blue sky. Two steps down and he's in paradise. Their south-facing backyard is all garden. The rosebushes Liza planted to celebrate the births of each of their children are in full bloom. Birds are singing and the pigeons are cooing in the neighbours' coop next-door, probably because their damn German shepherd hasn't smelled him yet.

He doesn't want to leave, but it's his kind of day, perfect for biking, midmorning after the rush hour traffic has died down. Except for a caravan of transport trucks on 401 East, the highway should be almost clear, full speed ahead in the passing lane.

Everybody wants something from him, but he can't help them. If it wasn't for Liza, he would have left Toronto long ago. She pulls at him constantly, but he's got to go. He really does. If he doesn't leave for Akwesasne right now, he'll never get back home in time to see that boy of his off to his first job. He's missed so much in his kids' lives; he can't miss that. Before he knows it, Micah will be out of the house and on his own. Dace was long gone by his age, first to the training school and then to the Pen. Where has time gone? He still feels like he's in his teens with a lifetime to make everything right.

He walks across the grass and takes the Harley out of the garage. It feels so good under his hands, almost as good as Liza. The station wagon's still parked on the front street. In his worst nightmares, he never dreamed of getting behind the wheel of an Oldsmobile with wooden side paneling, but there's enough seats for him and Liza and all six kids. There's a roof rack for their luggage, it's a safe second hand car and it was dirt cheap. Liza talked him into it. He would have picked a Crown Vic, even in this neighbourhood where people keep an eye out for the large, cushy cruisers that cops favour. Well, if they're smart, they do.

He revs up his bike on the driveway before he backs out onto the road. Down the street under that old oak right by the Giordano place where his son Micah's best bud Tony lives, a couple of teenage boys are smoking cigarettes or toking, but they beat it when he waves. If he didn't notice them, they probably would have skipped school, the devils. Unless they go to the collegiate, not many kids around here finish high school. A good job is being a full-time mailman, not just working construction for maybe half the year.

"We got a late start today," one kid mouths over his shoulder. *Sure you did,* he thinks. *Me too.*

It's better this way, he tells himself. Liza doesn't want him to go and she's in kind of a bad way, but she's busy with her job and the kids. She'll be okay. She's strong, his Liza, way stronger than most people he knows.

Yeah, and why's that? he asks himself, as if he doesn't already know. He can hardly ever get her on a bike now anyway, even though she used to ride one of her own. Maybe she wasn't born to the road, but she did all right. She loved biking because she loved him. And the freedom and the wind rushing into her face. But it was game over once Micah was born. Jesus, if he had just one leg and sixteen kids, he would keep his Harley.

I want you too, she said with a flicker of her old heart-stopping smile when they said good-bye, but she's still mad. He let her think that he had business down in New York State again. If he can help it, he never mentions Akwesasne.

Summer, or Summer Senior as he calls her in his own mind to distinguish her from his nine-year-old daughter of the same name, the girl who helped him out way back in 1973, still lives there on the reservation with her son Justin. Summer's brother Mac was shot dead by a dirty cop posing as a poacher back in 1977 and good riddance. Summer's a lot better off without him. The guy was nothing but trouble since the day he was born.

Here's the rub, the real reason he's reluctant to take Liza to the reservation never mind some of the stuff that goes on there — Summer Senior has the same name as his oldest daughter, though it sure wasn't his choice, not by a long shot.

He tried talking Liza out of calling their third child Summer, but he wasn't there when she registered the birth, so she got her own way. Again. There isn't any point in fighting with her about the kids anyway. It isn't worth it.

Kind of hippie, he said, loath as he was to remind her about Summer Senior. He'd told Liza about Summer way back in the days when they thought it was important to be honest with each other. Right. Man, they sure were green!

And she told him things — about that creep who stalked her in school and the bastard back in Ireland. Not that he was keen on hearing about her old boyfriends because he'd have to do something about them. He still doesn't know who got that Joe at the university. If he'd done it, the guy wouldn't have died so easy.

No way he's ever let on to Liza that he's still seeing Summer. As a freelance agent, he gets to do what he wants, way more than a plain old ex-con does. Working for so many different law enforcement agencies has given him more freedom and anonymity than he expected. The border guards still give him trouble, but a phone call here or there and they always let him go.

Maybe it's the smoke from the wood-burning stoves that keeps pulling him in, but the old Indian res has a hold on him. The res and the girl. Summer Senior might have put on a few pounds, but she still looks amazing. Best of all , she doesn't make any demands on him. If Liza ever decides to get back on a bike with him again, he doesn't know what he'll do.

This little road trip will also give him a chance to take a peek at his little airport on the way back. Maybe. He hasn't been there lately. He's run the little commercial operation for years, but it's gotten to be a real grind with this new partner of his. The guy looked real good on paper, but now that a couple of little unexpected problems have cropped up, Dace knows better than to trust the bastard. The only reason he's keeping the guy is because he needs somebody with a valid social insurance number to front the place. And he could do a lot worse if he doesn't watch out.

Like end up back in jail, the foregone conclusion of most of his 'friends' in the slammer. Even Rick Lowery, bad-guy-gone-good and a hero of the 1971 Maitland Penitentiary Riot, had landed back in jail.

Once Dace gets past the cloak-and-dagger stuff with the smugglers, it's kind of peaceful down there on the reservation. Nothing like the big city where everything's always jumping. Summer has upgraded from the trailer to a cozy little wooden house. She teaches the junior grades at the local school, but she's always so calm and collected, even with a cop on their tail. She's used to trouble.

Hello, Dace, she'll say and let him lift her straight up into the air. She definitely won't say, *What took you so long and when are you coming back?*

Why the hell can't Liza be more like that?

Dace often thinks of Summer. Especially in the midst of some domestic upheaval when a kid is sick or Liza is losing it over all their bills. But even in the good times when he and Liza pack the kids into the station wagon, roar down to Niagara Falls and across the border, Summer pops into Dace's mind. The way she lives on the reservation in her problem free one-child house. She got herself knocked up at eighteen when she went into Cornwall to finish her grade thirteen, but at least the girl had the good sense not to have any more kids.

What the hell is wrong with Liza?

It comes to him then, as it does so often when he's on his own, which is one reason he doesn't like being alone, that he and Liza are too much alike. They both want the same boisterous, busy life. They both crave the same high points, different kinds of highs, but they're still highs. And they can both get so low.

Maybe if Liza hadn't gone so mainstream and insisted on having babies they really couldn't afford, things might have been different, but she did.

Not that he doesn't brag about all his kids every chance he gets. As long as they stay out of trouble. The girls will be okay. They're pretty and equally smart and Eden is super sweet, but his boys — well, who knows?

Damn, this isn't working. Even when he's out on the highway and he's pushing seventy miles an hour, usually a sure-fire way to clear his mind, his mind replays the same stupid stuff.

So now it's all Liza's fault, Dace thinks as the warm wind rushes into his face, but he isn't proud.

I love her, he reminds himself. He always has. Lot of guys he knows are on their fourth wives.!

If Liza ever finds out about Summer Senior, what the hell is he going to do?

He has another reason to go back to the res today. Rick Lowery's meeting him there. After all these years! Fucking unbelievable. No way they could meet in Toronto. Dace still hasn't said word one about Lowery to Liza. He couldn't.

Liza never asks about Rick, which is just as well. The last Dace heard, Rick was just another dead man inside. But a month or so ago, he came by the farm and asked Norm about Dace. Sometimes Dace wishes that Norm hadn't told him about Lowery's visit and that he'd burnt the other guys' letters as well, but the old man's loyal to a fault.

No way Rick Lowery gets to meet his family, though! Partly to preserve his anonymity, but mostly for the sake of his family, Dace complied with the authorities and stayed away from all of his old friends, the people he grew up with in prison. To be honest, it wasn't that hard. A big chunk of his life went up in smoke, but he did it for Liza and his kids.

Liza will flip the hell out of her mind if she finds out he's hooking up with somebody like Rick, even if his old bud has made good.

Breezing by a slew of slow moving vehicles in the right hand lane, Dace catches sight of a couple of real old geezers driving with both hands on the wheel and shudders. You got to get old though, but it's the price of life. Dammit, he hopes Rick hasn't totally changed. It scares the shit out of him, the way some dudes age so badly. He sees their pictures in the newspapers sometimes when they're up to no good. Maybe the press doesn't take the best mug shots, but partying and boozing doesn't help either.

Is it just his imagination, or is his hair starting to feel a little thin? He doesn't need both his hands on this stretch of the highway. The Harley knows the road so well, it practically rides itself. He puts one hand up to his head, but his helmet's in the way, so he can't feel his crown. What a damn shame that everybody has to wear helmets in Ontario now. He slides his hand down his tied-back hair. It feels thick. There's lots of time to do all the things he wants.

At last he's at Cornwall. It should be a piece of cake crossing the border here, but it's not. There are multiple crossing points along the St. Lawrence, all bad.

Even though the border guard recognizes him from all the times he's crossed before or else he's even more stupid than Dace gives him credit for, the guy writes something on a piece of yellow paper and sends him into secondary inspection, hinting he can smell pot or cigarettes in the Harley's saddlebags. Yeah, sure, bub, like he's stupid enough to lug reefers in his bag. The guard's played this game before, but Christ it's getting old. Dace doesn't have much choice except to go along with the bastard though. For good measure and in spite of the line of vehicles piling up at his booth and everybody cursing Dace and his totally innocent bike, the guard calls a pal over to paw through the Harley's saddlebags. They even make Dace take off his leather jacket to shake it out. If they try to do a physical, they'll be sorry.

Then the second guy, somebody he's never even seen before, sizes up Dace and checks something in a computer. From the looks of it, the guy's just faking a search, but the recent introduction of computers to border security scares Dace shitless.

"You look familiar," the new guy mumbles, almost stopping Dace's heart on the spot, "but like from a while ago. Where you born?" he asks him again as if he looks too foreign to have been born in Toronto, Canada.

But they let him go, just like they always do. The fifty he slips the guy pecking on the computer keyboard definitely helps.

Summer's place is just across the border, a couple of miles in. He breathes easier on the reservation. The res has always had that effect on him. It really is another world. In the early afternoon, on a weekday, the road is empty of cars. Nobody's out in their yards.

They might be at work, but he doubts it. Most people around here don't have day jobs.

One right turn and then a left and he's at Summer's place. He gets off the bike on the little gravel driveway and parks it against a wire fence. He's got a key, but it looks like he doesn't need it. Smoke's coming out of the chimney. Dammit, it's a weekday, isn't it? Summer's supposed to be at work.

The front door swings open before he even reaches it. Summer's standing in the doorway, but she doesn't jump into his arms. She can't. An old, balding guy with long, stringy white hair is hanging off of her. The guy has one arm looped halfway around her neck, like he's her husband or a hostage-taker. A heartbeat later, Dace recognizes Rick.. He couldn't have picked him out of a lineup of old geezers, but who the hell else could it be? It doesn't look like the guy could take anybody hostage anyway, let alone a girl like Summer. Look at him shaking— he's barely standing up.

Summer isn't looking very happy, not that Dace blames her. She pries Lowery's arm from her neck, barely concealing her disgust.

"I came home for lunch to check on him, but I've got to get back. I let him in last night—he says he's Lowery, a friend of yours and that you knew he was coming. And he told me stuff about the riot, the same things you told me before, like the way you protected the hostages, so I was pretty sure that he is who he said. He's just stinko or he wouldn't have—"

"Wouldn't have—ah, Jesus, Rick, you didn't bother her?" Dace says, touching knuckles with his right hand and punching Lowery in his upper arm with his left, a little harder than he intended.

"Ah, man," Rick says, grabbing at Summer's arm and giving it a little squeeze, "C'mon now, is that any way to talk to an old friend? It's been a long time since I've been with a pretty woman."

Summer jerks her arm away.

"Dace," she says, looking longingly at the little black briefcase on the stoop by her feet, "It's okay. Except that he missed the toilet a couple of times, we've been getting along fine. I'm not sure he could have fucked me anyway, even if he wanted to. He's been in prison a hell of a long time. He talked and talked about the Pen, especially after he had a couple of beers."

"Did not!" Rick protests. "I never talk about that fucking place."

Summer ignores him. "He had a six pack with him when he got here. I didn't give it to him. I—he thought you were getting here sooner though. Like yesterday."

"I got kind of lucky for once, so I got here a bit faster than I expected," Rick says, swiveling his head back and forth between them like he's at some kind of spectator sport.

"I didn't want to call you and anyway you said you were coming soon, but I can't do this stuff, you know," Summer continues. "I've got my boy to think about. It's just me and him around here most of the time."

"Where's Justin?" Dace asks.

"He's not here right now—he spent last night with a friend. He got early admission to Concordia in Montreal so he's home working this summer at the border crossing."

Dammit, Dace thinks, *she sounds a lot like Liza*, but then the top of his scalp prickles. "Don't tell me the boy's a guard," he says. "Kind of a dangerous job for a kid with native blood, isn't it?"

"Yeah, and a suck ass job too," Rick says.

"Not that it's any of your business and you're not from around here anyway, but would you know about my kid?" Summer practically spits right back into Rick's face.

"We got Indians out west too," Rick says, taking a step backwards. "Lots of them in jail."

"Well, I'm his mother!" Summer says, looking like she wishes Rick would just vanish into thin air, but appealing to Dace instead. "I've got rights here in Ontario and so does he. Native rights, not Indian rights! Around here, Justin is either for the man or against him and anyway, he's over eighteen and it's good money gets, as clean as money gets. And we need money, Dace! You know what that's like, don't you with that brood of yours?"

"Summer," Dace protests, "I'm on your side and I love Justin. I've known him since he was a baby. You know that. If either one of you had wanted to talk to me about his plans or anything else, I would have been—"

"So give me a safe number, if you want me to call and ask your advice! Like I said, I didn't want to call you because, well, I just had to hope you wouldn't run into Justin at the border. He's figured out a few things about you after all these years, so it would put him in an awkward position, to say the least."

"I got family too," Dace mumbles with a quick look at Rick. Shit, he doesn't feel like sharing anything with the guy right now. He hasn't seen him in years. He can count on Summer to mind her own business, but once Rick gets into a drunken stupor, there's no telling what he'll do.

"I don't have a safe number where you can call me," Dace says. "Except my father's phone. What the hell's wrong with it? You've left messages with him before."

"I'm not calling there anymore, remember?" Summer says, standing there in front of her own doorway with her arms wrapped protectively around her chest. "That Millie, your stepmother, she never gives your father or you my messages. You know that! On account of her loyalty to Liza, I suppose. Not that I blame her, we women have to stick together."

"My stepmother? She's not, she's just—"

"Whatever, they're married, aren't they? And they've been married for years. That's what a stepmother is, the person who marries your father when your own mother's gone. I can take care of myself anyway—I always have! You know that. I've never taken a penny from you or any other man. It's none of your business what Justin does anyway. He can call you uncle, but you're sure as hell not his dad."

"Liza, did she say Liza? Don't tell me, that cousin chick, she's still got you by the balls," Rick says, trying to pat him on his shoulder but stumbling face forward over the doorstep into Dace's arms instead.

With one arm behind her, Summer pushes her front door open. Almost like he's dancing with him, Dace maneuvers Lowery inside the house onto the only easy chair, a beat up recliner in the front room.

"Yeah, Dace—you sure took your time getting here. I thought I'd never see you again, old man," Rick slurs. "I got kind of messed up after the riot, but from the looks of things, you been living the life of Riley. How's that? How'd you get so lucky? Me--I was the one who was supposed to turn over a new leaf."

Summer looks at Dace. He knows what she's thinking. Because whatever he's done—even the undercover stuff he sometimes tells her about—he hasn't made good. His family has, but he hasn't. Summer knows this from the noises he makes in his sleep, from the nightmares he'd rather not share with his wife.

But Summer's had enough. He can see that. You can only spill the beans so many times before people get tired of you. People have their own shit to deal with. They can't spend their whole life just propping you up.

"I've got to get back to school," she says. "It's almost the 1:30 bell. But I want you both out of here by tomorrow." She nods at Lowery. "Do me and my neighbours a favour and keep that one here in the house until you're good and ready to go."

Chapter Nine
Liza

Squashed into a double seat with the sort of man who keeps his legs open, Liza would prefer to stand all the way to the Yonge subway station, but she can't. If she does, she'll fall ass over teakettle in her stupid sling back high heels.

To complement her up-do and hastily applied mascara, she's wearing a grey lightweight summer suit with her maroon silk blouse. She would prefer to wear a long skirt and a granny blouse with no bra, but working downtown, it's best to look like everyone else. She'd be crazy to go braless after having six kids anyway, her mother says. She draws the line at wearing pantyhose, so her legs are bare.

She kept her briefcase on the seat beside her for as long as she could, but when the subway car fills up completely at Christie, she gives up the seat and perches her purse and her briefcase on her knees. A man immediately sat down. In order to avoid her seatmate's eyes which are riveted to the silver butterfly chain on her bare throat just above her trussed up breasts, she stares unseeingly at the dark concrete walls whizzing by in the window opposite her.

The underground, a favourite jumping spot of suicides, is so damn grim. A screech of a subway train's wheels and it's all over. All the angst, all the might-have-beens, all the what-the-fucks?

Why does the Toronto Transit Authority even bother with windows? Maybe so people won't feel like they're on a cattle car to Auschwitz?

Okay, so there's no comparison between the TTC and Auschwitz, but she hates the subway. It's a haven for oversized rats and other vermin, much like the man beside her. There's no other way for her to get to work downtown though. *Dazzle Publications* is on Queen Street West, right across from the new City Hall and Old City Hall Court.

Old City Hall's not much to look at, but it's so central. It really would be better if they hold the inquiry here. Better for her and Dace anyway.

Make the bad guys travel! She doesn't give a hoot about any of the perverts who worked in those awful schools. She can't stand to think about it, about all the creepy stuff that might come out at the inquiry or worse, about what might *not* come out. While all the bad priests go back to their well-cushioned retirements.

The fully paid retirement she and Dace will never have.

The man beside her shifts a little, but he doesn't close his legs. If only Dace was here. One look at him and nobody would dare violate his personal space or hers. Lots of girls cozy up to him though. Women from their neighbourhood are the worst. Not that she ever worries about them. Even if they're too needy and morally bankrupt to control themselves, Dace isn't the kind of man to be flattered just because somebody comes on to him. Definitely not. He's so secure.

The man next to her scratches his hairy chest through his open-necked shirt. Aside from this creep, infidelity is the one thing that might incite her to murder.

Or if somebody hurts her kids, but she can't even imagine that.

Thalia, that Mexican girl who lived practically next to them in Angangueo was hard to ignore, but she let that go even after Dace told her about Kathleen -Madame Butterfly—and that Indian chick on the reservation, what was her name? Great, she should watch herself. "Indian" isn't politically correct anymore, whether or not the wretched girl is a Native. And it was so long ago. What was Dace supposed to do ? He needed help from those girls when he was on the run. She couldn't blame him.

No way she'd put up with something like that now.

Stupid her, she's always been so boring, so faithful. Even when Dace leaves her for weeks at a time with a houseful of kids, with a wind blowing through her bigger than the one that's whistling through the subway tunnel right now, she never strays.

He was gone the longest time after he contacted his lawyer Gold about his outstanding charges. He owed for the time he hadn't finished serving and for the escape. Uncle Norm paid Gold. Who the hell else would? As long as Dace had an "affluent" parent, no lawyer would do it for free. Gold got him eighteen months in a minimum-security jail near Guelph, an hour and a half from Toronto. A sweet deal, everybody said.

Whatever. Dace had been real fed up living down in the States and sneaking back into Canada to see Liza and Micah, and real tired of not being able to see his father at all. This didn't clear his name exactly—most people were still convinced that he got away with murder during the Maitland Penitentiary Riot—but he was no longer "that man on the run."

Micah was only three when Dace came back to jail. Liza had taken the bus to Guelph Reformatory and visited Dace almost weekly, but she never took their son. She didn't want Micah Devereux anywhere near a prison.

Looking back, Dace really wasn't gone that long, although it sure was a grind at the time. He got paroled after six months and came back to live with them in Toronto. Well, sort of. He was only home for a few weeks before he started freelancing and flying here and there.

Okay, maybe she was tempted to stray once or twice, but she's kept her communication with her college boyfriend's family down to annual Christmas cards. Dear Mel and his not so dear mother. And she burnt the odd letter that used to come from that actor-guy in Ireland. Fortunately there are no real men at work, except for a couple of old guys who think they have a book in them and that they can still get it up for a younger chick.

She usually reads during the ride to Yonge station to change trains, but she it's impossible today. Her seatmate is still threatening to loop one of his big thighs over hers. Or else he's just thinking about something stupid to say.

The subway pulls into the Spadina station, disgorges a handful of riders and sucks in a boatload more. A woman comes and stands in front of Liza, almost on her toes. Her extra-large handbag is aimed at Liza's face, but she isn't pregnant or old, so Liza doesn't feel obliged to give up her seat. One thing's certain, her seatmate won't be getting off his fat arse, anytime soon.

Maybe I can get off here, she thinks, *and just walk the streets or have a coffee by myself in a park or go a little further, check into a hotel and just sleep.* For years, she's daydreamed about taking a hotel room by herself and sleeping for eighteen hours straight.

Determined not to give the creep beside her any encouragement, she closes her eyes.

She's not even at work yet and she's already exhausted. Getting Micah off to camp this morning completely wore her out.

Of course Dace came prancing back yesterday just in the nick of time to help Micah finish packing up, looking so good and so handsome, just like he always does. The kids all rushed him, but not her. She felt like socking him. The twins mushed their faces into his and nearly ate him up, they adored him so. Why? The guy's never there! He can barely tell the babies apart and he mixes up all the kids' names. The show the kids put on for him bugs her, but it's always this way, even if he's just gone for the day. The minute Dace gets inside the door, the kids start acting like she's just their caretaker and a hired one at that, somebody who's there to make sure they don't all disappear through a hole in the hardwood floor and the house doesn't fall into complete rack and ruin.

Little Liza, Dace said, coming over to her, smelling of a summer wind and kissing her neck while he held her hands in the small of her back. She caved in as usual, but really, the nerve!

He was always so wild—had she ever expected to keep somebody like him at home? He was always running from his past, just not very far. And no wonder, the things that have happened to him.

Not that she and Dace talk much about any of that.

Their last conversation at his father's was an anomaly.

For her own protection and their children's, he never talks much about his work down in the States, either. Which is fine with her. The less she knows, the better.

Don't tell me, she thinks even when they're making love. *I don't have to know!* Besides, he's getting out of his more questionable activities and concentrating on the airport. He promised.

Yes, he's always had needs and hopes that she doesn't, not to mention a whole lot of bad things happened to him that never happened to her.

But late at night she still remembers him on the ranch in Angangueo and up in the air when they flew together with baby Micah in that tiny, scary plane, all those years ago. When she was young and stupid. And brave, she supposed. Or maybe just gutsy. No way she's brave or gutsy now. What a blessing that she has wonderful memories to lull her to sleep. Like her memories of the monarch butterfly wintering grounds. She'd do anything to see them again!

Up there on the mountaintop, Dace was hers and hers alone. If she had the time—if she hadn't taken on so much and shelved her own dreams for so long—she'd grieve for the foolish people they once were. He was going to own and operate a commercial airport and she was going to write a book, fiction of course, but just look at them now. They have a houseful of kids. There's no time for herself or anything else.

Damn, they're getting old or she wouldn't be thinking like this. They're getting on and they still haven't done anything about clearing his name!

"Bellissima!" her seatmate finally says, jolting her to open her eyes, but she feigns deafness and looks away.

She'll be off this train in a second. Best to count her blessings—her many blessings. They really are better off now. Things were so much worse when Dace was on the run and he couldn't even stay in the same house as her.

But you still need to talk to somebody, a little voice nags her repeatedly, *get some professional advice for once in your life*. Her work benefits are only good for a visit to a psych once or twice. What good would counseling do, anyway? She went to Student Health Services after what that horrible Armitage did, but the counselor was less than useless…well, no point in thinking about all that now. Joe Armitage is long dead.

So she's a bit of a ruminator. She doesn't need some psych telling her this. She goes over and over things in her mind, every time she's trapped in the subway, every time she's left alone.

Lucky Dace, she thinks, *most people have probably forgotten about him and even if they haven't, he's not using his real name. So lucky me.*

Much to their mutual relief, the man formerly known as D'Arcy Devereux wasn't even referenced when that horrible Allan Legere escaped down east in Miramichi last month. The press listed other more recent escapees, but they never mention Dace. Few of their neighbours would know that the papers were talking about him, now that Dace no longer uses the Devereux name, but still. A certain kind of man, a narcissist, might have been offended at how fast he was forgotten, but not Dace. He and Liza had both been thrilled. A little disbelieving that Dace Devereux had been forgotten for once, but still absolutely thrilled.

All he had to do was give up his name.

Oh, God, maybe we aren't even legally married, she thinks, squirming a little. This is the real reason she avoids showing the kids their wedding pictures.

Not that she's one of those parents who feels compelled to share past mistakes with their children in the name of honesty, but she doesn't like lying either.

The only person she lies to is her boss, Irina. The less the woman knows about her, the better. Even if she came from a country rife with spies and corruption, where most people are just desperate to get out and it really isn't her fault.

The problem Liza has with lies is that they are just so darn hard to keep straight. White lies anyway. Lies of omission, like the illegal abortion she had in Ireland when she was sixteen and never tells anybody about except her friend Val Jaffe, are so much easier.

Talk about not sharing things—she's never even told Dace what happened in Ireland. She just can't.

Legal or not, marriage helped obscure Dace's identity. It was why she agreed to the ceremony. Both she and Dace were able to get a little bolder then. He moved completely out of Val Jaffe's place. He stayed in the bigger house on Southview with her instead, helped out a bit with Micah and then with the rest of the kids when they came along, infrequently at first, but then more and more.

Because she can't stop having kids. She just can't.

Yes, she's exhausted, especially this week, but her big, messy house, all their kids, her huge kaleidoscopic life, they're all right for her. She and Dace have lots in common, but she's not the exotic creature he is. Sure, she always wanted to write and fly to as many places as she could, but as a young girl she also yearned for everything she's got right now.

And Dace's love, especially his love. She smiles to herself. Because he loves her. She's gotten everything she ever wanted. She really has.

Maybe she's too lucky, though. Best not to acknowledge good luck or brag about it and tempt the gods, to attract the evil eye. That's what the Greek neighbour lady always says. Because what if the whole kit and caboodle suddenly comes crashing down? What if somebody gets sick or up and dies? Like Dace or her. Bad stuff happens to people all the time. Shit flies. There are horror stories in the news almost daily about somebody else's kids.

If anything ever happens to one of her kids, she'll go completely nuts!

Dammit, did she turn the coffeepot and her curling iron off? Well, Helen's there. If Irina isn't hanging over Liza's shoulder, she'll call her as soon as she gets into work and ask Helen to check. She'll notice if the coffeepot stays on in the kitchen, but she might not go to the upstairs bathroom for a while.

Or what if somebody simply blows Dace's cover? Little as Dace talked, Liza realizes he must have developed all sorts of underworld connections over the years, introducing undercover officers to their "targets" or "marks." How could he not? Once he even penetrated a Californian bike gang and passed on information about its activities to the authorities. The paper never named the informant, but that story had made the news and Dace just happened to be away in California at the time.

Dace wants the money this kind of work generates, but he doesn't have much choice anymore either. Even if he hadn't turned those bikers in, they would kill him for the simple reason that he once belonged to a rival biking gang. Give them half a chance and they'd go after her and the kids.

In prison, they call a person like Dace a stool pigeon, the last thing he ever wanted to be. Not that there aren't a whole lot of so-called stool pigeons already in there. But how on earth does Dace expect to testify at this upcoming inquiry and not get noticed?

C'mon, Dace, she thinks, *be sensible for once in your life!* Does he have to be the centre of attention, or the whole damn show, at any cost?

"Oh!" the woman in front of her suddenly squawks and then swivels her head around and glares down at the man beside Liza.

"I felt that, you creep!" People in the packed subway car turn in her direction, but through all the body parts, they can't see what's going on.

Liza gives him a dirty look, but he slides his eyes away, an injured look on his face. Then he takes out some worry beads and starts fiddling with them.

So why the hell do I feel guilty? Liza thinks.

"Sorry, sorry," she says, getting up and trying to push around the woman towards the nearest door as gently as she can.

She has to get up now anyway in order to get off in time for her stop to change trains. Another ten minutes on the Yonge-University line and she'll be down at Queen.

She's practically running by the time she gets off at Queen though, her briefcase thumping her side. If she's more than five minutes late, her boss will have already stuck six Post-It notes on Liza's telephone receiver. The last one will say something like this:

That writer's called three times before 9, insisting she 'sure as hell' isn't doing another rewrite. You're here to take people like her off my hands. You really must learn to manage your work and personal life better than this.

Never mind that Irina wastes an inordinate amount of time squeezing in breaks with her married lover, an eager-beaver delivery man.

Lucky for you, Liza often thinks, squelching the urge to kill her, that I both like and need my job.

And she does like her job, most of the time, even if she resents Irina for confiding in her and trying to justify the affair she's having.

Liza gets to work at work at three minutes past nine. Well, she's in the building anyway. She nods at the guard in the lobby who looks up briefly from her newspaper. For a moment, it's just her and the guard. Liza heads straight for the elevators, but they're all on upper floors. Maybe she should walk up the stairs. However she gets there, it will be way after nine before she reaches the fifth floor.

Behind her, the doors to the building open again and several people rush in. *Dammit, there's Irina.* She usually takes the stairs — for the exercise — but she must have spotted Liza. She stops and speaks to the guard about some garbage out on the sidewalk before she saunters over to the elevators.

"What's your excuse for being late?" she asks Liza, instead of greeting her. "I had to wait for my child's school bus driver."

"Well, I...there was a delay on the subway," Liza says, not caring to share that she was fighting with Dace half the night or even that he's home and she has help with her kids. To hear Irina talk, her own husband is totally useless. The less Irina knows about her business, the better.

Pulling the office keys out of her purse, Irina looks at her skeptically and purses her lips. She has a PhD in Art History from Bulgaria, she worked hard to get this job and she isn't averse to letting people know how far she's come. Sometimes she even talks about the men she had to sleep with in order to get this far. Life was and still is pretty damn hard in Bulgaria. Especially for women.

"I didn't have any problem. I must have been on a different car," Irina says. "Now if my husband had been home like yours probably was — you got some help with all those kids, right and it sounds like your mother's there half the time — but you know mine, he's still kind of depressed. It's me who always has to haul our son around."

I don't know what nightmare he left behind in the old country, but he's sure got another one here, Liza thinks, as they enter the main office with the Dazzle logo on the door.

Liza tries to escape into her little alcove, but Irina is following her, shaking her head and fluffing up her short stylish hair with her fingers.

"Hmm, looks like they didn't vacuum here again and Kim's taken the day off, so I can't ask her. I don't know what I'm going to do about him, though," she volunteers, presumably still referring to her cuckolded husband. "We get along okay and he's really not doing anything wrong, so I just can't—"

If she wasn't still worrying about the curling iron at home, Liza might be tempted to offer Irina advice or at least commiserate with her. She does this with her friend Val or even with a complete stranger in a long checkout line, but she just can't with Irina. The woman's her boss. Not to mention that the one time she confided in her, Irina threw it up in her face.

What's the matter, Irina asked when something didn't get done right away, are *you all worked up because your husband's away again?*

"Just hang on," Liza says, grasping at straws. "I've been married almost twenty years," she exaggerates, "and it gets better, it really does. There might be a rough patch here and there, but you've got your little boy to think about. It's complicated with kids, so don't give up because it can get better—really!" she repeats, nodding her head and smiling as sympathetically as she can. *As long as you're not already fucking somebody else*, she thinks, *and your depressed husband doesn't find out and blow out his brains.*

Fortunately Irina's delivery man buzzes the office right then, her face lights up and she vanishes for the next two hours. Liza checks with Helen the minute Irina leaves, but of course she'd already turned the curling iron off. Liza's debut author calls about 9:30 to say she's delighted with the changes she suggested, so the rest of her morning also turns out pretty good.

But her afternoon is something else, starting with Summer's teacher catching her on the phone at noon. She wants Liza to come in again for a parent-teacher meeting at 3:30 p.m. if you please, to discuss her girl's unreasonable behaviour. Summer isn't being very 'nice' to the rest of her class. The vice-principal should probably be in on their conversation...

"No," Liza says, feeling like the worst parent possible. "I can't take any more time off work this month. Maybe my husband—"

"No, no," the teacher says hurriedly, "I'll talk to the principal myself, maybe get her moved to another class. Have you considered putting her in the English stream? I really think she'd do much better there."

Over my dead body, Liza thinks, agreeing to come in at 8:30 a.m. the next day even though this practically guarantees she'll be late for work. Again.

Somehow she makes it to the gym just after 1:00 p.m. for her so-called lunch. If the gym wasn't in the same building as her office, she's not sure what she'd do. She walks on a treadmill for a good twenty minutes and catches up on the news, reading the paper back to front, before she realizes that the first section of the paper is missing.

The loud talking guy next to her probably has it. He's waving a folded newspaper around in his hand and railing away to his friend, while they both take a rest between weightlifting reps.

"I know one of those Newfie guys who was in Mount Cashel and came down to Toronto to work. He's going to be one of the witnesses at that inquiry thingy. It sounds like one of the sicko priests worked in both places."

"What inquiry you talking about?"

"The one here about the priests in Maitland."

"Oh, Jesus, that one. Yeah, what a bunch of total sickos. Those priests sure do get around, don't they? They get into trouble and the diocese just sends them someplace else."

"The thing is, the guy I know, the one that's talking about this shit, he's no innocent himself—"

"But he was just a kid, right?"

"He's still a jerk. Maybe life made him that way, but a jerk's a jerk. Yeah, the inquiry's set to begin the Tuesday after Labour Day. Kind of a stupid time if you ask me."

Chapter Ten

Courthouse Blues

Dace has no idea why he's going back to the Maitland courthouse to torture himself. Except that he still does stupid stuff sometimes. He's got lots of time to make things right, but what the hell has he done so far with his life?

He'll have to skip his visit to the airport, but that place is a lost cause. His new partner has him by the balls. And the guy knows it. But just wait, Dace will take care of the bastard someday.

I'm passing right by Maitland, anyway, he tells himself.

Except he's always passing by Maitland, he just never goes into town. The Devereux farm is about as close as he cares to get.

But with Lowery on the back of his bike, a link to his past, Dace heads into Maitland. It's been almost twenty years, but he finds the courthouse right away. Such a beauty she is, hiding so much shit and pain.

All sorts of people are milling around the courthouse grounds. He pulls up as close as he can on the road below and cuts the engine to his bike.

Holy cow, Maitland Courthouse looks like a tourist attraction! When did that happen? Well, why not, considering the stuff they spoof on *Night Court*? Dace catches the show on late night television when he's on the road sometimes. Watches it in sheer disbelief that court proceedings could be entertainment. What's wrong with people?

It's hot on the black Harley on the asphalt in the midmorning sun, but he keeps his helmet on. Except to take a couple of deep breaths and wipe the sweat from his eyes, he keeps his visor pulled down.

His face hasn't been plastered in the local papers for a long time, but he doesn't want to take any chances, to have some bastard rush up to him and say, *Hey, you sure as heck look a lot like D'Arcy Devereux, the guy who killed those perverts and got away with it. Bully for you!*

He was born in Toronto, but everybody thinks he's from Maitland. All his growing up was done here. *Or not*, as the prison psych would say.

The courthouse's mounted on an elevated piece of land, in the middle of a grassy parkland, overlooking Lake Ontario. It's been in use since the 1850s at least. Such a sprawling, stately, impressive building with the royal coat of arms of the United Kingdom carved into the stone front. The Big House, the prison here in Maitland, also overlooks the gunmetal waters of Lake Ontario. Kind of a wasted view, considering all he got to see from his cell.

"Hey, you got a light?" Rick asks, tapping Dace on his shoulder.

"Don't smoke near the engine," Dace says over his shoulder, but Rick has found his own light and already lit up. He puffs the smoke off to the side.

Real considerate of you, Dace thinks. *You're all heart.* Even with Rick's extra weight, it took less than two hours to get here from Cornwall. Dace worried the whole time, mostly about riding into Maitland as boldly as he pleased and having some old coot recognize him, but also about getting lost. He didn't feel like fumbling around good old Maitland town. Nobody has recognized him so far, but what if they do? Let's hope he looks like a tourist come to gawk at all the limestone architecture or line up for some damn fool haunted walk.

Looking around, he realizes that there's no way he could get lost, even coming in from the east on the 401. There's signs everywhere, including one for the Maitland Penitentiary Museum with a picture of the bell on it that some inmate smashed during the riot. Who the hell was that guy? It scares him, the way he's forgetting things.

His keepers led him here to the courthouse so many times from nearby Maitland Pen, like a dog on a chain, way back when. Well, there you go — some of it's coming back to him. Him and the rest of the ringleaders of the Maitland Penitentiary Riot entered the building through a makeshift corridor on the side. They got glimpses of the front of the building, riding into the grounds on the prison bus.

Ah, shit, what's Rick doing way up there on the lawn? Dace didn't even notice him getting off the bike. What's with him, butting out his cigarette like that on the grass? The guy has no effing sense at all. Security's going to be on him in no time.

Get your ass back here, he gestures to Rick, but then he drops his arm. No point in drawing more attention to himself.

The courthouse looks the same as it did at the end of 1972, the year of the Maitland Penitentiary Riot murder trial. Limestone, four pillars and three domes, the usual kind of overkill Maitland architecture. Except on this fine day in June, there's water instead of snow falling into that large, double-tiered fountain with the zinc nymph on top.

It was near Christmastime when he was brought here in chains, every day for two or three weeks. Too many days to distinguish and remember now, but not quite enough to get the job done. What a ball's up the whole fucking trial was. All that time and money wasted and nothing ever got resolved.

Liza used to hang out there. She taxied over from Maitland University and sat there in the courtroom looking so pukey-green.

It wasn't just the trial that was getting to her though. She was knocked up. Looking back, he knew she'd risked everything coming out to the trial for him. Doing what love and his goddamn lawyer told her to do: supporting him, her inmate cousin D'Arcy "Dace" Devereux as he was known then.

The worst thing she did was loving him. Even educated people still fall for all that hooey about bad blood. If he was a murderous felon, what did that make her? What had her classmates thought? A year or two later, she got out of Maitland and went to the University of Toronto. Lucky Liza. Nobody had a clue she was a convict's cousin down at the U of T.

He hadn't wanted her at the trial, but there wasn't much he could do.

Go home, he shouted inside his head and mouthed to her during the courtroom breaks. He hated her seeing him like that, in shackles, on the inside looking out. Hopeless, a loser. Again. They were all in shackles, thirteen men, the worst of the worst. Except the press eventually decided that Dace Devereux was the worst one of them all.

Well, dead is dead and somebody axed those two baby killers during the riot, but it sure as hell wasn't him. He was busy guarding and babysitting the six guards his friend Lowery had taken hostage.

Our collateral, Rick said. Sure thing, as long as the poor buggers didn't end up dead.

"Are you sure this is the right place?" Rick asks now, climbing back onto the Harley's bitch seat and twitching around so much in the process that he nearly unseats them both.

They had both showered out in Summer's yard under a cool hose, but Rick was shielded by Dace's back during the ride and worked up quite a sweat.

"What are you looking at me like that for?" Rick shouts in his ear. Christ, does the guy think he's deaf? "I know we were here that time when we were just kids and that old bootlegger died, but it's all kind of a blur. Bet they couldn't try us as adults nowadays, right?"

"Maybe not," Dace shrugs. "Except we had history. Even if we forgot about that fucking training school, the prosecutor sure hadn't."

"Sixteen—I guess I was stoned because I sure don't remember much. The headshrinker had a name for it—he said it was some kind of amnesia or something. 'Yak, yak,' he'd go, 'you just gotta talk things through.' But my old lady was right too, sometimes it's better to live your life and just let shit go."

"Sure," Dace deadpans. "I've heard that."

"That's why I'm kind of iffy about testifying at this upcoming inquiry thing you Ontario guys are so hot about. I was in a lot of courts after the riot, but I never came back here to this one, Bud. They didn't get me for the riot, remember? I never saw this place again."

Here we go again, Dace thinks, revving up the Harley. Get me the hell out of Dodge. The last thing he wants to do is relive somebody else's past. Lowery's right anyway. He wasn't charged after the riot and he didn't come forward, either. *Surprise, surprise.* And now he was yanking his chain about what had went on at St. Matthew's. Another surprise.

There's a lot of stuff Dace wants to forget too, but he doesn't have that luxury. So many other people are involved.

Rick is still nattering away, racking up excuses.

"Yeah, you lucked out," Dace finally says, taking pity on him. Because Ricky-boy was lucky. When he wrote about him, that Herbert Yonge journalist fellow had made the guy a fucking folk hero of the riot. Which he was, Dace supposed. Things definitely could have been worse. Look at what had happened at Attica.

But we sure got into a shitload of trouble, Dace thinks, *all in the name of glory, old friend. Your glory.*

Well, a leopard doesn't change its spots and neither does an ex-con. He's been around the block enough to know that.

Jesus, what's the quickest way out of here? Dace gives the Harley a good hard downward kick with his boot, instead of doing what he really wants to, which is boot Rick off his bike. He tears off down the street as noisily as he can, but there's still a hell of a lot of traffic on the road. A couple of little kids wave at him. A pedestrian who's about to jaywalk thinks better of it and jumps out of the way.

These days, the sound of a Harley drives Liza nuts, but it's still music to his ears. Back in prison, he dreamed of riding his bike all the time. And way back when, on his very first bike, he fled the scene after that bootlegger got shot. With only one regret—that he was leaving his good friend Rick Lowery behind.

If only he could ditch the bastard again. Turn him loose on the streets of Maitland until somebody starts bitching after him, *What are you doing here, Bub? We got your number. You spent a lot of time here in the joint and other prisons out west. You don't have no permission to hang around a prison town.*

Sure he owed Lowery for running out on him when the bootlegger got shot, but he doesn't owe him a thing anymore. Not after he took the heat for what happened in the Maitland Riot.

He doesn't need the guy either. He's strong enough on his own. Lots of other guys have agreed to come forward anyway. They aren't all chicken shits like Rick.

But for every guy who wants to testify, there's probably another one like Rick. Somebody who just wants to forget what went on.

And they might be right. Who the hell cared what happened when he and his little sister Rosie got sent to St. Matthew's, anyway? The past is the past. Nothing can be done about it now.

As for all the crap that went on at the training school, maybe he should just forget it. He's got big holes in his mind about the place anyway. He was older when he went there. He couldn't take care of everybody else, but he knew how to take care of himself.

St. Matthew's was something else though. A warehouse for throwaway kids, an orphanage of sorts. Turns out that lots of St. Matthew's kids had parents, they just didn't take care of them.

When he testifies at the inquiry and if the papers report it, his dad is going to feel real even worse. Which might explain why he never speaks about St. Matthew's or the training school if he can help it.

Or about what he read in the newspapers, when his only son was a bad guy on the run.

Christ, Dace hates the effing press. To give them their due, they usually report what they think is the truth, but they leave a lot of stuff out. You can't write what you don't know. And sometimes they just don't report things, bad things that might hurt friends of theirs.

Those Rollan Brothers did lots of good things in Maitland, too, that's what they're going to say.

"Well, I'm sure as hell going to have my say," he shouts over his shoulder to Lowery when they get stuck at a light. "People got to know what happened at St. Matthew's, even if the fuckers are all dead. The Church should know so it doesn't happen again."

"You're still on about those 'pedo-priests,' aren't you? Remember Father Danby?"

Something caves inside Dace. *No, I don't.*

"Ah, c'mon! Danby was the VP at St. Matthew's, but he wasn't that old. He just looked old to us. I heard he was related to a judge or something, that's how he got the job. You and me are like forty-something, right? So even if the rest of Danby's bastard crew are collecting pensions, I bet he isn't. You go get them, Dace. I don't have the stomach for all that shit, but you're a tough guy, you can do it. I know you can. I'm not going to lose any sleep if a bunch of those priests live out their twilight years in jail. And we all know what happens to old buggers in jail, right?"

Nothing happens to them, Dace thinks. *Nobody gets old in jail.*

Chapter Eleven

Going to Camp

Micah wants to go to camp, but he also doesn't want to go to camp. It's called being ambivalent, his favourite new word. Even his parents should be able to figure this one out. People want different things at different times in their lives. Sometimes you even do things you wouldn't do at any other time.

Like look the other way when your best friend breaks into the principal's office and steals an exam.

Or pretend you're not listening if somebody else tells a story about rolling drunks in High Park.

Or help somebody else's chick get an abortion when you're pretty sure you'd do the right thing and take care of the girl and marry her or whatever. Or wear a rubber, so you didn't get her knocked up in the first place!

Maybe he should have gone to summer school and beefed up his math grade instead. He already has over eighty percent. If he keeps it up, he'll qualify as an Ontario Scholar when he graduates from grade thirteen and get a little scholarship. But maybe he could do even better, get a bigger scholarship, help his parents out with his university tuition. Help a little with the younger kids when it's their turn to go school.

His math grade has pulled down his average this year, but if he spent as much time crunching numbers as he did reading English literature, practicing conversational French and dreaming over geography, he could raise his mark for sure. He has the brains or at least that's what his mother says.

Sure, he'd like to hear the loons at Arrowshot and canoe into all sorts of hidden bays again, he just doesn't want to be responsible for rotating groups of ten-year-old kids. Each group stays at the camp for twelve long, long days. Kids. He's had his fill of them. He's looked out for his brothers and sisters for years, but the camp kids are going to be an even bigger responsibility.

At least he'll be able to come back to Toronto every second weekend and unwind as long as his parents don't get on his case. But what if all his friends are busy working nights at McDonald's or down at the CNE? What if they don't have any money to spend running around town? Or what if one of the camp brats gets so homesick that he/she won't come out of the cabin? Or one of them wanders off and drowns in Little Joe Lake?

Or maybe the other counselors won't like him and he won't have any friends. You don't have to do much to get left out. If you arrive late or you do something differently, the clique's already formed. People usually like him, but you never know. Camp-types can range from kind of dorky, to wholesome religious nuts or crunchy granola nuts or just plain nuts. He should know. His parents have shipped him off to camp for years.

Where do they get the money from anyway? He's never really given it any thought until now. It had better not be from his grandpa. Camp used to be a whole lot of fun, but now it's just work. Also, he's new to the job, handpicked from last year's crop of counselors-in-training.

Some of the other counselors will be new too, but what if they're weird?

Unless one of them is that Mariposa girl. He heard she was offered a counselor job too, though she's still a little on the young side so she must have had some extra pull. Or maybe she just has a real pushy mum—the kind who wants her teenager out of the way. That doesn't mean Mariposa would be crazy enough to fall in with her mother's plans. Though she was already a bit flaky or maybe he just thinks about her like that because she mentioned flying back and forth between Montreal and Mexico several times a year and she has that goofy butterfly name.

Why do his parents want him out of the way anyway? It'll cause all sorts of scheduling problems with the younger kids.

His mother bugs him the most. *She* didn't want him to go off on the bike. Why the hell not? *She* ended up on a bike with his Dad, didn't she? Even rode one by herself, his Dad says, though that's pretty hard to believe. What's her problem anyway?

For the forty-eight hours before his bus leaves and his parents drive him to the pickup parking lot at a church in north Toronto, Micah tears up the house on Southview packing and repacking, creating a huge turmoil. For the first time in his life, he reduces his mother to tears.

"Why don't you leave my fucking stuff alone and stay out of my room?" he shouts at her, when he can't find his favourite sweater, his second pair of running shoes or half his socks or that journal he sometimes writes poems and other stuff in. Maybe Summer took it, but he doesn't think so. The kid's only nine. She just got the hang of reading last year. He doubts she can even read cursive, not that he's going to test her and find out. So it was Liza then. *Motor mother, motor cop!*

"You're always losing my stuff," he says, though stealing it is more like it. Even in his own mind, he can't repeat what he calls her under his breath, but from the look on her face, she hears him. As luck would have it, his father is just coming upstairs and guess whose side he's on? Dace's face darkens. He gets so mad that he slams Micah into the nearest wall and almost clocks him, but Liza pulls him back.

If Micah's supposed to be grateful to her, he's not. It's all her fault. His dad never would have lunged at him if it wasn't for her in the first place.

Nice, he thinks when he's finally seated on the bus and looking out the window, mesmerized by the pavement rushing past him underneath the big tires. *Nice*. He's going to have a lot more patience with his own kids. If he ever has any. Right now, he feels bruised and broken and worried about what's up ahead. Can't his parents see that he's under a lot of stress?

He might do a little after school tutoring next year, but this is his first real job. The campers on this bus have already been assigned to him. Every two weeks, he has to go through the same damn routine with a fresh batch of kids.

Out of the corner of his eye, he notices that the glasses of the kid across the aisle are fogged up with tears. He forgot to pack some Kleenex, dammit it— Why didn't Liza remind him? She stockpiles Kleenex and toilet paper in the basement like there's no tomorrow. He feels like crying too, but he can't. What the heck would all the little kids on the bus think if he did? He's practically grownup.

"Are you a grownup or a kid?" a kid asked him before they got on the bus, though when he looked down into the brat's face in the parking lot, he just about laughed. He might still be a bit on the skinny side, but this kid barely came up to his knees.

It really wasn't very nice of his parents to send him off this way. The look in his mother's eyes when he swore at her under his breath still troubles him, but Micah pushes the feeling aside. With his father staring daggers at him while he shook his hand, he turned around and hugged her before he got on the bus, but it was hard.

He leans across the aisle. The kid's name tag is slung around his neck on a cord and turned the right way out. "Those sure are cool runners, Kevin," he says. The kid bends over to retie a shoe, surreptitiously wiping his nose on his denim covered knees. "You want some gum?" Micah asks, pulling some Juicy Fruit from his pocket. They aren't supposed to bring gum and candy to camp, but people do, the repeat campers anyway. "Did you have any breakfast? They'll feed us when we get to camp — some okay hotdogs, I bet — but it's three hours before we get there."

God, it's always all about them. Just this morning while he was filching razors from his father's supply because he forgot to put them on the drugstore list, he overheard Dace talking about a phone message he had missed — what else is new? — about some inquiry into sexual abuse. The date for the inquiry has been set. Micah must have been too busy writing his math final, trying to improve his grade, to keep an eye on the newspaper. Nobody at school ever talks about such grim stuff, either. Half of them don't even read the paper, the big dopes. If it's worth knowing, they'll hear on the grapevine or something.

"Great," his mother responded to Dace in that snippy tone of hers, "so you'll be off on one of your little jaunts again, I suppose?"

"We could go together down to Cornwall and then on to New York," his father says, a little hesitantly for him, maybe because he knows she's just going to put him down again. "On the bike. We could pay Helen a little extra to stay overnight with the kids."

But Liza doesn't seem to notice how lukewarm the guy sounds. "Jeez, Dace, I'm tired of upper state New York!" she protests right on cue. "You always want to go there. You swore up and down that you were going to stay out of Massena and all the heat with the cigarette smuggling! And isn't that where you first met up with Kathleen what's-her-name, that butterfly person? It's been years, but the last time I checked she was still down in Mexico. Running some kind of monarch preserve, or a sanctuary, I'm not sure which — "

"Her place is called the Mariposa Monarca Mission," Dace volunteers. "And we didn't meet in Massena. It was just some hick little town in upper New York State. The kind you've always said you'd like to live in. The kind where nobody knows us. So you've been keeping an eye on her, have you?"

"Look, you can wipe that smirk off your face. It's really not that hard to see what she's up to! Kathleen Aldous is in the news sometimes, you know. She's got her PhD and she's, well—"

"Little Liza," Dace says, "If you just stopped having kids, you could get a PhD—"

"Oh, right, in my spare time! But you've got to admire Kathleen Aldous a little. I do, kind of. I don't know if she ever had any kids, but she's sure done something important with her life. Look at her—when she didn't get any recognition for helping to find the monarchs, she didn't just give up and die! She could have, but she didn't! When one door closed for her, she opened another. The woman's done something good with her life. She really has."

"And so have you, my darling. Maybe I haven't done so good, but look at our family and your job. You've got lots to be proud of! I'm a happy man."

If you say so, Micah thinks.

"Except you're always on the road, " Liza says and it sounds like she adds, "and you live under an assumed name!" but Micah doesn't believe his ears, plus he's still trying to figure out what she meant about cigarette smuggling. What the hell is she talking about now? His father's no smuggler. He's not a thief. He doesn't do bad stuff, he's the good guy in the 'hood. They even go to church on Sunday. Well, in the wintertime anyway.

"Never mind that we don't know what's going to happen with our kids and I'm fed up with office politics and cleaning up other people's prose. I have to leave my babies nine, ten hours a day! To do what?" Liza almost wails. "Trust me, I'm not doing anything that vital, that important. What's the matter with people who are English-speaking, but who don't know the difference between 'were' and 'where' anyway! I could understand it if they didn't think they could write a book, but they do. Why does everybody and their uncle think they can write a book, anyway? And that if they can't write one, that maybe they can edit one and tell me what to do? Oh, don't get me started!"

Oh, yes, Jesus, please don't get her started, Micah thinks.

"Maybe if we took a little holiday, you'd feel different when you came back. I think you need a little break."

There's a short silence. Liza is probably taking a deep breath in an attempt to sound more rational. It's her modus operandi most of the time, though once or twice Micah has known her to lock herself in the basement laundry room and just scream.

"Mum and Helen might be able to handle the kids for a few days," she says doubtfully, "but I don't have that much vacation time left. We need it for the kids. Why don't we take them down through some of the New England states later on in August? The girls and I would love to see where Louisa May Alcott lived and the babies don't really care where they go as long as they're with us. Or maybe we could drive down to Prince Edward Island, walk on those white sand beaches and see all the Anne of Green Gables stuff. "

Though he's still upstairs pillaging the bathroom medicine cabinet and listening the best he can through the door which almost opens onto the landing, Micah can practically see Dace rolling his eyes when Liza mentions the birthplaces of her favourite female authors. He sure would.

A bunch of stuff, little plastic bottles and one straight razor spills out of the cabinet into the sink and onto the counter. *Where the hell did that razor come from?* His parents are so careless with all the babies in the house. The little kids are down in the kitchen, mucking around in their cereal bowls anyway. He doesn't have time for this shit. Just watch, his mother will be upstairs in a moment to pester him. *If she likes cleaning so much, let her clean this stuff up.*

"Maybe," Dace says. He's probably got his face buried in Liza's hair by now. *Jesus, the guy can't keep his hands off her!*

Chapter Twelve
Camp Mariposa

There are already several cars in the parking lot when Micah's busload of campers from Toronto lurches off the last dirt road and careens in.

At first Micah doesn't think Mariposa is there. Through the open bus window, he looks over the campgrounds, at the log cabins to his right and further down the flagstone path to the big round dining hall, where a droopy maple leaf flag sprouts from the red roof. Looks like it's going to be a hot one, even way up here. He doesn't see her anyplace, but who knows, she might have already settled in, been here a few days, taken a sleeping bag outside and spent her last kid-free night sleeping under the stars.

It would make sense to stagger the arrival of the staff, bring in the out-of-province people first. Not that the camp administration is super organized. But you can work around anything if you have enough money, so maybe her mum drove her here early. He sniffs the air, imagining the scent of her, but all he smells are pine trees and maybe some chicken hotdogs and beans, the stuff they usually serve up for first lunch.

Mariposa wouldn't be on-site at this time of day anyway, not if she could help it. She loved tramping through the woods last year and going out in a canoe. Any canoe would do. At midnight, they'd sneak down to the shore, liberate one and paddle across the lake. It was pure bliss, navigating through the stars reflected in the water. Micah's view is obstructed by trees, so he can't really see much of Little Joe Lake yet, but Mariposa is probably out in a green canoe right now, tucked into a dip in the shore, surveying the chaos of his arrival from afar and laughing with the loons.

Montreal girls are so cool — they'd never arrive in a hot, sticky mess like this. That water sure is going to feel good on his skin and his dick if he ever gets a chance to jump in. It's real calm today, perfect for canoeing or just lying on your back and floating to heck away.

There's another camp bus right behind them, not that Billy the Busman gives a shit. He spends about ten minutes jockeying his big vehicle into place.

Maybe it takes him that long because he wants to torture the campers, payback for the racket the brats were making all the way up. They kept on rattling him even after he told them to shut the hell up. He sure as heck isn't getting any tips from a bunch of kids. Not that the dude deserves any. You don't swear at kids, plus he nearly drove the bus into a couple of lakes after they passed Huntsville and got onto a secondary road. For all Micah knew, the guy was on a suicide mission and wanted company.

By this time, Micah is sweating almost as much as the overweight driver, whose shirt is glued to his back. No matter what Micah promises, "his" kids won't sit back down. They're standing up in the aisle, pushing towards the front exit door like people trying to escape a burning building. He gives up trying to get the children seated again and works his way through them towards the front exit door. He faces them, his arms outspread. The kids are almost climbing over him. *Great*, he thinks, *I'm doing a great job.*

At last Billy the Busman pulls a lever and opens the bus door, the big jerk. The children tumble out of the bus. Somehow Micah stays on his feet.

A couple of the boys start running around the parking lot, weaving in and out of the cars, but the rest of the kids encircle Micah. They don't know where to go. Micah feels a blast of cooler lake air on his face in spite of all the hot metal cars baking in the parking lot. Most of these vehicles probably belong to staff members or a parent who decided to drive their little darling all the way from one of the States to this Canadian wilderness camp. That's a South Dakota licence plate over there on that Land Rover. Micah stares glumly at the jeep. He's miles from anywhere. This must be what going to prison feels like. If he doesn't make friends with some staffer who has a car, he'll die here an old man.

At last the bus empties out entirely. The campers from the other mix into Micah's. For one sickening moment, he can't tell anybody apart.

"I can't find my Polly Pocket!" one cries. Okay, that's one of his little girls for sure. She was playing with her bootleg toys on the bus. In the mad melee to sort out the rest of his charges and their bags and lead them to their assigned cabins, he wonders if he can take a leak.

He's really got to use the staff washroom, even though he hasn't drunk anything for hours, except for that large Coke his parents let him order from the drive-through at McDonald's on their way to the camp pickup at 8:30 a.m., along with two Egg McMuffins and a large order of fries. On this day of all days, they'd run out of milk. The twins guzzle the stuff like crazy.

After years of coming here, he knows the campground like the back of his hand. He finds the path through the trees. A big guy from the other bus brings up the rear of the campers. The guy's bigger than him anyway. He says his name is Gary or Gavin or something. Micah cocks his eyebrows at him, but he can barely nod "hi," much less come up with something cool or smartass to say.

His kids are still bugging him about this and that. One's hungry, one's got to pee, one's freaked out by a spider and a couple are having a spat.

"I don't think I'm going to like my cabin," a little girl no bigger than his sister Summer announces, oblivious to the fact that he's hauling six bags including hers and can't do a damn thing about it, "I'm supposed to be Chelsea's roommate. My mother said."

Micah spits out the cabin list from his teeth, securing it with his chin. *Tough bananas,* he thinks.

He looks back at Gary-Gavin, but there's no help there. The guy isn't even helping his own bedraggled campers with their bags. *Looks like I might not get my choice of roommates either,* Micah thinks, after sizing up the heavyset dude. He's never seen the guy before, which is kind of funny. Lots of former campers want to be counselors. Where the heck did the camp recruit this one from? The guy's at least six and a half feet tall and older than him by some two or three years. The big lug, he could be working in construction, putting his brute strength to good use.

Not that Micah couldn't take him on. Even if this Gary-Gavin character resembles a slightly better looking Texas chain saw murderer, except for a soft gut—at twenty! Micah isn't René Dace Gagnon's son for nothing. He's slowed down a bit, but he spent his early adolescence pumping iron at the 'Y.' He doesn't even remember the first time his father took him there. He's still kind of skinny, but everybody at the gym says that he'll fill out. He's got muscles where this Gary-Gavin guy doesn't. Yeah, he could bring this G-G down, especially if he surprises the guy.

The little girl is still whining in his ear. "We'll sort things out later," he promises her, hoping the kid will have a new best friend by evening if it turns out that her roommate isn't Chelsea.

Meanwhile the camp director has come out of nowhere and is standing around doing nothing, smiling at them like some kind of sleek Buddha. The woman's name is Anne Taylor, but even after seven years of coming to camp, he still doesn't know her that well. You don't see a whole lot of her if you're a camper, just at the beginning and the end of a session, though you might catch sight of her doing her early morning swim halfway across the lake and back. In her mid-fifties, with her still blonde hair cut in a chin-length bob, Ms. Taylor is wearing her usual lightweight camel-colored jacket and hat, like somebody on a safari. Or a journalist of some sort. Actually, he heard someplace that she writes travelogues for the *Globe and Mail* but he never bothers with that section. He won't be able to go anywhere for years unless he joins CUSO, which he just might. Ms. Taylor is a cool one all right, even cooler than his mum Liza. She makes him feel scruffy, like a day labourer hired to do her dirty work or some poor inner city kid she's brought up to Algonquin Park for a vacation. Some vacation!

On a plaque in the dining room, he suddenly recalls reading that Camp Arrowshot is Anne Taylor's lifelong dream. Boy, do some people ever have piss poor dreams! Micah wants to do something really important with his life. All his good friends do. He just doesn't know what that something is. How nice to have always known what you want to do, like Ms. Taylor and his mother! Irrationally and for his own sake he hopes, briefly, he hates the camp director's guts. It'll be a long summer otherwise.

Just then, somebody starts banging the camp gong, loud and long, the one that's in front of the dining room hall. It's used to regulate the campers' lives, but he's never heard it ring so loudly at midday or so urgently.

What the heck's the emergency? Unless the camp routine has changed, it's a bit early for a frantic lunch bell to announce that their food is on the table and in danger of spoiling. Maybe Martians have landed, there's a bomb threat or one of the campers, hopefully not one of his, is already missing and drowned. A couple of the younger kids, including crying Kevin, really start blubbering then—in abject terror, Micah supposes. Their cries get even louder when from out of nowhere, a long-haired girl in a one-piece tank suit streaks past them, dives straight into the lake and starts nosing around under the long wooden dock. She reminds him of somebody, but he doesn't have a clue who.

Then it hits him—it's Mariposa. Except she's got bigger boobs this year, probably because she's fully grown. And her hair's longer. Something like a drumroll fills Micah's ears. In spite of all the commotion, he takes a deep breath. Yeah, he likes her all right. He really does. So she's really, really here. *So pretty, so*—he doesn't know what to think. Well, thank God she's here and his campers are piping down. Maybe this job won't be so bad after all. He smiles until he notices Gary watching Mariposa bob up and down from under the dock. *The snake!* Yeah, he's a Gary all right, not a Gavin. *Look at that stupid grin on his fat face!*

Micah realizes two things then—that this big oaf Gary wants a little girl like Mariposa maybe even worse than Micah wants her himself and that this isn't some big emergency. Mariposa is just doing a practice sweep, he remembers from last year. He used to be able to just ignore that bell, but now that he's in charge of so many people, he'll have to do a headcount and assess the situation. They'll want somebody to do a safety check twice a day when the camp is in full swing, to make sure that everybody's accounted for, that nobody's drowned. Well, good for Mariposa. She can be 'It'! She's got the job of doing practice sweeps, one of the so-called perks of being here first. As long as it isn't his job, though he might have to take a turn eventually. He'd rather not poke around that rotting old dock though. A fresh coat of grey paint isn't hiding anything. Not that he's afraid of spiders or creepy-crawlies, having grown up in a hundred-year-old house in Toronto. And if the lifeguards and the counselors really do their jobs, no camper ought to drown so they'll never find a body.

Here be dragons, he thinks like he always does when he's confronted by things he doesn't want to know.

"Jesus, I love her ass," Gary turns around and whispers. "Just look at it when she dives down under the dock. It's so damn fuckable!" Yep, he's a Gary all right. A Gavin would be—well, somebody different, a cooler, smoother, nicer guy for certain. A polite Brit on a Canadian adventure or a holiday. A nice guy might think such things, but he wouldn't say them.

Micah knows he'll sound like a freak, but he doesn't care. "Isn't she a little young for you?" he whispers back, like he's the older dude, the one in charge. Like he has any idea about how to preserve a young girl's innocence and virginity.

If the director realizes what he and Gary are saying to each other, she doesn't let on. She nods at them approvingly instead. For all Micah knows, she's congratulating herself on handpicking them since it looks like they're getting along so well. Then she takes off for the shore. Maybe she wants to make sure Mariposa is doing a thorough job and has been properly trained. She wouldn't want any bullies at her camp, that's for sure. This place is for everybody. That's what all the camp brochures promise, after a parent has ponied up the big bucks for the camp fees.

Whatever, the director's not paying any attention to Micah or Gary anymore. Neither are any of the kids who are settling down a bit while they check out the campgrounds.

"I think she's from Quebec but she's plenty old enough here in Ontario," Gary grins, thrilled to death no doubt that the camp director is out of earshot so he can speak out loud. "As long as she's over fourteen and it looks like that chick is. I like my meat fresh—don't you?"

Chapter Thirteen
Illegal Logging

As soon as Kathleen opens the door, she knows something's wrong.

"Shit, shit," she groans, stamping her feet on the ceramic tile to shake the mud off her shoes. Why isn't she better prepared? Juan-what's-his-face didn't show up at the airport, but still. Freddie Nolan was along with her for the ride, so they took one of those rickety taxis—a rickshaw practically!—and she put her feelings of dread aside. With Freddie cupping her face and kissing her and slipping his hand in between her legs, it was hard to concentrate, anyway. God knows, if she acts on every misgiving she has, she'd go stark raving mad.

C'mon now, where's Juan? If he wasn't at the airport, he should be here. In the autumn, he goes up to Canada to work in the fields in Ontario or in British Columbia with a flock of his cousins, but he has no place else to go at this time of year.

Well, maybe he's sleeping out back in a hammock then?

Mexicans have no sense of time. *Just wait until I get my hands on you,* she thinks, depositing her house key back inside in her purse. Her nose is itchy and her throat's dry, but she stands stock still for a moment, trying to figure out why everything's so quiet, why her household isn't jumping with life, why it's so colorless.

What about the rest of her staff? Labour's dirt cheap in Mexico or she never could have afforded even this little ranch.

"Hola?" she calls out, taking a step or two.

The entrance way to her little adobe house is tidy enough, but there's a funny smell. It's not the odour of cooking gone bad either. Maria's a good cook, she'll give her that much. Where is the woman? Maria or one of her umpteen daughters always bustles in from the kitchen whenever Kathleen comes home.

"Catalina, Catalina," she'll cry out and continue talking in Spanish. Maria can't or won't say "Kathleen."' Luckily Kathleen has no trouble understanding the language after all these years. "You must eat, you lose too much weight!" Maria always says.

The excitability of Latino women amuses Kathleen, but it's a mystery to her. Except that they live in a virtual paradise, most Mexican women don't have much to get excited about.

Thank God Freddie Nolan is here getting her bags out of the taxi. Of course he wanted to come home with her. Why not? He's at loose ends. He works as a travel agent, so he can't travel to Mexico in high season. This is a good time for him to check out accommodation for the people he wants to send down here.

Kathleen has always had a kind of radar for trouble, so she's careful in her own way. His story—the parts she listened to anyway—sounds plausible enough. He can have a little holiday in Mexico City. Lots of ancient history there with the old city practically built by the Aztecs on a lake—or maybe he'll visit some of the Mayan ruins, if the rain lets up long enough.

She probably should go back outside until Freddie checks out the rest of the house, but she isn't going to be driven out of her own home, dammit. Her right hand reaches for the phone she had installed on the hall wall in the event of a calamity such as this. Maybe she should call those useless dicks, the Mexican police. But now that she gets a closer look, she sees there isn't any point. Not with the telephone wire down there on the floor.

Kathleen stares at the cut wire in disbelief. If the intruder hoped to scare her with this act of vandalism, it's not going to work. She won't let it. But with her temper getting the better of her, she takes the disconnected receiver off the hook and flings it to the unforgiving ceramic floor. It's damn nearly impossible to get a phone serviced in this place. To get tile. To get anything!

No way she can afford to go without a phone for months. She has so many responsibilities, to the butterflies, to her old mother and to her young daughter, even if they're thousands of miles away. Life used to run more smoothly when her mother had all her marbles. Things went even better when her stepfather was around. Her parents looked after Mariposa at least. If something happens to her family, she wouldn't be able to do anything right away, but with a goddamn phone, at least she'd know.

"Kathleen," Freddie says, finally arriving with their bags and almost making her jump out of her skin, "That spic taxi driver tried to stiff me, but I sorted him out. As if I wouldn't know how much to pay when I'm in the travel business—Mother of God, what the fuck happened here? What's with the phone? Are you all right? Are we in the right place?"

"Don't be ridiculous," Kathleen says, rushing off into the kitchen now that he's here. "I know my own house, you fool." What if something's happened to Maria and she's dead on the floor? And her butterflies, what if something's happened to her chrysalides and all the supplies she painstakingly collected? And oh, my God, what about her notes?

There's nobody in the kitchen, but what a mess! Maria would never leave it like this. Kathleen spots the sticky stuff on the counter right away. Somebody probably wanted her to think it was blood, but it's not. No flies. Kathleen spins around in circles in the empty room—empty except for the broken crockery all over the floor and the smashed taps in the sink.

Why, oh why, did they smash the taps? Just to scare her with their brute strength or alert her to the fact that they know how to swing a truncheon? Those taps are practically irreplaceable. They're all the way from Germany or Italy, someplace overseas.

Oh, God, there's broken glass leading out to the backyard! Her heart, which sped up the minute she entered the house, takes off on a real gallop now. What about the aquariums and her precious chrysalides? Is the glass from her aquariums? When she first came here, it took her nearly two years to get set up.

She steels herself to face the damage out back, but in the end, she just can't look. Not yet. In the doorway to her yard, she sinks down slowly to the floor and starts picking up glass from the floor, depositing it bit by bit into the palm of one smooth white hand. If she has to, she can retrieve the chrysalides from whenever they got flung and put them in a temporary cardboard box.

"It's okay, it's okay," she soothes herself. "You can fix this, you can make everything all right. Again. You're a healer, a fixer. It's what you do, it's what you've always done."

"Watch yourself," Freddie says, settling down beside her and wrapping his arms around her. "Don't cut yourself on the glass, pretty lady. What do you think they were looking for?"

"Nothing," she says, pointing out the open doorway to a painted scrawl on the wooden fence, "Look at that! *Get out betch.* They can't spell, but it's pretty clear they want me out of here so they can log wherever they want."

"Oh, c'mon," Freddie scoffs. "It's probably just kids. Sorry, but I find it hard to believe that a bunch of spics are organized enough to know what you're even up to."

"Well, they may not read the papers or follow my career," Kathleen says, "But unless they're complete imbeciles, they'll have friends who read the papers and their damn friends talk."

Chapter Fourteen

Canoeing

What the hell is Mariposa doing out on the lake with that clown in a canoe? She can canoe all right. She's been coming to Camp Arrowshot for years. They both have. She and Micah didn't pay much attention to each other when they were younger, but they got in lots of canoe practice together last year. It looks like Gary can canoe too, but the girl really shouldn't be alone out there with that baby-fucker.

You got to wonder about a guy like Gary, a big guy who drools over all the eleven and twelve-year-old campers. It's just weird.

From the dock at the shore of Little Joe Lake, Micah keeps an eye on his colleagues in the canoe. The campers are all in bed, but it's just after nine, so there's a spill of light from the setting sun. The moon is still hiding.

Micah puts his hand in his pocket and pulls out the package of Rothmans and the matches he bought on his day off in Huntsville. He lights up a cigarette on his very first try.

Inside her special cabin, the director goes to bed at the same time as the campers. She's been up since 6:00 a.m. A lot of other senior staff members are the early to bed, early to rise types too, especially the cook who gets up at five. Which gives people like fatso Gary plenty of time to get up to other shit, especially after dark.

Micah takes a big drag on his cigarette. *Hey, I'm getting good at this,* he thinks, when he doesn't even cough once. Maybe he won't finish this package, but it gives him something to do after his campers are in bed. Even if the light in the staff cabins wasn't so crappy, he's too tired to read at the end of the day. Gary came better prepared. He's got some pot in a tin can under some rocks in the bush, but he's saving that for the girls, man.

That little whiner Kevin delayed Micah. No wonder his parents signed the kid up for camp for the whole summer.

Mariposa could have and should have waited for him. They've gone out in the canoe together for the past several nights when it was much darker. They paddle by the light of the moon, just like last year. It's their thing, the time when they mostly just sit in the canoe and talk about the stars and stuff. For some reason, he hadn't really wanted Gary or anybody else to know what they were doing, but just look at the bastard now! He and Mariposa are out there in Micah's favourite canoe, as bold as brass.

He backs into a shadow where they can't see him. With any luck, they won't spot the lit end of his cigarette either.

Oh, Christ, what's that stupid dork Gary doing now? Don't stand up in the canoe — ah, good he's not, he's just edging forward on his knees with his big hands gripping the sides of the canoe so he can come up on Mariposa's behind. She looks over her shoulder. Maybe she's smiling, but Micah can't tell her facial expression from this far away. Looks like she's moving backwards into Gary's chest and his big soft gut. She'll have to if she doesn't want him to upend the canoe with all that weight in one spot, but she's not going to stand for that, is she? She's not going to let some slimy bastard touch her, she's not —

"Watch out!" Micah shouts, emerging from the shadows to run down to the end of the dock. They don't hear him, but it doesn't matter because the next thing he knows, they're both flopping around in the lake, grabbing at the floating paddles and making their way back to the overturned canoe. And Mariposa is trying to get all that mermaid hair out of her face. Micah still can't see her expression, but that goddamn Gary is guffawing his fool head off, scaring the wildlife for miles around.

Yeah, that's life. One minute they're in the canoe and the next they're in the water.

The lake is pretty calm though, just like it's been all week, so they're all right. Once they get hold of the canoe, they start shouting at each other.

Mariposa doesn't usually swear, but it sounds like she says "You stupid fuck!" Definitely, she didn't say dork, she said "fuck"!

She shouldn't have gone out there with the bastard, though.

What was she thinking? Can't she read the guy any better than that? Gary would take her sharing a canoe with him as carte blanche to do whatever he wants to do. Sure he would. When he talks to Micah around a late night campfire or in the staff washroom where he's usually waving around his dick, he's always blabbing about all the ass he's had.

Gary and Mariposa can take care of themselves, dog-paddle the damn canoe back to shore.

"What's the matter with you?" Gary berates Mariposa, his loud male voice booming out over the lake. Christ, they can probably hear him inside the cabins, the way sound carries at this time of night. "I was just trying to kiss you, you cold little bitch."

As if you have any right, Micah thinks. When they finally do get back to camp and haul the canoe up on shore right by his feet, he sees that Gary hasn't given up all hope because the fly of his shorts is undone. Well, what else is new? If he's had as much action as he says, maybe dog-paddling in his shorts has loosened his zipper, but Micah thinks the zipper got some help. Did the stupid bugger really think he could fuck in a canoe? Or maybe he thought he could cop a free feel, even if all the pleasure he got was kissing the back of Mariposa's neck and dick rubbing her ass.

One look at the shrivelled thing between Gary's legs and Micah can't help himself. He sucker punches the bastard right in the belly, which makes Mariposa even madder than she already is, the ungrateful little so-and-so.

Standing there just dripping, she wrings her long hair with both hands and squelches more lake water out of her shoes. She's tall, but she still has the face of a little girl. She reminds him of Summer and Eden after they've run through a lawn sprinkler, just before the game turns nasty and they shriek for the nearest adult.

"I can take care of myself," Mariposa says with barely a glance at Gary who's still writhing away on the ground. As if to underscore her point, she lands a good punch on Micah's shoulder before she takes off. When what she really should do is kick Gary in the balls!

Yeah, you can take care of yourself, Micah thinks, watching her climb the hill to the staff cabins. *About as good as the twins.*

"The little cockteaser sure can," Gary says, coughing-sputtering as he gets up awkwardly from the ground. He keeps a few steps back from Micah, but the dumb dork still hasn't zipped up his pants.

"That wasn't cool what you did — sucker punching me like that. Is that the kind of dirty shit that they pull in that wop neighbourhood that you're from, you son-of-a-bitch? What kind of daddy you got? Or does your mummy even know who he is, Micah Devereux? Don't worry, I'll get you, you just won't know when it's coming either. Or how. It doesn't look like Mariposa's going to let you into her pants either, but I'll help myself to her the minute you're gone. She wants it, she just doesn't know it yet."

In addition to wanting to kill Gary, even if it's in his sleep with a pillow over his head, Micah is sorely tempted to tell somebody that the guy is bothering Mariposa and maybe even some of the younger campers, but he doesn't. You just can't tell. The Director wouldn't do anything about it anyway.

Tell us, tell us, adults always say, but when it comes right down to it, nobody wants to know. Also, from what he's found out so far, Gary is the son of the director's good friend, which might explain how he got the job in the first place when there were so many other more qualified candidates around.

It doesn't explain why Gary wanted the job, but it was probably to get away from something. Why else would somebody want to work up here?

Back at the staff cabins, Micah tries to sleep but eventually he hears the door of the girls' staff cabin opening. When he goes outside to check, the first thing he sees is Mariposa. It's midnight, but she's sitting on a log beside their dead staff campfire. She's crying. Judging by her swollen face, she's been crying for hours.

When he sits down beside her, she collapses against him into his arms and cries some more. He's reminded of his sisters again, of Summer clutching her Pound Puppy and Eden snuffling into her pink teddy bear when she's in distress.

Great, so I'm a teddy bear, that's me, he thinks. Well, better that than playing out some *Lord of the Flies* crap here at camp.

"I want to go home," Mariposa says. "Gary's always making a fake grab for my pussy or my breasts. 'You're all wet. You know you want it,' he'll say. I didn't think he'd be stupid enough to try something out in the canoe though! What took you so long, anyway?"

"Kevin."

From what Mariposa's told Micah this summer, she can't really go home, unless she wants to head on down to Mexico where her mother is and practically die from the boredom and heat. Murder stirs in his chest, but he'll just have to do his best not to kill Gary. And try harder to protect Mariposa.

The next morning, Mariposa acts like nothing's happened. What's that all about? *You don't have to be so nice,* he thinks, but

169

that's a girl for you. Mariposa even smiles a little at breakfast when Gary cracks a stupid joke.

The next time Micah sees her, she's coming out of Director Taylor's digs and she's not smiling anymore.

Did she really think the director would do something about Gary?

They'll have to do something about the bastard themselves.

Mum, Mariposa. Even Grandma, the way she lives her life. I really don't get women. I just don't get them at all.

But he doesn't have to understand all women.

Just Mariposa will do for now.

Chapter Fifteen

The Canadian Schmuck

*A*h, men. What a bunch of stupid buggers. Whatever their age, whatever their nationality! But the ones born before 1970 are definitely the worst. Gay or straight. Kathleen has yet to meet a guy who doesn't think he's the be-all and the end-all and a super stud to boot. Look at her thesis advisor when she was twenty-one. And once they get something into their heads, watch out.

It's the same if they want you. Or even if they just say they want you. You have no say. They bulldoze right over you. They're cavemen all over again. And God help you if you marry. You're lost.

Look at Freddie Nolan! What was she thinking, bringing him here to her place in Angangueo? They've known each other a few weeks and now he wants to marry her. As if he could. Mr. Super Stud isn't even divorced.

Of course it's the butterflies he's really after, not her. He'll do anything to get his greedy hands on them.

Once she realized the full extent of Freddie's plans, she did her best to talk him out of messing around at the Sierra Chincua colony. The monarch colony is her baby. She's researched and coddled monarchs for almost twenty years. The big jerk never even heard about the Sierra Chincua colony until he met her. Oh, but he's a smooth operator. All that talk about checking out the local tourist digs for his company. His plans for ecotourism are way bigger than that.

Fortunately Sierra Chincua's the only colony open to the public right now so he can't do much harm. Unless he persuades the Mexican authorities to open up more colonies to tourists, but that isn't going to happen. It just isn't. Not if she has any say. And most Mexicans are so lazy anyway.

A fat-cat American might stand a chance, but Freddie Nolan is just some poor Canuck schmuck. He flashed a couple of twenties when they went to see the police, but he's as poor as she is. Poorer maybe if you factor in the ex-wife.

Him and his damn ecotourism!

I feel real conflicted about this, she tried telling him, the more he yammered on. But did he care?

You gotta promote it, babe, he said, finally rolling off of her when they were in bed. He smacked her rear as if to emphasize his point, so she smacked him back.

What's to lose? he seems to think. It's a win-win situation for him, her and the monarch colony.

Maybe. She's been thinking about organizing an annual monarch festival. She'll have to give it some more thought, but a festival might help.

Kathleen has no idea what Freddie said to the business bureau to sell them on the idea of ecotourism because she refused to go with him, but she went with him to the police station in Angangueo. It was her house that the bandits trashed and her monarchs that were threatened, not his. She managed to retrieve most of the chrysalides from the underbrush in her yard, but still.

The Mexican cop shop was straight out of the movies, with a wooden ceiling fan circulating stale air. Freddie Nolan's face broke out into a sweat the minute they went inside. Two uniformed officers welcomed them.

Kathleen might have met these fine examples of the Mexican police force on a previous occasion, but it was hard to tell. They all looked the same to her in their greasy uniforms. Neither of these men nor their representatives deigned to come out to her house when she reported it broken the week before. If they recognized her, a pale-faced blonde and practically the only güera living in the region for the past sixteen years, they never let on.

They made a huge fuss over Freddie though, probably mistaking him for a privileged American male.

Not that she or Freddie got a chance to say much. The part where she told the police that "bitch" was spelled wrong was completely lost on them.

"Si, si Señora," they kept interrupting, nodding their heads so much that she was afraid they might both fall off. "They shouldn't say. That's not nice. It was just some chicos, we'll take care of them."

"No, it was illegal loggers," Kathleen said flatly. "Leñadors, you, you—" *You big dopes*, she finished under her breath.

"Ah, Señora, nobody come to your casa if your Señor's there."

"Freddie Nolan is not my Señor!" Kathleen finally started shouting. "He's not going to be here with me all the time! Why the hell don't you people care about the monarchs?"

Freddie started pulling her out of the smelly little office right then.

"Don't worry," he said. "They know who the guys were. They'll talk to them, they just don't want to let on."

Chapter Sixteen

Letter

Kathleen's phone still isn't working by August, *surprise, surprise,* but for some reason the Mexican mail is way speedier than up north, so that helps. Word-of-mouth works pretty well here, too, so she gets everything else repaired inside her house in less than six weeks.

She takes care of the back fence herself with a couple of coats of thick paint. Like she tried telling the police, the misspelling of "bitch" really bothered her. Errors and omissions, especially spelling mistakes, drive her insane. There's no room for error in her business or any business, and no excuse if you graduated high school and paid enough attention to detail.

Her household staff showed up, the minute everything was squared away. Money helps. It really does. But they would never come back to a place trashed by a drug cartel, further evidence that the intruders were probably friends of the illegal loggers.

Who knew, the hoodlums who trashed her home might even be friends or family of her "loyal" staff. Everybody's related around here. Funny how none of her staff were in the house when it happened.

The Mexican police were asses, but they got after some of the illegal loggers, maybe because of all the noise the international press was making about illegal logging in the monarch wintering grounds. Okay, so Kathleen tipped the press off herself. If the Mexicans didn't wake up and listen, local tourism in out-of-the-way Angangueo was going to be even more compromised. Nobody in their right mind would want to visit here.

Even if he is a penniless Canuck, it probably hadn't hurt that Freddie Nolan went to the local business bureau with his idea for organizing expeditions to see the monarchs. He's a bigger gun than she is with her little girly job of chasing butterflies while Mexicans starve.

At least the major cleanup's behind her now. But there's always something to worry about, isn't there? She picks up the letter that came in the mail today and reads it for a third time. Strange. It looks like the letter was typed on a Smith-Corona electric and posted on the first Saturday in August from Toronto, but it purports to be from Anne Taylor, the director of Camp Arrowshot:

> *I regret to inform you that your daughter isn't safe here, probably because she's too young and immature to be working as a camp counselor. Even so, she's such a lovely and enthusiastic girl that we would love to keep her, except we're concerned about our own liability.*

Hmm, Kathleen thinks, fanning herself with the hand scrawled envelope. The second sentence sounds like Anne Taylor, kind of pompous, but the first part doesn't.

What a nuisance! Well, she doesn't have much choice. It's already midmorning—if Kathleen wants to get Mariposa a ticket, she'll have to leave for Mexico City right away. With any luck, she might get to the airline counter before two. Her whole day's going to be shot, but what else can she do?

She could make a call from a wealthier neighbour's house, but you can't trust people over the phone. If she doesn't stand there and watch what the ticket agent is doing, her kid might end up in Tunisia.

"I'm off," she says to Maria before she leaves the house. "But I'll be back for dinner for sure." They never eat until eight or nine anyway.

Tearing out of her driveway in the little car she keeps down here for emergencies, she wishes she could get in touch with Freddie Nolan. He might be able to fly down with Mariposa or at least help her get off. No, wait a minute, he can't. He's finalizing his divorce. Well, of course he is. He didn't fool her. He kept saying the woman was an ex, but Kathleen knows a married man when she sees one. The only thing she didn't suspect and should have, is the threat he poses to the monarchs.

Well, if she can't beat him, maybe she can join him. This long drive into Mexico City will give her a chance to think some more about her idea for a monarch festival.

At the rate she's going, she'll have all day. The stupid car in front of her is slowing everybody down. *What's the dumbass driver doing anyway, slamming on his brakes like that all the time?*

An annual monarch festival might be a win-win situation for everybody, especially if it's promoted right. If the locals had a chance to sell their handicrafts, they might be happier too, or at least less inclined to sulk and destroy the monarchs' habitat.

As for Mariposa, she'll have to get herself down here, the little brat. Just thinking about her errant daughter nearly makes Kathleen floor the gas pedal and force the car in her way off the road.

She doesn't have time for Mariposa's nonsense, she really doesn't. And she won't have time to pick her up at the airport either. Juan can go get her. Well, Juan and Maria. It's a nuisance giving up two of her staff for the whole day, but Juan's the driver and Maria will have to chaperone him and the girl. Juan had his eye on Mariposa the last time she was here. Or maybe Mariposa had her eye on him.

The girl's never been much trouble before, but she's definitely making up for it now. Screwing up her first real job!

What has Mariposa done to upset the director? Had sex with that Micah boy she was hanging out with last year? As long as they used some protection, it doesn't matter! What does the camp expect when they hire teenagers?

On the bridge just ahead of her, the slow-moving car almost comes to a complete stop, so she honks. Jesus, just keep moving! Honestly, the shape people keep their cars in down here. And why is it suddenly so hot? The last she heard on her radio, the day was on the cool side for Angangueo at this time of year, about 70 degrees.

Maybe it's perimenopause, she thinks as a second wave of heat and irritation engulfs her. She honks at the stupid driver again. *It's not menopause, I'm just coming on forty-seven!*

Well, never mind that. It can't be.

As for Mariposa, the girl's just going to have to shape up.

Chapter Seventeen
Letting Micah Go

Liza grips the wheel of the station wagon with both hands.

"Oh, for God's sake, just break it in two and give them each a piece!" she cries.

With the animal crackers practically all gone, she has zero hope of keeping her troops in order. It's her own fault. She's got to keep the car, this rolling madhouse of hers, better stocked. But all she could think about was Micah when she left. She wanted to get to him fast, so she threw everything and everybody into the station wagon and fled.

Neither her mother nor Helen is available today. She's not sure how long she'll be gone anyway. At least it's a fine day for a drive. If only this had happened during the week, though! All she'd have to worry about is missing work and Irina's sour face.

Dace, she thought, staring at the useless phone earlier that morning and wishing she could get in touch with him. *I hate living here alone.* Of course she doesn't have a number for him! She never does. He's probably on a plane anyway.

Well, they're almost at Camp Arrowshot now. In the passenger seat beside her, Sammy certainly isn't being much help. He's pawing through a stack of comics, oblivious to all the cut rock and pristine lakes they're passing. He's just turned twelve, so he's allowed to sit in the front seat now.

In the backseats, Summer and Eden are pretty useless. They're okay with the twins sometimes, but if Liza really needs their help, forget it. Eden's pretending to sleep and Summer, who's evidently fed up entertaining "her" twin, announces she wants to take a nap. As if the little brats ever sleep at this time of day!

"We're almost there, girls," Liza says. Her hands are aching and her right thigh is beginning to shake. It's all she can do not to reach over the back of the seat and slap someone. She never drives much if she can help it, but she's been hanging onto the wheel like a life preserver for the past three hours, with one quick bathroom break at a gas station just outside of Huntsville. The place was busy with cottagers who had missed coming up the night before. What a commotion, getting everyone in and out of the car. All five children pestered her for more treats, as if they hadn't just finished a week's worth.

Even when there aren't a lot of trucks, she hates driving on the highway by herself with such precious cargo. At least the twins are still in their car seats, though they've been straining at their straps like little prisoners for miles. Based on previous experience, she has separated them, with Cory in the middle seat next to Eden, and his noisier twin Cole in the narrow rear seat beside Summer, but it hasn't helped. Even though the little boys aren't identical, they have this weird connection—or least a disconcerting sixth sense of what the other is up to. In just three short years, they've become remarkably adept at keeping score.

His is bigger! was the first complete sentence either spoke. Other people find this cute, but Liza doesn't.

They're just a few miles from the park gates now. She really can't take much more of this, she thinks guiltily. It isn't the kids' fault. They should be home, doing kid things, enjoying a day off school.

The twins were fine until they reached Barrie, an hour into their trip. Then all hell broke loose. Cory screamed first and then Eden started.

"I'm supposed to go to Sarah's birthday party today!" she sobbed. "Grandma helped me with my princess costume!"

"Well, you can't!" Liza snapped, though for some reason it seemed particularly heartbreaking that she couldn't let Eden play princess today.

Because something awful has happened and you don't want to think about, she thinks as she drives into the park, ignoring the booth near the gate. It's okay though. She isn't going to stop at any of the campgrounds or the attractions, so she won't need a pass.

The ride along the dirt road into the camp is interminable. At last she spots some signs of human life up ahead, several cars and two trucks. Anne Taylor, that director-woman, and some other people must have been waiting for her, because the minute she pulls into the parking lot, they descend on her car.

For a split second, Liza almost fears for her life and her children's, but then she takes a deep breath, flings open the door of the station wagon and gets out. She's got to do this. Whatever happens, she can't cry. *Overwrought mother, too many children,* that's what they'll say. Still inside the car, all five *kids* are miraculously quiet, but even if they were making their usual racket, she wouldn't notice.

"Where's Micah?" she asks. "I want to see my son."

Anne Taylor drops her outstretched hand and purses her mouth. Lines Liza has never noticed before radiate from the woman's upper lip.

"Can I get you a coffee or some tea?" the director asks. "Don't worry about the children. This is Mariposa Aldous. She can take your little ones over to Arts & Crafts with her campers and entertain them for a while."

Hearing the name Aldous, Liza shoots a quick look at the tall teenager's tear blotched face, but it looks nothing like Kathleen's.

Mariposa comes forward then. When Liza doesn't say no, the girl lifts the rear door of the station wagon and starts getting the kids out. Liza is reluctant to abandon her younger children to a complete stranger, but the girl works at a children's camp, so she lets her kids go.

Anne Taylor is pulled together as usual and she looks at least outwardly calm. The woman's always seemed competent enough. She's also very enthusiastic about her work, which counts for a lot in Liza's books, but she's never really liked her.

What the hell makes this bitch think that she can just fire Micah with only a few weeks left to go at camp anyway?

"I think you'd better come get your son," she said during their telephone conversation, that and a little bit more which Liza wasn't really able to take in. All she could really grasp during their brief telephone conversation was that Anne Taylor wanted Micah out of camp and fast. But why? Doesn't the woman know anything about children? An experience like this could scar him for life! This can't be happening to Micah, Liza's golden boy.

Liza has to do something. She is going to do something. She just doesn't know what.

Anne Taylor is introducing the two adults with her, a man and a woman. Liza nods like she's listening, but she doesn't catch either person's name, just the fact that the woman is the camp chaplain.

"I want to see Micah. Now," she repeats, despising her own trembling voice.

"As you wish, Ms. Dev — uh, Ms. Deb — ?" Anne Taylor says.

"You know it's Devereux, it always has been, the same as my son's! And you do remember his name — you called me about the right kid, didn't you?"

"It's going to be all right, Ms. Devereux. We'll get everything sorted out. Let's go over there where we can talk," Anne Taylor replies, pointing out the way, "the senior staff has a little meeting area just inside the woods."

Liza follows the director and her colleagues down a short trail. Micah had better be there. Thank God she sees him right away. He's seated on a rock by a dead campfire, whole and unbroken. He doesn't get up when he sees her.

"Nothing happened," he says, stiffening when she rushes over to hug him. "They got it all wrong."

He's just embarrassed, Liza thinks, sitting down on a log as close to him as she dares. *Please don't push me away in front of all these people*, she prays. *In fact, please don't push me away at all. It breaks my heart.*

Out of the corner of her eye, she takes stock of the man and woman who are here with Anne Taylor, no doubt to give their director moral support. Or be witnesses. They sure as heck aren't here to support her and Micah. *Where's my help?* she thinks irrationally.

Think, she tells herself, *just think. But just what the hell did these people do to her son?*

"Now," Anne Taylor says when everybody's finally seated, "Micah's a fine boy, he's been a good camper for years and he's a fine student I'm told, but we just can't have this sort of thing here. I'm not sure he's done exactly what's been said — And it's a new world and people are free to make their own sexual choices, just not here, so nobody's pressing charges."

"Oh, no, no charges," the chaplain-woman jumps in, a little breathlessly.

"Who's they?" Liza demands.

"Just that shit Gary," Micah mutters. Liza's eyes dart to him, but Anne Taylor and her staff ignore him.

"Gary who?" Liza asks Micah.

"A counselor," Anne Taylor says evenly, "But let's not bring him into this. He's another fine young man. He didn't want to say anything, he's just worried about some of Micah's campers. Micah has a cabin full of boys this week, older boys. Well, almost full. Somebody contacted one of the boy's parents and they came up and pulled their son out almost the minute he got off the bus. Like I said, we're not sure anything was going to happen, they just didn't want to take any chances, um, based on what they heard. Their son's fifteen years old, so he might be almost as big as Micah, but that's not the point. There's a big difference between fifteen and seventeen and your son is well grown. But as long as Micah goes quietly and nobody talks to a lawyer or goes to the press, we can let him go with a good reference."

"Yeah, nobody has to know what happened here," says the chaplain, a blowsy sort of woman in her late forties with a kind face.

Or just a stupid face, Liza thinks uncharitably.

"As the camp chaplain, the kids tell me lots of things, but we don't—"

"I never would have thought it," the only man in their little group says.

"Sorry," Liza says, "what is that you do here at camp?"

"I'm the cook. I only ever seen your son with the girl. But you don't know about guys sometimes. I had a good friend—"

"But what on earth's happened?" Liza interrupts, ducking her head into her shoulder to blot the tears coming out of nowhere. God, why isn't Dace here? Why is he never here? Why does she even expect him to be? "Micah's great with kids and he's—"

"Mum," Micah groans.

"He's just maybe not our kind," the chaplain says, utterly oblivious to the effect this comment might have on Micah and Liza, though the woman shrinks back a little at the pained look on the director's face.

"Well, now," Anne Taylor says, jumping right in again, "I'm—the camp—we're not saying anything like that. And we most certainly welcome all kinds here, so that's not to say Micah wouldn't be welcomed back at a later date—maybe if he talks to somebody, like a psychologist and gets a doctor's note saying he won't ever, uh, you know, act on anything..."

"Act on anything?"

"Look Ms. Devereux, there's no need to say things that can't be unsaid. That's the camp's philosophy. Boys are boys, so this just might all blow over if it's handled in the right way. The camp's reputation will be protected and so will Micah's. I'm just trying to look out for your boy, I really am and that's what you should do. A psychologist might have another take on this, uh, situation or at least be able to offer us some assurances."

"But camp's almost over," Liza says, wondering how she can afford a psychologist even if Micah really needs one, but he doesn't. He doesn't!

"People have urges and we like Micah, we really do," the chaplain says, warming to her topic while she pushes some wispy greying hair off her forehead, "but we don't want to encourage him to act on his urges, to put him in harm's way. What's okay for grown men isn't necessarily good for young boys. I—we can pray for him if you like."

Anne Taylor purses her lips again, but she doesn't say anything. Oh, God, Micah looks so exhausted! He has black circles under his eyes. Has he lost weight too? The last time he came down to Toronto, he looked fine. He was in and out of the house all weekend running around with his friends.

"I'm not just going to sit here and listen to this crap!" he says, getting up. At just the sight of his long limbs moving away from her, Liza's heart clenches. Of course her baby is embarrassed and ashamed. Who wouldn't be? The director has practically fired him from his job and hinted at sexual misconduct. He's wearing shorts and just flip flops on his feet, the gear he probably wears most of the time at camp, but he's surefooted enough. Liza starts up too, almost stumbling over a rock on the ground, but the cook puts out a hand and stops her, his hand lingering just a bit on her leg.

Micah needs a haircut, she thinks, focusing on the mundane, anything she can control. *I'll drop him off at the barbershop when we get back, if there's time.* From the direction he's going, it looks like he's headed for their station wagon. She hopes so.

It's okay, she tells herself, he's got no place else to go and he's no Tom Thomson. And surely to God he won't drown himself in the lake over sorrow and shame… But wait, didn't she read about some private schoolboy doing just that when he was accused of cheating on an exam? Walking home, the sixteen-year-old had just jumped off the Don Valley Bridge that separated east and west end Toronto.

A boy. She just doesn't get it. This is Micah they're talking about. She knows her own son. Whatever happened, it must have something to do with a girl! It's all right even if it is something to do with a boy, but not with a younger one in his care.

Liza faces Micah's accusers again. "Is it that girl, that Mariposa? Have they done something?" she asks, suddenly recalling the girl's tearstained face. Yes, that's it, the staff here is just confused. If something happened, it's got something to do with her. Liza clearly remembers Micah mentioning her lovely butterfly name before. Still, Liza can see why the camp wouldn't want their counselors fraternizing or worse. The girl's so young.

She can still see Micah up ahead. Like some kind of zombie, he's slowed down to a walk. My God, she's losing him. Whatever happened here, someday he's just going to walk away from her and start a new life.

"Micah," the director calls, "do you want us to all go away so you and your mother can talk privately?"

But Micah isn't interested in talking. *If this was television*, Liza thinks with her eyes on her son, *I'd kill all his accusers right now or at least have the pleasure of socking somebody in the jaw.*

And no she isn't going to ask Micah about what "really" happened here. There's nothing to ask. She'll have to let this sink in, but it looks like the camp staff think that Micah did something with a boy in his care. Or that he wanted to do something, which in some people's books is almost as bad.

Micah hasn't, though. Liza's heart clutches again, fearing what this might do to him. Who is this liar Gary, anyway? Liza's pretty sure that Micah said one of his fellow counselors was called Gary something and that he's a bit of a suck up or worse, but that he's also the son of Anne Taylor's good friend.

Oh, Dace is going to be so mad when he hears!

And if Micah's dad can't take care of things, she'll sue the goddamn camp herself and take away all of that cool bitch's dreams! Liza will fix her, yes, she will.

When Liza gets back to the parking lot and she doesn't see Micah right away, she almost panics. Then she sees him coming towards her from the direction of the staff cabins. He looks like a packhorse. He's carrying two duffel bags, his backpack and his guitar, everything he's lugged up to camp over the past six weeks. Without sparing her a glance, he drops his things through the open window at the rear of the station wagon before going around to open the front passenger door.

"Don't you want to say goodbye to anyone?" Liza asks before he climbs into the car.

"No," Micah says. "They're all going down to the waterfront." He says something else but he's slamming the door after himself at the same time, so Liza can't hear him.

Leaving Micah to sit by himself in the car, she goes off to round up the rest of her kids. It takes a lifetime, but finally all the kids are accounted for and strapped into their seatbelts.

It's stupid to try and talk to him, especially with the kind of mood he's in, but she does anyway. At best, it's three and a half hours back to Toronto. In a low voice that she hopes only he can hear, she pulls out all the comforting words she knows. He's such a wonderful boy. All this will pass. Someday, the director will realize Micah's done nothing wrong and what a mistake she's made. But it'll be too late because he's going to get another great job. Nobody else has to know anything about this. Liza speaks for a good ten minutes before Micah says a single word.

"I'm tired, Mum," he says, staring out the passenger window at trees and rocks.

"Maybe we can get you to a psychologist on Monday," Liza finally says in desperation, although she has no idea where she'll find one who can see an adolescent on such short notice or where she'll come up with the hundred bucks or more that such a professional will almost certainly want up front, "Get you back into camp on Tuesday—I could put you on the Greyhound to Huntsville and somebody from camp could pick you up."

"Stop the car," Micah says, staring out the window.

"Why?"

"I want out."

"But what did you do?" Sammy asks from the seat behind Micah to where he's been demoted.

"Nothing," Micah says with a quick look at his mother.

"That girl Mariposa said she was your friend and that she was real sorry to see you go," Sammy persists. "But then this Gary guy came into the Arts cabin and he said she didn't know what the heck she was talking about."

"He didn't think I saw him," Summer pipes up, from the other side of the infant car seat separating her from Sammy, "but he kind of squeezed Mariposa's bum when he came in. 'Gary,' she says and her teeth were like this," Summer says, demonstrating with her own clenched mouth and her lips drawn back, as if in extreme pain. "I don't think it was a good touch, Mum."

"No, that wasn't a good touch," Liza says automatically. *Gary*, she deduces, feeling like the only recourse she has left is to learn to read minds, *he's at the bottom of this, somehow he must have got hold of that camper's parents and told them lies about Micah and their boy. But why?*

"Shut up," Micah yells. "For God's sake, everybody shut up!"

"Shush—I know you didn't do anything wrong and being let go isn't the worst thing that could happen," Liza tries again. "It might seem that way right now, but it isn't. You've got nothing to be ashamed about, darling. Do you think maybe that Gary guy just wanted you out of the way? He sounded like a bit of a jerk when you mentioned him before. A co-worker can be a good friend or he can be your worst enemy. Especially if he's jealous or just plain bad. It depends. You know, some bad stuff happened to your father and he—"

"So what," Micah says, almost conversationally. "And stop trying to make me feel guilty by crying. This is your fault. Why'd you have to make me go?"

Liza grips the wheel again and focuses on the road. It feels like Micah has kicked her in the gut. But it's no use talking to him. Not when he's like this. The boy isn't in his right mind.

Somehow she's got to make things right.

Don't hurt me, Liza thinks all during the long sleepless night following their return while she stares up at the ceiling in her bedroom, alert to any movements from Micah's room.

She ordered pizza for them, a Saturday night treat, but he didn't eat a thing before he went to bed. His camping gear is still all over the dining room table where it will no doubt stay until she takes the sleeping bag to the cleaner's, washes his clothes twice to get the sand out and stores everything else in the basement closet.

And please, please, don't hurt yourself. There really are worse things than getting fired from your first job. I should know. Look what happened to me when I was your age, look what happened to your father. No way she's going into the past, though, even in her mind. The stuff happening now is hell enough.

But by dawn the next day, she feels a little better. When she awakes from the briefest of sleep, Mariposa's face and name pop into her mind and just like that, she knows what to do. Funny how life can get clearer in the bright light of a new day.

Mariposa Aldous, that's what Anne Tyler called the girl. And Aldous is definitely that lady scientist's, that butterfly person's name. The girl would probably have her father's surname though.

So maybe Mariposa is Kathleen Aldous's niece, a cousin or a brother's child?

Liza waits two hours. Most of the older kids are waking up, going down to the TV room to eat granola bars and watch cartoons. She hears Summer helping the twins out of their cribs. But at 8:00 a.m. when Micah is still sleeping and with any luck will stay that way until at least noon, she goes downstairs to the dining room to call the one line into Camp Arrowshot. She doesn't expect Anne Taylor to answer the phone herself, but she does.

"This is Micah's mother, Liza Devereux," she says before rushing on. "I don't know what exactly is going on at Camp Arrowshot, but—"

"Really, Ms. Devereux, I don't think I care for your tone."

"—I want you to do something about that counselor Gary," Liza says, speaking as fast as she can before the director gets it into her head to hang up, "I heard he's your friend's son, but..."

"Now see here, it's your son who's in trouble, not Gary Pu—uh, not Gary. Really, Ms. Devereux, it's not good to always take your child's side. A young man of seventeen has got to learn to take responsibility for his own actions."

Yes, Liza thinks sarcastically, *the jails are full of felons whose parents always took their side.* "It doesn't matter what your friend's son did to Micah—well, actually it does, but I can't do anything about that right now and I can about that girl Mariposa Aldous or at least I can try. I'm pretty sure he's bothering her, that Gary, that he's doing things to her that she doesn't want."

"You don't strike me as the kind of person who believes everything she hears and reads or even what's in the newspaper, Ms. Devereux. Have you even met Gary Ptak?"

So his surname's Ptak, Liza thinks, mentally filing the information away. "Well, no, but I heard what he—" she starts to say, not caring to mention her daughter's name.

"I thought not, because Gary is really a most exemplary young man. As for Ms. Aldous, I'm sure she's mature enough to take care of herself or I wouldn't have hired her. Girls mature earlier than boys, don't you know? Besides, this is a children's camp, they don't, well, our counselors just don't have that kind of privacy here. You know, not one of our girls has ever left here pregnant!" she adds triumphantly. "But we can't always help what happens off the campgrounds, especially if the girl chooses to go off with a young man. That's natural, at least, whereas your son might have, or well, at least he might be interested in both sexes. Which is fine, just fine, bisexuality is just fine," Anne Taylor hastily adds, "just not at Camp Arrowshot, if it involves a boy in his care!"

"I'm talking about the girl's safety," Liza says doggedly, her head reeling from the endless circle she and Anne Taylor keep traveling, "I want you to do something to protect that girl."

"Well, I'll certainly review this matter —"

Review? Liza thinks, suddenly wondering if Mariposa has already tried to complain about Gary.

"I know Mariposa Aldous's aunt from university," Liza lies. "And she'll no doubt be very interested to hear that her niece is being harassed or worse. Whatever, she runs a butterfly sanctuary down in Mexico, so I'm sure she has lots of media contacts. Maybe you've seen her in the news too?"

There's a pause on the other end of the line before Anne Taylor says, "Well, no, that's not right, it's Mariposa's mother who's —"

Liza speaks over her. "As for my son Micah, his father and I will be in touch with you real soon. But if I don't have a note saying he's on a paid leave of absence by the end of this week, as well as a glowing handwritten reference from you and an invitation to work at the camp next year as a senior counselor which my boy will no doubt be happy to refuse, his father and I will have to consult a lawyer! And we do know some!" *Unfortunately,* she thinks. "Not to mention," she continues,

191

warming to her task, "I'm also very good friends with an author and journalist myself—Val Jaffe? She works for the *Toronto Star.*"

"Val Jaffe? Well, yes, I know her from a few press functions and I know her work, but she's a bit out to the left for me. Look, Ms. Devereux, you're evidently taking time out of a busy morning. We can certainly review things here at Camp Arrowshot—there's always room for improvement in any organization—but I have to go now. The dining room is just closing. I like to make sure everybody goes where they're supposed to. I'm sure you can appreciate that the safety and well-being of our campers here at Arrowshot is paramount. We have ninety-two campers here this week. I also have a staff of ten to supervise, which rather surpasses even your large household—"

"I—" Liza interjects again, but Anne Taylor is still talking.

"And like I said yesterday, nobody has to know what happened here. But don't worry, I've been thinking while we were talking and I'm sure we can meet your demands. I really don't appreciate being threatened like this, though. And you should think about not making perpetrators accountable—that's partly where the residential and the training schools went wrong with those uh, bad priests. I'm more of a teacher than a parent, so it's not my job to tell somebody how to parent, but it seems to me that you're making a mistake with your son."

Screw you, Liza thinks, staring down at the black phone which she's already slammed back into its receiver. Belatedly she recalls Anne Taylor didn't actually guarantee Mariposa's safety, but there's no point in calling her back now. She'll just get some underling to answer the phone.

No, she's burned all her bridges as usual. Christ, what's wrong with her?

Turning back to the doorway, she sees Micah standing there in his pajama bottoms with his chest bare and his face still unshaven. Not that he has to shave every day, so he must have missed a couple of days. *Damn, how much has he overheard?*

"Micah," she says guiltily, gesturing back at the loaded dining table, "why don't you get yourself some breakfast and then clean up your camping gear? Or I could make you some pancakes and eggs. Sammy and the girls might want to go to church today, but I don't have to go."

"Can't. I've got stuff to do. You know, I really wish you'd stay out of my business."

"Micah, I can't, I just want to help you and your dad isn't here. That woman, Anne Taylor, she's not, well, I don't know — she's just kind of strange."

"But I don't want your goddamn help! And Dad's never here! What the hell is he, some kind of criminal or is he just on the run? He doesn't need to be here anyway! I'm seventeen, so I'm pretty sure I can take care of myself. I always have! As for Mariposa, that's none of your business either. I wrote to her mother three weeks back after I socked that pervert Gary in the gut."

Liza looks at her son then, knowing full well that they both wished he'd done more than that, damn the consequences, like his father would have.

"Three weeks ago? So why hasn't the mother replied or gotten in touch with the camp at least?"

"She has. Mariposa got a plane ticket in the mail from her just the other day. Her mother's way down in Mexico though, so I guess that's why it took so long. It's hell getting mail into the camp anyway. I think it's delivered by canoe. I also heard that Mariposa's mother lives someplace where she doesn't even have a phone. Whatever, Mariposa and I are both out of camp and away from that asshole, not that I couldn't have taken care of him myself a long time ago if he wasn't Anne Taylor's protégé."

Kathleen Aldous? She couldn't possibly have accomplished so much if she had to look after a child too, Liza thinks. How old is Mariposa, anyway? And where's the girl's father?

"Mariposa's mother is what, she's who?" Liza asks. "You're not telling me that Mariposa's mother is Kathleen Aldous, that monarch expert? I thought Kathleen might be an aunt."

"Well, I guess she is. And who said she was her aunt? Look, I told you last summer that one of the campers' mothers was that famous lady Kathleen Aldous. You're the one who's always yapping about monarch butterflies. What's the matter with you? You never listen to a word I say!"

Chapter Eighteen
Mariposa's Refusal

Mariposa can hear the phone ringing before she even opens the screen door and unlocks the heavy door of her grandmother's home in Montreal.

Thank God I still have my key, she thinks, letting herself into the hallway. She leaves her bags and camp gear on the veranda. They'll be okay there for a while.

True to form, the next-door neighbour's dog is barking, but she can't do anything about him right now. If she shuts the door, she'll boil to death so she just latches the screen.

The damn phone is still ringing, practically vibrating the hall table. It's her mother for sure. Knowing her, she's probably been calling the house ever since Mariposa failed to show up at the airport in Mexico City. Mariposa feels badly about Juan who was supposed to pick her up, but what makes her mother think she can tell her what to do? She's not a kid anymore. It killed her to waste the plane ticket, when her mother could have spent the money on those monarchs she loves so much, but she had to. She couldn't have gotten on that plane. She was too sick.

Because the camp director Anne Taylor, basically fired her, right after she complained about Gary the second time. Gary goosed her right in front of those little kids! She couldn't stand what the big shit was doing to Micah, either.

The money and the plane ticket she'd gotten from her mother had arrived just in time. Even if when she first opened the letter, she thought, *No way, I'm not leaving Micah, I'm not! Even if the director is a bitch and Gary's a total jerk!*

The plan was for Mariposa to depart from Pearson Airport in Toronto, a four hour bus ride from Algonquin Park, but it was just as easy for her to go the other way and hop a bus to her grandmother's place in Montreal.

When she's good and ready, she picks up the phone, but only because the ringing is getting on her nerves. It's her mother all right.

"So you're there," Kathleen says.

"Where else would I be?"

"I've been calling the house for hours! I even called the camp in case you changed your mind about leaving but nobody answered. What's a parent supposed to do if there's an emergency? And what the hell's wrong with them anyway, letting a young girl just take off by herself?"

"It's not like it's the first time I ever traveled on my own. I told them that when I— And the chaplain drove me to the bus stop in Huntsville, which probably left them kind of understaffed, not that I give a f—"

"Don't use that word! If you got to Huntsville, why the hell didn't you take the Toronto bus?"

"Because Granny's place is here."

"Well, you can't stay there all by yourself. For a weekend maybe, but not for the whole school year."

"But if I stay here, I can keep an eye on Granny, visit her and do stuff for her and the house and anyway I'm seventeen! She doesn't have anybody except us."

"Your birthday isn't until October and seventeen's still not old enough. Granny doesn't know us anyway, so don't worry about her. Listen, kiddo, I won't pay the bills, the hydro, the phone, the taxes or for any of the groceries. And God help me, I'll sell that house from right under your lazy tail if I have to. Granny can't use it and she gave me power-of-attorney, not you. Legally speaking, you're the child here and I'm the adult. And speaking of bills, that plane ticket was totally wasted! And what about me? How do you think I felt when Juan came back here empty-handed and told me you weren't on that plane? For all I knew, you had been kidnapped."

"And sold into white slavery!" Mariposa snickers. "You watch too much American TV, Mum."

"You know perfectly well I don't waste my time watching television! The only reason I have one here is to get the weather and the news, such as it is! Not that anybody would blame me if I did zone out on TV—there certainly wasn't any TV in the San when I was a kid! That's not what we were talking about, though. I want to know this and only this—what the hell happened at that camp? What went wrong?"

"Nothing went wrong!"

"Oh, really! Well, what am I supposed to think when I get some cloak-and-dagger letter from somebody claiming to be the camp director saying that you're 'in harm's way'? You were at a children's camp for God's sake, in a perfectly safe place, the same place you've gone to for years. It's God's country up there! What could possibly go wrong? How could you be in harm's way?"

In what century is her mother living? Lots could go wrong, Mariposa thinks. At least her mother doesn't suspect she was fired. That would be the last straw. Not that Mariposa gives a flying—well, you-know-what. One way or another, she had to get away from Gary. Things got even worse after Micah left. Gary just couldn't or wouldn't keep his hands to himself! What a pig that guy is, just her luck that he's the son of the camp director's friend.

"I was fine, Mum and you know it. Camp just wasn't much fun this year—"

"What, because you had to do some work for once?"

"No—well, sort of. It's different, being staff. There's this really creepy guy—"

"You mean the one who was hanging onto you last year when I picked you up, Mike somebody?"

"No, no, Micah Devereux was still there—we were working together — but it wasn't him."

"Devereux?"

"Devereux. What's the matter with you, Mum? It's not like you've never heard his name before. I told you his mother's always writing him these big long letters just like you do, but you never listen to me."

"And you got all mopey when you didn't hear from him last year. He never answered your letter, did he? Mariposa, listen, this is very important. You didn't uh, do anything with him, did you? Please tell me you didn't because I—"

"Of course we did something! We're teenagers," Mariposa lies, puzzled as to why her mother gives a hoot if she's having sex. If anything, her mother has always seemed in a hurry for her daughter to lose her virginity.

Have you? Kathleen asks her every six months or so. *We can get you a prescription for the pill. Just keep away from my Mexican boys when you're down here, dear.*

No problem, Mariposa thinks. Though Micah would probably do better than that kid down the street did, the one who came all over her.

"Why shouldn't we? I'm almost seventeen!" Besides, she and Micah did almost kiss but it was only the once.

There's a long silence at the other end of the line, the kind that really creeps Mariposa out, the kind they usually have. She thinks frantically about just hanging up the phone and running out the front door to God-knows-where until her mother says,

"And where is young Micah Devereux right now? Not there in the house with you, I hope."

Honestly, the notions her mother gets! It never even occurred to her to ask Micah to come here, but she should have. Because he was fired like her. What's he doing until school starts?

"No, he isn't," she answers truthfully this time, tempted as she is to scare her mother just a little bit more. "There was a big powwow at camp so his mother came and got him, unlike some people who are always down in Mexico doing their own thing! She had all these younger kids with her —

"Who had kids?"

"Micah's mother!"

"Well, she probably doesn't do anything except look after her kids then. No wonder she could come running up there to pick up her baby! You should have gotten on that plane, Mariposa. I could help you if you were down here with me. And you could help me. The monarchs —"

"No way I'm coming down to that dung heap in Angangueo!" Oh, God, she's losing it again. But maybe if she yells loudly enough, her mother will listen for once.

"Okay, I'll just drop everything to look after you! I was going to come back to get you ready for senior year in three weeks anyway, so I'll just come back early. The papers have all been signed, but we still need to get you some school uniforms."

"You really don't have to do that, Mum. I'm not going back to boarding school here in Montreal anyway, not when there's a perfectly good house —"

"Now listen here, you're not staying up there alone with all sorts of strange men running around and you getting up to God knows what. And I know about that pot you smoke! No wonder you've got so little ambition! That stuff's not good for young people. Mark my words, someday they'll find out that pot plays havoc with developing brains. Enough of this! It's your senior year. If you don't want to go back to school in Montreal, we'll get you into another private school so fast your head will spin and then it's off to college for you. Or you could come down here, get into the University of Texas and be that much closer to me. But you're going to have to smarten up and get some good grades this year, even if all you do is go into journalism. It's a win-win situation for both of us. You can concentrate on school and I can tidy up down here. Things are going pretty well for me right now, not that you asked! I had a bit of a scare when I flew down here back in June, but the authorities surprised me. They got rid of a lot of riffraff. Better for tourism— Mariposa, are you still there?"

More business shit. The monarchs are okay, but all her mother thinks about is her work. And men. "Yes, I'm still here. Where else would I go?"

"And as for that boy Micah, uh, Devereux, if he's in the same grade as you are, he'll have to do another year of high school because they have that stupid grade thirteen thing going on in Ontario. Where's he from? Ottawa, I think you said?"

"Yes, he's from Ottawa," Mariposa lies again, for the simple reason that it's always best not to tell her mother everything.

"Listen, Havergal might be a good fit for you if you don't want to go back to school in Montreal. I've met some smart women who came out of there. Even if you have to do grade thirteen in Ontario. But maybe you won't. You've got a late birthday, but I think you could probably get some extra credit for your high school there in Montreal."

"Havergal?" Mariposa protests automatically, but then she shuts up. She'll have to go to a boarding school anyway with her mother away in Mexico so much. No way she'll get out of that. And Havergal's a posh girl's place in downtown Toronto, isn't it? How far from Micah's place can it be?

Later that night as she unpacks her bags and gets ready for what is likely her only night alone in the house, she's puzzled. What the hell does her mother have against Micah? She doesn't even know him. Micah's the sweetest boy that ever was.

Chapter Nineteen

Conception and Deception

All the kids are back in school. When the monarchs fly down to Mexico in the fall, kids go back to school. In Liza's mind, these two events are forever linked. With the long summer behind her, life seems to slumber a little, but she usually gets a second wind in the fall.

All her kids except the twins are in school that is. They won't be eligible for half days in junior kindergarten for another year. Helen's taking them to a co-operative nursery a few times a week. They'll have to travel on a bus a bit out of the neighbourhood, but it's something for them to do. The little hellions!

She worries she's raising Cain and Abel, but Cole and Cory are still little guys. They're just turning three. They'll be all right.

The monarchs have already all flown south or so the *Star's* reporting, lots of them. Kathleen Aldous and the rest of the people trying to help the little creatures must be doing something right. Liza hasn't seen that many monarchs herself. A few came to her backyard garden, but except for work, she really hasn't gone anywhere. Maybe she needs to plant some more milkweed.

The monarchs have gone but Dace is here for once.

"When does Daddy sleep?" Eden asked this morning. Great, so even her six-year-old notices Dace pacing their house and yard half the night. He spends the rest of the night in their room, not that Eden needs to know this. Or that he makes love to his wife like a guy with something to prove. He's here, isn't he?

Don't go, Dace, please don't go. Don't leave us again.

But he's different. "I'll kill you if you get pregnant again," he keeps on saying. Not that he takes any chances. He hates the things, but he uses a condom all the time now. "The twins nearly killed you last time. You've got to do something for yourself."

As if she could have another baby right now! She isn't that crazy. The background research she was doing for the upcoming inquiry has already sickened her. Totally. And she gets so sick when she's pregnant. Let the anti-abortionists come after her if she gets pregnant again. Look at those poor kids in some of those priest-run schools. Some of them would have been better off unborn.

Besides, she's got a husband and six kids to take care of and she's weary to the bone.

She might not even have anything to worry about. Maybe she's in perimenopause, headed for the same early menopause as her mother. She feels a stab of grief at the thought, but it looks like her periods are slowing down. She's only had a few since the twins were born. Dace is right, the birth of the twins has knocked the stuffing out of her. A woman's body is only designed to carry one baby at a time. By the seventh month of her pregnancy with the twins, she'd gained so much weight she could barely move.

On her doctor's advice, she actually stopped taking the pill last month. If her mother had gone into premature menopause, those light periods Liza is still getting are probably triggered by the pill. So many hormones aren't good for you, especially if you don't need them. Everybody knows that, or should.

Liza's doctor, a general practitioner who supports the midwives in Toronto, is big on natural remedies and natural birth control. He wasn't thrilled about prescribing the pill for her anyway, not that he's had to write her many prescriptions. She's been pregnant or nursing for much of the past fifteen years.

"Just make sure your husband uses a prophylactic religiously until you haven't had a period for at least a year," he said.

So Dace did. There was just that one night when the condom broke, so she's probably safe. They were both a bit wild that night.

At least Micah's okay now. A lot can change in a few weeks, especially in a teenager's life. Even before he brought Mariposa home to meet Liza, he walked around with a newfound spring in his step. The boy isn't sleeping much either, but his eyes and skin glow. The little bit of acne on his cheekbones has vanished. Teenagers! Micah behaves like he wasn't practically accused of sexual misconduct, that nothing bad ever happened in his life. Well, it hasn't. Even if Micah never gives her any credit, Liza fixed things. The references and offer of employment she demanded from Anne Taylor came in the mail just the other day.

And Mariposa Aldous got away.

There's just one problem. The girl has ended up here in Toronto of all places!

Liza almost died when Micah brought her home. A closer look at the girl and Liza knew she was Dace's daughter. Dace must have known about her existence—how could he not? How then could he let her grow up almost parallel to Micah for nearly seventeen years? Leaving Liza to explain everything! Well, what else is new? But just what is she supposed to say to Micah now?

Uh, about your little friend Mariposa Aldous, I think she's your half-sister, dear.

One thing's certain, Micah won't blame his father. He'll blame Liza instead.

It's horrible to consider, but once Micah realizes Mariposa is his half-sister, it might even push the two kids closer together. It's weird, but Liza has heard about such things happening when children who were adopted get together with people from their birth families.

She has no proof that Micah and Mariposa had or are having a physical relationship, anyway.

I've met Micah's friend Mariposa Aldous, she nearly tells Dace several times, but she can't, not with the shit going on in his life.

At her craziest, she even thinks about getting in touch with Kathleen Aldous to talk about their kids, but she can't summon up the nerve for that either. *Oh, God, I'm such a coward*, she thinks.

How much control is the woman likely to have over Mariposa anyway? Look at her. She has zero control over Micah and not much over the rest of her kids.

But maybe Mariposa isn't Dace's daughter after all. For all Liza knows, the girl is Dr. Gene Sheridan's daughter with that whimsical butterfly name of hers. Why else would a smart, practical woman like Kathleen choose such a name unless she wanted to honour the man? And Sheridan was Kathleen's adviser, wasn't he?

Liza met the great man in Mexico when everybody showed up at the butterfly wintering grounds at the same time. She remembers him quite well. He was very charismatic, just the type to attract an academic like Kathleen. But no, Sheridan was an old man, even back in 1973, not to mention too loyal and committed to the monarchs he'd loved and pursued his whole life.

Mariposa might still be somebody else's daughter though. She doesn't have to be Dace's, she doesn't. What about that other professor Kathleen brought to the monarch wintering grounds, the American? He wasn't a very nice person, but he might have fathered the child.

What a relief that would be.

Except Mariposa is Dace's daughter, all right. She looks more like him than even Summer and Eden do, especially around the eyes. And she walks the same way as he does, with a lithe, graceful gait. Liza's little klutzes must have gotten their awkwardness from her.

Chapter Twenty

Another Can of Worms

L iza misses the first day of the inquiry. At the rate she's going, she won't make the train to Maitland this afternoon, either. One step forward, two steps back. *Push, push.* It's like she's in labour again and she can't get the kid out.

Cole and Cory can be pretty adorable, but they aren't being too cute right now. No sooner does she fold some clothes into her suitcase than they dump them out on the bedroom floor. They're looking for the treats she sometimes hides in her luggage. And fighting with each other and screaming loud enough to alert her neighbour Donna through the brick walls.

They're driving her nuts, but it's not a nursery school day. And her head's so full of lists. Lists of food, lists of who's babysitting the smaller children hour by hour, lists of after school activities, lists of plants to be watered, cats to be fed, bills to be paid and an appointment with the twins' pediatrician and one with Summer's teacher, again, dammit! What's going to become of that girl? All the time she wastes worrying about her, the little drama queen! When she should be worrying about Sammy. He's spending a lot of time out in the garage. And he's so quiet.

Quiet ones are always trouble, her own mother used to say. But what did she mean? Liza's twin brothers were lots of trouble and they sure weren't quiet. *Dammit, where's the belt to that green dress?*

At least Micah's settled down a bit, she thinks, momentarily so paralyzed by anxiety that she can hardly move. Maybe Sammy is just reading old cartoons in those newspapers out in the garage.

No way she can be in Toronto working and coming back to her children at night, and in Maitland with Dace and all the rest of that sad, desperate crew. God help them, she hopes Dace isn't hanging out with those guys. He isn't supposed to be.

But are the inquiry people be stupid enough to put up all the witnesses at the same motel? She doesn't think so. There's quite a few potential witnesses though. Especially considering the number of St. Matthew's alumni who are dead or in jail. They called it a model school, but students didn't get much of an education. Many of the surviving former residents can barely read. At least they can talk. Over sixty men, former residents of St. Matthew's, called the hotline that Dace helped organize. But only some will have the balls to testify. Look at Dace's buddy Rick Lowery. He's not talking. After all Dace did for the guy!

Trying to tug the suitcase off her bed and almost flattening Cole in the process, Liza briefly envies her husband.

"Get out of my way," she says, tapping Cole a little harder on his rear than she intends, while Cory quickly dances out of reach.

On his Harley, Dace will have ridden through leaves just starting to fall. He left late Sunday. He's holed up in the very same hotel where all the lawyers representing him and twelve other inmates after the Maitland Penitentiary Riot once stayed.

The bedside phone rings just then. Her stomach lurches.

Shit, she thinks, knowing full well what the call is about before she picks up the receiver. It's twenty after nine, so she should have phoned work by now. She really feels sick now, so at least she won't be lying. The twins are carrying on so much that she can't remember the last excuse she used, more than six months ago.

Happily it's just Kim, the office secretary calling her, and not that damn Irina. Somehow Irina usually contrives to be out of the office at the same time as Liza, leaving her lowest paid employee to run the place. It's like she has some sixth sense that Liza won't be there to see what she's getting up to, which also means that she cares about her opinion for some reason. Even though Irina always says she's home tending to some emergency, she's frequently sighted with her special friend, hoping to dodge the hundreds of people who work in their building.

"I'm sick," Liza lies hastily and easily to Kim. They've always been united in their unwillingness to have their work schedules dictated by the time that Irina spends with her boyfriend, but no point in asking Kim to deliberately lie for her now.

"Shit," Kim whispers back, "She's here, you-know-who! What am I going to do with her? Yeah, her, the one who wears the big floppy hats and has just finished writing her twentieth bodice ripper, *Heart's Desire.* You know what she's like. She's sitting in Irina's office right now correcting all the grammar in our memos and phoning everybody she knows to complain we're not doing enough to promote her books. And that our coffee's no good."

As for Irina, Kim confirms that she has another emergency at home, or she might just be trying to avoid her client, who knows? Though come to think about it, Irina's delivery man friend hasn't been around yet either. Just last week Irina tried to pass off this particular client to Liza, but the woman wouldn't have it. At the time, it annoyed Liza just a bit.

"Can you come in for just a little while?" Kim begs.

Great, Liza thinks, after she double checks the train schedule, but somehow she finishes tossing her suitcase together, passes the twins over to Helen and is out her front door by 10:00 a.m.

Bye, bye she waves. Both boys look so darn angelic now that they have the sitter to themselves. She'll check them again when she comes back to pick up her suitcase, make sure they're all right and that her lists of do's and don'ts are strategically placed next to the front and back doors.

Her next-door neighbour Donna, a woman in early middle age, is sweeping some imaginary dirt off her sidewalk, but she's watching her. Though she has three dogs and a pair of half-grown kids, Donna's no baby lover, so most of her comments have to do with the comings and goings of Dace and what's wrong in Liza's house. *We've got mice in our house again. Looks like they're coming from your place.* Donna thinks the world of Dace, though. *Ah,* Liza sometimes thinks in amusement, *if I'm such a bad housekeeper, I wonder how you'd feel about living next-door to an ex-con?*

"I heard screaming coming out of your side window yesterday and wondered if I should go over there—" Donna says with what might pass for a sympathetic smile to anyone who knows her less well than Liza does.

"And helped out? That must have been Eden. She's usually so calm, but she got a splinter stuck in her thumb. I had a heck of a time getting it out. Funny, I heard some screaming coming from your house the other night, but it sounded like your husband—"

"Oh, that, that was just—" Donna says to Liza's retreating back. *Stay out of my stuff, you fucking bitch* is what Liza actually heard him say, that and a few other choice words before she slammed her side window shut.

Two hours, Liza thinks as she walks to the Dufferin subway station, *this writer gets two hours and then I'm on a train out of Union Station to Maitland. I'll tell Madame Hot Pants how great her books are, how I've read every single one and never spotted a single grammatical mistake or font error and that if there's one in this latest book, it's somehow the printer's fault because it sure as hell isn't ours. I'll give Irina this much: there's no way she would ever miss a grammatical error.*

No way Liza wants to drive all the way to Maitland, which is why she missed the first day. The recent trip up north to get Micah and the horrible trip back home have completely undone her. Great God in heaven, why is her life always such a mess?

Chapter Twenty-One

What Sammy Knows

Never mind what his mum thinks, Sammy loves it when both his parents get the heck out of the house. He can do whatever he wants. It isn't easy living in a house with so many people milling around. It's still warm enough inside the garage, so maybe they think he's out here drawing caricatures and getting ideas from the funnies in the old newspapers piled sky-high here, but he's not.

If they think about him at all. If they remember he's their middle son. He had a real nice spot in the family, but then the twins came along. He was Liza and his grandparents' baby boy, a second son born five years after their precious Micah, but he's nobody now. His dad's still good to him when he's home though. They watch reruns of *The Three Stooges* all the time.

His mother's always telling him what to do. *Hang up your coat. Don't pay any attention to Summer, she's just trying to get your goat. Put that dish away. Your backpack's full of half-eaten lunches. Empty it all out. When did you last brush your teeth?*

"Mum," Sammy managed to grab Liza's attention before he left for school this morning, "Can I sleep over at Jason's on Friday?"

"Yes," she said, "But just this once. And we can't have him back. We've got enough kids here and well, never mind. Did you make your bed and is that your homework on the stairs?"

Uh, oh, Sammy thought. She never wants him to sleep at other people's places, so something's wrong again. She thinks he doesn't notice the way she's always crying or parking Cole and Cory in front of the idiot box, but he does. He just doesn't care that much. She should give the twins to grandma, get them out of the way. They've got enough kids here. Grownups always have problems, but they look after themselves. Kids' problems are worse because they can't fix things themselves. Anyway, she'll come around and start taking care of them again. She always does.

He can't remember the last time she tried to hug him, not that he'd let her. *My little man,* she sometimes says, *what are you thinking about?* He hates it when she calls him that or when she coos at the twins. It's even worse what she says to them, *My little baby boos. What am I going to do when I don't have a baby anymore?* She doesn't think he hears her, tucking the boys into bed at night and catching them in her arms at the foot of the stairs, but he does.

She was after him to enter that cartoon contest at school, but he wouldn't. He left the torn up entry form on the staircase for her to find. It's some stupid lame contest and it's rigged anyway.

Everything's rigged. Even Grandpa says so.

Sammy looks up at a cardboard box high on a shelf and grins. He can't help himself. There are horrible things in that box, but his chest swells with a kind of a pride, like it did when he passed that dumb science test or he catches the ball. Any ball.

His goal is to put at least one article in the box every day. His mother's going to have conniption fits when she finds out that the nail scissors are missing from the downstairs bathroom. She'll be even madder when she finds out that he's cutting up all the old newspapers in the garage, but at least he's not cutting himself like some of the dumbass girls he knows.

It's not the first time he's cut stuff out of the newspapers. He's been cutting articles out of the *Star* for his school projects for years, the stories with pictures. Micah and Summer do too, but so far they've left the *Maitland Spectator* alone on account of it being mostly just full of small-town news.

He wouldn't have bothered with these articles if he hadn't come across the name D'Arcy "Dace" Devereux in the *Star*. That's got to be his dad, right? Who else could it be? There's so many stories about this Dace fellow, Sammy doesn't know how he missed them, but the ones from the nineteen-sixties and seventies are way down at the bottom of all the newspapers, almost rotting on the damp floor. They start when his dad's about sixteen. The earliest ones are mostly in the *Spectator*. Sammy has to tug them out from under newspapers that are stacked well over his head. If this was last year, he probably wouldn't have had the strength.

Somebody has gone and circled the articles with this Dace guy's name in pen and written, *Lies, all lies* in a couple of places. If they hadn't, Sammy mightn't have even noticed them. It kind of looks like his mother's tiny printing, but he's not sure.

Summer's so nosy, she would love to see these articles, but she can't. He won't let her. They're his, just his.

These news stories are all about his father, imagine that! They must be. The name's a bit different, but there are a couple of photographs of him too, pictures of him looking super tough and besides Devereux is the name most of them use. If his dad's cool now, he was even cooler then. Yeah, his dad was such a cool dude in the Big House all those years ago. In Maitland Pen, near where Grandpa lives. He wishes he could talk about this stuff to somebody, but he can't.

He tried telling his best friend, but Jason thinks he's making stuff up again.

Is this another one of your kickass cartoons? he says.

Yeah, Jason, he thinks, *kaboom!*

Sammy has cleaned up all the newspaper mess by the time Micah appears. He used to leave the newspaper cuttings on the cement floor, but his eagle-eyed mother spotted them and thought mice had gotten into the garage again. It was funny to see her flip, but no way he wants her messing around in here and finding his treasure box.

It's suppertime anyway and come to think of it, he's starving.

His big bro, who's not so much bigger now because Sammy is coming into his own fast, is always turning up like Superman. Or at least Micah thinks he's Superman, but he's not. He's just Liza's sidekick, the stupid dick.

"It's suppertime," Micah says, looking around. "Grandma made Shake and Bake. She's staying the night. What are you doing out here anyway, buddy? Smoking or something? You have to watch it with all those newspapers around. The battery in that smoke detector hasn't been changed for years and there's nobody to hear it anyway."

You're not the boss of me, Sammy nearly says, but he doesn't. Summer's already such a pain in the ass, he'll be in a bad way if Micah gets on his case too.

"I'm not doing anything," he says instead, thrilled to high heaven to know something Micah doesn't.

What would happen if he said, *Listen, Mikey bro, Dad killed some bad guys! I bet you didn't know that!*

Well, tortured them to death.

But the stuff those guys did to their own kids! Sammy skipped over most of those parts in the paper, or he would have been sick. If it made him sick, what's a guy, a real stand-up guy going to do when he gets his hands on a baby killing pervert?

Those guys on that new *Law & Order* show would do the right thing too.

Chapter Twenty-Two

Still Waters

Dace looks so drawn. His dark eyes are as flat and opaque as stones. As the newspapers used to say about him, *the accused showed no emotion*. Or as Liza's mother likes to put it, *still waters run deep*. Well, no wonder he looks so terrible — he's scarcely slept for the last ten weeks. What's he staying awake to protect them from? Or maybe he's just going crazy and trying to make her crazy. Reflexes and memory aren't the only things that suffer if you don't get enough sleep.

It's Wednesday morning already.

"It's okay," Dace remarks as she tries half-heartedly to read the newspaper that was shoved under their hotel room door. "You really haven't missed much. And I'm okay. I'm drinking lots of coffee and I'm off the booze. A police officer finally testified yesterday afternoon and spilled some beans, but it was just the lawyers before that, yakking and setting up the stage about what they think went on at St. Matthew's and pitching their own version of events."

"What would they know? They weren't even there!"

"C'mon, you know how these kind of guys think. They have stats on situations like this. They've got it down to a science. Witnesses are so unreliable, lawyers say. It's like everybody's looking through a kaleidoscope. Most people know what a kaleidoscope is, right? Each one sees a different picture when it's their turn. The first guy sees one thing, the second guy sees something else and some bright lights see nothing at all. Maybe the stupid dicks are colorblind, I don't know! You've got a real advantage here, darling, at least you've been in a courtroom before."

"Lucky me," she says, slouching down behind the newspaper while he paces the perimeter of the room.

"Well, it's the same story at an inquiry. Once a lawyer, always a lawyer. From what I saw the last couple of days, lawyers act the same way at an inquiry as they do in regular court. They're here to protect their clients' rights and pull in some cash, but it's like they're playing a big game. And like most gamesters, they want to be on the side that wins."

"So screw the truth and nothing but the truth, is that what you're saying?"

"Well, not exactly. Call me a jackass, but a real good lawyer doesn't tell lies. He doesn't have to. But he or she might put a slightly different slant on things. The next thing you know, they're not telling the same story at all. I've had to sit outside the room by myself because I'm a witness and I haven't testified yet, but Gold swore that's all the lawyers did, the first morning anyway. They went over the history and the good works of St. Matthew's to put everything in perspective for the judge. Spoon fed him, kind of. This Judge Clemens will try to be as fair and impartial as King Solomon when he produces his report down the line, but the newspapers are a different story. You can't believe anything those lying rags say. They take what they can get and they don't get everything."

"Gold?" Liza asks, still staring blindly at the *Maitland Spectator*.

"Yeah, he came through after all. I was real glad to see him, but he should've given me a heads up. He never returned my calls in Toronto, so he must have been pretty busy."

"Why didn't you tell me before?"

"I tried calling you a couple of times."

"I doubt that—I mean I doubt Gold was too busy to give you a heads up. He hasn't been in the news much lately, so maybe he's just losing his edge. Believe me, there's something in this inquiry for him or for his career. Something besides you."

"Remember this is just an inquiry," Dace says, "I don't really need a lawyer, you know. Gold's just here as my advisor. He's in complete agreement that I should use an alias to protect my undercover work. I asked him about that."

Tears spring into her eyes. She tosses the paper aside onto the carpeted floor. "Jesus, Dace, I don't want to know anything about your undercover work! I'm not even supposed to. And you swore up and down that you wouldn't do it anymore, that you'd stop, that you haven't done it for months and that most of your money comes from the airport! You said—you promised that we were all right now, that we didn't have to worry about those effing bikers coming after our children anymore!"

"They won't, little mother. It was the Angels giving the Wolfhounds all that grief. The cops are cleaning them up in Montreal right now."

"Shit! I can't—we can't—I mean our children! What if your cover gets blown and the wrong person comes after you? I know you're not with the Wolfhounds anymore, but when you infiltrated the Angels down in Cali— Dammit, I told you I had enough of bikers! And what about the rest of your enemies? It's not just the Angels who were after you. They came later."

"I really wouldn't worry about anybody else," Dace says, although it infuriates Liza even more the way he's putting on this big act, acting so calm. "That Maitland guard, Savage, would have been after me like a pit bull if he had any balls, but I don't see him, do you? He was trouble and a lone wolf, so my guess is the Pen just cut him loose. I haven't heard word one about him for many, many years and he's never contacted you."

"Why should he? He didn't know me!"

"All the guards at the Pen knew who you were, Liza, my little college chick."

"They did not!"

"So forget about Savage. Either he's still stumbling around Mexico looking for me or he's six feet under, at the bottom of a shovel, just like that old song says."

"That's a Bob Marley song. It's not that old."

"Well, don't worry about Savage. He might do it just for spite, but it would be a waste of his time to come after me. I came back up here and did my time."

"Don't remind me. Micah was only three!"

"I'm even on the good side of the FBI now, way, way down on their line. Especially since I've turned a lot of bad guys over to the feds during the past ten years," Dace shrugs. "A couple of my marks might still have enough juice left in them to come after me, but I doubt it. They were old when I stung them and they were all shit deep into drugs with the life expectancy of some poor slob in a third world country. It was them or me. If prison or drugs didn't get them, they might still have some life in them though. We do, even if we do have a teenage son!"

"Yes, well, we're not in prison. Or on drugs. And it's not the olden days. My mother's life was practically over when I was seventeen."

"Let's just hope that my old enemies all got themselves killed just like that bastard you knew back in university. What the heck was his name?" Dace adds, scratching his head.

"Joe Armitage." Liza stares at him, reddening. No way Dace has forgotten the name of the lecturer and journalist who caused her so much trouble back in the Journalism Department at Maitland U. If only she'd forgotten it! Why on earth are they talking about Joe when they should be talking about anything else, even Micah and Mariposa? Probably because it's easier than talking about their current concerns.

"Nobody just gets themselves killed. Joe wasn't a very nice person, not by a long shot, but I never thought he'd come to such a bad end. I still don't know what was wrong with him, but when it comes right down to it, a sociopath is really just a sick person."

"Yeah, a sociopath like that jackass is just a poor sick slob!"

"You have to feel sorry for people like that. Or at least for their families. I see that now, now that I have my own. Joe was so young when he got killed. He seemed a lot older than me at the time, but he was only in his late twenties. Looking back, it really was kind of remiss of the university to let him stay in a co-ed residence with all those young girls, all his 'sweet young things'! When I first met him, I was just a freshman myself, three floors under him on an all girls' floor. Do you know that the following year, they actually mixed the sexes on the same floors?"

"Lucky him," Dace says, "Sounds to me like he was a real fox in a henhouse, mixed floors or not. I bet he hurried back there the next year—"

"No, he got an apartment."

"Oh, yeah, right."

"He had, uh, more flexibility that way. I wouldn't call what happened to him lucky, either. Dead's dead. Sure he did some terrible things and he hurt all sorts of girls—but he also wanted to make good, to do something important with his life. And he didn't. He couldn't. He got warped growing up. I used to want to know why, what happened to make him like that. You know me, I always liked knowing what makes people tick."

"And me," Dace says. "You wanted to figure me out."

"And you," she agrees. *But not anymore. I'll leave that to your descendants, to your biographers,* she thinks. *The ones who'll just think you were an interesting character in a story, not a flesh and blood human being. I don't care about who or what made you anymore. I just care about you.*

"Um," she falters slightly for she almost never asks about Dace's old friends, especially the ones he knew in jail, "I know they're bound to have issues, but how did some of your old buddies from the training school make out?"

And from the Pen, she thinks, but she doesn't say.

"Not as good as me!" Dace quips.

"I bet they still get to use their real names! You know, Joe Armitage did one good deed before he died: he gave me lots of ammunition, all those awful stories about Judge Silverton that I mailed off to the press, that trophy file full of pictures about those teenaged delinquents he'd sent to training schools for his own use or not depending on what they did for him in his judge's chambers behind closed doors. Oh, God, that man was so sick and he had so much power over those boys!"

"Liza, darling, please don't upset yourself."

"But you can't imagine the stuff that was in that file!" she says, wiping away a tear.

"Yes, I can."

"Judge Silverton was such a vile, vile man. So compelled! Worse than Joe. I still don't understand it. People looked up to Silverton. Well, not us. We didn't. We knew better. But it just didn't make any sense. He had everything to lose, a judge like him. He was such a respected member of the community that I can hardly believe it to this day."

"He didn't think he'd get caught."

"There are so many other people like him, too! Doctors, teachers. How can that be? They've got so much to lose."

"Money, power, it's not enough. The greedy bastards always want more."

"I couldn't read all the file. It made me sick. It even made Joe sick and that guy was about as bad as bad can be. He stole the file for me, you know."

"I remember."

"Joe was going to hold onto the file himself, but he wanted to be a big time journalist and a lot of the pedophiles in that file were Maitlanders, people his family knew and liked."

"Yeah, that was one book he couldn't write, so the dumb cluck went after the bikers and tried to build his career on them. He must have thought that a bunch of hairy bikers were too ignorant to read a newspaper, but even bikers have friends who can read."

Like you? Did you arrange Joe's murder? Did you guess what he'd done to me? "I didn't know what else to do about Silverton, but I had to get him off the bench, especially after that old bastard sent you right back to jail."

"Well, I knew too much and let's face it, I hadn't been exactly a good boy."

Liza narrows her eyes at the cocky expression on Dace's face and winces. No way he's responsible for Joe's murder. If Dace knew the terrible price she'd paid Joe in exchange for that file, he'd have sent his friends to pay Joe a little visit all right, but they would have just roughed him up. Wouldn't he?

She could hardly even admit to herself what Joe had done to her! And that university counselor had as much as said that it was her own fault.

And it was, she supposes. Or maybe she'd rather take responsibility for what happened than feel like a victim.

Dace was way down in Mexico when that fucking pervert Joe Armitage got killed anyway. And Joe was a pervert, no matter what that stupid counselor thought. She must be getting sentimental in her old age. Sometimes when she remembers Joe, she almost forgives him. She's forgetting stuff too. She's got to.

It could have been so much worse. Look at what some women put up with. Joe really didn't hurt her much, except no way she was the only girl he ever raped. She knows that now, knows it better with every passing year. You could never know everything about a person, though. There's good and bad mixed up in everybody. It's just that some people get more than their share of bad. And you've got to stop them. All the girls a twisted man like Joe would have hurt and raped if he lived any longer.

And what if he had kids? What would have happened to them?

Whoever killed him, they did good.

And even if Dace somehow helped kill Joe, directed it from afar, she'll never let on to him that it even occurred to her that he could have blood on his hands. Dace is her children's father. No way she wants him to know that she imagines he's capable of killing for her. It would give Joe Armitage way more importance than he deserves in their lives.

Anyway, they did say that the bikers went after Armitage on account of that exposé he'd written about them, so Dace couldn't be guilty of arranging a murder on her account nor is she responsible for inciting him to murder.

But Judge Silverton was even worse than Joe Armitage.

"You know," Liza confesses to Dace when he finally stops pacing around for a moment, "As time went on and my memory dimmed a little, I almost felt responsible for that nasty old man shooting himself, especially after his family pulled the plug. But it was years before I found out that he was dead for sure and then it was quite by accident. Remember?"

"Kind of. I was just glad the bastard was dead."

"Well, I heard somebody talking about him on the way to work. You know when all that stuff about Gordon Stuckless and those poor boys at Maple Leaf Gardens was going on? So when Judge Silverton finally did die, it wasn't real big news. No doubt his family and his colleagues wanted it that way. And sure, I wanted him dead, but not at my hands. I never liked playing God."

Leaning across the small table between them, Dace takes both her hands in his. "Listen to me, you did real good. Stop this guilty conscience stuff, all right? I think you might be forgetting a few things. People do that to protect themselves. You know that. And they do worse things. My guess is that somebody in Silverton's family, maybe that fucking priest nephew of his, pulled the plug."

"But why would he do that?"

"Because he was afraid his old uncle might finally get a conscience on his deathbed and tell everything he knew. Some people do, if they haven't already started leaking out stories in their demented, drunken old age."

"*A demented, drunken old age*, that's good!"

"As for your old pal Joe Armitage, I think my biking buddies liked taking the rap. There was bad blood between Armitage and them, so it made sense. But he was probably killed by the priest's friends because they were afraid he knew too much about Judge Silverton, his pedophile nephew and the rest of their fucking crew."

Liza stares at Dace. He's so much smarter than she is. It's never occurred to her that Silverton might have figured out that Joe stole that file from him and that somebody — she! — had leaked the contents to the press. But of course he had. "So you still think that it wasn't just Silverton, that there was a bunch of professional people involved in a child sex ring? But Silverton's nephew? What ever happened to him anyway?"

"How the fuck would I know?" Dace says, as he lets go of her hands, then gets up and goes into the bathroom.

Liza follows him. She watches him brush his teeth, which are almost as perfect as the rest of him, in spite of all the trouble he's seen.

"Look," he finally says, when he finishes rinsing his toothbrush and shuts off the noisy cold water tap, "let's forget about Silverton's nephew. That's another guy who really makes me sick. He got sent off to some safe place — for him anyway! — just like the rest of them so he's probably still doing some real bad stuff, may he rot in hell. But no way he stopped doing what he was doing cold turkey. He couldn't."

"Why not?" she asks after they curl up the unmade bed together.

"Maybe it's just my opinion, but most of the perverts I've heard about have low IQs and they're on the small side. Physically, I mean. And they don't have any friends. They might have partners-in-crime, but they don't have friends. Somebody ought to do a study on them someday. Or maybe they have but nobody reads the shit or none of the right people do anyway. It's like you say though—why the hell would they keep doing the same thing over and over, no matter what the cost?"

Like you and that undercover work, Liza nearly says, though it's hardly the same.

"Hey, you swore you'd give up that undercover work," she repeats, just thinking about it again.

"And I am!" Dace says happily.

Liza looks at him skeptically. Knowing him, he's probably just grateful she's changing the subject even if he is still on somewhat shaky ground.

"The airport really is making money, darling," he continues. "It's done real well this past year, in spite of my jackass partner. I'm going to start putting more effort into it as soon as I can get him tossed. I've done some good undercover work, but it's so time-consuming. Micah's already seventeen. I want to spend more time with you and the kids."

Liza smiles. If only she could believe him. And what are they going to tell the kids about him—about them—when he finally comes home for good? Should they say that they're cousins? And what about Mariposa? She and Dace will have to tell them, they've got to know.

"I'll believe that when I see it. But getting back to Gold—I'd still like to know what's in this inquiry for him. If he had lots of work, he might have sent a clerk, but he never would have wasted time coming here himself."

"You don't like him much, do you?" Dace asks, laughing a little as he loops a leg over hers.

"I like him okay. He sure lives in a different world than you and me. But he did all right by you. I just think he's led kind of a privileged life and that he could have done more for us. I was just sort of disposable and I was pregnant with Micah, something I was just beginning to realize. I didn't know how vulnerable I was then, but I do now. If somebody treated one of our girls that way! Okay, so he didn't have much choice if he wanted to stay on the right side of the law but he sort of threw us to the dogs after the riot. 'Tell me where he is, Liza,' he said and you know that was real bum advice. What was I supposed to do, rat you out and send you back to prison to be tortured and killed by Savage and his crew?"

"Yeah, but Gold's still on the side of good, don't forget that. He's one of the good guys, he really is. He wants those dirty priests taken down. Even if he's super privileged and has never been in a place like St. Matthew's or known anybody who has. Okay and maybe his career's taken a bit of a nosedive lately, so the inquiry just might be the vitamin shot it needs. If it gets enough press and—"

"And, what?"

"There might be a big settlement coming out of this. The church will have to pay for what their priests did."

"Here we go," she says. "And Gold will get a nice cut if he helps out. So when's your testimony? Is there like a schedule?"

"Tomorrow, I think and then we're out of here. I don't need to hear the rest of the shit. I already know most of it anyway and what I don't know, we can read in the inquiry report. There's some kind of method to this madness at the inquiry, you know. They're calling witnesses chronologically, according to the years they lived at St. Matthew's. It's going to take a while. I've heard that the witnesses span thirty years! Honest to God, I think I recognized a witness in the motel bar last night. Some tough dude who was a year or two ahead of me at school. I looked over and he was sitting there just kind of bawling into his beer. I hope he doesn't sound like he's making things up when he testifies. I don't care what people say, they hate seeing a grown man cry."

"That's not going to be you, is it?" Liza says, patting him on the chest and laughing a little. "Not my guy, so strong and tough!"

"Not me," Dace agrees, lifting one arm and flexing it. "I'm tough as nails! I don't know, though," he adds more soberly. "I've never testified before. And I've been accused of being a hothead."

Like after the riot. "I remember," she says, quirking one eyebrow and twisting her mouth.

"Maybe I'm the kind of person who falls apart, how do I know? They wouldn't let me say anything at the riot trial. It's not a good sign when the accused doesn't testify."

"It's not that they wouldn't let you," Liza says. "They wouldn't let anybody. That was another big, stinking cover-up until somebody finally decided not to waste a lot of court time and money defending felons. But those guys at St. Matthew's were just little boys. And Rosie? How did she end up in there? I tried to ask Uncle Norm once but he gets so upset that he let you guys go there after Aunt May died."

"They took in a few girls from time to time, if they were siblings, on a temporary basis in an emergency situation. And Rosie looked a whole lot like a boy when she was a kid. Maybe Dad passed her off as a boy! How the fuck do I know?"

"What?" Liza pulls away from his arms and stares. "But she wasn't even Eden's age! I can't imagine Eden—"

"Come back here, I'm just joking. Dad didn't do that. She was just supposed to be there for a few weeks. She wasn't school age and she certainly couldn't work. We worked like devils at those places, you know, especially in the training school! I'm pretty sure 'idle hands are the devil's workshop' was the motto over the main door."

"But that's crazy! About Rosie going there, I mean."

Dace is silent for moment. "She was so little," he finally says. "Christ, I need a drink."

"It's not even 10:00 a.m.! You act like we're vacationing at an all-inclusive resort."

"Well, if I do get through this, I swear on my mother's grave that's what we're going to do. We'll take the whole damn family to Mexico during March break, go swimming and see the monarch butterflies again. Maybe Auntie Maeve and Dad and Millie and Dawn can come—"

"Wait—what about Rosie and her family?"

"Sure, let's take everybody! No way I'm paying their way though. Good old Vincie is making enough money to bring Rosie and the kids. Heck, let's throw in your brothers for good measure. I bet they'll come south with us even if they never show up for much else. Especially if they can squeeze some more money out of Auntie Maeve for the trip."

"But the monarchs fly north at the end of March!"

"Okay then, so we'll go earlier."

"And take the kids out of school? I don't think—"

"Look, I'm not sure I can do this, Liza! I'm getting cold feet and you're not helping! And look at today's headline," Dace says, pointing to the newspaper down on the floor. "It's just like what happened at Mount Cashel, 'documents lost!' They mean that old report from 1960, I guess."

Liza strokes his arm, trying to placate him. "But how can that be? St. Matthew's has only been closed a few years, so that old report's got to be somewhere. Has anybody looked into the Ontario Archives? I did a course in research methodology. It's been a big help, working on my PhD. Lots of old hospital reports and all sorts of school reports end up there. You'd be surprised, the stuff they keep."

Dace rolls the other way from her. "How am I supposed to know? Gold and the rest of them have their own researchers, don't they? They should be able to find anything, the fucking moles. "

"Darling," she says, getting up on the bed and wrapping her arms around him from behind, "even if you do get upset when you give your testimony, it's okay. You're bound to have upsetting things to talk about. You can't just pretend it didn't bother you."

The bedside phone starts ringing, that annoying hotel sound. It's Gold.

"No point in coming into the inquiry today," he says. "The proceedings have been put off until tomorrow. A key witness or a lawyer is delayed."

Chapter Twenty-Three

What Lies Beneath

With this latest hiccup in the inquiry, they could have gone back to Toronto for the day, but they don't. Liza's just gotten to Maitland. But she feels so guilty about wasting unnecessary time away from work and the children that they decide to spend the afternoon and evening out at the farm. At least they'll be with some family.

This is a mistake, Liza rolls her eyes at Dace when no one's looking. She feels like an amputee without her kids. She's nothing by herself, as far as Millie's concerned. The kids are always popping up from behind the couches in the cavernous family room, running up and down the stairs, in the kitchen eating Millie 'out of house and home' or outside in the bushes, up to God-knows-what. It's Millie's fault—she's the one who encourages them to go wild.

"I miss them," she says while rummaging in her freezer for some dessert.

"They've got school." *Oh, God,* Liza thinks. *The luxury of staying home all day and just baking and cooking.* She does enough on the weekends. She'd go nuts, staying in the house all the time, but she can see the appeal.

"What am I supposed to do with this stuff?" Millie asks, taking stock of her butter tarts and rice crispy squares. "We can't eat all of this. You'll have to take some home."

But they all try. The really do. Liza and Dace play cards and shoot pool with Millie. After Dawn gets off the school bus and Norm comes back home from work, they eat dinner and watch *Miami Vice* on TV.

They just don't talk about anything that matters. Even when Dawn goes to bed early, Norm and Millie don't ask the obvious question: *So how's the inquiry going?*

Miami Vice includes a subplot about a violated child, but they still don't say anything. Maybe they don't know what's happening in Maitland? Well, of course they do. The newspaper lands on the bottom of their driveway without fail and they read damn nearly every word.

They always have, even if it's just so they can say, *Well, they didn't get that one right. Somebody's got it in for our Dace.* Right or wrong, there might be clues in newspapers, stuff they ought to know. Years ago when Dace was on the run, the newspapers were their only hope of finding out anything about him at all.

What a repressed lot, Liza thinks, but when it comes right down to it, she isn't much better. If the guys got into the beer or the women had a glass of wine, they might have talked a bit about what really matters, but they don't. Norm doesn't drink during the week anymore and Millie never did.

"Christ, I sure could use a drink," Dace mouths to Liza the only time both Norm and Millie are out of the room. "Dad probably has some whiskey out in the shed. But there's no way I want to be hung over when I testify tomorrow and give them a chance to doubt my word."

"Typical," Liza whispers back to Dace, "if we don't talk about this, maybe it'll just go away." Of course Norm and Millie know they're staying in Maitland to be closer to the inquiry. Or else they would insist that Liza and Dace stay out at the farm instead of in an expensive hotel.

That doesn't mean they want to talk about it though.

Uncle Norm finally cracks just a bit when they're getting into their car to leave.

"Be careful," he says as he first shakes Dace's hand and then decides to hug him instead, "Sometimes things can't be set right no matter what you do."

Norm hugs Liza fiercely. "Take care of my boy," he whispers. "Just like you always have."

But Millie still isn't letting on why they're in Maitland midweek. She kisses the air next to Dace's cheek and does the same with Liza. "Bring the kids next time," she orders before she escapes back into the house. Darn it, she's left the stove on again. She's always doing that.

There isn't a bar fridge back in their room at the hotel, a mixed blessing. Because if Dace could have had just one good stiff drink, he might have fallen asleep earlier. He mightn't have tossed half the night and the rest of the night just dreamed.

For years now, drinking to forget has worked so well.

He smells them first in his dreams, their bodies and the sour urine smell of unwashed clothes. And then he hears them: the rustle of cassocks, approaching footsteps on a dorm floor.

If it was just him, he might have left the guy alone, he wouldn't have poked Father Danby in his soft gut and in his eye, but it wasn't. He was a tough kid, he could have taken it, but Rosie couldn't. A little girl has so many soft places.

The first time he wakes up in-between dreams, he remembers briefly, but when he runs to the toilet, it's like he's throwing everything away. They ate chili at his father's house earlier that evening, not good. Liza stirs a little in bed, but she doesn't wake up. Maybe he isn't awake either. Maybe he's still dreaming. He lies back down beside his wife and presses his face up against the back of her neck. Liza moves a little, settling into his arms. This is his real life. It's all that matters. He's just had a bad dream.

Until he dreams and remembers again. It wasn't just him and his sister, the unlucky ones who the bad guys were after. The dirty men came from the same place, they nodded at one another: *I know your ilk.* And they never went away unless they got sent away.

It was the same at the training school, they crept into the beds of so many boys over so many, many years. Trying most of them out, why not? Because they wanted to, because they could and because there were so many bad, needy little boys right there in their care.

Everybody knew this or should have known it.

What's wrong with people?

And what was wrong with him?

Chapter Twenty-Four
The Handyman's Tale

S orry, folks," Hubert Gold says to Dace as soon as they meet inside the small entrance. The three storey government building where they've scheduled the inquiry is just a short walk from their hotel.

"I was sure we'd be ready for you by today, but it looks like we're still not."

"Shit," Liza and Dace say simultaneously.

I don't suppose you could have phoned and told us that, Liza thinks.

Gold, who's wearing a conservatively cut suit and tie, gives Liza a cursory glance and nods approvingly. "Looks like you've kept your figure in spite of all those kids," he says, oblivious to the way she's bristling. "I like that suit you're wearing too, especially the skirt. It's perfect for the occasion."

"What are we going to—a wedding?" Liza asks as they head deeper into the building. With both her and Dace dressed in suits and holding hands, it almost feels like they are. If only.

"And what about me? Don't I look good too?" Dace smiles sardonically as he fingers the lapel of his suit.

"You look like a fine upstanding citizen too," Gold readily agrees. The lawyer has lost much of the hair on the crown of his head and there's broken blood vessels around his nose, but maybe life isn't treating him so bad. He still doesn't look much older than he did at the murder trial following the Maitland Penitentiary Riot.

"When will they want him, then?" Liza leans around Dace's chest to ask.

"Well, at the rate this is going, we'll be collecting background information for another week or so."

"Another week!" Liza protests. "My kids will be orphans!"

"Be a good girl. Stay here in Maitland, Dace needs you."

"No, I don't, I mean I want you to stay Liza, but—"

"These kind of proceedings take time." Gold taps the overstuffed portfolio he's clutching to his chest. "There's tons of upset people in there and upset people need a lot of breaks. To pee, to pull themselves together, whatever. It's such a crapshoot when a person testifies. No matter how much you prep them—"

"Prep them?" Liza asks.

"Yes, 'prep' them," Gold explains patiently. "Not coach them to tell lies… But you're still never sure what's going to come out of a witness's mouth. Or what the other lawyers will dredge up. The press can be unpredictable too—"

"The fucking press," Dace says, "This is supposed to be an inquiry. Why doesn't the judge just keep them out and let the buggers read his report?"

"You don't want that," Gold says. "We have freedom of speech here in Canada. The press will probably be on our side anyway. If they come. It depends what else is going on. We may not be the biggest show. But I also want to impress upon you both that this is an inquiry, not a trial, so the usual courtroom procedures—and sometimes the usual safeguards—may not be in place."

Safeguards, Liza thinks. *When the hell were they ever in place?*

Dace sits down on the first bench they come to outside of some double doors. He pats the seat beside him, but she doesn't sit down.

"Why can't he go in?" she asks.

"He can—after he testifies," Gold says. "But you can. Just don't advertise who you are. And don't talk to anybody or you might compromise Dace's testimony."

Dace leans his head back against the wall and closes his eyes. A man who looks like a reporter brushes by their little group and heads into the room. Is he one of those newscasters from CTV news?

Liza bends down to kiss Dace before she goes in.

"Everything's going to be all right," she whispers, the same mantra he always uses with her.

Once she gets inside the room, she doesn't feel as bad. She takes a front row seat in what looks like the spectator area, feeling almost calm. It's a good twenty minutes before the judge comes in. More and more people pile into the room. After yesterday's testimony and what was reported in the paper, they might reach full capacity today. Reporters go to one corner, the priests and what looks to her like lawyers, go to another. She must be in the right spot.

The *Globe* is up from Toronto, but the *Maitland Spectator* has also been following the inquiry. She caught up on all their coverage, staying up late last night to read the newspapers while Dace tried to sleep.

The last witness at the inquiry was a police officer called Clarence Downing who said he tried to bring charges against several priests from St. Matthew's in 1960, but that he was forced to drop them.

According to the *Maitland Spectator*, Gold asked Downing why he dropped the charges.

I had to, the officer reportedly replied. *On the police sergeant's orders. The school got rid of the bad priests anyway.*

When Gold finished with Downing, he turned around and smiled at the spectators, probably expecting some well-deserved applause. Liza could just picture Gold grinning away.

He's grinning now. The man who just sat down in front of the judge must be Gold's witness because he's heading towards him. If Gold is hoping to provide corroborative evidence for Downing's testimony, this witness is about as far a cry from a respected officer of the law as he can get. Why didn't Gold get the guy to at least shave?

"Quiet, please," Charles Clemens, the presiding chair, a retired Justice of the Supreme Court of Canada says. For the benefit of any newcomers, the judge introduced himself as soon as he sat down, but Liza could barely hear him. She remembers his name from the paper, though. An unidentified person comes over and adjusts the judge's microphone.

"This guy is well-known to the local police," somebody behind her whispers.

Today's witness certainly has a good loud voice. He doesn't need his microphone. He's always gone by the name "Lonnie Kendall." But he doesn't want the press using his name today.

"Reporters, please take note," Judge Clemens says. "In fact, I would appreciate if you all left the room while this man is speaking."

There's a collective groan from the clutch of reporters, but they do what they're told.

Kendall sure doesn't look like a victim to Liza. He's a big, burly man in his late forties, with a black beard that still has no grey in it.

A big strong man just like Dace.

He's never been abused, Lonnie Kendall alleges, stating instead that he's a long-time resident of Maitland who worked at St. Matthew's from roughly 1957 when he was nineteen-years-old until the mid-sixties. Kendall did mostly odd jobs and some gardening so he was there a lot. He saw things he shouldn't have.

"I saw that Brother there when he was a director," he says pointing at an old man sitting with the rest of the frocked priests, "bending over a ten-year-old boy and when I went back to his office later, he had the youngster by the head and was banging it against the wall, bang, bang, bang—"

"Did you see anything else?

"I didn't have to. That was enough! I went right to the director of child welfare—"

"Let the hearing show that at this time, the director of child welfare in Ontario was—" Judge Clemens says, but Liza doesn't catch the name.

"But the director did nothing!" Kendall continues. "He told me: 'The Catholic Church's on a pedestal. We can't touch them.' 'Well,' I said, 'you do something or I'll put you and your pedestal on the front page of the *Maitland Spectator* and the *Toronto Star*!'"

Laughter ripples throughout the room.

"Quiet," Judge Clemens says to the spectators, trying to hide his own smile with his hand.

"So you left it at that?"

"No, I went to the cops too, but you know them—"

"Please, Mr. uh, Kendall, the Maitland Police aren't under investigation. You're not here to attack them."

"Well, I told two cops but they didn't do anything about it either."

"Maybe they couldn't," a lawyer who hasn't spoken before suggests. "Maybe it's like our friend, Officer Downing said here yesterday. My guess is that the police had orders from people higher up, maybe they moved some brothers out of province. That's what happened out at Mount Cashel."

"Your Honor, my friend here disputes that," the same lawyer speaks again. "He says that they tried to get Mr. Kendall to give a police statement the next day but he got all testy and refused."

A second man, who must be another lawyer for the Rollan Brothers, finally steps up to the witness. "But aside from this incident with the director, you never actually saw any sexual abuse, did you, Mr. Kendall?"

"No, but I heard—"

"And when you saw the director bouncing a ten-year-old boy off the wall, you did nothing to stop him?"

"Look, sir, if I had intervened, I'd probably still be in jail and I wouldn't be here. There'd be no inquiry, there'd be no nothing!"

Judge Clemens calls a break then. Liza seeks out Dace in the hall where he's still sitting, methodically working his way through a package of cigarettes.

"This is going to get real bad," she says speaking as quietly to him as she can, hoping nobody in the nearby cluster of reporters can hear her. Not that any of them are paying any attention to her right now. Six or seven of them, all men, are staring at the inquiry room doors, waiting for Lonnie Kendall to emerge, she supposes.

"It sounds like today's witness was basically saying the same things about St. Matthew's as that policeman did," she says to Dace. "The guy speaking wasn't even one of the victims and he was still pretty upset. Do you think there's going to be any counselling available for the witnesses?"

"Don't make me laugh," Dace says. "I bet those poor saps out at Mount Cashel never got any counselling."

"Actually, I think they did."

"With all the money this inquiry is costing, they sure as hell aren't going to want to spend money on shit like that— Whoa, there," Dace interrupts himself as somebody bursts through the doors Liza has just exited and shoves the nearest reporter.

It's the man who just testified, Lonnie Kendall. "Give me your film!" he shouts at the terrified looking reporter who's trying to protect his camera.

"I didn't take any pictures," the reporter tries reasoning.

"Give me that film right now or I'll rip your fucking head off!"

His hands shaking, the reporter opens his camera and gives Lonnie Kendall the film. "Here you go, man, it's all yours."

The next day, the inquiry begins hearing from the men who were residents at St. Matthew's. The very first man who gets up to speak starts to cry. His name is Josh Curran.

Man up, Liza thinks, but then she can't help it, her own eyes tear. Why shouldn't a man cry? Josh Curran is only about thirty. Whatever happened to him, he still has the wide-eyed innocent look of one of her own boys. She counts off her sons in her head, stringing them along like pearls: Micah, age seventeen, Sammy twelve and Cole and Cory who are still just three.

Maybe Josh Curran wasn't hurt by a priest.

Yes, maybe he was mistaken about what had happened, the lawyer for the Rollan Brothers suggests.

"No, I'm not mistaken," Curran says, "but I've been a mess ever since I heard about what happened out at Mount Cashel. For years, I thought it was just me. I thought that I must have done something to make the brothers do mean things to me. It so bad that I didn't know if I was queer or if I was straight."

"Nothing wrong with queer!" a spectator shouts. Out of the corner of her eye, Liza glances in the direction the voice came from, but she can't see who spoke. *Shut up. Would everybody please just shut up. Don't sidetrack people, don't make this about something else.*

"Now Mr. Curran," the lawyer says, ignoring the interruption, "let's leave aside any discussion of your sexual orientation, which is neither here nor there—"

"But it is, I got so confused! And I'm not saying there's anything wrong with queer guys, I just didn't know what to say, if I should come out or not, if my family—"

"Is it not fair to say that you were already a mess when you came to St. Matthew's?"

"No, it isn't."

"That your own mother had left you there because you wouldn't go to school and that you lied all the time?"

"No, that's not true. She couldn't look after me, that's all. My dad had just taken off and I was the youngest of five. And I was kind of sickly so she thought I might be better off—"

"You were never a well child, were you, Mr. Curran? What about those terrifying temper tantrums of yours, the way you acted out all the time? I have your admission records right here and the truth is that both your parents were alcoholics. They never made it past age forty, did they?"

"No, but—"

"And isn't it a fact that you like to drink too, Mr. Curran? And that you drink quite a bit?"

Josh Curran looks down into his lap and balls a piece of paper, his notes perhaps. He mumbles something else, but nobody else in the room can hear him.

"What's that?" the lawyer asks. "We can't hear you. Would you please repeat yourself?"

Josh Curran shoots so suddenly to his feet that the lawyer steps back. "This is pure bullshit! Get me the hell out of here! I've said everything I want to say..."

"Well," the lawyer says, "if this is too difficult for you to talk about, we completely understand, but surely you don't expect us to just believe the story of an overwrought young man—."

"That's enough, sir," Judge Clemens.

"But good men's reputations are at stake," the lawyer insists. "For years now, the Rollan Brothers have done a lot of good working with at-risk youth—"

But at a nod from the judge, the spectators are already getting up and dispersing. A friend goes up and leads Josh Curran away.

Chapter Twenty-Five

Mariposa and Kathleen

Kathleen stares at the butterfly on the back of her freckled hand. *Mariposa Monarca*. She loves the name. The pretty little creature suits her. If she could, she'd wear nothing but filmy scarves and skirts, patterned in butterflies instead of her more practical jeans.

At least she can still fit into her Levis. Her long-time housekeeper Maria can't, but then Kathleen hasn't had ten children nor is she cooking all the time, all those tortillas and beans. Kathleen's finally got some seafood into their diet, even if she does have to shop for it herself.

Going to the market also gives her a chance to pick up some tequila to calm her nerves. No way she wants to end up on valium, but she needs something. It's nerve-wracking around here.

She's surrounded by petty criminals, the kind who feel no compunction about destroying the monarchs' winter habitat, while they—the local men at least—flee up to Canada in the summertime to make their living working in fruit fields.

Still, things could always be worse. She's a long way from most of the illegal drug trade. Those drug cartels are bad, real bad. A neighbour's missing teenage son has just turned up in a mass grave. What a horror, a dead teenage child! Kathleen can't even imagine it.

Inside the house, the way Maria is singing away in the kitchen is getting on her nerves, but she lets it go. The woman sure is loud, though.

The monarch butterfly on her hand twitches a little, tickling the webbing between her outspread fingers with its proboscis. It's already tasted the sugar sprinkled on the back of her hand with its feet. What a dandy little girl she is, but she can't go anywhere right now with her broken wing. If Kathleen doesn't watch out, a bird might fly down from that tree overhead and nab her. Monarchs are toxic to a lot of birds, but not all of them. She's lost a fair number of monarchs to Mexican birds over the years. Kathleen glances up to see if she can spot a bird lurking around, but she can't.

Once this monarch is mended and after the long winter is over and March finally comes again, she might easily lay up to five hundred eggs, one at a time. As long as she finds some milkweed on her flight up north, most of her predators will leave her alone.

His destiny fulfilled, her male companion will die just after he fertilizes her.

And what a smart little girl she is! A maternal ancestor left Mexico four generations before her and died long before she could pass her story along, but this northern-born descendant was still able to find her way back down south all by herself. This little monarch might have come from anywhere, Ontario or Quebec or from the northern US, but if she came from Nova Scotia, she flew almost three thousand miles.

If only Kathleen could figure out how she does this! She could contribute so much to the body of knowledge about monarchs then, get herself even better known. Her name would be on all sorts of scientific papers then: *Dr. M. Kathleen Aldous.*

This monarch is definitely a female because unlike the male of her species, she doesn't have two black spots on her hind wings. Kathleen's been nursing stray monarchs back to health for more than fifteen years, so she should know. She gives a lot of credit for her knowledge to Dr. Gene Sheridan, her former professor, the scientist who first realized how far monarchs migrate and located their wintering site too, but she's just being polite. The way women and Canadians should be.

The fact is that Dace Devereux and his cousin saw the monarchs first up in Michoacán all those years ago, except Kathleen was the one who stayed to care for them while Dace— well, what did he do? Got himself into more trouble, no doubt. She's never heard about his recapture, but she doesn't get a lot of Canadian news here.

So she stayed in Mexico. Not that she had much choice, given the state of affairs at McGill University and the complications of getting her PhD. She got it though—eventually—in spite of the Dean! What a misogynist that old man was. Girls have it so easy nowadays. North American girls anyway, she hastily qualifies. The old guy would never get away with that kind of crap now.

Ah, but those were the days. Even if when she first set up shop, illegal loggers were already messing up things. She made a little more headway this fall after she cleaned up from the break-in and sent Freddie Nolan packing, but not much. Too many other distractions, like her daughter. Maybe someday Mariposa will realize the sacrifices she's made.

What with everything Kathleen has on her plate, she had no alternative. She had to let her helpers locate all the damaged monarchs along the sides of the roads leading uphill to the Michoacán wintering sites. Juan brought her this monarch just the other day in his brown, cupped hands. A little creature worth up to five hundred males.

For the past two days, Kathleen has gone out into a screened enclosure in her backyard to feed her new baby sugared water or just sit there watching it for long periods of time, like an obsessed mother watching her sleeping infant.

Judging by the tattered shape of her wings, the little creature has come a long way, an early arrival for some reason, something to do with the weather conditions where she lived or maybe she just lucked into a more favourable wind than her companions. No way she started out alone though. Monarchs travel in packs, all for one and one for all. Most of them come to Angangueo the first of November, arriving auspiciously on the Day of the Dead when Mexicans honor their ancestors.

One of this monarch's wings is quite askew, the price of her haste or whatever else drove her south, several weeks ahead of her mates. Kathleen examines the odd angle of her monarch's rear wing. It looks like it can be fixed. She has repaired these injuries and even trained some of her helpers in her technique, a practice they're well-suited to with their deft little hands. But she wants to fix this one herself.

"Caterina," her housekeeper says, bursting out from the kitchen and blocking all the sun, "It's your girl, your Mariposa, she's on the phone again."

"Dammit, Maria, " Kathleen says, "I told you to stop taking collect calls from her. I'm not made of money."

It's too late anyway, Kathleen thinks, heading into the cool darkness of her house to speak to her errant daughter. *Even if grandmother doesn't know it, she's paid the first term fees to Havergal, so you're staying there and that's that.*

But miracle of miracles, Mariposa isn't trying to escape her posh school. She likes it there. Sort of. Well, it's okay. She isn't calling about that, so maybe she's accepting her cushy fate. But she just met her friend's mother and the woman looked at her kind of funny.

"Which friend's mother?" Kathleen asks sharply. Honestly, she doesn't have time for this.

"Micah Devereux's mother!" Mariposa shouts, nearly taking off her ear. "First she goes, 'If your mother's really Kathleen Aldous, I had the pleasure of meeting her a long time ago.' And then she goes, 'If you're just turning seventeen, you were probably conceived in February.' Who the hell talks about when somebody was conceived?"

"Don't swear, dear," Kathleen says automatically, never mind that she herself often does. "I thought you said Micah's family lived in Ottawa," she adds, but she's just playing for more time. Her head is spinning. Mariposa isn't making any sense.

"Well, I couldn't have said that because they don't! They live right here in downtown Toronto except they've been off a lot at some inquiry in Maitland—the parents I mean—and they left that houseful of kids on their own—"

"They're home alone? How many kids are there?" Kathleen asks. "Well, you know, your friend Micah must be at least seventeen and in some cultures—"

"I don't know, there's five or six of them. And they're not exactly alone. The mum comes back from Maitland every few days, but she's going nuts. She actually said that! I get the feeling she always says exactly what she wants, which is real strange. Poor Micah! And there's a babysitter or something and a grandmother butting in but you know what I mean. Micah says his twin brothers have been kind of upset and that his sister Summer or Autumn or whatever she is, is acting out. He told me the situation when we went over to Dufferin Mall to get some french fries. Mum, do you think you could send me some money for some winter clothes? The camp still hasn't paid me and I look kind of stupid wearing this uniform all the time."

"Okay, Mariposa," Kathleen says, "you've got my attention now. Is that what you want—to be the centre of attention as usual? I don't have time for this now, kiddo. I really don't. But I'll drop everything the minute I can get a flight out of Mexico City.

I'm doing this for one reason and one reason only. I want you to stay away from that Micah Devereux, do you hear me?"

"No," Mariposa says, but whether or not she was saying *No, I won't see him anymore* or *No, I won't stop seeing him*, Kathleen isn't sure.

"My guess is that he's not such a 'poor boy' as you think," Kathleen says. "A boy like him, with the kind of father he has, is bound to be able to take care of himself. I'm sure he's always had to and he looked, uh, quite muscular if he's the same kid who was hanging around that time I picked you up. I'll explain everything to you when I get there— Damn, I suppose I'll have to talk to his mother."

At this point, Mariposa yells so loudly that Kathleen has to hold the phone away from her ear. She checks over her shoulder, but Maria has disappeared. The poor woman doesn't like swearing and doesn't approve of the way she's raising her daughter either, that's for sure. Kathleen can still hear Mariposa, though.

"What's wrong with him?" she's wailing. "And how would you know? You can't talk to his mother, I'm seventeen!"

"Micah's not the enemy. It's his father who is—that Dace Devereux."

"But his father's not even there! Micah says he hardly ever is—"

"Why, has he been in jail?"

"Why would he be in jail?" Mariposa seems genuinely perplexed, so that's good. "And anyway," she says, "I'm pretty sure that Micah's father's name is René Gagnon, not Devereux. The kids in his family use their mother's name, just like me. I actually thought it was kind of cool, don't you? Why the hell do kids always have to take the father's name even if the parents are married? It's just so sexist—"

Oh, God help us all, Kathleen thinks. So maybe Liza had the good sense not to hook up with her cousin Dace after all. Kathleen has never known Liza's surname nor did she care enough to find out. But if Liza was Dace's paternal cousin, she might have the same surname as he does.

"The father's name is René Gagnon?" she asks weakly.

"Apparently," Mariposa says. "That's the name Micah's always put on his camp forms as next-of-kin. And he worships the man. He talks about him a lot, maybe because he's not around much."

That's not the way it worked with you and me, Kathleen thinks. *Mothers are different, I guess.* "I'd still like you to stay away from him and his family. Please believe me, the family is — well, strange..."

"Oh, my God!"

"You don't know what goes on in some families."

"Shit, Mum, this isn't one of your horror stories about child abuse, is it?" Mariposa explodes again. "You're always on about that kind of crap and about how fathers are really kind of unnecessary — your explanation for why I don't have one, I suppose!"

"I'll tell you about your father someday, but it's kind of complicated —"

"I don't care about him!" Mariposa says, but Kathleen knows she's lying because she can hear her crying. "And anyway we were talking about — or you were talking about Micah's rotten father — not mine! What could you possibly know about Micah's dad or his family, anyway? And who's Dace?"

"Like I said, I'll explain to you face-to-face." *Which is a whole lot more than my mother ever did for me,* Kathleen thinks, desperate to get off the phone. She has a sudden urge to relieve herself. If she doesn't get to the toilet soon, she'll burst. Honestly, in spite of all she's done, her kid is as spoiled as the rest of Generation X.

How did this happen anyway? Kathleen thinks as she finishes up in her little bathroom and washes her hands. She's living out some stupid woman's story in the kind of book she hates to read.

She did everything she could to prevent this nightmare. She really did. Mariposa grew up in Montreal, not in Toronto or Maitland after all and there are all sorts of children's camps. What were the odds of the girl running into her half-brother at a children's camp, even if it is in Ontario?

Well, maybe this kid wasn't her half-brother. Maybe Micah really is this René Gagnon's kid—whoever the hell René Gagnon is! Sure, Liza had a kid with her when they found the butterfly wintering grounds and Dace was looking quite proud, but maybe she was just trying to pull a fast one. Some girls are like that. If they accomplish nothing else in life, they get a man. Well, let's hope Liza Devereux conceived that Micah boy with somebody else for all their sakes.

Dace Devereux was Liza's first cousin anyway and that isn't exactly right, not these days.

As for Mariposa, why didn't she mention that the boy was a Devereux before? And then she outright lied about the boy's hometown. Just wait until she got her hands on the little brat!

Oh, God, she thinks, heading back to her beloved monarchs, she really should have kept better tabs on Dace Devereux. Not that it's all her fault. She read the *Montreal Gazette* and the *Globe and Mail* and she didn't see Dace Devereux's name in the news for years. It's like he's dead.

Well, maybe he is. When she goes back to Toronto, she'll find out once and for all.

Chapter Twenty-Six
Bad Blood

At the ripe old age of seventeen, Micah finally acknowledges what he's always known. That his parents must be cousins of some sort. Sammy and Summer are too young, so no way they've figured this one out yet, but he sure has. Lucky him. He just didn't want to admit it, didn't want to add two and two. It made him so effing mad and he didn't like feeling that way about *them*, about his parents.

How could she? And how could his father? And even if Micah was a slip-up during a momentary lapse of common sense, why did they blithely, carelessly go on having more kids bang, bang, bang: Sammy, Summer, Eden and then twins!?

Leave it to his mother to start popping out kids two by two. Cole and Cory are kind of cool though.

It blows his mind what some adults—what some parents—do! And they're still together, sort of.

It's really selfish of them, to say the least.

But he's ready to deal with it now. More than ready, ever since he got fired from camp. *What doesn't break you...*so there's some truth in that.

He misses camp more than he expected to—dumb stuff like canoeing and hearing the forlorn call of a loon. But the goddamn smugness of the director and the chaplain and that cook who was supposed to be his friend! He doesn't miss them at all. As for that Gary Ptak, the next time he sees the lying bastard, he'll tear him limb from limb. Or worse. Ptak's from Toronto so he's bound to run into the guy someday. Toronto's big but it's not big enough for both of them.

Those nights that he even misses the howls of the wolves or the moon shining in his eyes and keeping him awake, he just won't think about how he messed up. Or was messed up, which is even worse. Why's that? Why's being victimized so much worse than just plain old fucking up? Yeah, if he can deal with that kind of bullshit—the utter effing injustice of it all—he can face this stupid situation with his parents.

On one of Liza's return trips from that inquiry thingy in Maitland, Micah finally gets up the nerve to confront her. Stuck in the city, he hasn't noticed the trees start to change color but it's late September so maybe they have. The nights are cool now.

As soon as he hears his mother's key in the front door lock, he's in the hallway. He knows he should wait until she comes in and at least uses the bathroom after her long trip, but he can't. His sisters and brothers are still up. They're downstairs in the recreation room watching TV right now, but the minute they hear their mother's voice, one of them will be right up here.

"Are you and dad cousins?" he blurts out before she's even closed the door.

Liza locks and deadbolts the door.

"I thought you knew," she says, coming a little further into the hallway and instantly bending down to clear some clutter from the floor.

I bet, Micah thinks, feeling his stomach heave. He probably should stop right here and flee upstairs, but he backs into the living room instead. It's only then that he realizes that he half-expected her to say, *No, no, darling boy, that's not true! Why would you even think such a thing? Who's gone and filled your head with such lies?*

The nerve of the woman! Sure he's taken her by surprise, but how can she answer him so nonchalantly? He's seventeen, both his parents should have sat him down long before this and said — well, what? They could have held some kind of family conference, that's what mature people would have done. Called in a shrink or a priest or some kind of professional to sort out the whole mess.

Or not done something so effing stupid in the first place! Oh, the Christly carelessness of his parents! Yes, *the Christly carelessness of them*, he repeats to himself. Contraception was available in the early seventies when he was conceived and therapeutic abortions were legal in Canada. Well, weren't they? All he knows is that other people in Toronto, in Canada, weren't having kids all over the place. With their own cousin, yet!

He's thought about this for a while, so the idea that he wouldn't exist if his parents had been more responsible doesn't faze him. When does the soul enter a foetus, anyway? The soul is transferable, duh. It's the only way life makes any sense to him. For that reason alone, the idea of somebody aborting a foetus has never bothered him. An acorn isn't a tree. A foetus isn't a child.

Those flyers that some of the anti-abortionists, the so-called pro-lifers send around his neighbourhood are just plain nuts. There was one hanging from the front door handle the other day supposedly depicting the bloody mess of a late abortion. What a damn lie! He's been around babies enough. That dead or sleeping baby in the picture was at least three months old.

He took the card off the door handle and tossed it in the outdoor garbage can where it belonged. Before Summer could see it, anyway. Summer isn't the only one who cries when she sees that kind of crap. His mother gets kind of teary-eyed. But not because she's anti-abortion, that's for sure. A woman's body belongs to her alone, she always says.

"How was I supposed to know you and Dad are cousins? Did you think I had inherited your memories of something, that your memories were imprinted on me?" he asks her now, madder still that he's gotten momentarily sidetracked. Now that he's talking, he can barely control his rage. It's a wild horse he doesn't dare let loose. "Because they're sure as hell not!"

"Micah, please stop swearing and just let me hang up my coat. I'm not swearing at you!" She takes off her coat and piles it over another one before following him into the living room. The shoes and backpacks she's picked up on her way in are already lined up near the foot of the stairs ready for tomorrow's stampede.

"Yikes—what's all this mess in the living room?" she asks, surveying the assortment of take-out containers and dirty napkins on the floor. Micah hasn't even noticed the soy sauce spilled on the hardwood floor near the fireplace, but she does. She goes straight over to the black sticky mess and nudges a crumpled napkin over it with one foot.

Wow, Micah thinks as he sprawls out in the only easy chair, *she's pretty tired if she's not cleaning up that shit!*

"I ordered Chinese food for the kids after Helen left," he says, a little sullenly for him. "It was Summer's idea, so she's supposed to clean it up, but the little brat's gone downstairs. They're watching TV. *Full House* or something wacky like that. There's nothing violent on at eight."

"So the money I left for an emergency got used up on take-out! For God's sake, Micah! Why didn't Summer make some mac and cheese? Are the twins still up too? What did they eat? Please tell me you didn't feed them chow mein!"

"I thought you'd want to see them." The twins are all revved up now that it's past their bedtime, but they aren't his brats.

Liza sits down on the couch across from him. The undersides of her eyes are pitted with bits of black mascara. *She's old,* Micah thinks. *All of a sudden, she just looks old.*

"I can't," she says. "I can't see them right now. They're just little boys and the things that have been happening at the inquiry have upset me to say the least—"

Micah stands up. "You never want to talk about anything! First you're on about Chinese food and now you want to talk about that stupid inquiry. What did I just ask you about, anyway?"

"Sit down, Micah. You were asking about your father and me," she says, staring off to the side like she can see Dace and she's not all alone. "And our relationship. And how you're afraid it's wrong. Because even if you didn't say so, that's why you're afraid. It doesn't make you wrong though. And it doesn't make your brothers and sisters wrong either."

"Wrong!?" Micah shouts so loudly that a kid pops its head up from the basement stairwell and peers around the corner at them before beating a hasty retreat. *Just my luck. There's probably a commercial on.* "It's not that it's wrong exactly, it's just not right," he says, a little more quietly, but he's still yelling. "I looked it up and here in Ontario, you can marry your first cousin if you want to, but nobody effing does!"

Well, that's not true exactly. A Pakistani boy called Sunny has just enrolled in his grade 12 form. The kid's name is bad enough-- *Sunny one so true, I love you*, some of the girls sing — but as it turns out, his parents are first cousins too. Sunny made the mistake of mentioning this in History just once, but he shut his trap pretty fast after that. A lot of kids' parents are from other places so they didn't say anything, but the looks they gave him and the way the girls giggled at their lockers that day!

Is that why all those people look so much alike? laughed Sveta, a girl with Eastern European parents.

What, said another girl, *spectacularly cute?*

But Sunny's parents didn't get married here, did they? Also, they're from another culture, so it's sort of okay.

"I know," Liza says, finally smiling a little, though even in his own agitation Micah can't help but notice her exhaustion again. She wore her blue jeans home for the trip home, but she never wears them that rumpled and stained. They're looking a bit baggy too, like she's lost weight. "We did though. We got legally married in an outdoor ceremony on Centre Island, hired a minister and then for good measure, we went to City Hall. We were all alone or almost. It was hard, real hard not to be married if you had a baby in those days. Even if your dad wasn't around a lot, he still wanted to put a ring on my finger. I didn't care that much myself because we couldn't get married in the Catholic church, so I still never felt truly married, plus your father's name, well, never mind that—"

"Jesus, you're not even Catholic!"

"I know, but Dad is and even if you're distant cousins, you've got to get a special—I forget what it's called, but the Church makes you pay for it and it just seemed kind of silly to me. Plus your dad would have had to prove he's Catholic and we couldn't—"

"I don't care if you weren't married before I was born! Lots of people's parents aren't married! One guy I know practically came out of a test-tube! He's never going to know who is father is and he's mad as hell. He's got some weird condition and he doesn't know where it came from! Plus he just wants to know who the hell he is. But I do care that you and dad are related to each other. It's surer than shit embarrassing! What am I supposed to tell people?"

"Nothing. Just keep your mouth shut. It's nobody's business, plus if they find out about that, they might find out about—"

"They might find out about what?"

"Oh, I don't know!" Liza says, stalling him again for some reason. She grasps her hands together and leans in closer to him.

"There's nothing wrong with you," she repeats. "You're okay, you really are. You know that. Look at your grades, look at how good you are with people, how athletic—"

"Yeah, I'm a real prince," he mumbles. But he does know he's okay. Sort of. His uncles, the other twins, were clean crazy in their heyday. His grandmother's always yakking about them. *So don't smoke that pot stuff*, she'll say, like she knows anything about marijuana and as if that's all that was wrong with her boys. Yes, what about his uncles' bad blood, some of which they must have inherited from Liza and Dace's shared grandparents?

Well, at least Liza and Dace aren't double cousins, Micah rationalizes or they'd be related to each other on both sides of their family tree.

Oh, yeah, he groans to himself. *Things could always be worse.* But his parents' relationship has been worrying him ever since Mariposa ended up at Havergal, that la-di-da girl's school right here in Toronto. He doesn't know why he's so worried. Mariposa just seems kind of familiar to him.

At Gladstone Public Library and then onto the Reference Library downtown for some more scientific articles this past week, he researched consanguineous relationships and the relative risks to the offspring of such couples.

Newer articles say the risk of genetic defects is very small to the offspring of first cousins, but some of the older articles say it's not, the American ones at least. Although it's not common knowledge here, over in Europe and lots of places in Asia, but not in China for some reason, cousins have interbred for years.

Great Britain, where Micah's ancestors apparently all originate, is rife with first cousin marriages. He probably shares his genes with half of Europe and God knows who else, what with all the invaders who paraded through the British Isles. Even Charles Darwin, the great English biologist who first established that people descend from common ancestors married his first cousin! And they had ten children.

Micah still doesn't like it though.

Nor does it explain why his mother did such a stupid thing. And kept on doing it!

Love, he's half-expected her to say. Naturally. A fool of a guy might say sex, but what's a woman or a girl going to say? And what's more, believe? That doesn't make it any better or any less disturbing. His mother loves his father, loves him in a crazy obsessive way, he supposes. And his father loves his mother. Micah has never doubted that. *Oh, great, so I'm the offspring of a love match. That makes it all better.*

Mariposa comes to his mind again for some reason, but he doesn't love her like that. He could but he doesn't and he really doesn't know why. She's such a cool girl, he just wants the daughter of the butterfly lady to stay in his life.

Dammit, his mother looks so stressed. She's clutching her throat like she can't breathe while she culls her mind for the right words to tell him, to make everything all right. That's what she's like. He really should go over and hug her, he knows that, but tough luck. She's on her own here.

Plus she was kind of funny about Mariposa last week when he brought her over to visit.

He gets up to go to his room, but Liza won't let him.

"Please sit back down," she says.

At first he thinks she's going to try and make him clean up the living room while she rounds up the younger children for baths and bed, but that's not it. Summer will get everybody to bed that night, even Sammy.

So he sits down and waits while she stares off into space.

"Micah," she finally says, "I need to tell you something about Mariposa. I'd like to talk to her mother to make sure, but I just can't— And this one really isn't my fault, but I don't want you to think it's your father's fault either. People were chasing him and he was so alone…"

"No," Micah says, meaning, *I can't take anymore*, but Liza just keeps on talking. Why didn't she just stay in Maitland? On and on she goes, rubbing her eyes, raising her voice so she can be heard over the squeals of the younger children coming from the basement.

Ah, shit, the stuff that comes out of her mouth! All her hopes and fears. Her dreams for them. And some stuff about Mariposa. He doesn't believe it. With any luck, his mother is just crazy and everything she says about Mariposa is all lies.

"Enough. That's it!" he says when he can finally get a word in edgewise. He bolts up from his chair while she just keeps sitting there like she doesn't have enough strength left to move.

He'll go stay at Tony's where people are normal. It's that or shoot the whole place up. Not that he has a gun. Let her figure out what to do with her gang of kids. It's crazy here.

But crazy or not, there's absolutely no way that Mariposa is his half-sister! *She's not, she's not,* he thinks, scrubbing furiously at his eyes. His mother's not even sure. Why'd she tell him then?

Chapter Twenty-Seven

See No Evil, Hear No Evil, Speak No Evil

Away down in Maitland where Liza first went to university and fell in love with an inmate at the penitentiary, the inquiry into certain activities at a local school drags on and on. Some people love their alma mater, but after being gone from the University of Maitland for over fifteen years, Liza doesn't. She hates it, or Maitland anyway.

And everybody in Maitland, the way they act so holier-than-thou. After what they've done, after they've hidden something so monstrous.

She hates them, even if she isn't sure what she would have done if she were in their places. They probably just wanted to protect their families' and their friends' reputations, to protect their own jobs. Or maybe there's an even simpler explanation. If you're raised to respect and revere priests, you can't face what's going on.

See no evil, hear no evil, speak no evil.

Most of the boys from the training school were just plain bad anyway. *Bad bastards*, some of the witnesses for the priests will say. They should talk.

How on earth did she finish a degree here? As a nineteen-year-old, she was torn between two lives, her life as a student and her life as a visitor of a prison inmate. The same thing shouldn't be happening now.

Except this time it isn't just about Liza and Dace, two young people alone in the world. They have a family. *Six kids, what was I thinking?* When she was twenty, she thought she'd be strong and make the right choice, keep her perfect baby Micah and let Dace go, just let him go, but she didn't. She couldn't. Instead, she took what little Dace could offer and had five more kids. Love—for it must be love, what else could it be?— got her every time.

And her babies, she loves her babies, all the hope and promise in them. Well, she's just going to have to juggle better, maybe even take an unpaid leave of absence from her job.

No way she can be in two places at once, but both Dace and the kids need her. He needs her more right now, that's all. He's been here in Maitland for nearly three weeks now, for much of that time on his own.

Seated at a little table by the window with her typewriter open and ready to go, Liza listens to Dace showering. He won't be satisfied until he's drained the entire hot water tank. At least he isn't singing. Not that anybody sings much in this place. It's weird, like something in the *Twilight Zone*, the way the townspeople's code of silence has infected them all.

The hotel staff have wisely spread the men and their family members throughout the five storey building. But in public areas like the breakfast room and the parking lot, Liza recognizes other witnesses from the inquiry, men from Dace's side. Nobody lets on though. Earlier on, a few witnesses got together to share their memories about their school lives, but it was game over once the lawyers found out. Occasional flickers of recognition still pass between Liza and some of the wives.

At least the old men from the other side, the priests, the ex-priests and their colleagues are all staying someplace else.

Thank God, Liza thinks, still focusing on Dace. His clothes are starting to hang on him. Sometimes when he turns his head away from her, she's startled to see that he looks like an old man.

We're getting old, she thinks. *We're running out of chances.*

If only Dace could run away and start all over again. Like he did before.

But if he does, the children might find out about their father's past. This is the worst she can imagine now. Or wants to imagine. *I should tell them, Micah and Sammy, anyway.* But what would she say? If Micah is so upset that his parents are cousins, how's he going to feel when he finds out that his dad is an ex-con?

We'll just have to make sure you testify under an alias, Gold keeps promising Dace, but how is that going to work?

A knock on the door interrupts her thoughts. Liza feels safe enough in the hotel, so she opens the door without even looking through the spy hole. It drives Dace crazy when she does this, but it's just the chambermaid Lorraine Somebody, not some nightmare from his past. Lorraine smiles over her stack of white towels. Liza takes the fresh smelling laundry from her, staggering backwards a little under the weight. They need a lot of towels with Dace showering twice a day.

"Do you want me to come back later?" Lorraine asks, staring into the room at the unmade bed. She's a rounded woman in her late fifties but her eyes still light up whenever she sees Dace. *She isn't that old*, Liza supposes.

"Yes, please," Liza smiles, determined not get into another lengthy conversation right now. Uncomfortable with having somebody wait on her, she had gotten personal with Lorraine and now all the woman talks about is herself. "Any time this afternoon will be just fine." Oh, God, if she doesn't watch out, waiting tables or cleaning up other people's slop will be the only jobs she can get. Much to her relief, Lorraine lets the door close and goes on her way.

With everything going on right now, who the hell cares about work, anyway? she thinks as she piles the towels onto the dresser by the television set. She should just quit. Her pension and benefits will be unaffected because she doesn't have any. She could collect a little employment insurance and look for a better job later on. *Oh, sure.* She really wouldn't miss her Irina and her shenanigans, but she'd never make enough money on EI.

Maybe Uncle Norm can help them out a bit financially—again. God, she hates depending on Dace's dad. At their ages!

Gold still thinks there might be some financial compensation for the training school victims down the road—and a percentage for himself—but he's just dreaming. They all are.

What would Dace be entitled to anyway? He isn't a victim. Liza sits back down by the window and stares at the blank page in her typewriter. Several unfinished projects nag at her. Just like the letter she's writing to Kathleen Aldous, the storyline in her novel is going no place.

I can't focus, she told Irina, which went over real swell, *I'm having marital problems.*

Marital problems? Irina said, as if she'd never heard of such a thing, *I can let you have three weeks off max. Unpaid. Kim wants time off too, but she won't be able to go. Lots of people have marriage problems and still manage to work, you know.*

Thank God she didn't tell Irina the truth. Whatever happened to Dace, Irina's tale of woe and war was sure to trump his. Irina still managed to immigrate to Canada and set up her own business, didn't she?

Back to her typewriter. Released from her daily grind and doing a lot of just waiting around, Liza finally has some "free" time. To write, in theory. To figure out what to do about the Mariposa situation which is making her even crazier. To distract herself from what's happening at the inquiry. To distance herself from whatever Dace might say if and when he finally does testify.

Because she can't, she just won't think about it. Especially after hearing what some of those other men had to say.

At the hotel in Maitland and at home in Toronto on the nights she spends there, Liza types and retypes her letter to Mariposa's mother, the renowned Kathleen Aldous. She keeps a copy of this letter in her briefcase along with her unfinished novel, a fistful of unpaid household bills and the latest missive from Summer's teacher. Everything in her screams out not to contact this lady, an accomplished person and a scientist of some repute. It was in her own best interests to keep an eye on Kathleen Aldous for the past fifteen years, so she did. But she still doesn't know everything about her. Just what they put in the newspapers, which may or may not be accurate.

But she admires Kathleen, she really does. For her to have done so much, she can't have made the mess of her life that Liza has. It's embarrassing really. Liza still remembers the dismissive glance Kathleen gave her when they found the monarchs' wintering grounds.

You're nothing, she might as well have said.

She can't just come out of the woodwork and question Kathleen about Mariposa's paternity, she just can't.

At the very least, her inquiry might spur Kathleen to ask about the whereabouts of Dace. Who's not Dace Devereux anymore. Oh, God, will they really let him testify at the inquiry under a pseudonym?

Liza should talk to Kathleen about the girl though. For Micah's sake, for all their sakes, for… Ah, bleh! It all comes back to Dace.

Let Kathleen come up from Mexico to Toronto, then! Let her look up Liza if Mariposa told her about Micah Devereux and if the woman even remembers Liza's name.

Why would a scientist like Kathleen elect to have her only child with a man like Dace when she's been affiliated with a university all her life? She must have had so many brains to choose from. From a purely biological point of view, such a choice of a baby daddy makes no sense.

"What are you doing?" Dace asks, finally opening the door of the bathroom and steaming up the bedroom too, "Writing a book?"

Liza looks up. Seeing Dace pat his muscular chest dry, something in her stirs. But they don't have time today. They never do anymore. They have to get ready for the inquiry, maybe even eat a little before they go. If they can. Neither one of them ate much dinner last night.

"Yes," she says. "In my spare time."

And why in hell did Dace conceive a child with her all those years ago when he was on the run? True, he always "blamed" Liza for the children they had, but he could have done something himself. Like not had sex with Kathleen or used a condom! How about that?

"Is it about us?" Dace asks, just like he always does. "Am I the sex interest?"

"No, it's about vampires," Liza says, snapping the cover of her typewriter shut. "It's what's selling right now and we need money."

"Hey, little girl," Dace says, diving headfirst back into their bed. "Why don't you come on over here?"

Liza smiles, but she doesn't bother answering. She doesn't have to. He can't. And she can't. Not now. It doesn't matter, though. When this is all over and they're back home in Toronto, they'll…

Oh, for God's sake, focus! she tells herself, drumming her fingers on the hard shell of her typewriter case. She's been up and dressed for nearly two hours while Dace has just gotten out of the bathroom, but it didn't help. She hasn't accomplished a damn thing.

She can't keep her mind on one problem let alone two or three. It's making her schizoid. How does she manage everything when she's working? Though her mind keeps shying away from what happened at Dace's school, she's going to have to deal with it sometime. Sooner or later, Dace is going to testify.

He keeps on getting jerked around, though. His testimony was bumped yet again by some priest now living in British Columbia who alleged that he couldn't have been at the school during the time in question.

Yak, yak, yak!

So maybe that man really isn't a pervert. Or maybe he changed. It could happen. The idea of spending your golden years in prison and maybe even dying there might do that to some people. Right! Of course, the priest's surprise testimony had a ripple effect and delayed other people's testimony.

Dace is still lying on his back, staring up at the ceiling. Never in their life together has he sat around so much.

If you get the chance, what are you going to say this afternoon? she nearly asks. *About all those old men in their stinky robes?* He rarely speaks about the past, but the closer his turn comes to spilling the beans at this inquiry, the more miserable he gets. Much of the time, he's just plain mad, though not at her unless she's determined to take things the wrong way.

Don't, Liza, he'll say. *Just don't.* And at night, he thrashes around and gnashes his teeth when they both want to just sleep.

Here they are alone together in a hotel room—and how often does that happen?—but they certainly aren't having much sex. She can't read his mind, but making love for her is almost an ugly, indecent thing to do. Hearing or even reading about the testimony at the inquiry is enough to kill anybody's passion.

We're old, she thinks again.

One good thing, Dace is talking a bit now. Each night when they're in the dark, he confirms the testimony she shares with him from the inquiry.

Just watch, they're going to say that the witness is lying and he's just out for money, he says, which is exactly what happens, the very next day. A lawyer for the priests implies that the witness is a gold digger, out to get whatever he can from a wealthy institution like the Catholic church.

You ought to be a fortune-teller, she tells Dace.

Yesterday in the hallway, she overheard more of the same from the priests' friends. That the priests here at the inquiry are innocent of such heinous sexual crimes, that the witnesses are lying for cash.

Witnesses mention some of the priests by names, but they aren't allowed to point them out, at least not in public. But people know who the witnesses are talking about, all right. Liza has started to sort them out herself. What priest would come to the inquiry unless he's got reason to believe that somebody might say something bad about him?

Real bad.

He's innocent and this is a witch hunt, each priest's friends say. Well, of course they do. Sometimes bad guys have friends. There's one priest, a little younger than the rest, who wears a patch over his left eye. If he was at the school when Dace was, he must have been a fairly young man. People hover around him all the time. Why? From the very first time Liza saw this man, she detested him on sight. More than the others, who are just a bunch of nondescript old men, a herd of buffalo trying to protect their last overgrown calf. She tried to describe this younger man to Dace, but he didn't know who she was talking about. He looked a bit funny when she mentioned the eye patch, though.

If only they would let Dace into the inquiry, but they won't. Because he hasn't testified yet and he might get contaminated, what a sick laugh!

She doesn't care about the old men, she really doesn't. Why should she? Can you ever decontaminate a child?

Because unless the witnesses are all pathological liars, many of the priest-teachers at the inquiry were sexual deviants who targeted the most vulnerable boys in their care, the smallest ones, the ones with no one to look out for them.

In the room where the inquiry is taking place, Liza can't even look at the men in robes. Their very presence implicates them.

The sickening thing is that they look so normal. Because they just aren't.

This isn't a trial, Judge Clemens has to keep reminding everybody. Or a witch hunt, he implies. It's just an inquiry. As if some of these old men might really be normal or normal enough to have never abused a little boy.

Whatever, the dirty fuckers never touched a boy like Dace. A strong boy. A strong boy who became an even stronger man.

Aloud she says to Dace who's finally standing by the bed like a man risen from the dead, "Do you want some more coffee? Or some breakfast? Maybe the continental breakfast is still on downstairs."

"Nah. I'll just make another cup of coffee here. It's not half bad. What the hell's wrong with me? It's only ten in the morning and I'm already as tired as hell."

Chapter Twenty-Eight

Adversary

They get to the inquiry that afternoon, with time to spare.

The usual suspects are here, Liza thinks, watching the gathering factions in the hall: the priests, the lawyers for both sides, the press , the spectators. She recognizes everyone by now and they recognize her. As far as she can tell, Hubert Gold is the only lawyer missing. Why's that? He better not be sick.

At precisely 1:00 p.m., the doors open and everybody, except Dace and a few other lone men, goes in. Liza takes her usual seat in the front row. It's funny how spectators have appropriated specific chairs. It's a good thirty minutes before Judge Clemens arrives.

Oh, good, there's Gold, coming in the side door. Finally. He goes right up to Judge Clemens to speak to him.

"Mr. René Gagnon is the first person up today," Clemens announces. For some reason when he says this, everybody looks at Liza or at least it feels this way. She starts up to go get Dace, but Gold shakes her head so she sits back down, feeling a little foolish.

Somebody else fetches him from the corridor, a man, she's not really sure who. This man leads Dace to the seat near Judge Clemens. By now, Liza's nerves are so shot that she almost bursts into tears.

She can't believe this is finally happening.

Dace is cool, though. Every eye in the room is on him, but he knows exactly what to do. He's been rehearsing for days. A hush descends on the room the minute people see him. Oh, he's such a good-looking man, even if Gold told him to wear glasses. The glasses make him look like a lawyer, anything but what he is.

He goes up to the chair between Gold and Judge Clemens, affirms the name they agreed upon and sits down. The judge and the lawyers have to know Dace's real name, but nobody else should.

Dace has ignored the Bible. Very few of the other witnesses have sworn in on it, either. In their hearts they may still be Catholics, but a lot of them are conflicted about the Church.

He sits down and smiles at Gold. Whatever else lurks in Dace's genes, he's a born actor. He always was. At age ten, he auditioned at the training school and then at seventeen, he debuted at the penitentiary, following a time-honored path. Lots of boys who got sent to training school turned bad. If they weren't already well on their way, that's just the way things went.

Dace looks strong and confident, an expert in whatever he wants to share, nothing like an ex-con. Nor is he a reluctant witness like some of the other men were. This is something he has to do. Something he's wanted to do for a very long time.

Liza sits up even straighter. She feels like she does when she sees little Eden in a play, Summer swimming a race or the boys playing hockey. She wants Dace to score, to show everybody how wonderful he is, for him to blow the moth-eaten robes off the old men priests and all their good works.

But she's also afraid of what he might say. *Spare me*, she prays, *the same way you always have.*

She can't have it both ways, though. Dace has a job to do and she's got to see it done. She leans forward in her chair, trying not to spook him. As if she could. The lawyers bunching together at the front of the room aren't paying any attention to her, but a couple of reporters are keeping their eyes on her.

Here I am on trial again too, she thinks. Well, good for these reporters for still coming here when so many of their colleagues have already given up. She just doesn't want them to focus on her. The other day one of the Maitland reporters wrote about another woman: *A spectator whose husband had been in St. Matthew's dabbed at her eyes with a handkerchief.*

Ah, Dace looks so cool, so handsome, he really does. Some witnesses have broken down, but he's going to hold up just fine. Maybe she won't, but he will. His self-confidence is contagious. All around her, other spectators sit up straighter and smile at him. He's wearing a blue shirt and a dark, double-breasted suit, the one they bought together in Maitland.

This is his chance, maybe his only chance, to tell his story, to set things straight and everybody wants him to have it. Well, almost everybody.

Go, Dace, go, Liza thinks, settling back in her seat and clasping her hands together in her lap.

Gold starts off so kindly that she could have kissed him. He leads Dace through his early life, bit by bit.

René Gagnon had just turned ten he said, when he went to live at St. Matthew's, for the usual reasons that kids got sent to that kind of school in those days. They weren't all orphans exactly. In his case, his mother had died when he was nine and his father, a small auto repair shop owner whose business was expanding, was having trouble raising him and his little sister on his own. They stayed with their father's mother in Cornwall for a year or so, but then his grandmother got sick or maybe she just got too old. She passed away a year or two later. It was St. Matthew's or temporary foster care, Dace explained. On the recommendation of their local parish priest, St. Matthew's even took his four-year-old sister in.

"Is your sister here today?" Gold asks, knowing perfectly well she isn't.

269

"No, she just wants to forget what happened," Dace says. "She's got a husband and kids of her own. And she was only at St. Matthew's for a while. She slept in the nurse's room. The nurse was the only other female in the school and she took a shine to Ro — uh, to her, to my little sister. We were just supposed to be there for a few weeks, a month at most."

"But you stayed longer?"

"Not exactly. Our father came and got my sister right on time, but Social Services wouldn't let him take me. I had to go to juvenile court instead. My father came. They said I didn't need a lawyer, a decision he later regretted."

Shit, Liza thinks. Does Gold know this or is Dace just pulling it out now? Liza always thought that Dace was sent to training school for truancy. The men who testified earlier had offered similar reasons for their expulsions from their homes — pilfering from the church box, stealing a loaf of bread, the usual *Les Misérables* stuff, to hear them tell it.

"He regretted many things, including sending you to St. Matthew's in the first place," Gold says.

"Conjecture, that's just conjecture," a lawyer called Arthur Garbutt interrupts, shaking his head.

Just the sight of Garbutt scares Liza half to death. Now that she hears him talking, she feels even worse. Gold pointed out the well-fed looking man to her just yesterday. Rumour is that Garbutt was brought in from Toronto specifically to attack Dace's credibility. According to Gold, the general counsel for the Rollan Brothers are bragging that they spent mega bucks to probe Dace's past. What exactly they found out is anybody's guess. Dace's documented history at Maitland Penitentiary for sure, maybe something about his sojourn in Mexico, but hopefully nothing about how he currently makes his living.

"Right, Mr. Gagnon is here to tell us about St. Matthew's, what some of the priests did to the kids there," Gold agrees.

"Mr. Gold, please don't lead your witness," Judge Clemens says.

Dace looks from one man to another. "The next thing I knew I was in training school, the youngest boy there," he says.

"And why was that?" Gold asks.

"It was on account of Father Danby at St. Matthew's," Dace says. "He hurt my sister, so I hurt him," he blurts out. "And I hurt him bad. Because he wouldn't stop."

Liza closes her eyes.

"Slow down, Mr. Gagnon, slow down," Gold says. "Some people here are hearing this for the first time today. It's hard to keep track. Who was Father Danby? Was he from St. Matthew's? Is he here today?"

Dace looks over at the clutch of priests in one corner. He looks a little shell-shocked to Liza, not that anybody else could tell. *My God, he hasn't seen any of these creeps for thirty years.*

"It's kind of hard to tell," he says. "Some of these guys look a lot different now. Balder, you know, and they didn't used to need canes. Back there in the fifties, they had crew cuts and horn-rimmed glasses. And they weren't near as fat."

A few spectators give an uneasy laugh.

"But I'm sure that the younger one over there is Father Danby. That eye patch is a dead giveaway. Unless there's a whole bunch of one-eyed priests, I'm pretty sure that I did that to him."

Arthur Garbutt leaps forward. "Oh, you're *pretty sure* are you? Nobody else mentioned Father Danby. I want to cross-examine this man on his credibility," he appeals to Judge Clemens.

"Maybe because they weren't there at the same time as Danby and I was," Dace says.

The door behind him suddenly opens, so Judge Clemens must have pressed a button. The judge gets up and at a nod from him, Gold and Garbutt follow suit. *What the hell is going on? Liza needs to go to the bathroom, but what if they don't let her back in?*

From his seat, Dace seeks out her face and cocks a questioning eyebrow at her, but it doesn't help. She has so many questions, such as *why didn't you tell me any of this before?*

The spectators grow increasingly restless. The woman behind her spills a contraband container of coffee on the floor, narrowly missing Liza's shoes.

Five excruciating minutes later, Judge Charles Clemens, Arthur Garbutt and Hubert Gold finally re-enter the room, in the same order as they left. It doesn't look good, not with the triumphant look on Garbutt's face.

This is just a game to you, Liza thinks, *all this awful stuff that these boys were forced to live through and it's just a game to you,* but then her mind stops. She can't bear to relive all the tales of buggery and the strappings of small boys' behinds that she heard about during the last few weeks. Not even in her own mind. And God help any boy who got sick at St. Matthew's. At least two boys died for want of medical care.

Garbutt's cross-examination of Dace starts.

"Have you ever used any other name than René Gagnon?" he asks.

Both Liza and Dace looked over at Gold who's shuffling through some papers, but there's no help there. Knowing Dace, Liza is a little surprised that he doesn't just get up and leave. *Run,* she thinks. *Just run.* But he can't. He's come too far.

"You know I have," Dace says evenly. "Especially if you investigated me, like they say you have. And you know why I can't use my real name. I work for a lot of law enforcement agencies. "

"Oh, so, it's not because your real name is connected to violent crimes? Like maybe manslaughter and a murder or two? And all this before you were twenty five? Well, even if you can't tell us your real name, you can tell us some of your other names, can't you?"

"I don't remember them and whatever I did or didn't do, I served my time."

"This here news article says you were on the run for two or three years down in Mexico."

"Well, read a little more. I came back and finished my time at Guelph Reformatory."

"You got eighteen months, but you were paroled after six."

"I was."

"Have you used a lot of names? More than three?"

"Way more than three," Dace agrees.

"So you tell a lot of lies then?" Garbutt then asks.

"I think everybody lies occasionally!" Gold protests.

"Not everybody. And not like this man," Garbutt shakes his head.

"You don't have to answer that," Judge Clemens concurs, nodding at Dace.

"All right, let's get back to your undercover work. Are you good at your work?" Garbutt asks.

Please Judge Clemens, stop him again, Liza thinks, but he doesn't.

"I'm considered good." Dace looks at Liza. "Maybe too good. My wife wants me to get out of the business."

"That's neither here nor there," Garbutt says. "So why did you get sent from St. Matthew's to the training school—wasn't that also on account of a lie?"

"Indirectly. But it's those priests who were lying, not me, and Silverton was the juvenile judge. Father Danby is Judge Silverton's nephew, or he was."

Finally Gold holds up his hand. "That's enough," he says. "This may not be a courtroom, but if people are giving testimony, I think we should at least try to follow some protocol."

Garbutt nods, but he keeps going at Dace, making references to all sorts of American cases Liza has never heard about before this. Who the hell has? And why is he exposing Dace's undercover work? And why is Judge Clemens letting him? Is he half asleep or does he just want to be entertained?

With access to all sorts of law books and newspapers, Garbutt or his crack shot assistants have certainly done their research.

First off, Garbutt asks Dace how he explained to his drug dealer connections why he wasn't convicted in a 1985 charge of dealing amphetamines down in New Jersey.

"I told them that I had a brilliant defence counsel just like you," Dace says. "And they believed me because they were poor boys and money buys a lot of stuff."

Garbutt smiles thinly at Dace's backhanded compliment, but he isn't through. He notes that Dace testified at another trial in Boston that he was able to beat the charges as a result of his political connections.

Dace rubs the back of his neck. Beads of sweat are popping out on his forehead, a telltale sign that he's getting a headache. "Sir," he says, "If I told the truth—that I had negotiated a deal to sting a drug dealer—I would have gotten myself killed."

"I suggest you have only one motive for concocting so many stories. You want money and with six children to support, you need a lot of money—"

As if I'm not working too, Liza thinks.

"—and you know that if you continue doing work for various police agencies, you'll continue to be paid by those agencies. The money's a sure thing. It's as simple as that."

"Right," Dace says.

"It's the same motive that brought you here today. You think there's lots of money coming down the pike. You're just like the rest of the men who have testified here. You know that you won't see a penny of any settlement if you don't lie."

Dace glares at Garbutt, but he speaks out as clearly and loudly as he can. It's costing him, though. Anybody can see that.

"This is not about money," he says. "It's about my sister and what happened to a whole bunch of other kids at St. Matthew's."

"We're not talking about other kids, Mr. Gagnon, we're talking about you," Garbutt says.

"About me and what happened to my sister, you mean," Dace says pulling at his tie and starting to rise a little in his chair.

"All right, Mr. Gagnon," Judge Clemens says. "I think it's time we all took a break."

Gold rushes forward to congratulate Dace as he steps down.

"Well, that went better than I thought," he says. "Hang in there. You're doing really good."

Maybe Dace looks okay, but he's not. *Please,* Liza thinks, *please end this fast.* She tries to hold his hand during their lunch, but he can't even pick at the french fries they're sharing. His fingers are trembling.

Worse, when they go back to the inquiry, they see a strange man, somebody who hasn't been at the inquiry so far. The stranger is talking to one of the Rollan Brothers. When Garbutt shows up, he joins them.

As soon as Dace sees the man, he stiffens by Liza's side.

"Who's that?" she asks, holding onto his arm.

"Breeze," he says succinctly.

"Breeze who?"

"He's an Angel, a biker. One of the guys I helped put away."

"For what?"

"Drug trafficking," Dace whispers to her quickly before he resumes his place near the judge.

All the breath goes out of Liza, but she sits back down.

Has Garbutt dug up this Breeze himself? If he didn't, why was the lawyer talking to him? It's obvious that Garbutt is just trying to freak Dace out. But surely intimidating a witness at an inquiry is illegal. If it isn't, it should be. It is on American TV! Maybe. Oh, God, she isn't sure. Why the fuck doesn't she know more about Canadian law? She should by now. Glancing over her shoulder, she sees Breeze coming in. After looking around a bit, he settles down in the middle of the spectator seats and fixes his eyes on Dace.

Almost immediately, Garbutt starts questioning Dace about his former drug habit.

"That was fifteen years ago," Dace says. "I've been clean for years."

"But would it be fair to say that whole chunks of time are gone from your memory as a direct result of your abuse of street drugs?"

"No," Dace says. "It wouldn't be."

"Well, then," Garbutt asks, "what about your constant visits to Akwesasne? Do you remember any of those?"

"Akwesasne?" Judge Clemens asks.

"Your Honor, Akwesasne is that Indian reservation down near Cornwall," Garbutt says.

"Ah, you mean St. Regis," Clemens says. "That's what we call it here on our side."

"There's a lot of illegal cigarette trade on both sides," Garbutt says. "And drugs too."

Cigarettes, Liza thinks, *that's all.*

"But I don't think that's why Mr. Gagnon goes there," Garbutt continues.

"I really don't see what that's got to do with these proceedings," Gold says.

"Maybe nothing," Garbutt admits. "But according to border control, this man—or a man who calls himself René Gagnon—has visited the reservation at least twice a year and sometimes more for the past fifteen years. He stays there with a schoolteacher called Summer uh, sorry, I had her names in my notes but I can't find it right now. What's that all about?" he asks, turning his attention back to Dace. "Is it just an attractive young native woman that you're into or are you into the drug trade there too?"

"Neither," Dace says. "Summer—she's just an old friend."

Liza nearly stops breathing. She could swear that Garbutt turns around to check her reaction, but maybe he doesn't. An important lawyer like him has bigger things on his mind than her.

Later that day, in a private room adjacent to the big one where the inquiry is taking place, Dace meets with his RCMP handler who's finally made it in from Ottawa.

What a bunch of cloak-and-dagger stuff, Liza thinks, fed up to the teeth by everybody and everything. Gold must have alerted the bland, grandfatherly looking man who can't or won't give his name. The guy sure doesn't look like he works for the RCMP with that great big gut, though.

At least Gold has done something for Dace because he sure as hell didn't do much else today. Gold practically let that Garbutt walk all over Dace. The RCMP man blabs on and on, but when he hears what happened today, his biggest concern is that Dace's unmasking as a police agent will put him in imminent danger.

"You and your wife and the kids too," the man says with a sidelong look at Liza. He talks for another three minutes or so, until she almost tears out her hair.

"The RCMP will want you to go into a witness protection program," he finally says. "Especially with this Breeze guy here. You can do this, once everything's wound up at the inquiry, of course. We'll assign an officer to watch you for now."

"That's just not happening," Dace immediately says. "I'm not leaving my family and my dad again."

As for Liza, it takes all her strength not to go back to the hotel, jump into her car and make a run for Toronto. Where her children are, where there are other people who love her besides Dace. Where she's something else besides a sidekick, an ex-con's little wife.

And a cheated-on wife at that.

But she can't. Because Dace needs her. Back at the hotel, she follows him into their room. He sits down on the bed and holds out his arms.

"Come here," he says, but she doesn't move.

All this shit, she thinks *and he still hasn't said anything about what happened to him and Rosie when they were kids*. Well, she's come this far with him. Whatever he's doing with that other Summer, the twit isn't here. What has he done with her, though? Had a kid with her too? Or maybe he really is into the goddamn cigarette trade. Or something else. God, Judge Clemens sure is naïve. Cigarettes? The reservation is chockful of other drugs as well. Everybody knows that.

Damn, she thinks, fiddling with some of her errant hair in the mirror near the door, *and I was so sure he'd never cheat on me. That I wouldn't put up with this kind of crap if he did. Oh, no, not me. But I'm such a good little loyal wife. I can't walk away from him now. I just can't.*

Outside of their hotel, an OPP officer armed with a shotgun has been assigned to guard Dace and herself, she supposes. *Great,* she thinks, *so now I'm a target!* There's nothing to worry about, though. Garbutt probably just paid Breeze to come and scare Dace, to put him off testifying about anything else. Hard to believe a lawyer would do something like that, but that's what he must have done.

"He's a bugger, that Garbutt," Dace says, pounding his right fist into his left after he shares some more repugnant details with her about Breeze.

Liza is only half listening. She's so humiliated by what she heard about Summer at the inquiry today that she almost doesn't care. Just thinking about Dace's infidelity, his *disloyalty,* she flushes again and again.

Garbutt really is a bugger in more ways than one. "I don't like him either," she agrees, just to make Dace stop talking about him and Breeze. She gives up on her hair then and walks a little closer to the bed. "But I guess a lawyer has to do everything he can to defend his own client."

"Yeah and the priests will do everything to protect their own kind. Liza," Dace adds offhandedly, though when he says her name, she already knows what he's going to say, "all that shit about Summer Senior, it's not —"

"It's not true?" she asks, just before she whacks him with a closed fist in the side of his head.

Right then, one of the hotel fire alarms starts going off outside their door. Of course. No matter, they aren't going anyplace.

"Not exactly. Not how he tells it," Dace says, grabbing both her hands. "You're the one I love, you know that, don't you?"

"I guess," Liza says, lowering herself slowly into his arms. Tears are running down her face. She blots them on his shoulder. The fire alarm stops ringing then, but a little voice is still yapping in her head.

What made him do this to her? *Don't let this go. You don't want to just be loved the best. You want to be the only one. You want all of him.*

"I'll kill you if this ever happens again," she says into his chest. "You, just you. I wouldn't waste my time on the bitch."

Of course he promises her the moon and the stars.

Later that night, safe in Dace's arms, even if it's just for a moment, she dreams of her sister-in-law Rosie. Aka Rosie McCaud, mother of two, to whom she's never really given much thought. Who didn't get into trouble like her big brother did. Long ago little Rosie Devereux must have wanted to be loved too, just loved. Liza has seen a few old pictures of Rosie, a little girl who looked more like a boy. A sad and confused child who wanted to fit in. Daughter of a dead woman and second child in a family where the firstborn was a fêted son.

Waking up from her fretful sleep and still thinking about her, Liza tries to put herself in little Rosie's shoes.

And what about those awful, pathetic young priests? Was that all they wanted? Love, but Jesus, it was all just too sick. A lot of priests must have been poor boys from big families who fell in love with the church, though. Or maybe they just didn't know what else to do. Lots of people went into teaching or to grad school for similar reasons. The priests were male, full of testosterone. Young men think about sex all the time, don't they? Maybe even priestly wannabes. They weren't eunuchs after all, though from the sounds of it, a lot of them should have been. They may have wanted affection, but they craved sexual gratification more. The gratification that the church said they couldn't have. And in their special cases, the kind of gross indecent gratification that nobody has a right to have!

It's morning, but she's still trapped in a bad dream. Propped up beside her on a couple of pillows, Dace is yammering away to Rosie on the phone, as if he calls up his sister every day. He doesn't. The man can hardly keep up with her and his own kids.

"Rosie, Rosie darling," he keeps calling her, the same thing he always calls Liza, "I've got to tell them. A four-year-old can't agree to nothing, you know that."

Chapter Twenty-Nine
Rosie

Somebody *else would have just collapsed after yesterday,* Liza thinks, *but not him. Not Dace.* Pride surges in her, the wrong kind as far as his enemies are concerned. She can almost hear them thinking: *Such a cocky bastard.* Or something even worse.

They let themselves into the inquiry room. They're all psyched up for Dace to resume his testimony until they see Gold.

"Sorry," he says immediately, "I just found out myself. The defence has called another witness to refute your testimony about Father Danby."

Sorry, Liza thinks, *we'll be lucky to get that.*

"Shit happens," Dace says.

Oh, stop it, Liza almost says, *stop oversimplifying and playing things down.* She wants to run for the door, but she can't. Dace isn't going anyplace. They sit down on the edges of their chairs and hold hands.

Breeze is already there. When he spots them, Liza is pretty sure he licks his chops.

Today's witness, Dwayne Hurley, a former student at St. Matthew's, describes himself as a local schoolteacher who teaches grade two. Teaching is his second career. He sold cars before. He's short and stocky with the usual black frame glasses that he keeps pushing back on his nose, a nice man, the kind you want for a neighbour. He has two kids of his own, both boys. He's been married a long time.

Nothing wrong with him, Liza thinks. Straightaway, Mr. Hurley volunteers that he was never abused at the school. So he very much resented the call he got from somebody at a helpline asking him to participate in this "mockery of an inquiry" and implying that he was abused. Well, he wasn't abused and he doubts anybody else at St. Matthew's was abused either. The papers are getting it all wrong.

"Whatever, I don't think anybody was abused," Hurley repeats. "St. Matthew's was a good school. There's all this talk about tearing it down, but it still is. Me and my brother—I mean, 'my brother and I'—lived there for a couple of years, off and on. We both made good. St. Matthew's had all sorts of sports programs, lots of healthy activities. Where do people think this abuse took place anyway? The showers were like an echo chamber. And a watchman was always on duty when we slept."

"Were you at St. Matthew's the same time Father Danby was?" Garbutt asks.

"Yes, I was. And no way Father Danby was a child molester either. If you ask me, the guys that have been doing all the talking are just out for blood money."

"By blood money, I assume you're referring to the compensation some former students hope to get from the diocese whether or not any of their priests are charged?" Judge Clemens attempts to clarify.

"Yes," Hurley says, looking a little distracted.

"So is it fair to say then, Mr. Hurley, that when somebody from the helpline called you, you felt like you were being asked to make a false complaint?" Garbutt redirects him.

"It was some fella called René Gagnon who called me. He had a list of people who'd been at St. Matthew. And I remember this Gagnon kid from the school when I was there..."

"I'm sorry, but that's impossible, sir," Gold interrupts Hurley, "There wasn't any kid called René Gagnon at your school. I'm also going to suggest that Mr. Gagnon didn't ask you to make a false complaint, but that you were worried about your position as a teacher. Maybe you were even worried about losing your own boys if it ever came out that you'd been abused and that you'd done nothing to—"

"No, sir, that's wrong," Hurley says, his voice shaking. "The difference between me and that René Gagnon fellow, is that I'm not a stool pigeon like the papers say he is."

Liza hears Dace suck in his breath. If Dwayne Hurley wasn't in prison, he knew somebody who was. "Stool pigeon" wasn't what the papers said. They referred to yesterday's witness as an informant. Stool pigeon is prison talk.

"A stool pigeon?" Garbutt asks.

"Yes, sir."

"Like he gives evidence against people?"

"Yes, sir. And he doesn't just rat out drug pushers either, like the papers said. He rats out other people."

"Like Father Danby?"

"Yes, like him. Father Danby never did anything! He didn't. I know, I was there."

"Now just a minute," Gold says. "Mr. Gagnon is telling a different story. Let's get him back up here to tell us what really happened to the kids at St. Matthew's."

"Your Honor, Mr. Hurley should be allowed to finish his testimony," Garbutt says.

"No, it sounds to me like Mr. Hurley is finished," Judge Clemens says, "Please bring Mr. Gagnon back up here."

"Right," Garbutt mutters to nobody in particular, "let's hear the whole sordid tale."

But Dace is already on his feet. No way he'll let this go. He turns around briefly to rub Liza's shoulder and then goes back up to the front of the room.

"It's true," he says. "I was the one who organized the helpline back in the spring. I made some calls from the States where I had a job and some from my house in Toronto. I worked from some enrolment lists I got from Social Services, me and a couple of other people did. When I called them up, I remembered a lot of the guys who were at St. Matthew's the same time as me, but I don't remember Mr. Hurley. I'm not saying he wasn't there, I just don't remember him. I'm forgetting more people than I know now. But maybe he was one of the teacher's pets, maybe he didn't hang out with the bad boys like me."

"Mr. Gagnon," Garbutt says, "Surely you aren't suggesting that Mr. Hurley here was somehow complicit—"

"He's not suggesting anything," Gold says, "but he's going to tell us exactly what happened with Father Danby."

Liza's eyes hurt so she closes them, but she has to open them again. She's put off knowing a lot of things for so long.

"Father Danby had a thing for the school's nurse, or at least he pretended to. Father Danby was a priest or maybe he was just a priest wannabe then. He wasn't supposed to be interested in a woman, not like that—"

"Come now," Garbutt says. "Most of us are Catholics here. We know all about the priests and celibacy."

"Celibacy sure didn't stop him from poking boys when he was making his nightly rounds."

"And yet he never poked you?" Garbutt says.

"No," Dace says. "But he went after some of my friends. They never told nobody, but they told me. Because after me and my sister came, he stopped bothering them. For a while, anyway. And they were glad, real glad. The smaller the boys were, the more Danby liked them. That's what my friend Rick Lowery thought anyway. Lucky Rick, he figured out how to keep out of Father Danby's way. Rick had already been in St. Matthew's for several months before me and my sister came."

"Rick Lowery?" Garbutt interrupts. "Is this Mr. Lowery here today?"

"No," Gold says, "and it doesn't matter. Please continue, Mr. Gagnon."

"He started off by strapping my little sis any chance he got — "

"Whoa," Garbutt says, "what are you talking about? Where's all this coming from?"

"Who?" Gold asks.

"That man there," Dace says, pointing out the priest with the eye patch. "Father Danby. He went after her the first day we came and locked her in a closet until she peed her pants. The nurse came and got her out. And he strapped me too, any time I tried to interfere. I didn't do much though. I thought the nurse would take care of my sister, but she always slept on her good ear so when Father Danby started going in there at night — "

"Really now, Mr. Gagnon, you weren't there — "

"No, but I heard her crying one night and nobody was going to her, so I went."

"Where did you go, Mr. Gagnon?" Gold asks.

"I don't see how this is pertinent," Garbutt says, "There's no record that a child called Ro — of a little girl ever being at St. Matthew's. They didn't take girls."

"If there are any reporters here, I don't want the sister's name mentioned at all," Judge Clemens says. "Go on," he nods at Dace, but he doesn't have to. Dace has started talking. They can't stop him now.

"I went to the nurse's room. My sister was crying and a man's voice was saying, 'Shut up, shut up or lord Jesus I'll give you something to cry about!' The door wasn't locked, so I went in."

"And," Gold prods gently, "what was happening?"

"I couldn't see much at first. It was dark and I'd never been in there before. But it looked like my sister had been sleeping on a little pallet at the foot of the nurse's bed. The lady had a single bed and she was still snoring away."

"And yet you heard her snoring over everything else?" Garbutt asks.

"I did. She—the nurse was stone deaf in one ear, so she slept on her good side. Everybody knew that. It was the only way she could get some sleep in that place." At this point, Dace pauses, looking almost lost.

"What was happening with your sister?" Gold asks.

"She had stopped crying," Dace says.

"Mr. Gagnon, you must have heard lots of kids crying in an orphanage," Garbutt says.

"I knew my own sister's cry. And she had stopped crying by now, she was just making a sick kind of squealing sound. I couldn't see her—"

"So you couldn't even see her," Garbutt says.

"Please, Mr. Garbutt," Judge Clemens says.

Yes, please just shut the fuck up, Liza thinks.

"But I could hear her. He—Father Danby—was on top like a big buffalo, wearing that robe. I could smell him too, the pig—"

Liza stops hearing for an instant. When she tunes back in, Dace is saying something about the nurse's umbrella. "The nurse had left her umbrella standing up in a big empty tomato soup can that she kept by the door—"

"A soup can?" Garbutt says, raising his eyebrows in surprise.

"It was one of those big industrial cans," Dace says. "Like they buy for institutions—"

"Really, your Honor," Garbutt says, "I don't see the relevance. In any case, St. Matthew's didn't use canned foods. They grew all their vegetables on the grounds. For whatever reasons, this man is lying again. I'm going to suggest he was never even in the nurse's room."

"Mr. Garbutt," Judge Clemens says, "You're a well-respected lawyer. I've already told you this once in private, but I'll say it once more. This an inquiry, not a trial, and this inquiry just wants to find out what went on. In case you've forgotten how a commission of inquiry works, this is what happens: people testify, I evaluate their stories later and then I write my own report based on facts."

"So we can get the fucking priests later!" a man from the spectator portion of the room shouts.

"Security," Judge Clemens says smoothly. "Remove that person from the room. Now. Mr. Gagnon, please go on."

"So there was an umbrella?" Gold asks Dace, looking unperturbed. "And what did you do with this umbrella?"

"Well, nothing at first," Dace says. "I just grabbed it. I won't lie to you, I wanted to ram it up Danby's ass, but I couldn't. I was shouting and shaking too much. And I wasn't that big myself. 'Get off my sister,' I said. 'Leave her alone!'"

Oh, God, Liza thinks. *Is this really necessary? What the hell do you want? Maybe he should have just said, 'Please get off my sister, Father Danby, sir?'* Down the row from her, a woman retches as quietly as she can into something in her purse.

"Well, you've gone this far," Garbutt says. "So go ahead and tell us what you did to this man here, this man of God." Garbutt walks up closer and pushes his face into Dace's. "I'm going to suggest that Father Danby went into the nurse's room to comfort your sister. She was prone to nightmares, wasn't she?"

"I didn't mean to," Dace says.

"Oh, so, now you didn't mean to!"

"It looked like Father Danby was having trouble getting up off the ground, in that robe and all. Or maybe he was just too far gone. You know, like when a guy… I didn't know exactly what he was doing to my sister, but I'd seen a dog once or twice. And she was still making those little yipping sounds, so I—"

"You what?"

"I didn't mean to," Dace repeats. "I was just jabbing the umbrella at him, trying to make him get off, but then when he turned around, I must have caught him in the eye. But I was sure glad because he got off my sister pretty damn fast then. He had his hand over his face and blood was streaming from his eye. I thought he was going to start hollering, but he didn't make a sound. It was weird."

"Weird—the man had just lost an eye on account of a delinquent! My guess is that he was in shock—"

"Sir, I believe that this inquiry is about St. Matthew's, not the training school," Dace says. "Because I wasn't a delinquent, not then. Not even by your standards. And Father Danby didn't lose his eye that night either. I'd like to tell you that it was dangling from his empty eye socket out onto the floor, but it wasn't."

Garbutt checks something with his assistant. "You're right," he agrees, resuming his interrogation, "Father Danby lost his eye later because it got infected. But it was because of what you did! When you were what, all of ten? The whole incident kind of predicted the man you would become, didn't it? A violent man and a liar to boot. If we had access to your prison records today, we'd find out all about that—"

"I'm not lying, I'm just here to tell people the kinds of things that happened at St. Matthew's so we can all move on, so people can get some closure."

"Okay, I can probably be a little kinder than that. You don't exactly tell lies, you just exaggerate things to make yourself look good. A rather common attribute of orphans and kids raised in institutions, I'm told. Take this business about you being the saviour of your kid sister— It's pure bunk."

"That's a real interesting interpretation of the facts," Gold says. "But we've already heard from several witnesses that abuse of all kinds was rampant at St. Matthew's, so why shouldn't we believe Mr. Gagnon? The only thing that surprises me is that he wasn't sexually abused himself."

"I wasn't. Not there. But I was scared shitless after what happened with Father Danby and the next place I got sent, the training school, it was even worse. At least I knew better than to try to help out anybody at the training school. I never helped anybody when I was there, nada. I didn't even help my best friend, not even when a couple of the priests there went after him real bad."

They must have gone after Rick Lowery, too, Liza supposes, watching Dace practically limping back towards her, a broken man. To her astonishment, it looks like tears are running down his face, but he's looking at the floor. If he is crying, he won't want anybody else to see him. She stands up, prepared to flee with him out the door. She doesn't want to know any more, she just doesn't. Nobody here at the inquiry does. What kind of sicko would?

When Dace reaches Liza, he puts his arm around her shoulders like he never wants to let go. *Time enough to deal with whatever happened at the training school down the road,* she thinks, hanging onto him.

It will all come out when they finally charge Father Danby and some of the other priests who've been implicated during the past few weeks. God knows they have enough evidence now and lots of those men worked at the training school. Unless they were all sent away like Father Danby. Where did he go next? As far away as possible, no doubt. To some northern residential school, people always said. After that, who knows.

Gold approaches. "I've made arrangements for Dace to talk to a psychologist tomorrow." He holds out a small white appointment card to Liza. "He's—well, I'm not sure what's happening to him," he says, speaking like Dace isn't even there.

Oh, really, she thinks. *It never occurred to you to wonder what kind of effect talking about such things would have on a man?* She feels like kicking Gold, but she reads the card he gave her instead. It isn't Gold's fault anyway. Nothing is.

Dr. Fred Cooper, the card says. Cooper's a common enough name, but it's the same last name as the guy she saw at Maitland University Health Services all those years ago. She isn't sure what his qualifications were then, maybe he was just in training, but he's probably a qualified psychologist by now. Cooper was another one of Joe Armitage's family friends. She only went to him a couple of times. The guy was totally useless, but he might be better with men.

Dace is still flushed and breathing heavily. If the tears in his eyes are from sadness or from anger, she can't tell. Jesus, all that terrible stuff about poor little Rosie. Thank God she isn't here and pray God she's forgotten everything.

Dace might be faking a breakdown and bailing out on everybody, but he'd never cry in front of people if he could help it. He never has.

"What's this?" he asks, trying to read the card upside down in her hands.

Please don't cry. You're scaring me. "Gold wants you to see a psych tomorrow," she says.

The room has nearly emptied, but they sit back down in their chairs. One of the last people to leave stops by and introduces himself as a doctor. In her terror, Liza couldn't describe him. She doesn't catch his name either, just the doctor part. She's still holding onto Dace.

The doctor asks Dace a couple of questions—*What year is this? Who's the prime minister?*—but he doesn't get much sense out of him.

"Has Mr. Gagnon ever been suicidal?" he finally asks Liza. *No, but I have*, she feels like saying. *Kill me the fuck now.*

"No," she says.

"I don't think he has to go to hospital. You can probably take him home, but go see a psychologist as soon as you can. And he probably shouldn't testify anymore."

"No," she agrees, "He's said enough."

Back at the hotel, Dace just seems quiet, but it looks like chunks of his memory might be gone, just gone. Twice that night, he pushes her down onto the bed and sinks into her, more like a man in need of a transfusion than a lover, but it doesn't matter. At least they're making love. Anything is better than just watching him lie there like she's done for the past three weeks.

They even talk a bit that night or at least he does, even if it's about nothing relevant. He knows her and he recalls the names of all their children and the two family cats, so that's good.

He even remembers to call Rosie and say "Don't worry about the news, everything's all right, they won't use your name."

But when he gets a call about the helpline, he has no idea what the person is talking about. And when Liza asks him more about Rosie, he's as clueless about her as he is about everything else to do with St. Matthew's. He remembers some stuff, but the orphanage and the training school are all mixed up in his head.

One look at Dr. Fred Cooper the next day, Liza's stomach turns over and she's a raped twenty-one-year old again. Not that he remembers her, so she's safe enough for now.

"Ah, Mrs. Gagnon," he says, "I'd like to talk to your husband alone for a while if I may."

Devereux, I'm still Liza Devereux.

Watching Dr. Cooper lead Dace away, she realizes that either he doesn't have a real good memory for faces or else she's changed a lot. He sure hasn't. He's a bit more pudgy, but he looks more like Jon Voight now than ever. The doctor and the actor are aging together in real time.

Dr. Cooper and Dace stay inside his office for a little over an hour while she paces up and down the doctor's tiny waiting room like a fitness buff on a treadmill. And revels in being alone. The doctor's receptionist, if he has one, must be out on an extended errand. The desk phone rings several times but is quickly silenced, probably by an answering machine.

Liza hears the murmur of their voices, but no distinct words. She resists the urge to put her ear against the office door and keeps on walking.

But she's standing in front of the door when it finally opens.

Liza's always been under the impression that psychs don't like to share their diagnoses with relatives, but Dr. Cooper does.

"Your husband is suffering from post-traumatic stress disorder," he says without any preliminaries, in the same voice that he might volunteer that his new patient has an IQ of 152. Dace doesn't react when he says this, but Liza can't help smiling, it's such a relief to have any kind of diagnosis.

"It can happen," Cooper explains, "when somebody starts reliving the same traumatic events every day. That's why Mr. Gagnon was fine until the inquiry." The doctor says this and a whole lot more as he rocks back and forth on the balls of his feet, but he's talking so fast that Liza has a hard time getting in a question.

"His memory, the parts he's lost, will it all come back?" she finally interjects.

For the first time since he started talking to her or rather at her, Dr. Fred Cooper looks her in the eyes. "That depends," he says. He must have learned something in the past fifteen years though, something about people, or maybe he really is better with men because he seems to have connected with Dace. Well, good for him.

"I'm sure this is the furthest thing from your mind right now, but after talking about the things he did at the inquiry, Mr. Gagnon will either have an increased desire for sex — to prove himself as it were — or he might not have any desire at all. Either's fine and it probably won't be permanent. But if he does try to perform, he might not be able to. And he might not be sleeping very well either—"

"He's not."

"I'm right here," Dace says.

"I can prescribe something for that. I can even prescribe something for erectile dysfunction if you want," Dr. Cooper volunteers with a little smile. "There's some good products on the market now."

"For Christ's sake!" Dace growls, grabbing Liza's hand and pulling her towards the exit door. "Let's go."

"I'm not concerned about that," Liza says over her shoulder, flushing at Dr. Cooper before she's out in the hallway. "The sex part, I mean." Everything was fine last night anyway.

Cooper follows them a little ways. "As for your husband's memory, which is what you should be concerned about, it will definitely come back, Mrs. Gagnon." Liza doesn't bother correcting him about her name this time, either. "It could come back whole or it could come back a bit at a time. But ask yourself this — do you want it to?"

Chapter Thirty
Sorry

Three days after he broke down at the inquiry, they try to get Dace to testify again. It's against Liza's better judgement, but what does her opinion matter? She's just his little wife after all. He sounds cogent enough until Garbutt asks him exactly where the nurse slept at St. Matthew's.

"It was in the basement, near the kitchen," Dace says firmly.

"Are you sure?"

Oh, Liza thinks, clenching her fists in her lap, *please, please just let me smack that self-satisfied look off your fat face.*

"Yes."

"I'm going to suggest to you that it was on the main floor near the school office." From somewhere out of a suit pocket, Garbutt pulls out an old floor plan of St. Matthew's, producing it with a theatrical flourish. "I'm also going to suggest that you were never even in the nurse's room, that in fact you attacked Father Danby out of the clear blue — "

"I did not!" Dace roars, just like any liar would.

"In fact, all your school reports including those from the training school — and I have them here too — describe you as yet another violent child, prone to fits of rage."

"Ask the witness a question, please," Judge Clemens says. "This inquiry is more interested in what happened at the school than it is in Mr. Gagnon's character."

"Well, then, perhaps you can tell me where the school gym was?" Garbutt asks Dace while Liza squirms in her seat. "That should be easy. As a St. Matthew's boy, you must have spent a lot of time there."

"Your Honor, I fail to see what any of this has to do with Mr. Gagnon's testimony," Gold interjects.

"Your Honor, it has plenty to do with Mr. Gagnon's honesty and memory. The events we're describing took place over thirty years ago. I intend to show that Mr. Gagnon's long-term memory is faulty at best."

"Mr. Gagnon," Judge Clemens says, "you can answer the question. It seems simple enough."

"Just what's the fucking question?" Dace asks, his voice trembling.

"Where was the gym at St. Matthew's?" Garbutt repeats.

"I don't fucking know! You think that just because I can't remember where the gym was that I don't remember who buggered a four-year-old?"

"Please control yourself, Mr. Gagnon or I'll have to ask you to step down," Judge Clemens says.

Dace refuses to even look at Garbutt. He looks at Judge Clemens instead. Liza's heart turns over. Dace is making a tremendous effort just to cooperate.

"This isn't about me and my memory," he says, a little more calmly. "And I'm not out to get the Church. Honest to God. All the priests who did this stuff, they can die in their own beds for all I care. I just want them to admit what they did. And I want to make sure that nobody like them is ever in a position to hurt a little kid like my sister again."

Liza leaves Maitland on the 6:00 a.m. commuter train the next day. Who are all these nuts who spend four hours traveling back and forth to work in Toronto every day? She's got some business at Women's College Hospital that will take her away from work again, but maybe she can sneak out in the afternoon while Irina's doing her own thing. The appointment she made is still a week away. Too bad it isn't her only problem.

"Trust me," she said to Dace when he took her to the train station, "working for Irina is much easier than staying at home. I'd have to let Helen go and being on my own with the twins all the time would drive me nuts."

"Go back," he insisted just last night, "You've got to," but it hadn't looked like he was thinking that.

On the platform with her train almost huffing away without her, he hugs her fiercely.

"I don't like it, little darling, but it's the right thing to do. You've got to take care of yourself for once."

In the fresh light of day, he's talking about her hospital appointment, of course, not about her going back to work. As far as he was concerned, she should just quit *Dazzle* anyway.

But who's going to take care of Dace when she's not there? Somebody has to keep him out of trouble. Poor Uncle Norm. He had once hoped she would do just that, though she'd been barely more than a girl. *Just don't do anything stupid*, she thinks. Dace had gotten so drunk in the hotel bar the previous night that he almost got into a fight with a complete stranger. If he blows up again at the inquiry, all's lost.

Part of her is scared he'll cry again, but he doesn't. The train blows its last whistle. Dace pushes her away, steering her towards the door with his hand in the small of her back. Though his memory is still shot full of holes, his physical strength has come back in just a few days.

But all this strength has come back at a price: his fury.

On the train in one of the window seats she usually prefers, Liza's mind plays Dace's testimony over and over. That and the anger he brought back to the hotel and almost took out on her. She tries not to think about these things, but she does. Lucky that sex still appeases him.

Even if she's somehow ended up pregnant again. *Ah, sweet Jesus.* But she can't, she just can't pull another pregnancy off even if her damn eggs are still good. *And let's face it*, she thinks, *they probably aren't. I'm thirty-eight!* She has so many other people to think about now. Twins are born deprived of individual attention, her girls are turning into little old women before their time and as for her sons, this would make the oldest one pretty nuts for sure. In the final analysis, it's Micah she just can't do this to.

I'm sorry, she told Dace over and over. She wasn't just apologizing for her pregnancy or herself, she was apologizing for what happened to him, long, long before her time. And Dace knew this.

Stop saying sorry, he said. *I never wanted you to know all this, it's not your fault.*

And maybe it wasn't even theirs. Shit happens. But it's got to stop.

Chapter Thirty-One

Poison

Dace is wrong, Liza thinks, listening to him rant on the phone later that night after she's got all the kids to bed. *Just wrong.*

The priests, those men, those adults were all totally at fault. They still are. But the shame and even the guilt most of the boys experienced is working in the priests' favour. Just like it did with the boys of Mount Cashel. The man who testified earlier that day is a perfect example of this.

It's after 10:00 p.m. but this call will still be costing them a small fortune. Dace rarely phones her, so today's testimony has really freaked him out.

I should have been there, Liza thinks.

Down the road, what was said today might end up in Judge Clemens's report, but it didn't make the six o'clock news. It wasn't scintillating enough. One more witness just felt guilty and sorry about what he'd done or should have done.

But listening to Dace recount this man's story, Liza can see why a witness like this would bother the hell out of him. The witness's name is Matthew "Matt" Mathieson, yes it really is, Dace tells her, not that it matters.

The last time Dace saw Matt, he was a good-looking kid of twelve or so, the kind who liked reading and who stayed out of harm's way, a useful ploy if you ended up at St. Matthew's. But Mathieson told the inquiry he had walked into the school library to see a small boy on his knees fellating Father Danby. Not long after, Father Danby had come up behind Matt in the same room — a place hardly bigger than a walk-in closet— reached around him and squeezed his genitals.

"I didn't know what to do," Mathieson told the inquiry. "So I just stood there for a moment. When Father Danby put my hand on his penis, I even squeezed it a couple of times. Then I turned around and just looked at him. I guess he knew I was mad, real mad, so he stopped."

Was it really that easy to refuse? Well, maybe if you were a confident, well-built kid like this Matt kid was. But he was still scarred. Of course Mathieson never spoke to anybody about the incident out of fear and shame. Who the hell would? Even at the inquiry, Mathieson sat there for so long staring at his hands that Dace worried he wouldn't go on.

But he did. "In my opinion," Mathieson continued, laughing a little nervously, "what happened to me was more of a sinful act than a criminal act and that made me a sinner too. It was the fifties. We didn't talk about stuff like that. Sex stuff was real taboo. It never even occurred to me to tell anybody. I was—well, I was embarrassed, I guess. If I said anything, people might have called me a queer, like I had invited him to come on to me. What the hell was I doing in the library alone?"

Mathieson said that he was only here thirty years after the fact because his therapist told him that if he didn't confront the past, it would poison the rest of his life.

Oh, the power of a psych, Liza thinks. *They're like modern day seers. We all should have one.*

Upstairs, one of the twins cries out in his sleep, Cole probably. Liza waits a moment, with one ear cocked towards the ceiling.

When she doesn't hear anything more, she whispers into the phone receiver, "Do you want to talk to a therapist again? That Cooper fellow was okay."

There's a long pause. If they weren't lovers and she couldn't still hear him breathing, she'd hang up the phone.

"I can't, Liza. It's no use. I'm just going to have to go into a witness protection program, you know that."

And what about us, what's going to happen to us?

"I'm sure they have therapists in witness protection. They must. Mathieson's right. You got to do this, Dace. You've got to talk some more. You've just got to. Or it'll poison your life."

If it hasn't already.

Chapter Thirty-Two

Old News

Editing a romance novel, riding the subway back and forth, bathing the twins and reading the *Tales of Narnia* to Eden, Liza believes in magic for a full forty-eight hours or more. That Dace will be made whole again, that he won't have to go into a witness protection program, that the inquiry and all the dirt it's digging up will soon be over. It's the only way she can cope with everything else on her mind.

She wishes she had an alternative, that there was a door into another world for her. A way out of this hellhole. But she's got to let this pregnancy go, even if it's her last chance to have another baby. At least she isn't sick yet with this pregnancy, which is strange.

Come Saturday, the *Maitland Spectator* publishes a full page article called "Will the Real René Gagnon Please Step Forward?" and that's it. She's totally focused on the inquiry again. Dace is a drowning man. They're all drowning. Who should she save first? Dace calls to say that on a back page, the weekend *Globe and Mail* is carrying the same article. How could they?

Micah and Sammy are still sleeping. Another parent stopped by to take the girls to their dancing lessons.

Considering what the article apparently says about him, Dace sounds pretty calm, but he can't talk for long.

After she hangs up the phone, Liza stares at the twins in their highchairs. They're happily eating dry Cheerios and drawing on bits of scrap paper with their oversized crayons, but their calmness won't last long. It never does.

As if on cue, one of them starts squawking, "Lello, I want lello, mine!"

"Yellow," Liza says automatically, tearing the editorial section out of this morning's newspaper and tucking it under one armpit. She needs total quiet right now. She scoops the twins out of their highchairs so quickly that they both squawk, but their protests die down when she carries them one by one down to the basement, turns on the TV in the family room, and plunks them in front of a cartoon show. Heading into the adjacent laundry room, she closes the door and sits down on the floor in front of the vibrating washing machine. It's cold on the cement floor, but as long as her boys are fixated on the TV, she can read the article in relative peace.

The article expands on many of the accusations that Garbutt has already leveled at Dace. Oh, joy, there's even a photo of Dace. It's a younger photo of him — a mugshot which Garbutt must have purloined from some file — but it's still a photo.

"René Gagnon," Garbutt told the reporter, "is a pathological liar. I'm not allowed to say he was a juvenile delinquent, so maybe he wasn't, but you see this kind of behaviour in the product of a training school. Maybe not in all the kids who get sent to a training school, but in some. Or it could be that Mr. Gagnon's just a born liar. What he said here last week at the inquiry about one of the brothers is pure creativity on his part. And I'm willing to bet that all his neighbours say the same thing too, that he's a real nice guy, but he tells stories all the time. That he's always the hero. You can bet on that."

The Christian order's whitewash, Liza thinks, getting up from the floor with some difficulty and folding every bit of clean laundry that she can find on top of the dryer. *Of that pervert and my Dace.*

When the twins are finally napping, Micah and Sammy are flaked out in front of the TV watching football, and the girls are back from ballet, but have gone off to the corner store for a treat, she talks to Gold on the phone. For once, he's calling her.

"Don't worry," he assures her. "This character assassination of his won't go unnoticed. The women's groups and a lot of other people are going to be all over this. After all that's been said about putting a rape victim on trial, people will be appalled that the *Maitland Spectator* dedicated an entire page to doing basically just that."

"And what about the *Globe and Mail?*" Liza asks, but at least it's on a back page and to be fair, the *Globe* has reported everything else from the Maitland inquiry too, drawing the obvious parallels to the situation at Mount Cashel.

At first Liza's too numb to even feel angry, but she sure is confused. Even if Dace lied to protect his undercover work, what does that have to do with the issue of abuse? He practically initiated the inquiry here in Ontario. He got things rolling on the helpline when nobody else had the courage. He deserves a medal, for God's sake, he doesn't deserve to be pilloried and hounded into hiding! And he doesn't deserve to lose them all again.

But later on when she's in the back garden raking leaves with her own precious little boys, she knows this much. In the matching sweaters coats that their Grandma knit for them, her sons deserve the best, whatever happened to her and Dace. How could she leave them to go into a witness protection program with Dace?

Oh, God, she just can't. She's got no one to leave them with, there are no more of those awful orphanages and nobody's going into foster care. She'll give them to Millie first. What kind of mother gives her children to somebody else to raise? *A sad and desperate one.* Micah might be okay on his own, especially when he goes away to university, but the rest of her children are hardly half-grown.

Just thinking about Micah's imminent departure, she drops the rake and catches up the first unsuspecting little boy in her arms. *They still smell like babies*, she thinks, crushing first one and then the other against her chest. *I'm making the right call.* They can both be her babies for a little while longer now.

"Mama, Mama," they both giggle in turn. "Let me down!"

Yes, she and Dace have both done right this time, no matter what the stupid paper says.

And he'll do the right thing again. Whatever that is.

And so will she.

Chapter Thirty-Three
Women's College Hospital

The inquiry's wrapping up. In a few weeks, the parties concerned will attempt mediation and Father Danby, at least, will have to go back to court. He's been charged. Then off to jail with him, lickety-split. Or so Liza and Dace and his other victims hope.

Just like she knew he would, Dace drives down from Maitland to Toronto to meet her at Women's College Hospital. It's a Thursday, the day after Hallowe'en. On the side streets, smashed pumpkins still litter the ground. The hospital's downtown, not far from where Liza works. So far everything's working out in her favour. Irina's off "sick."

"Once upon a time, this was a happy place," Liza says, walking into the lobby off Grenville Street. "I'm not sure how thrilled my mother was, but I was born here."

"I think I was too," Dace says, wrapping his arms around her. "I should ask my dad."

A volunteer points them towards the nearest elevator. They take it to the third floor. There are doors everywhere. The doors all look the same, but after walking through a maze of waiting rooms, they find the right one. They join the gowned women there.

"I had to check in with the doctor yesterday afternoon," Liza says. "She put something on my cervix to soften it, but I think I could still change my mind. She said I can't, but if the embryo is really strong, maybe it'll just hold on."

"I can't stay, Liza, I've got to go. You know you can't do everything by yourself—I mean, can you?—do you think you could do this all over again? The twins are almost three. They'll be four by the time— Maybe Auntie Maeve can move in with you or Helen could board at our place."

"No," she says, "I've done this before, this will be easy—"

"Of course, you've done it before, you've had six children, you could have this one in your sleep, but you're not, it's not good for you—"

"Because it's in the hospital," she says. "I don't have to worry about doing myself irreparable harm, much less dying and leaving my children motherless."

Dace looks puzzled. Liza knows he's trying to focus on her. That he wants to be there for her. He really does. But she still can't tell him what happened to her in Dublin when she was sixteen, what she and her poor grandmother had to do. She just can't. She always thought she would, but it's never the right time. How ironic that she can't tell him certain things, either. What a joke.

"But you had the twins in the hospital," he says, "Did you really worry about dying when you were having a baby? Why were you so determined to have the other kids at home then? Jesus, did the doctor already give you some drugs last night?"

Because I hate hospitals, Liza thinks, *hate other people having control over me, hate that they take a happy event like giving birth and turn it into some kind of high-tech power show. Hate that they know my business and judge me for what I did or didn't do. Another baby? Really now, Liza.*

"Go in there and put a gown on," a nurse from nowhere says to Liza a little patronizingly. She would never be in such a predicament, her face says. If only Liza's midwife could be here, but this isn't her kind of work. Long ago, midwives must have helped women out in a situation like this, but then the medical profession got in on the act. Maybe the good doctors hadn't liked it, but they had. *We just want to help you*, they said. *To keep you from hurting and killing yourselves.* This when so many women died in childbirth.

Or maybe, Liza thinks, *they just wanted to knock all the midwives out of their male-dominated profession. That makes more sense.*

Well, nobody liked doing stuff like this, but the alternative for her and everybody she loves is so much worse. *Concentrate,* she thinks, *concentrate on your future, not your past. You have one, you know. You're not your mother, girl.*

She'll feel a hell of a lot better when this is all over though, when she gets her life back. *I won't do this again,* she thought when she was sixteen. *Whatever happens, I won't have to do this again* and now here she is, a geriatric pregnant woman with an embryo she dares not bring to term.

A tag on the nurse's uniform says her name is Julie. Such a pretty name.

"You haven't eaten anything today, right?" Julie asks.

"No," Liza says. It's already one in the afternoon, but it isn't that hard to starve herself. On the advice of her doctor, she hasn't drunk or eaten since midnight. *Whatever the hell happens, go ahead and sedate me this time,* Liza thinks. It was hell when she was sixteen to be awake and go through a mini labour, all to produce an embryo, twelve weeks gone.

Dace gets up and tries to follow her into the dressing area, but another nurse stares him down. Liza finds it surprisingly difficult to shuck her clothes in a small cramped cubicle and tie the robe at the back of her neck. Her fingers tremble. She glances briefly, fleetingly at her stomach before she tugs the robe down over her front. It's the increased size of breasts that betrays her pregnancy, even if she's only eight weeks gone.

She knew almost instantly she was pregnant and had phoned the privately paid Morgentaler Clinic but even they wouldn't do a thing before now. *It's so small, the doctors are afraid they might miss it if they do anything before eight weeks*, the nurse had said apologetically.

So she would have had a few weeks to think about it, if she wasn't so busy. While inside her, the embryo grew and grew, faster than the speed of light. *Even if it's still only the size of a raspberry right now.* God help her, they better find it. She hasn't been that sick which in her case might mean the pregnancy isn't viable anyway. She can only hope. Or maybe she and Dace have just been too stressed for her to feel anything else, who knows?

I'm putting Dace through hell, she thinks, sitting back down in the waiting room with him and letting him stroke her hand. They're surrounded by robed women, most of them about twenty to forty years old, like something out of *The Handmaid's Tale*. A lot of the women are accompanied by a man, but not all. Funny, because they sure didn't impregnate themselves. Thank God, there aren't any teenage girls here. Maybe they schedule the young ones on different days or do them at the Hospital for Sick Children. The idea of Summer or Eden doing this down the road horrifies her. But the idea of one of her girls forced to have a child she isn't ready for horrifies her even more.

Please, please don't ever let this happen to them, she prays.

Dace's hand brushes her cheek. "You're so beautiful," he says, just like he always does.

She doesn't want to hear him though. She feels just like she did when she was sixteen and pregnant in Ireland, old and used up. Abortion was illegal then in both Ireland and Canada, a dangerous business fraught with mess and uncertainty. You had to be pretty desperate, maybe even half out of your mind to get one. But you did. Yes, if no other alternative presented itself, you jumped at the chance. Or you jumped someplace else.

Because if you didn't, you, your baby, your whole family was doomed. Everybody except the father, who had been so insistent on having sex with a sixteen-year-old girl, whom you had gone back to because what did it matter when you weren't a virgin anymore and besides he was so handsome and he had wanted you.

A relative or a friend helped you, but you didn't tell anybody else what was going on. In Liza's case, it was her grandmother's friend, a nurse who performed the procedure in her bedroom. Or maybe you tried telling your sad story a few times, but they didn't understand, they didn't get you. They would never end up in trouble like you, they said. Ergo, they would never do what you did. But you did what you had to do because nobody was going to help you if you didn't help yourself. You just stopped talking about it after a while. When you weren't half out of your mind.

Her grandmother took her to the nurse abortionist three times before the poison took. Liza never knew exactly what was injected into her womb to induce a miscarriage an hour before dawn, but she thought it was lye.

Abortion is illegal in Ireland to this day.

But she isn't going to feel old for long. She knows this precisely because she was once an abandoned teenager whose desire for love, whose fertility and lack of access to contraception threatened her whole future and all the family she had.

She leans into Dace and smiles up at him. She has to, for his sake. Because even if she feels badly right now, all she'll feel afterwards is an immense sense of relief, when she's herself again, when she's just Liza Devereux.

Like she did before.

Oh, God, why did this have to happen again?

Chapter Thirty-four

The Kids Need New Shoes

Dace doesn't tell her exactly when he's leaving. He never has. Less time for despair. Which she's gotten really good at lately. She could teach a class in it. But he's probably left some cash in the station wagon, behind the padding of the child's car seat closest to the driver's side.

She wakes up just before dawn with a sob in her throat. He isn't there in the bed beside her. The house that's so full of their children feels empty without him, but she can still smell his body on hers.

Feeling her way along the still dark hallways of her house, she passes the younger children's bedrooms and on the lower level, the living room where he sometimes falls asleep on the couch.

"Dace!" she feels like roaring. Just "Dace." His name fills her head. How are they supposed to keep in touch? How many times can he call from some out-of-the-way phone booth? Will that even be possible this time?

At the back door off the kitchen, she drapes one of his forgotten coats over her nightgown and pulls on her high boots.

She has a script for almost everything else she's been in her life: the unwanted child, the pregnant teenager, the convict's cousin, the woman with too much ambition and too many children, but she doesn't have one for this. Or maybe she does: deserted wife.

God, she's tired of being left behind. He might be down in the basement or outside in the garage, but she doesn't think so. She goes outside into the backyard to look around. The windows surrounding their property are still unlit.

She walks round to the front of her house on Southview. All the windows are dark here too, except for a couple of dim ones that look out and wink at her, the only person in the neighbourhood stupid enough to be up now. If she wasn't responsible for so many people, she'd be a bag lady. She looks like one right now, creeping across the empty street.

At her car, she bends down to feel for the emergency key taped to the chassis. She opens the rear door of the car with the key and is rewarded almost immediately. As usual, there's money in the car seat closest to the driver's side. She shoves it into the pocket of the coat.

Dace hasn't done any undercover work for ages and the guy managing the airport is up to no good. He must have gotten the money from the people in the witness protection program. How does that even work? Did he go to them or did they come to him? Did he get up one morning and just say, *There's a mortgage on my house and the kids all need new shoes?* He doesn't need to tell her everything, but she wishes he told her this.

Shit, it's almost light. She crosses the street again and slips back quickly through the alleyway separating her house from her neighbour Donna's. She plows through melting snow on her back lawn just to reach her garage. The side entry door to the garage is jammed with snow, so she lifts up the door for the car, cursing quietly to herself. Dace's bike is still there, but that doesn't mean anything. He usually leaves it behind when he takes off to God knows where. He has to. It's a dead giveaway to an ex-biker's true identity, to somebody with his notorious past.

Liza leaves the garage. At least she has her boots on, the black leather ones that go all the way to her knees. But her thighs are still prickling with cold. The rolling aluminum garage door makes a hideous screeching noise as she pulls it back into place, loud enough to make her neighbour Donna look outside. Does the woman ever sleep?

Donna slides open her window and clicks her tongue.

"He left about 4:00 a.m.," she shouts down, loud enough to wake the rest of the neighbourhood.

"I know," Liza says "He—he had to go out of town, go someplace early for his work." Why's she even talking to this woman? She chokes back another sob. If only Val was next-door instead of this witch. When's the last time she saw Val anyway?

At her back door, Liza grabs a snow shovel propped nearby and quickly clears the stoop, as if that was her sole purpose in coming outside. It's no use though. She doesn't just look like a crazy woman, she is.

He had to leave them. Again. He isn't any use to her dead. That old bastard Father Danby can't get at him or his sister Rosie anymore, but those guys he helped put in jail while he was working undercover sure can.

Something that asshole Garbutt had to know when he blew his cover at the inquiry.

Watch you language, she admonishes herself, but God, both Garbutt and Danby sure are creeps.

What wouldn't she have given to run around the room at the inquiry screaming, *You're out of order! The whole inquiry is out of order! They're out of order!*

She doesn't know Dace's exact plans, but she knows this much. Somebody must have gotten him a car and parked it on a side street near here for ten minutes or so. A car with New York licence plates or maybe plates from Ohio or Michigan, it doesn't matter. His new identity papers would be in the glove compartment. If he left at 4:00 a.m.—why, oh, why didn't she wake up?—he's almost be in Maitland. Drinking takeout coffee or some such slop, with just one careless hand on the wheel, the same way he always drives if it's just her and the kids aren't with them.

We're going to live forever, Liza.

Sure they will.

Oh, God, she took an allergy pill last night to fool her body into sleeping. No wonder she didn't wake up.

Dace wanted to attend the last day of the inquiry and say goodbye to some of the people he's met there, but he won't. He can't. Maybe he'll cross the border at Thousand Islands, pretending he's a salesman of some sort after some big American bucks. Why not? After that, she's not sure. Or maybe he isn't doing that. Maybe he's headed in the other direction for a crossover at Niagara Falls.

Who the hell knew that the witness protection program in Canada is such a big thing? After all her personal dealings with Dace and the justice system, she's never even heard about the program before.

If only they hadn't fought before he left.

In her agitation, with her hormones crashing for nearly a week after she came home from the hospital, they finally had it out about Summer Senior. Sort of. Funny how you can talk and talk about some things and never get anyplace. No wonder some people just get up and leave a marriage. It's a hell of a lot easier than what she tried to do. No wonder other people say, *I can't take this anymore. Your philandering. Your disloyalty. It hurts so much.* Which was why she took that allergy pill to help her sleep.

Even after he said, "Stop worrying about her. I can't cross the border at Akwesasne, anyway. You heard Garbutt at the inquiry. Somebody will be waiting for me back there at the reservation."

"Except it won't be Summer," Liza said, pushing him hard in the chest.

"No, it won't be," he agreed, hugging her.

"Do you love her?" she asked.

"I love you and only you," he swore. "But she helped me out a long time ago. She's a real nice girl."

"Nice girls don't fuck other another woman's man!"

"No," he said, pulling her by her hands into him. "Not like you fuck me."

"I love you and only you. And you're the only man I ever loved." She wanted to punish him, to be cool, to be reserved, to be the way she presented to other people, but she couldn't. She wasn't going to say she loved him again, to give away the last little bit of herself, but then she went ahead and did just that.

Liza does her best with the shovel, but she's freezing by now. Both steps of the stoop are still rimmed with ice. She leans the shovel back against the house and opens the door, entering the kitchen as stealthily as she can.

The house is still quiet. She goes upstairs and nothing moves. With any luck, the kids will sleep for another twenty minutes or so. Like some kind of a mantra, she repeats *I love you* in the privacy of the master bedroom, counting the cash Dace had left her, five thousand dollars this time. It will do. But he's going to have to find some way of getting her more money, three or four months down the line.

It will be spring by then and Micah will get accepted into a university. Their firstborn is practically grown up. How has he ever survived them? Maybe he'll escape to McGill. Anyplace except Maitland U. He can keep his own name as long as he cuts off all apparent contact with them.

Sammy and Summer will probably squawk about leaving their friends, but she's going to take them and the rest of the kids away then. Poof, they'll vanish into thin air, just like that. Even if it's pure lunacy. They can do that, right? Go wherever Dace is. Be with him again. She might even talk her mother into going with them. If Dace can assume a new identity, so can they.

Uncle Norm and his family are something else. She'll worry about them later.

All she has to do is hang on for a while.

She can do that, yes she can. Even if her stomach aches all the time now.

From downstairs, she hears the rumble of the TV, the one in the living room. A couple of the older kids must have gotten up and snuck downstairs, the girls probably. They aren't supposed to be watching television before school. She'll get after them in a minute, shoo them off to get dressed.

Quickly, she starts making her bed. She'll get the twins out of their cribs next. She stubs her big toe on the leg of her own bed and yelps. One of them hears her.

"I want to go potty!" he roars.

I'm going potty.

Unless she leaves Dace once and for all. The way she always said she would if he had another woman.

What's wrong with her that she just can't?

And what's wrong with him that he's always needing somebody else?

Chapter Thirty-Five
Start Over Again

No *more rain.* Dace makes his way to Farmington, Connecticut, a place where he's never even been old news. The way he drives, it's less than eight hours from Maitland in the cold November rain. He knows this road almost as well as he knows the one between Toronto and Akwesasne.

When he first got into the car, a one-year-old Ford Taurus, the radio was tuned into a blues station, but he leaves it on. It's not the kind of music or the kind of car he'd choose, but the ownership papers in the glove compartment are in his new name. The radio signal stays with him almost all the way. *No more roses.*

The drive's pure pleasure. With his glasses on, a new identity and a New York licence plate, he makes it across the border at a Thousand Islands, with the minimum of questions asked. Minding his own business, he looks like a regular Jack. Sure there's a lot of things he can't erase, but maybe he really can just drive away this time and start all over again.

Go, the border guard motioned him when he sat there for a moment, totally expecting to be asked something else.

He checked and double checked before he left. Nobody was asking questions about him down in Connecticut either. If that dick Garbutt knew about Mountain View, he would have blown his last cover sky high just for kicks.

Aside from Liza and his kids, this is one of the best things he's ever done, getting himself some property in an upscale neighbourhood with the proceeds from his very first undercover job. Something you could still do back in 1977.

Heehaw, he thinks, *back on the farm.* His place is hardly a farm though. It's more like a ranch, the site of a former sawmill. Brunson's, people called it from the early 1600s and for the next three hundred years. After that, it got called Mountain View. For years now, he's owned Mountain View, ten acres with a four-bedroom clapboard house and several out buildings, just on the edge of Farmington up against a mountainside. It's got a white picket fence. Houses are spread out down here, nothing like the cramped neighbourhoods in the towns near the American-Canadian border or in Toronto where his family lives.

He kept the dark nineteenth century furniture and the handmade quilts that came with the pretty house. Liza loves them.

Tools and a motorbike or two gradually filled up the outbuildings, but the only signs of him in the house are a couple of fresh scratches on the antique furniture, some Tunxis arrowheads he found when they were digging out the swimming pool and an old tin washbasin he wants to make moonshine in. The stars and stripes blow boldly from the house's veranda.

The outbuildings serve many purposes, but the property's most attractive feature — for rentals anyway — is an artist's studio. Painters, mostly ladies from New York City who fancy themselves watercolorists, came to stay for a week or even longer in the summertime. They rave about the way the light hits the water in the millstream. And autumn rentals are good when all the leaves are falling. Painters still come or the odd parent who's settling a daughter in at Miss Porter's School.

The small in-ground swimming pool by the millstream probably also helps. It's warm enough down here to keep the pool open from mid-May until Hallowe'en. Once upon a time, you could probably swim in the millstream, but you can't now. The stream runs slower and slower every year. It's a half-frozen trickle right now.

You could use the studio for a writer's retreat too, he said, trying to lure Liza, but she's never been here by herself. He comes to this house three or four times a year, usually with different friends. He purchased the house through a third party with the understanding that a property manager would care for the place in his absence.

I'm Bill, is how he introduces himself to the local busybodies who show up on his doorstep, selling Girl Scout cookies and bringing invitations to the Kiwanis Club. Just Bill, which is why he's going with William "Bill" Hudson now.

Like any self-respecting outlaw, he probably should have hidden out in a cabin in the woods somewhere, maybe in upper New York State, but he isn't. Mostly because Mountain View's less than a day's drive from Toronto, but also because who the heck would expect to find him in a place like this? From the sounds of it, there's already a lot of lunatics and loners hiding out in the woods, anyway.

Less than ten miles from the state capital of Hartford, the town of Farmington is an affluent community with low, spreading houses, pretty white churches and several large corporations. It's got a good history, the kind Liza and certain Democrats favour. Way back in the nineteenth century, the majority of Farmington's residents had been abolitionists, active in aiding escaped slaves. Several former "stations" on the Underground Railway still remain.

Little do the people of Farmington know that they are providing him with a safe house too, never mind that he's an ex-con. It's enough to make a guy feel guilty. For a privileged white boy, he sure has made a mess of things. He still is.

It can't be helped, though. He had to testify at the inquiry. What choice did he have? At least some good has come out it.

Although it hasn't hit the news yet, they've finally charged Father Danby.

Gold's the one who told him, trying to calm him down. *Just get out of here and don't fuck this up,* were his exact words. *I'll help you keep in touch with Liza and your brood.*

It sure would be nice to have a woman here, Dace thinks, as he walks through the house checking for nests of mice and bugs. But the house has been recently and thoroughly cleaned. It smells of Pine-Sol.

He doesn't want just any woman, though. He wants Liza, just Liza, no matter what she thinks.

In his parlour, he sits down in a plaid wingback chair by his cold fireplace and stares. There's a gun hidden up inside the chimney. And a knife and some cash and a bottle or two. The cleaner isn't that thorough, but just to make sure, he gets up and checks. He takes the pistol and a bottle out and leaves everything else. The chimney looks like it's still in pretty good shape.

He leaves the bottle on the coffee table, but he tucks the gun in his belt, wipes his sooty fingers on his jeans and goes upstairs to check the closets. For good measure, he peers into the crawlspace the real estate people call an "attic" and then underneath all four queen sized beds. Even the crawlspace is totally empty and recently swept. A rubber ball, probably a dog's toy, rolls out from under the last bed, but there's nothing else.

He feels a bit paranoid, but he didn't go through all that crap at the inquiry and leave his family just to come down here and end up dead.

It was all that goddamn Garbutt's fault. No wonder some lawyers get shot. He'd go back and kill Garbutt himself if he really was the murdering kind.

Chapter Thirty-Six

A River To Skate Away On

Micah hears fragments of lyrics from the music piped into Nathan Phillips Square and not much else. *It's coming on Christmas.* He's trying to catch sight of Mariposa through the skaters, all the joyous skaters. It's the first Saturday that the rink is open in late November. *I wish I had a river I could skate away on.* Not him, though. He wants to be right here in Toronto with a little fresh snow falling, waiting for the girl with the butterfly name.

A huge holiday tree, the kind of white spruce that's brought in every year from northern Ontario, has been hoisted and decorated in front of City Hall for several weeks now, but it's still a ways to go to Christmas. It's only a week since he took his brother and his sisters to the Santa Claus parade, with Cole and Cory bundled up in a sleeping bag inside their double stroller. His mother said the same thing she always does, that the parade is held earlier and earlier every year. His parents were both home for once, but Liza wanted to linger in bed. She had some female complaint or other, or so she claimed.

I'm bleeding a lot today, Micah heard her saying to Dace.

He'll wait for Mariposa to get here before they rent some skates. She plays women's hockey at Havergal. All those girls' legs, he'd sure like to see that.

She sounded so eager to hear from him on the phone this time. They still have a lot to figure out. It's been weeks since they saw each other, nearly two months. But late at night, especially when his parents were out of town, they talked on the phone. Constantly, until a housemother or somebody at Havergal got after Mariposa. They spoke about how much they miss each other, said all the things they can't say to anybody else. Even if she really is his half-sister, they could still be friends. He wasn't going to let the fact that they might be related put them off each other, but it had. For a little while anyway.

Especially after Mariposa's mother flew up at Thanksgiving and informed her that yes a man called Dace Devereux had been her dad.

It hadn't taken long for Micah to put his mother's name Liza Devereux and his father's name René "Dace" Gagnon together after that.

It had taken Mariposa a little longer to figure things out though. For one thing, she didn't know that Liza always called her husband "Dace."

So Micah had to tell her. That and a few other things. There was such a long silence on the other end of the phone, he thought she'd dropped the receiver and fled. In shame or horror or something else, something far worse. He didn't know what else to say to her anyway. But he could hear a bunch of foolish girls carrying on in the hallway where her dormitory phone must be, so he hung on.

"Yuck," she finally said, "Gross. That's really more than I want to know."

"I don't want to know either," he said, "But we have to."

"People can't help who they love, can they?" she asked in a voice so small that he wouldn't have heard her if he wasn't thinking the same thing. "And we didn't know."

"Yes, they can," he reassured her, the way any sensible adult would.

But this Sunday afternoon when he finally catches sight of her wearing a red scarf and a red tam o' shanter on her bright head and walking over the ice towards him through throngs of skaters, he isn't so sure.

"No boots on the ice," a rink guard calls out to her but she ignores him and walks straight up to Micah. Pretty and perky, just like a guy likes a girl to be, with her eyes full of him.

She smiles, just smiles. So he does too, like the doofus he is. He's so glad to see her and it looks like she is too, but they don't hug. It doesn't seem right. What are they supposed to do? Shaking hands seems pretty dumbass too.

"So how's it going, bro?" she asks.

"Okay," Micah says. "How's your skating, sis? Look at that guy over there, the one with the turban! I guess he wasn't born here, but at least he's trying. Do you think we can show him how it's done? You can skate, right?"

"Of course," she says scornfully. "My grandmother took me to girls' peewee hockey and then we did figure skating for a while. Well, I did. She just came and watched."

"My grandma used to take us to hockey practice sometimes. But no figure skating. That's my sister Summer's thing."

Of course she's your sister, too, he thinks. Maybe Mariposa would like to get to know her and Eden and his brothers. Maybe she should. But she doesn't want to, at least not right now. She never asks a thing about them. Silence comes over Micah and her, the bad kind.

It takes forever to get their skates. A bunch of people have come out of nowhere, so there's a real lineup now. They read the rental prices posted over the counter. Micah doesn't have the right change or even enough money for his own skates. Mariposa has to give him some, part of her allowance from her mother. It's real awkward at first, this date of theirs or whatever it is. But he doesn't care. He's happy and so is she. When it's their turn at the counter, she asks for a size eight and a half. He's been wearing size eleven, but it's a tough squeeze until he ditches his socks. They kneel down on the cold cement floor and lace up each other's skates. He holds one of her slender ankles in his hands for a moment, but then he lets it go.

If they do nothing else together, he hopes they meet here every Christmas for the rest of their lives. Long after he builds his real family and long after she gets hers. And long, long after they both figure out what to do with their lives. Screw all three of their parents and the messes they left behind. He won't make the same mistakes Dace Devereux and his women did, he just won't. And Mariposa won't make them either.

Just look at her—she's perfect the way she is.

Out on the ice, they're even more perfect together. They skate the length of the rink together, hand in hand, cutting a wide swath. They're so good that everybody else gets out of their way. *Maybe I'm dreaming,* Micah thinks, except his face feels cold.

"Cute," he hears another skater say, "they look like they were born for each other." Is the woman talking about them?

On a return run, Micah raises Mariposa's hand and twirls her around. Where are the cameras? They're skating so well, a kind of story dance—*first I met you, then I lost you, but then you came back to me*—that he wants a keepsake. Maybe Mariposa comes by her grace naturally or else she just has music in her blood, but years ago, he and his mother used to dance together in the kitchen when his father was away all those Friday nights.

He's tempted to fall down with her on the ice, just so they can have a good laugh, just so he can say, *See, it's not all that serious, this stuff. We don't have to make such a big deal out of everything. We're not doomed to repeat our parents' mistakes.* But he doesn't.

Because it's not the same for her. Her eyes are full of him. He sees it every time he spins her around and she gazes at him. She loves him. But it's okay. Sweet girl, she's only seventeen. She's got a lifetime ahead of her to fall in love with somebody else and she will.

When they part in the subway to travel in different directions, *He doesn't love me like that,* Mariposa thinks. Well, that's good. But it isn't. Her stomach hurts. She wants to go back almost eighteen years ago to when she was conceived and change things. Get hold of her foolish mother, shake her out of her trance. If it was possible in some kind of *Brave New World,* she'd never even have a father. Dace Devereux was practically just a sperm donor after all. Maybe someday she'll want to know him too, but for now it's enough just to know his son. Besides if she had a different father or her mother had a different sperm donor, she wouldn't be the same person she is now.

It's okay, though. Because she can do what her mother couldn't. She can find somebody real to love, a love to last. Somebody like Micah, somebody who's not her brother. Or her half-brother. Same difference. And she'll do other things.

Hockey's tomorrow. It's the semi-finals. They'll win the Hewitt Cup this year for sure. And after that, she has to get cracking on the article she's doing for the school rag, *Behind the Ivy.* She's got lots of ideas.

"Yes, but what about that chemistry class?" she hears her mother saying on the phone. "I'm not drawing on your grandmother's money to pay those kinds of fees just so you can flunk science again."

Chapter Thirty-Seven

Rancho Paradiso

Life's like this, it always is. Liza's anyway. It changes in a heartbeat. *Kaboom!* Sammy says when they first arrive at the Hotel Rancho Paradiso near Zitácuaro and he's running around checking everything out.

Watching Sammy, she sighs in relief. She hasn't seen him so happy in a long time. She's done the right thing, no matter what Dace's RCMP handler thinks. The looks he gave her when he handed over her new driving licence and the kids' altered birth certificates! She'll be able to apply for more documents later if she needs then. Her kids need their father and she needs him too. They'll just have to be extra careful.

The Devereux family are at Rancho Paradiso, just after Christmastime. She went to the library and checked out a *Frommer's* travel guide to find out about this place. It's a terrible risk, but they're all together again, chasing butterflies. At least that's the plan. If she always did what she was supposed to do, none of her kids exist. And with no kids to anchor her, where would she be?

The bus ride from Mexico City to Zitácuaro was wild. Liza could only clutch one twin at a time, while the other one ran up and down the narrow aisle. Even with all her children there, the bus was only half full, so the older kids had each sat in a window seat, transfixed by the Mexican landscape and the different kind of lives they glimpsed. Liza's mother was there too, but it was all the poor lady could do to hold onto her seat.

"Pinch me," Liza begged her giggling little boys as they bumped along. "Mama's dreaming again."

Never give up, don't jump, nothing's so bad, she told herself. Stopping for a moment at a roadside hamlet, they saw richer Mexican children coming home by themselves from school in taxis, still dressed in their uniforms.

Dace is coming down a day later on his own. They really haven't been separated long. No need for all that despair! Liza, the kids and her mother flew down to Mexico City from Toronto, while Dace is going to fly US Air from New York, or at least that's his plan. He likes to change plans at the last minute, to keep everybody on their toes. He wanted to fly down in one of his own planes, but the little airstrip where he'd once worked here in this area is long gone, so there's no place for him to land.

The cabins at Rancho Paradiso each have two double beds and a fireplace. It's colder than Liza remembers here in the mountains, especially at night. Ah, but she had spent most of the time in Dace's arms when they were last in Mexico. She'd hardly needed a sheet.

Not so at Rancho Paradiso. The beds are all piled high with two duvets each. She stays under the duvet most of the time she's in her room. She keeps the twins in the bed beside hers, bolstering them in on the open side with extra pillows. The boys are so small that they can almost get lost in the duvets. It's a new game for them.

Mama, Mama, they cry whenever they're in the cabin, *You can't find me.*

The older boys, Micah especially, spends most of his time in the dining room where Dulce, the owner's wife and the chief cook, gives him all the food he wants, so he's in heaven. Sammy's still picky about his food, choosing beans and tortillas most of the time, but Micah's open to anything new. He praises the resort food constantly, anything to keep it coming. Dulce's two children are almost grown and away at a good school most of the time, so she dotes on the entire Devereux family, but Micah is her favourite, a young man at the start of his life.

And there's something at the ranch for the girls. As long as the sun shines, they swim in the heated pool, boldly flirting with the young Mexican boys who make the water sparkle and gently, teasingly flirt with them in return.

My God, Liza thinks, observing her little girls, *they're not even teenagers!*

But ten-year-old Summer is already sprouting breasts. Early puberty's around the corner whether Liza likes it or not. There are three years between her and Sammy, but Summer's catching up to him fast. Although Liza knows this isn't supposed to make her feel sad, it does. She wants to stop her children from growing up and away from her, but she can't. She can't stop it any more than she can stop the monarchs from flying away from here in March.

She picked Rancho Paradiso because it's close to the monarch butterfly sanctuaries, three of them. For years, Liza has dreamed of seeing the monarchs in their wintering place and she's finally here again.

Dace arrives the next day. He registers in the cabin right at the end as William Hudson, a cargo airline owner from Connecticut.

When they first meet on the patio by the swimming pool, they pretend to be strangers. It's kind of sexy, even if the first thing William Hudson/Dace says is: "Are these all your kids?"

Yes, Liza thinks, a little miffed, *if you weren't their father, I guess you wouldn't want a woman with six children. Lots of men wouldn't want a woman with just one.*

Descending on them with a special welcoming drink, the owner Rafael and his wife Dulce probably think: *how charming. That this woman with so many children should meet such a nice man.*

For a while at least, the children don't blow Dace's cover. The older ones, Micah, Sammy, Summer and Eden are kind of cool to him for once. He's got a good excuse for being away for so long, but still. Couldn't he have figured out another way? The way the girls make up to the pool boys so easily, they certainly aren't shy, so this alone might have been a clue that they already know Dace, but it isn't.

I'm going to stay this time, after the inquiry. I'll stay with you guys for good, I just have to put some things right, he'd told them, but he lied.

Even the twins hang back with their thumbs in their mouths, shy with this fine, handsome, strapping man that they haven't seen in so long.

As for Liza, all through the late fall, they watched her cry and run around in her car when she should have been working and looking after them. She even quit her day job and was doing God-knows-what up there in her room. She perked up a bit once she starting making plans for this trip, though.

"It's over," Liza whispers to Dace on the terrace after they're introduced, "Danby has gotten the stiffest sentence so far—fifteen years—probably on account of what he did to your sister. I don't think people care much what happens to bad little boys." She doesn't say anything else about the priests and the inquiry though. Dace stiffens and pulls back from her even when she tells him this. She knows what he's thinking—that even if they couldn't put it all behind them — they should try.

They're here to see the monarchs again. It's Dace's Christmas present to her, to all of them. But Liza really should have been more cautious because Mariposa is down here too, visiting her mother. Of course. Their lives are so hopelessly intertwined.

Stupid her, she never gave Kathleen and her girl a single thought until Micah opened his big mouth.

I want to see her, he insisted on the flight down, this after hitting her with the fact that Mariposa was spending Christmas vacation at her mother's. What's wrong with teenagers? Why did they have to try to spoil things for everybody else, too? And what's wrong with her? She should have foreseen this. But all she could think about was Dace and butterflies and getting Micah on one last family trip. God, she really is losing her mind.

No, Liza said, while she tried to entertain the twins with a storybook, *No, just no.*

The airline stewardess took a special interest in him too, so Micah shut up for the rest of the plane trip, but then when they got on the bus, he was troubled by the view.

Do people really live in those shacks? he asked.

The resort's a different world, though. Now that they're here, it's easy to forget about poor people and how through sheer good fortune, the Devereux family has a different life.

Except Micah keeps at her, wearing her down, pestering her the way that only a privileged teenager can.

He can go see Mariposa by himself, he really can. Zitácuaro isn't that far from Angangueo where her mother Kathleen Aldous lives.

"Mum," he runs up to her the very first time she's sitting by the pool, drinking a glass of white wine, with one eye on the younger kids while she tries in vain to read a book with the other, "Can you please call Kathleen Aldous about me and Mariposa getting together? "

Besides, Mariposa's family, isn't she? And if Liza doesn't do something, he can hire a driver and go himself or borrow the resort owner's car, which is probably a nonstarter, but you never know. All Liza needs is Micah driving all over the Mexican countryside and running into drug cartels.

"Micah," she tries reasoning with him, "How would you feel if you were in my place? I don't want anything to do with that woman."

But he can't or he won't put himself in her place, even if he is seventeen. Liza's his mother. When it comes to her, he wants what he wants. Dace isn't even with Kathleen anymore. Rightly or wrongly, he's with Liza. From the sounds of things, Dace hadn't even known about Mariposa.

What kind of woman doesn't tell a man that he has a kid? Micah asks.

Me, Liza thinks a little guiltily. Her situation was different, though. Dace had been on the run, so she wasn't able to tell him about Micah for several months.

Yes, Mariposa is Micah's half-sister. She's family, so he really has Liza there. God, Liza's brothers don't have that much to do with her. Why can't Micah be more like his uncles? Yeah, right.

"Maybe we can meet at one of the colonies," Kathleen hedges when Liza finally calls her from the one working telephone in the resort office and reintroduces herself. "El Rosario probably has the most going for it right now."

The whole conversation is as awkward as hell. Not that Liza expects anything else. She half-expected, half-hoped that Kathleen would hang up on her right away, but she doesn't. When she hears another female voice babbling something at Kathleen's place, Liza almost groans. The voice sounds like a teenage girl's. Great, so Mariposa really is there. How can Kathleen talk in front of the girl?

"Please be quiet, Mariposa," Kathleen even says at one point.

"Our kids," Liza says, after fumbling around a bit, "Micah and Mariposa, they know each other, you know that."

"I don't want—"

"They'll get together here whether we like it or not. I think we should be there."

"Look, I'm kind of busy right now."

"Me too, but—"

"Well, they can't come here," Kathleen says. "You can't bring all those kids here. One of the colonies really would be better, as long as they can keep their hands to themselves. And what about your husband? Is he going too?"

"Dace? Well, yes, of course I haven't talked to him about this yet, but yes, the whole point of this trip is to visit the monarchs again. He's been promising us a trip here for years, but you can't say his name, his real name. Please! I don't know how much the twins will get out of all this, they're only three, but— Oh, God this is just so damn awkward. Dace used to go by the name René Gagnon, but he's in a witness protection program so he's got a new name now. I can't say what it is. But this is a real small place, so you might hear something. If you do find out his new name, please, please don't reveal that you know who he really is."

Jesus, Kathleen wouldn't, would she? But what if they're keeping tabs on her and the resort's phone bugged in case she tries to make a call to Dace? *Shit, they probably are.* '"They" being his enemies. Dace is the one in a witness protection program, but his whole family might be under a microscope. Her, especially. But Dace is Mariposa's dad, no way Kathleen is going to want him dead. No way she'll blow his cover. Would she? *Shit, shit, why did she go and open her big mouth?*

There's a short silence while Kathleen processes all this or maybe she's just biting her nails. Finally she asks, "What's he in a witness protection program for now? Not that I was looking, but I haven't heard word one about him since I moved down here. I thought he was dead. When I knew him, it sure looked like he was going to flame out."

"Not for a crime," Liza says. "He's been working undercover, but then he set up a helpline for the abuse victims from St. Matthew's and all sorts of people came forward. Former students of the school as well as local people. I told him not to testify, but he did and some stuff got out that shouldn't have."

"Isn't that the purpose of an inquiry? Getting 'stuff' out?"

"The 'stuff' I'm referring to had to do with his undercover work. I'm sure you'll understand if I can't repeat what it was. It wasn't Dace's fault, anyway. It was that lawyer, Gar—uh that lawyer working for the priests. He played real dirty. Did you follow the inquiry at all?"

"I couldn't, even if I wanted to. I don't get all the Canadian news down here," Kathleen says in a voice that implies, *thank God.* "But the situation in Maitland, it was just another one of those sexual abuse scandals, wasn't it?" she asks, sounding a little wary.

"Yes," Liza agrees. "It was just another one of those sex scandals involving little boys and little girls too, I guess. They're happening all over the place. Almost every time they put a child in an institution, it attracts predators. Some of the witnesses were told by a psych that it's best to confront the past, but I wonder. The whole thing was highly stressful to say the least. It made Dace a bit crazy — and I — well, never mind about me."

"Crazier than he already was? Somebody who pursues a life of crime really is crazy, don't you think? Did you really have all those kids with Dace? Really, Liza —"

Liza's face goes hot. Who's this woman to tell her how to live her life?

"And did you really have Mariposa with Dace?" she asks. "A man you knew for a week, a man who wasn't even yours? What were you thinking? I wasn't married to him then, but I don't like it. And what are you thinking — dragging that poor girl all over the continent and leaving her in private school? Maybe if she spent more time with you, she wouldn't be so interested in her own brother, at least not that way!"

"Mariposa isn't the problem here," Kathleen says.

Well, of course, she's not. You are!

They hang up on each other then. Liza's face is still burning when she leaves the resort office. She hates losing control like this.

She heads back to the pool where Dace and the kids are, sits down in a chair beside him and tries to calm down.

Nobody even notices that she's upset at first.

"Why in God's name did you take up with a woman like that?" she finally asks Dace after she drinks a little wine.

"Who the hell are you talking about?" he asks her right back.

Micah has just pulled himself up from the water to the edge of the pool. "Dr. Kathleen Aldous," he says flatly. "Did you talk to her, Mum?"

"I did," she confesses.

"Jesus," Dace says, "Are you trying to sell me out?"

"I sure didn't tell her your name. And she wasn't very friendly, just like I said. If we run into her, we'll just have to pretend that we don't know each other. You will anyway, Dace. She didn't say, she didn't need to say, but she doesn't want us to have anything to do with Mariposa," Liza says. "Especially Micah."

"I'm not, I'm not interested in her that way!" Micah yells so loudly that Dulce materializes out of nowhere with a couple of cold drinks.

"Well, I told you to stop bugging me about her, Micah. Just because we're living parallel lives, it doesn't mean we have to acknowledge each other or share space."

But nothing can stop the inevitable from happening, Liza thinks later, so of course Kathleen and Mariposa show up at El Rosario, the same day as Liza and Dace go there with all their kids. Micah and Mariposa might have had a hand in the meeting, but it's also fine and sunny, for the first time in several days.

Some of the other visitors are on horseback, but neither the Aldouses nor the Devereuxes are. As soon as they see the horses, the twins want to ride "horsy." It's Liza's fault. She made the mistake of telling them that Micah did when he was a baby.

"Why does Micah get to do everything?" Summer immediately demands.

The Devereux family passes by the souvenir stand under the mountain. They follow the path halfway up the mountainside before they see them. Kathleen and Mariposa are staring into the trees, one fair, one dark, both of them so beautiful that even Liza gets a lump in her throat.

Of course, Liza thinks bitterly. But it really is the best day to see the butterflies this week—what else can she do? When it's sunny, the monarchs are always at their liveliest.

Thank God they're at one of the most magnificent shows on earth, so she doesn't have to think about the mess they've made of their lives.

The older kids understand the need for quiet and caution in such a holy place, but her little guys Cole and Cory have to be pulled back and restrained. A few monarchs flutter on the ground the twins are scrambling along, but thousands upon thousands of butterflies are flitting through the oxymel trees.

Liza and Dace carried the twins uphill. Their guide led the way, holding Summer and Eden by their hands. Both girls got real quiet, awestruck by the beauty of their surroundings.

Sammy had been walking with Micah, but the minute Micah spots Mariposa, Sammy's on his own.

Are there really fewer butterflies than when Liza and Dace first saw them back in 1973? The papers say so, but it doesn't look that way. There are even more than she remembers, with lots flying around and so many butterflies clumped and clustered high up in the oxymel trees that they look like great bunches of grapes.

The Devereuxes have had a slight advantage, coming up the hill and partially blocked off by their guide, but they're spotted by Kathleen almost right away. Kathleen's eyes cut briefly to Liza and Dace, lingering a little longer on Dace. She ignores the children.

Kathleen puts her arm around her daughter Mariposa instead. *She's mine,* her eyes might as well say, *you can't have her. And Micah's not getting her, either.* Kathleen looks like she wanted to step in between Mariposa and Micah, but she can't. Micah has come up too close.

Watching the butterflies, Mariposa doesn't even notice the Devereuxes at first. She's crying soundlessly, tears of joy spilling down her face. "Mum," she says, "there's way more monarchs here than you've ever got."

As soon as they see her and what she's looking at, Summer and Eden start crying too, but more loudly than Mariposa.

"Mama," Eden tries to whisper, looking up into a canopy of trees, "Are they real?"

"No, it's just animation, you little dope," Sammy says.

Micah wipes Mariposa's tears away with his own fingers. She's not startled at all. She smiles brilliantly.

"Shush," Micah says to the sister and brother who are jumping up and down on the other side of him.

None of them say anything else to each other, not even when some of the butterflies come down and land on their fingers and their sunhats. Even if somebody wanted to blow Dace's cover to complete smithereens, they couldn't have. Kathleen's still trying to hang onto Mariposa and everybody else is too dumbfounded to speak.

A crowd of spectators has pushed up the hill behind them, but none of them are talking, either.

Once, we practically had this place to ourselves, Liza thinks. *We found heaven and then we just left. How could we do that?* she wonders, forgetting Micah and Mariposa, forgetting all her yearning and her ambition and watching butterflies instead.

This is what I should have done with my life, she thinks. *If only I could have been Kathleen and had Dace and all our children too.*

Chapter *Thirty-Eight*
Reconsidering

Micah gets early acceptance into all three of his university choices, but he won't go. All that work and he just won't. Liza isn't sure, but she thinks he started to change his mind shortly after he saw the monarchs' wintering grounds.

Liza remembers feeling the same way too, except Dace made her leave him and the monarchs and go back up north to school. He hadn't given her a choice. It was almost March and the monarchs were ready to fly home anyway.

Micah still comes out with a new vocabulary word almost every day. He tries his new words out on her, he reads the newspaper and books all the time, but he's made up his mind. He's had enough of school for now at least.

"I'll work and travel," he promises. "It's not going to cost you guys a dime."

Please, please don't be like your father. It's Micah's choice, it has to be, but it gnaws at Liza that Micah claims he isn't ready for university no matter what his grades say, no matter how grown up he seems.

Let him go, her friend Val counsels her. *He'll come back to you.* But what does she know, she with her one spoiled little girl?

Micah isn't that grown up. He's such a sullen sourpuss half the time. She was so sure he'd go away to university, just to get away from her and Mariposa and Toronto, the whole sticky mess. But apparently an out-of-town university isn't quite far enough.

Wrapping up her china in newspaper and carefully placing the items in discarded grocery cartons, she wonders if kids ever do what you thought they'd do. She and Dace sure didn't. They aren't even now. Considering how old their parents are—both Maeve and Norm are in their early sixties—Liza finds this especially heartrending or she would have, if she had the time.

Why do you all have to move so far away? her mother asked, a little plaintively for her.

Uncle Norm wasn't much better. *It's time you stopped following that boy,* he said.

But it sure had looked like Micah was university-bound, that he was going to follow in Liza's footsteps and do even better than she had. Not that it would be hard to beat her track record. Here she was almost forty, penniless and unemployed! All Micah had to do was stay out of trouble, get his PhD and write lots of books. Why shouldn't he fulfill her dreams? He's a boy after all and their eldest child to boot. Why did she insist on having him if he was just going to throw everything away?

The planning it took! Way back last September while his parents were screwing around in Maitland—Micah's words, not hers—he switched from Bloor Collegiate, got himself into the semester system at City School, finished up his grade twelve and then got a head start on his grade thirteen credits. Liza had no idea how he accomplished this with everything else going on in their lives, but he had. He forged his permission forms, not that she cared about that. When she found out, she was actually quite proud.

To say she was preoccupied with other matters was putting it mildly. Her kids could have taken a space shuttle to the moon and back that fall and she wouldn't have noticed. Micah would still have to take a full load of courses at summer school to finish grade thirteen by September 1991, but he could do it.

And he would have done it, followed the path he'd laid out for himself if he hadn't got hold of that damn bike! The way he talks about it, she can see that a motorbike means the same thing to him as it does to his father. A bike offers a wild, thrilling ride out of some private hell, although in Micah's case, it's surely a self-made one. Why's he acting this way? Nothing really bad had ever happened to the kid!

The bike's parked out in the street in front of their house right now. Neighbours leave their handprints on the shiny chrome, checking it over.

No, Liza tells the bike's admirers, *we didn't buy that for Micah. He did it all by himself.*

It took him a while to save up his pennies from his camp job and a little bit of after school tutoring that he sometimes does, but he found a second hand bike, a Yamaha, the Japanese kind that his father thinks is pure shit. Is this his way of getting back at his dad?

Because Dace is never there, is he? Liza can almost see their son thinking. *So screw him and whatever the hell he thinks!*

No, Dace is never there, so here she is, packing up their five younger kids and taking them down to Connecticut at the end of June. Wherever Dace is, they'll be okay. As long as Dace's handlers don't decide to move them someplace into the woods and make her homeschool her brood.

At least they've made enough money from the sale of the house to finally pay back Uncle Norm. There's even enough money left over to keep Micah in university in Ontario if he wants.

Liza surveys the sealed boxes she's stacked in the living room and sits down on the one she thinks is the strongest, the one labeled "Pots." Micah's almost halfway out the front door, his helmet in hand. Wearing a helmet is the law, so he doesn't have any choice. He wants to show his new bike to Mariposa, he says, before she leaves Havergal to go back to her mum's place for the summer. Ah, Mariposa. The girl's trouble, but at least she's the kind of trouble that Liza knows.

"You could stay at Grandma's for the summer, keep going to school here," Liza says, grasping at anything that might steer him back on course. "You and Grandma could keep an eye on each other."

"I want to go now," he says. "I'm eighteen. I've got to get the hell out of here. Besides, you know Grandma. If I don't stay with her, maybe she'll change her mind and go to Connecticut with you."

Oh, sure, Liza thinks, burying her face in her hands. *She's just like me. She'll never go anyplace. Or I'm just like her.*

And Dace is going to be stuck in Connecticut forever, too.

Chapter Thirty-Nine
Hell-Bent for Havergal

Roaring along Dupont and onto Bathurst a bit too fast on his new bike, Micah wonders how he can ever leave Toronto, he loves it so much. But after hitting fifty stop signs and pressing his luck gunning it through a couple of amber lights, he changes his mind. Make him fucking Easy Rider, give him the wide open road, that's all he wants. Get him away from his mother. From the looks of her, he'll end up a paraplegic at Sunnybrook if he doesn't end up fried eggs right out there on the pavement in front of their house for all the neighbours to see.

Being an alarmist isn't really her style, but she says this, anyway:

"Do you know how many of your dad's friends are dead or crippled?"

"I'm going to live forever," he says and she almost smiles. It's the only line he remembers from *Fame,* maybe because she hums it sometimes. They saw the movie together when he was nine or ten.

"Your father's friends felt the same way," she says, "but most of them are dead now. They put one leg over a bike and their number was up."

Damn the woman, it's like she can read his mind. When he's on his bike, he feels like he'll live forever, but he also thinks about death. Are all women like his mother? He sure as hell hopes not. He definitely wants to be with a woman, with a girl, someday.

Who are all these guys that his father knew anyway, these total losers who hit the pavement at such an alarming rate? Where were *their* parents? Not nagging them like his mother is, that's for sure. Some of them must have survived, not that Dace is hanging around a bunch of ill-fated bikers now. At least Micah doesn't think he is. As usual, Dace has left his precious Harley behind him. Not that he had much choice. He's such a centre shot on a bike like that.

"It's your father's fault," his mother keeps fussing, "always taking you out on that Harley."

"What, that I got a bike? Why'd you let him then?" he shouts at her and that shuts her up.

"Don't go," Mariposa begs him unexpectedly when he finally locates her at the café where all her Havergal friends hang out in their spare time.

What, he thinks, *you too?* "Why not?" he asks, rearing back from her in the little booth where he's jammed in his knees. "I thought you were spending the summer at your mother's? I'll be back in September to finish grade thirteen anyway. We'll get together then."

"Will you really? I don't know, I just have this feeling— And I like knowing where you are, I like knowing you're safe."

"Jesus," he says, "you sound just like my mother." Little does she know it, but it's exactly the right thing for her to say, especially if she wants to push him away.

Why's everybody always leaning on him anyway? He can't stand all this pressure to be what his father wasn't: the kind of man who isn't always running from something, the kind of man who can use his own name. He dumps some cash on the table, mostly coins, and gets up.

He's got to leave now, he's got to get away from them all. The future beckons him, all the things he'll be able to do without his mother and everybody cramping his style.

He feels lighter already, just like he knew he would.

Chapter Forty
Longing for Micah

Mariposa's got good instincts. She always has. Maybe she got them from Kathleen. She's pretty sure she got zero from the mysterious Dace. She's right about Micah, anyway. He doesn't come home to finish high school and head off to university, at least not right away. And when he finally does, he wraps it up in a dizzying six months.

Micah even goes to his high school graduation, but he's the only person with the Devereux name who's there.

Liza or somebody claiming to be her sends flowers when he graduates. *Congratulations and all the best to you, my darling,* her note says. *You've done real well. It breaks my heart not to be there.*

Then he's off again, this time to Trinity in Dublin of all the damn places. At least nobody has to worry about him on that bike anymore. That sure didn't last long. His bike really must have been a piece of Jap crap. He wiped out on it in Central America someplace, left it in a gully for the locals to pick over for parts.

He flits here and there, backpacking through Europe and Asia in the summertime. But two years in and Dublin's his home base.

The Devereux name's still good in Ireland, he tells everybody with a little smirk on his face. So his father's an ex-con. Nobody's heard about the guy in Ireland. And people are forgetting about Dace Devereux in Canada too.

Where did Liza and all her kids go? Not that Mariposa has much in common with them. Micah's the only Devereux who matters to her.

Maybe she should be more interested in her sperm donor daddy Dace, but she isn't.

D.M.D.Y.R.M? Mariposa doodles all over the wall beside her bed. It's short for *Dear-Micah-do-you-remember me?* words she can't say out loud. She also prays a lot to Micah, *Please come back to me,* but just in her head.

It doesn't matter, though. If Micah can run around doing good things, so can she. After she finishes university, after she goes to work. There's probably more newspaper work in a city the size of Toronto, but she can be a journalist down in Mexico. As long as she's an investigative reporter, not just one of those well-dressed dorks who looks pretty and regurgitates the news. She'll scare up some good news for her mother's monarchs. She doesn't have to stay here in Toronto where nobody knows who she is, where even the Devereuxes don't want to be.

The first year, after he leaves for Central America, is the worst. Micah spends the whole twelve months in Guatemala. Christmastime in Toronto is a real bust. First off, there's no reunion with Micah at Nathan Phillips Square. Then Kathleen calls Mariposa to say she's got some "good" news. She and Freddie Nolan have just gotten hitched!

Really? Mariposa asks. *But – but – are you sure he's even divorced?*

She's not sure why she's surprised. Kathleen has never done what Mariposa expected her to do, not even once. On the plus side, Freddie Nolan is closer to Kathleen's age than those other juvenile Don Juans were. And he's not really a creep. He's also big enough to keep some of the bad guys away. It was so scary when they broke into the house that last time. Not that Kathleen's any slouch. She'd kill the bastard who came between her and those monarchs.

The monarchs really are so magnificent. When Mariposa saw them at El Rosario, life became wonderful but insignificant, all at once. *Look at them,* she thought. *They're just doing what they were born to do. That's all I have to do, too.*

She wants more than monarchs want, though. She wants somebody like Micah. She wants her own true love.

Liza, Kathleen and Dace wish with all their hearts that she never met Micah. All three adults will do everything in their power to keep her and Micah apart.

But if Mariposa never met Micah, how would she know what kind of man to wish for?

Chapter Forty-One
Deconstructing Dace

Summer walks a block from her car to the therapist's office on Avenue Road for the exercise, but that's it. She's not staying out here a moment longer than she has to under this grey and gloomy November sky. Maybe she can get some laps in at the Y later today, but it's hard with kids. If you leave them alone for five minutes, somebody's on your case. Her older girl is ten for God's sake. Now when she was ten...

The therapist is running behind schedule. Summer has ample time to clean out her purse and dump a pile of used Kleenexes and restaurant bills into the wastepaper basket next to the receptionist. Why in God's name is some doctor's time more valuable than hers? She's going to be a doctor, too.

"Yes," Summer jumps right in and tells the woman, when she finally gets in and settles down into an upholstered chair, "I guess a lot was expected from me. I was the oldest girl in what you call a big family now. There's six of us. My father has another kid too, but she doesn't really figure in my story." *Nor do I want her to*, she thinks. "But I didn't mind. Until we moved down to Connecticut. My oldest brother was almost grown up, so he didn't come and Sammy, the next kid in the family—well, he was a bit clueless then. There's an artist's studio on the property. My mother used to hole up there to write, especially when she was revising — in fact, she still does — and she'd leave me in charge."

The therapist has been sorting through some papers, her notes from the last patient perhaps, or maybe what she asked Summer to write, but she stops now.

"Your mother's a writer?" she asks, finally focusing on Summer. "You didn't say that."

"Well, she's not as well-known as somebody like Sandra Brown or Clara Coulter or Norah Roberts, but she makes a pretty good buck writing romantic suspense."

The therapist looks like she wants to ask more about her mother, probably because she's got a book or two in herself, but she doesn't. *Jesus, is everybody a closet writer nowadays?* It's the last thing Summer wants to do. It's hard enough coming in here and spilling your guts all over the place.

"And your father? Or is there one? A lot of women from your mother's time were raising children on their own," the therapist says instead.

Just like you, Summer thinks, noticing a framed photo beside the therapist of a young woman in a graduation cap.

"Well, of course, we had a father and we all had the same one."

"Why do you feel obliged to say 'we all had the same one'? Was there some question about your paternity?"

"No, no— It's just that with six kids in this day and age, people tend to assume that my mother had a bunch of different baby daddies."

"And your father is —?"

"Bill Hudson, that's what he calls himself now."

"That's what he calls himself 'now'?"

"Yes. Because of him we don't use our real name."

"Was he able to have a job?"

"Yes, he owns a cargo airline near Farmington. In his new name. He's pushing seventy now, but he's not even close to retiring. For as long as I can remember, he's been off flying somewhere, like to his father's place in Can— Uh, I really shouldn't say where he goes. He doesn't like people talking about his activities. But I really think he's happiest when he's up in a plane."

How to explain her parents? Well, duh, doesn't every child want to? Because if you could figure out those guys, maybe you could explain you. And nobody wants to figure out their parents as much as Summer Hudson aka Summer Devereux does late in 2017. Even if her parents are still very much alive down in Connecticut. Never mind if her mother floods Amazon with pot boilers under a penname and Summer might end up as a subplot in one of her stories if she doesn't watch out. Or if her father sleeps with a loaded gun under his pillow while he holds his wife's hand. And she lets him, she lets him! Liza, her mother, who always told her kids stories about how much she hated guns.

Back here in Canada, having finally gotten her PhD from the University of Toronto, the Hudson name just sounds ridiculous, but Summer's stuck with it. She can't take back the Devereux name. Ever.

She's always known that, but it still bothers her. *It really does*, she tells this woman, this therapist person that she doesn't even know. For one thing, she always liked the name "Summer Lavinia Devereux." It bothers her even more with only two children to show for all her effort and a crazy ex-husband who's after her for alimony.

She's got full-time custody of the kids, but she's been pulling in more money than him for the past ten years. Or so the damn court documents say. How the hell can that be when she's just been on a contract at the U? Man, that bastard can lie!

Where does love go? Why can't she be more like her parents? Why did they get to be so lucky in love?

"You could have taken your husband's name," her therapist points out. To keep calling the woman her therapist is a bit of a stretch, considering she just met Dr. Alma Fischer for the first time today, one last step to Summer becoming a proper psychiatrist. She doesn't have to see a psychiatrist, her programme director just recommended it, but why not? There are all sorts of whacko weirdos out there calling themselves therapists. She might as well start out right.

"No," Summer says, looking at Dr. Fischer incredulously. Where did she come from? From some repressive place like Russia? It looks like the woman's in her fifties, but she should know better than that. Taking your husband's name is wrong, just wrong, not to mention totally unnecessary. Summer's ex-husband, the father of her girls, was crazy-wonderful like lots of artists are when she first met him, but he's just crazy-strange now, with those visions of his. Of course it's not his fault and she thought she could fix him! She was young then, only twenty-four or something. But what if she had been head-over-heels in love and taken his name? One of her biggest regrets is that she gave the girls their father's name, but she's not about to change it now.

"I couldn't do that," she says, righting her face. If she's going to be a proper psychiatrist, she's got to learn not to show her emotions. Like her father. You never know what that guy thinks unless he says. He's still real good at that.

Why didn't her parents consider what it would be like for their children to just change their names, what it might do to their self-esteem and their sense of identity? It was okay for the twins and that little suck-up Eden. They were only four and seven at the time, but it was harder for her and Sammy. Sammy was thirteen, a real vulnerable age for a boy; and she was ten, a young girl in early puberty.

It's practically the reason she decided to go into psychiatry. That and because she'd really like to find out what makes her parents tick, her dad especially.

The things her parents did never made much sense to her — at least before they moved to Connecticut. She gets Connecticut, she really does.

It's what happened before that. Why did her father turn to a life of crime? And why did her mother, an educated woman, go along with him?

Because she loves him, Summer thinks, *loves him like crazy.* Oh, God, maybe if she had loved her own soon-to-be ex enough, they could have made it.

"Yes, what about your mother?" Dr. Fischer tries to interject. Oh, psychoanalysis, it's still all about mummy, isn't it? Look at Tony Soprano and his warped mother in that Mafia series on TV. The woman was worse than him. Who the hell was Tony's father, anyway?

"Oh, her," Summer says. "People say I'm a dead ringer for my mum, but don't get me started. Not today. Anyway, I understand her, I really do. It's my father's story that shaped our lives. I'd like to focus on him." Even if her father didn't have much education, which apparently is one of the biggest determinants of criminal behaviour, and he wasn't a big time criminal, his behaviour was still kind of stupid. C'mon, why did the guy get into so much trouble when nobody else in his family did?

"There's nothing in our family history to say something was lurking in his genes," Summer says. "Grandpa didn't have a whole lot of education, but he did real well with his automotive businesses in Maitland. He started out with one and ended up with four or five, all in the area near Cornwall."

"The Grandpa who was your father's father?"

"And my mother's uncle."

Dr. Fischer looks at her blankly for a moment, but then she says, "You mean your parents are cousins?"

Summer nods, a little hesitantly, though she really doesn't know why. It's just that some people are so stupid about this cousin shit. She's known her parents were cousins since she was sixteen. Her brother Micah apparently went a bit crazy when it finally sunk in, but it didn't bother her much then and it sure doesn't now.

There was so much else that Micah could have and should have flipped out about. But he hated the past, hated delving into wherefores and whys.

"But your grandparents weren't cousins, were they? Is that what you mean when you say there's nothing in your family history?"

"Of course my grandparents weren't cousins too! We're not the Hapsburgs."

"The Hapsburgs?" Dr. Fischer looks puzzled.

Summer shakes her head a little. Another person who hasn't studied history.

"The Hapsburgs were a very influential European family who went extinct because of inbreeding," she explains. "I just mean that one of my great-aunts did our family history and she found absolutely no evidence of criminal activity in previous generations, except for one of my great-grandfathers who bootlegged in Quebec a bit."

"Bootlegging was and still is a crime," Dr. Fischer says. "And lots of criminal behaviour goes unreported."

Good for you, Summer thinks, *so you know that much.*

"Well, yes, but times change. Bootlegging's more on par now with selling weed."

"Are you thinking it was environmental then?" Dr. Fischer asks. "Your father's issues, I mean."

"Yes, if it wasn't something in his genes, it must have been environmental unless it was because of his damn good looks. Good looks are kind of wasted on a man. Or so my Grandma used to say."

"But you went ahead and married a good-looking man anyway?" Dr. Fischer asks.

"Yes," Summer says, smiling a little, "How did you know? Because girls marry men like their fathers?"

No need to explain the problem with good-looking men. *Good looks tend to make a man narcissistic,* Summer thinks, *more than they do a woman anyway. Show me the woman who thinks she's attractive in the first place!* A woman knows her looks are fleeting, no matter how much she exercises, no matter how many calories she cuts, no matter how much Botox she tries. *You have to love a woman who doesn't give a shit. Like this Dr. Fischer person right here, who really could stand to lose a few pounds.*

But even if her father was just too good-looking for his own good, it doesn't explain everything.

"Well," Dr. Fischer says, looking down at the papers in her lap, "what about all these things you said about your father in this little pre-assessment? Any one of these factors would have had a profound effect on your dad: his mother died before he was ten; he was driven to assault somebody in that horrible school; he was probably sexually abused himself or forced to stand by and watch his friends or family be abused; he was briefly addicted to heroin. Or so you say—" the doctor says, her eyes darting to a clean ashtray on the table beside her. "In my professional experience, nobody is ever 'briefly' addicted to anything. And although he was only convicted of assault, never of the murder of two fellow convicts during the Maitland Penitentiary riot, everybody was convinced that he orchestrated those terrible deeds."

"He did not!" Summer says crossly. "My brother Sammy had fun digging up all that shit, but it was lies, pure lies. He always acted like our dad had done the world a favour, even if the kid couldn't kill a spider himself without worrying about karma." *My God, Sammy's a computer animator now. And he teaches a college course in cartooning part-time.* "Of course, I'd—we'd all prefer to think our father wasn't a murderer, but it's kind of hard to care about a couple of child molesting perverts. Do you?"

There's a slight pause. "No," Dr. Fischer finally says, "but if you ever repeat what I just said, I'll deny it. As professionals we can't express such opinions. What are you going to do if somebody with, let's say, child molesting tendencies comes to you for help?"

"I don't know," Summer says, her mind suddenly darting to her own little girls, who are eight and ten. Just a little younger than she was when her mother dragged her down to Connecticut. No wonder she's thinking about all this stuff and about her father. Maybe Dr. Fischer expected her to go on about her ex-husband, but Summer can't. The last thing she wants to do is talk about her ex! The poor bastard really is just sick. She knows that. Maybe she could have done more to help him, but she's got to think about her girls.

"That isn't the kind of work I want to do though. I'm much more interested in forensic psychiatry."

"Like your brother Micah? What did he get his PhD in? Psychology or sociology?"

"No, no, not like him! He's a criminologist, a theoretical criminologist. He just writes papers and stuff. He doesn't *do*. Not anymore. He wouldn't enjoy testifying in court at all. We're just glad he's settled down. He tripped around overseas for years, doing a bit of this and that in-between semesters at Trinity. It took him years to get a proper degree! He taught, he built schools, he helped people get clean water. My mother was so proud, but she cried almost every day, she missed him so much. And almost every June, she hopped a plane and met up with him! The twins were only six, the first time she took off! And I—"

"How long was she gone for?"

"Only a couple of weeks and my grandmother was usually there. But I—well, both my parents kind of favoured my brother Micah. I don't know what she was prouder of, my big brother's good works or the fact that he graduated from Trinity in Dublin. She lived in Dublin when she was a teenager herself. She was supposed to go to Trinity, but something happened. I don't know what."

Dr. Fischer smiles triumphantly. Is a psychiatrist allowed to do that?

Ah, shit, so it's back to her mum again. How did that happen?

Chapter Forty-Two
All She Ever Wanted

Liza looks out of her window onto the stream and smiles. If she doesn't, she looks old. Especially when she Facetimes with the children.

Is that a blue jay squawking over there in the walnut tree again? If she looks long enough, she might even spot a stray monarch heading down south. There were several monarchs in the garden just last week, but they're probably all gone by now.

There's a lot she doesn't like about the States, but she loves it here at Mountain View. Even if she still sleeps with a man and his gun, though they've been safe and sound here for more than twenty five years. Even if they had to become part of the American Dream. The younger children are all practically Americans, especially Eden—her lovely baby girl Eden—who's close by in New York, appearing in her tenth Broadway play.

"I learned how to act in my family," the girl tells reporters, tongue-in-cheek. "It was better that way. My mother's a writer. For a while there when I was growing up, I thought she was making us all up. My parents did their best—yes, they're still together after all these years—but I felt invisible sometimes. I was a middle child followed by twins, so I had to put on a pretty good show if I wanted to get any attention."

"And your father? What does he do?"

"My dad's another dreamer. He owns a small cargo airline. He loves to go places and fly."

Ah, Eden, sweet Eden, she's such a great little ambassador for them all. She makes the Hudson family sound almost normal, no matter how hard some of those reporters dig. But it's high time she put her acting career aside for a while and became a mother. How old is she now, anyway? Thirty-three? Whatever, she's running out of time.

Micah and Summer both have a couple of kids. And Sammy's got six! A mirror image of his birth family, two boys and four girls. Thanks mostly to Sammy, Dace and Liza have ten grandchildren now, such a unique bunch of little individuals.

Even Liza's twins are doing okay. Her mother's twins, not so much, but things could be a lot worse. Not that Cole and Cory can afford to get up to much trouble, kept undercover all these years.

She picks up the latest framed picture of Sammy and his family that she keeps on her desk. It looks a bit like Annie Leibovitz's work, but it's not. For one thing, the two-year-old and the baby aren't growing out of flowerpots. It's amazing what you can do with digital photography these days. All eight people in the photo are smiling, with red maple leaves cascading around them. Even the cocker spaniel looks cheerful.

True, it was easy enough for Sammy to father all those kids, but he did it and he sure didn't run out. Look at Summer. Now that the poor girl's on her own, she really has her hands full, not that her ex ever was much use. If only Liza was up in Toronto, she could help her out more. Or if Summer would come back down here. But she hates Connecticut. It's too white bread for her.

Not that Summer's really "poor." The girl's always been so smart and so organized. Sure she had help from her husband's mother, but she got her PhD even with two kids.

Sammy, he's real good with his kids too, but his wife or his partner, whatever, she's the one who birthed them and from what

Liza's seen, she does most of the work. But six kids, that's really something in this day and age. The world's so different now. Liza's address says Farmington, Connecticut, but with almost everybody on the Internet now, the whole world is her home.

Damn, is that her mum or Dace she hears coming up the path? Her mum's over ninety now, so she usually sleeps in late. *Thank God!* Except Dace has started bothering Liza when she's working, bringing her news about the latest stupid thing the US president has said or done.

Liza smiles at him anyway when he opens the door. She can't help herself. The pull between them is still there. If anything ever happens to him, she'll die. Dace's hair is totally white, but he still looks the same to her as he did when he was twenty-five. Not so her, although Dace swears she hasn't changed a bit, maybe because she's never let her hair turn grey.

This is why we start to lose our sight, she thinks, *so we can't see what's happening to each other.*

"Little Liza," Dace says right out of the blue, the way he always speaks to her, convinced as he must be that she can follow the meanderings of his mind. "Enough of the politics here. If this new president really starts digging around and cracking down on illegal immigrants, we're all sunk. It's time to go home."

"But we have papers—"

"Which are only good as the next security breach."

"Except there hasn't been one in twenty five years! Ah, Dace, you know we can't go home," she says, getting up from her desk to hide in his arms. *Nor do I want to,* she thinks. She's just so tired having this same old conversation all the time.

"Sure we can. You know me, I've been thinking about this a lot for the past few years. All my enemies, all the bad guys are dead and gone. We can go home, Liza, we really can."

But they can't. Dace is just dreaming again, that's all. Anything to keep the past at bay. Is it good or bad to bury the past? She no longer knows or cares. And anyway they are home down here in the States.

"You know, we don't have to stay here in Connecticut year-round."

"We don't?" Dace holds her from him with both hands, playing dumb.

"We could stay connected to the children on the Internet, spend the winters someplace warm. They could come visit us on spring breaks."

"What — in Florida? We're not that old, Liza."

"Mexico then?" she says hopefully. Except they'll have to fly. They can't drive all the way down to Mexico like so many snowbirds do to Florida, all the way from Canada or from the northern states. Not anymore. It's just a daydream of hers, the one she wants so much, she's afraid to even share it. Dace doesn't say anything at first, but she can see that he's thinking about it at least.

"Maybe," he finally says. "Maybe we can work something out."

ACKNOWLEDGEMENTS

Many thanks again to my first reader — my long-time husband John R. Allen, who has always encouraged me to finish Liza and Dace's story, difficult as some aspects of their lives were.

Thanks also to the survivors of institutions like St. John's in Uxbridge, Ontario who found the courage to speak up for those who couldn't. I only knew one survivor, but for the past thirty years, their stories have been in the press. From the survivors in David Henton's and David McCann's 1995 book *Boys don't cry: the struggle for justice and healing in Canada's biggest sex abuse scandal,* I also learned much.

Last, but not least, thanks to Ann Pullum at Word Detailer; Tatiana Villa at Vila Design and Raymond Hoy's team at The Fiction Works who helped me put the finishing touches on *Take to the Sky.*

ABOUT THE AUTHOR

Karen E. Black lives mostly in Toronto, Canada close to much of her well-traveled family. Black's coming-of-age novel *From the Chrysalis* about Devereux cousins Dace and Liza begged for a sequel, so she wrote *Feeling for the Air*. This second novel focused on Dace's escape from a corrupt penitentiary system and his and Liza's dual mission to clear his name and find out where the Canadian monarch butterflies really made their winter home.

Take to the Sky, the final novel in this trilogy, is not only a sweeping saga of the life that Dace and Liza dared to dream for their large family, but of the monarch butterflies in Toronto, Canada and Michoacán, Mexico so many people have fought to save.

In January 2016, Karen Black finally visited Michoacán, Mexico and saw the monarchs' wintering grounds. At the El Rosario colony, high up in the rugged forested mountains, millions of monarchs colored the oyamel trees orange and bent their branches under their collective weight. Black's timing seemed perfect. She could still get on a horse. Also, the monarchs, long threatened by illegal logging, the use of pesticides and the eradication of milkweed, had made a big comeback. Six weeks later, at least 1.5 million monarch butterflies were hit with a deadly freeze during an unusual ice and wind storm. The storm hit the colony just as the spring migration to Canada was beginning. Luckily, many butterflies had exited the mountains before the unexpected freeze.

Black did her Master's in Library Science at the University of Toronto and completed several certificates at the Institute for Genealogical Studies, but she did her undergraduate degree in sociology at the University of Western Ontario. Though Black's first loves will always be English literature and family history, she's grateful for some of the insights she gained into social problems, human social relationships and institutions when she studied sociology.

Please feel free to contact her at: karen.black@sympatico.ca

Books in the Devereux Cousins Trilogy

www.ingramcontent.com/pod-product-compliance
Lightning Source LLC
Chambersburg PA
CBHW051526250626
47156CB00001B/244